MISSING:
PRESUMED DEAD

James Hawkins

A Castle Street Mystery

THE DUNDURN GROUP
TORONTO · OXFORD

Copy-Editor: Julian Walker
Design: Jennifer Scott
Printer: Transcontinental

Canadian Cataloguing in Publication Data

Hawkins, D. James (Derek James), 1947–
    Missing: presumed dead

ISBN 0-88882-233-2

I. Title.

PS8565.A848M57 2001   C813'.6   C2001-930650-4
PR9199.4.H38M57 2001

1   2   3   4   5   05   04   03   02   01

 Canadä

THE CANADA COUNCIL | LE CONSEIL DES ARTS
FOR THE ARTS | DU CANADA
SINCE 1957 | DEPUIS 1957

ONTARIO ARTS COUNCIL
CONSEIL DES ARTS DE L'ONTARIO

We acknowledge the support of the **Canada Council for the Arts** and the **Ontario Arts Council** for our publishing program. We also acknowledge the financial support of the **Government of Canada** through the **Book Publishing Industry Development Program, The Association for the Export of Canadian Books**, and the **Government of Ontario** through the **Ontario Book Publishers Tax Credit** program.

Care has been taken to trace the ownership of copyright material used in this book. The author and the publisher welcome any information enabling them to rectify any references or credit in subsequent editions.

J. Kirk Howard, President

Printed and bound in Canada.

Printed on recycled paper.

Dundurn Press
8 Market Street
Suite 200
Toronto, Ontario, Canada
M5E 1M6

Dundurn Press
73 Lime Walk
Headington, Oxford,
England
OX3 7AD

Dundurn Press
2250 Military Road
Tonawanda NY
U.S.A. 14150

MISSING:
PRESUMED DEAD

For those who have brought sunshine into my life
For those I love, and have loved
For those I have lost
For my Mother and my Children
For the memory of my Father
For Sunshine

Chapter One

The chill of emptiness unnerved Detective Inspector Bliss the moment he strolled into the foyer of his new station. The public enquiry desk seemed abandoned: not simply unoccupied; not merely devoid of the usual mob of whiners – seeking or leaking information. It was, he thought, more like the *Marie Celeste* – hurriedly deserted. An early morning cup of Orange Pekoe still steamed; a ledger, opened, had been neglected mid-entry; a gold Waterman fountain pen, nib exposed, ink drying, lay across the page.

David Bliss tested the air carefully, almost fearing something noxious, but found only the familiar scent of pine disinfectant and floor wax. He sniffed harder and the sound of his snort echoed off the bare walls and subsided to silence, absolute silence. A tingle of unease rippled his spine and prickled hairs on the nape of his neck. A sudden inexplicable wave of fear told him to run, but the same fear nailed his feet to the floor and made him suck in a sharp breath. What's happening? he puzzled, spinning nervously around.

Then a vivid memory came flashing back – a memory of his early days in the police, working a shift on a similar public enquiry counter at a station in the leafy suburbs: fender benders between Jaguars and Rolls Royces; stock market fraudsters and bent C.E.O.'s; shoplifters nicking Foie Gras and bottles of Veuve Clicquot from the Deli.

A disgruntled queue had formed as he patiently took a detailed description of a missing cat from a faded old dame, her few remaining teeth as green as her blouse, but her pearls still gleamed. "This is the sixth time in two weeks," she admitted, making P.C. Bliss wonder why he should bother. Behind her, an Andy Capp figure in tweed jacket and flat cap stood patiently in line and, when his turn came, he slung a jute sack on the counter.

"What d'ye make of that then, Guv? Found it in me garden when I wuz diggin spuds."

Young P.C. Bliss, unthinking, mainly concerned at getting the grubby bag off his desk, quickly picked it up and unleashed an unexploded twenty pound WWII bomb which rolled across the desk and dropped to the floor with an almighty bang.

"It's a bomb," breathed Bliss, and all twenty people crammed into the office froze in a moment of absolute terror. Waiting – for what? The police to do something? An explosion?

"Everybody out!" he had yelled, coming to his senses, and had never forgotten the sight of a dozen people piled in an untidy heap at the foot of the station steps.

"Yes?" said a face peering round a door, startling him out of his memory and breaking the tense silence. "What d'ye want?" the face continued with irritation. Why irritated? wondered Bliss, aggravated by the sharpness of the man's tone. Had he interrupted some important police business? More likely, he guessed, he had put a temporary brake on the morning rumour mill that was just getting steamed up for the day over a coffee in the back room – who's screwing who; who's in the shit; who's been passed over for promotion. He let it go, thinking it pointless to make enemies the first day in a new job; a new force, and, wiping his sweaty palms on his trousers he carefully controlled his voice. "I'm the new detective inspector. Is Superintendent Donaldson in his office yet?"

The counter clerk's expression metamorphosed from annoyance to deference and a body emerged round the door to support the face. "Sorry, Sir. I didn't recognise you."

"No reason why you should, lad – I've never been here before. Just transferred from the Met. Now where do I find the Super?"

"Come," called a muffled voice a few seconds later as a half packet of chocolate digestive biscuits disappeared into a drawer marked "confidential." Bliss wiped his sweaty palm down his trousers again, preparing for a handshake, and swung open the door.

"Breakfast," mumbled the senior officer, turning away, dusting crumbs off his shirt, ignoring the outstretched hand. "You must be D.I. Bliss," he said, picking up a file, using it to wave Bliss to a deeply buttoned leather armchair. "I hope this has nothing to do with your arrival."

"Sorry, Sir," said Bliss, dropping his six-foot frame into the proffered chair, smoothing the creases out of his new suit. "I'm not quite with you."

"Bit of a coincidence," continued Superintendent Donaldson with a trace of maliciousness, his head buried in the file. "God sends us a hot-shot detective from the hallowed halls of New Scotland Yard, and we get our first murder in six months." By the time he looked up, he had found a welcoming smile to mask the sarcastic smirk.

Bliss let the jibe go. "Murder," he breathed as his pulse quickened again. So that's it, that's the reason for the unnatural quietitude. A murder in a small town – enough to wipe a Royal scandal off the front page of the local rag and fill the marketplace tea shops with a knot of nattering spinsters who, on other occasions, might sit silently aloof, absorbed in the *Church Times* or *Victorian Gardens*.

"You didn't arrange this, did you?" added Donaldson, tapping the folder, now smirking. "You Scotland Yard types have a reputation for pulling clever stunts ..."

"Actually, Sir. I was never at the Yard. I kept my distance – too many chiefs and not enough Indians for my liking."

The superintendent lowered himself behind his desk, studying the newcomer with a censorious glance and toying with one of a number of stainless steel stress relievers that littered the leather surface. "So how do you feel now you are one of the chiefs?"

Brilliant start, thought Bliss, feeling the sting of the remark, "I didn't mean ..." He paused as the other man raised a hand.

"It's O.K., Inspector, I know what you meant," said Donaldson, speculatively teasing a silvery ball on Newton's Cradle, as if deliberating whether or not it would crash into the other balls on release – almost daring it not to cause an equal and opposite reaction. "Felt the same myself at times," he continued, "Still do on occasions. But you'll soon discover, if you haven't already, that however far up the ladder you go, there's always another bastard above waiting to kick you down – chiefs have other chiefs on their backs you know." Then he released the ball, flinging it forcefully against the pack and smiling as the silvery balls swung and smashed back and forth in gradually decreasing reverberations.

There's no answer to that, thought Bliss, refusing to be drawn. "What's this about a murder, Sir?" he said, easing himself forward in the chair.

The superintendent smoothed his moustache thoughtfully, loosening a flurry of biscuit crumbs. "It happened yesterday, last night ... I tried to get hold of you ..."

"I was up in town tidying up a few bits and pieces – if I'd known ..."

"Oh, don't apologise, you weren't due here 'til today; I just thought you'd like to get your feet wet as soon as possible, but I'm winding you up really."

"You mean there wasn't a murder."

"Oh no, *au contraire*. There was certainly a murder, but even us country bumpkins could solve this one." He flicked open the file as if needing to check details, but the bags under his eyes confirmed he'd been up half the night keeping his finger on the pulse. "I'm getting too old for this lark."

You look it, thought Bliss, guessing he might find a copy of the pension regulations uppermost in the other officer's desk.

"About 9.30 pm. Disturbance in the Black Horse public house on Newlyn Road," began the superintendent, skimming the page.

"Bar fight?"

"No – it was upstairs." He paused, looked up and explained. "They let out a few rooms – bed and breakfast. Damn good breakfast it is too; you should give it a try – Bacon, sausage, mash ..."

Bliss coughed pointedly. Donaldson caught his look of impatience and returned to the file, "At least twenty witnesses in the bar heard the commotion. Mind you, another twenty or so claimed to have been in the bog at the time – you know the deal – 'Sorry, Guv – didn't see nor 'ear nuvving.' Four people came forward claiming they saw a body being dumped in the back of a pick-up truck behind the pub, then driven off like a bat out of hell. There were obvious signs of a struggle in the room: broken ornaments; smashed glasses; blood all over the shop; duvet missing off the bed." He looked up again, "Used it to wrap the body we suspect. Bloody fingerprints on the door handle and more on the banister rail down the backstairs. We've recovered the weapon – steak knife, absolutely plastered in blood and dabs. The landlady identified it as one taken up to the room earlier."

"Do you have a suspect?"

"Not a suspect, Detective Inspector," he said, rising in confidence, "we have the murderer. He's made a full confession, on tape, properly cautioned. In fact the tape's being transcribed right now. He is one: Jonathan Montgomery Dauntsey, 55 years, of this parish."

"And the victim?"

"Believe it or not he stabbed his own father ... sad that." He paused and waited while his face took on a sad mien. "Tragic ... It turns your stomach a bit to think someone's own kid could do that."

"It's quite common actually."

The superintendent brightened. "Oh I know – anyway it keeps the clear-up rate healthy. Where would we be without domestics, eh? We used to call 'em Birmingham murders you know."

Bliss nodded, he knew, but the superintendent carried on anyway, "We used to reckon that the only murders the Birmingham City boys ever solved were domestics."

"I know, Sir – but it's a bit different today."

"Oh yes, Dave – political correctness and all that. Gotta be careful we don't upset anyone, eh," he continued, his expression giving the impression that political correctness was fine – in its place. "Anyway," he carried on cheerily, "Welcome to the division – and welcome to Hampshire. I'm pretty bushed after last night's shenanigans so I've arranged for one of your sergeants to show you the ropes while I get a few hours kip this morning. Everything's taken care of with the murder – just a few loose ends ..."

"Loose ends?"

Superintendent Donaldson hesitated, deciding whether any of the loose ends were worthy of mention, even rifling through the slim folder as if hoping to find a missing clue. "Well, we haven't found the body yet," he finally admitted. "But," he pushed on quickly, "that's just a formality. It was a bit of a fiasco last night to be honest. Coppers rushing around in the dark bumping into each other, falling into ditches, that sort of thing."

"You know where the body is though?"

He nodded tiredly and gave the Newton's balls a gentle workout. "The general area – I'll introduce you to your staff and they'll fill you in. The deceased was a pongo by the way, at least he had been during the war, a Major Rupert Dauntsey. One of those who insisted on keeping his title after the war," he continued, disapproval evident in his tone. "You know the type: pompous stuffed shirt, wouldn't make a brothel bouncer in real life. Shove a swagger stick in his hand and poke a broomstick up his ass and bingo, an ex-C.O. with a snotty accent and a supercilious way of bossing the locals around and weaselling his way onto every committee going: golf club; church restoration; anti-this; anti-that; pro-this; pro-that."

Bliss caught the drift, "Not one of your favourite ..."

"Never met him," cut in the superintendent shaking his head. "Although I probably bumped into him at the Golf Club Ladies Night or Rotary Dinner ... I just know the type." Then he spat, "Army," as if it were a four letter word, pulled himself upright in the chair and punched a few numbers on the intercom. "I'll get D.S. Patterson to brief you properly," he said, studying the ceiling, listening to the distant buzz of the intercom, awaiting a response. "Sorry to throw you in at the deep end like this, but I'm sure you won't find it heavy going."

Ex-Royal Navy, thought Bliss, recognising the older officer's vernacular and diction and found confirmation on one wall where a serious-faced young naval officer peered out of a row of rectangular portholes against a background of ships, dockyards and exotic landmarks.

No-one answered the intercom. "Might as well take you below decks – show you your office on the way," he said, coming out from behind his desk. Then he paused with his hand on the brass doorknob and turned, his face taut with seriousness. "Dave, it's only fair I put you in the picture ... I know why you've been sent here. The chief has filled me in." He caught the look of alarm on Bliss's face, put on a reassuring smile and added quickly, "Don't worry. No-one else knows and it's entirely up to you what you tell them. But a word of warning – the other ranks will be watching to see how you perform. Keep an eye on them. There's one or two not above putting a spanner in the works just to see how you handle yourself."

"I understand, Sir," replied Bliss, immediately knowing that the local detectives would undoubtedly find sport in trying to put one over on a new boss –

especially an outsider, particularly one from London. "And I would really appreciate it if no-one else is told," he added.

"You have my word, son. Your secret's safe with me – just keep your head down for a while."

"I intend to."

Introductions were brief, the C.I.D. office had suffered a similar fate to the enquiry office. The previous evening's shift had worked all night and gone home. The early shift had already taken their place, donned rubber boots and were forming search teams and fanning out into surrounding areas of woodland and wasteland. Only Detective Sergeant Patterson remained. He had been on duty for fifteen hours and it showed in his dreary eyes and slept-in appearance.

"How's our murderer this morning, Pat?" said the superintendent, waving Patterson back into his chair as he languidly signalled his intention of rising.

"Sleeping like a bloody baby actually, Sir. It's alright for him – some of us have been at it all night, tramping through the bloody woods – look at the state of my ruddy trousers ... it's not s'posed to be a mudbath in the middle of June."

"No joy with the body, I guess ..."

"Not yet – but we've got half a dozen more dog-handlers coming over from H.Q. They'll soon sniff it out; he couldn't have taken it far."

"It," thought Bliss, rolling the monosyllable round in his mind. "It" – the Major would have been a "Sir" yesterday, a man with a lifetime of knowledge and experience, a commissioned officer no less – a man of substance. One ill-tempered jab with a steak knife, and now he's just an "It."

Leaving Bliss cogitating on the frailty of human existence and the D.S. worrying about his trousers, Donaldson excused himself. "Call me at home as soon as the body turns up," he added on his way out.

Bliss slipped into a convenient chair. "The Super tells me that apart from finding the body everything else is sewn up."

Sergeant Patterson's face screwed in mock pain, exposing prominent gums and yellowed teeth. "Actually, Guv, the scenes of crime boys have been on the blower – there's been a bit of a fuck-up at the pub I'm afraid. Everyone was so excited running round after matey last night that no-one thought to tell the landlady to keep her hands off the crime scene. Apparently she's cleaned and disinfected the whole place. Scrubbed the backstairs – 'Not having people tramping blood in and out of the bar,' she told the forensic guys. As if anyone'd notice."

"Shit – what about the weapon?"

"We've got that alright. One of the uniformed lads marked and bagged it."

"Thank Christ for a woolly with a brain."

"A woolly, Guv'nor?"

"Metspeak for uniformed officer, Pat. I'm surprised you've never heard it before. Woolly ... woollen uniform?"

Patterson sloughed off the information with a grunt then returned to the investigation in hand. "It's a good job we got the confession."

"Anything else I should know?"

"We haven't told the old boy's wife yet. She's in a nursing home ... Cancer," he mouthed the word with due reverence. "She's not got long by all accounts. We went to tell her last night but the matron said the shock might kill her so it'd be best if we left it 'til about ten this morning when the doctor does his rounds." He checked his watch. "You'll have plenty of time to get there."

"Thank you very bloody much."

"Tea – Sergeant Patterson."

Bliss, still jumpy, jerked around in his chair and was disturbed to find that a diminutive grandmother figure in a blue polka dot dress had crept up behind him.

"Are you the new ..." she began.

"Detective Inspector – Yes." Bliss finished the sentence for her. A delicate hand shot out in greeting, and Bliss found himself rising in response.

"Daphne does a bit of cleaning up around here," explained the detective sergeant.

"A lot of cleaning up, if you don't mind," said Daphne in a manicured voice, straight out of a 1940s Ealing Studio movie.

Bliss took the hand and was surprised at its softness – none of the bony sharpness of old age he'd expected.

"I suppose you've heard about the murder last night," she said, peering deeply into his eyes, keeping his hand a few seconds longer than necessary. "Awful business – killing the old Major like that."

"You knew him."

"'Course I did – everyone round here knew him – well, did know him – if you take me meaning. I could tell you one or two ..."

"You wanna watch our Daphne, Guv," butted in a young detective wandering into the room and perching himself against a nearby desk. "She'll have you here all day ... Tell him about your UFO, Daph."

"Shut up, you," she said, bashing him playfully with a hastily rolled *Daily Telegraph*, forcing him to retreat from desk to desk.

Bliss smiled, amused at an elderly woman behaving like a playful adolescent.

"No respect," she panted, returning. "Would you care for a cuppa, Sir?" she asked, looking up at him with smiling eyes, not at all embarrassed by her youthful exertion. She looks exhilarated, thought Bliss, noticing the slight blush in her cheeks, although there was no doubt that overall Daphne was fading – her skin, her hair, even her clothes, had a washed-out look, though her eyes were as sharp as her tongue. Despite the fact she was old enough to be his mother, Bliss found himself attracted by her eyes. She's still got teenage eyes, he thought to himself, entranced by the sharp contrast between the burnt sienna pupils and almost perfect whites.

"Wouldn't have the tea if I were you, Guv," called Detective Dowding from across the room. "She makes it from old socks."

"Don't listen to him, chief inspector," she said making eye contact, crinkling her crows feet into laughter lines.

"Inspector ... Daphne," he reminded her. "I'm only a lowly detective inspector."

"You look like a Chief Inspector to me," she said, then amused herself and the others by summing up her reasoning as she closely inspected him. "Distinguished, greying a bit around the edges; chiselled nose with an intriguing kink in the middle, puts me in mind of a boxer I dated once – he became a politician, ended up in the Lords – never stopped fighting." She paused as an obviously pleasurable memory flitted across her face, then returned to Bliss. "Well-spoken, not like this crowd ..."

"Bit of a beer belly," interjected Bliss with an embarrassed laugh.

"Um," Daphne sized up his midriff with an approving eye. "Comfortable, I'd say. Well fed – good home cooking – doting wife, I suspect – plenty of steak and kidney pies and rice puddings."

He wasn't going in that direction. "So what was this UFO?"

The detective constable laughed from a safe distance and put on a suitably alien voice. "It was real spooky, Guv – Ooooooh. Go on, Daph. Tell the boss."

Indignation sharpened her tone. "I didn't say it was a UFO. All I said was there were some strange lights in the field."

"It was an extra-terrestrial abduction," continued the detective, still in alien character, clearly enjoying tormenting her. "They grabbed an earthling and right now they're dissecting his brain somewhere on another planet." Pausing to laugh, he went on, "And the aliens made crop circles, didn't they, Daph?"

"I didn't say they were circles," she shouted, "I just said the corn had been trampled, that's all." Then she stomped out muttering fiercely about how in her day people were taught to be polite to little old ladies.

"What's that all about?" laughed Bliss.

"Somebody nicked a pig from the farm at the back of her place and drove it through the cornfield," explained the sergeant. "She must have seen the bloke's torches."

"Pig rustling?" queried Bliss with surprise.

"Yeah, Guv. You ain't in London now. They used to go for cattle, but too many people are scared of mad cow disease."

"And chickens," chimed in the detective across the room. "Then there was the sheep over ..."

"Alright," shouted the sergeant. "This ain't *All Creatures Great and Small*, Dowding; we've got work to do. And you'd better start by getting Inspector Bliss and me some tea, seeing as how you've pissed Daphne off."

"Daphne's always pissed off, and always nosing and ferreting around in other people's business."

"You don't like her 'cos she solves more crimes than you do," laughed Patterson.

"That ain't true."

"What about that fraud job?"

"I could see it were a forgery."

"Funny, you never mentioned it until Daph pointed it out."

Ten minutes later, fully briefed on the murder, Bliss found himself in the cells being politely, though firmly, told to mind his business by a rather serious man with a gold-plated accent. A man who, in any other circumstances, would have been placed as a bank manager or gentleman farmer.

"Mr. Dauntsey, Sir," Bliss had begun deferentially once he'd introduced himself. "I'm simply asking you to be reasonable. It must be obvious to you that we will find your father's remains eventually. Wouldn't it be sensible to tell me where we should look?"

Bliss sat back on the wooden bench studying the government grey walls – wondering how long it would take for the blandness to drive you crazy – awaiting a reply, realising the incongruity of the situation, realising that in past similar situations, confronted with obstinate prisoners holding back crucial bits of evidence, his language and demeanour had been entirely different.

"I'm afraid I really can't tell you that, Inspector. I'm sure you understand," said Dauntsey as if he were a lawyer claiming the information was privileged.

"But you've admitted slaughter ..." he started in a rush, then paused, slowed down, and sanitised his words. "You've confessed to a homicide. What possible difference would it make if you were to tell us where to find the body?"

"None – probably. But, as I've already made perfectly clear to the superintendent and the sergeant, I cannot tell you."

Bliss, realising that civility was unlikely to get the answer he required, briefly considered switching to something more assertive, even aggressive – "Look here you little ... " – but found his confidence draining in the face of a man with whom he'd prefer to be playing golf. He was still thinking about it when Dauntsey rose and waved him toward the door. "Now if that's everything, Inspector – I'm sure you have many things to do."

Dismissed! By a prisoner. "Now look here," he began forcefully, then he let it go. "I'm just on my way to inform your mother. Do you wish me to tell her anything on your behalf?"

"There's no need to distress my mother, Inspector. She's sick enough without having to worry about all this."

"Are you crazy? Are you asking me not to tell your mother that her husband's dead, and her son did it?"

"All I'm saying is, she is so terribly ill that she might not understand that it was for the best; that it was just something I had to do."

"You had to kill him?"

"Yes – Like I said in my statement, it was for the best all round. I'm sure you understand."

"Is that your defence?"

"I don't have a defence, Inspector – I don't need a defence. Ultimately, there is only one judge to whom I have to answer; he will understand I am sure."

"That may be so, but in the meantime you'll have to explain yourself to twelve befuddled jurors and a cynical old judge, and they'll take more convincing than you saying that it was something you just had to do."

"Inspector. Have you ever read *The Iliad*?"

Bliss paused to allow the spectre of deep thought to pass over his face then answered, "Not as far as I recall. No."

"You wouldn't understand then," said Dauntsey turning away, leaving Bliss feeling somehow diminished. It's not my fault, he wanted to explain, Homer wasn't exactly flavour of the month at West Wandsworth Comprehensive School.

"Try me," he said, unwilling to let Dauntsey think he was in control.

Dauntsey took in a slow breath. "Then the father held out the golden scales," he began, speaking softly to the wall, "and in them he placed two fates of dread death."

The silence held for a full minute before Bliss could stand the tension no longer. "Sorry – I don't know ..."

Dauntsey spun round accusingly. "I said you wouldn't understand."

"Enlighten me then."

"Sometimes, however unpleasant it may seem, we are each confronted by impossible choices and, when that happens, all we can do is let fate take a hand in the outcome."

"And you're saying that the circumstances were so compelling you had no alternative."

He nodded, "I believe the Americans call it being caught between a rock and hard place, Inspector."

"Could you elaborate?"

"I think I've said enough – good morning, Inspector, and thank you for your understanding."

"He's round the twist." Bliss's voice echoed along the cell passage to Sergeant Patterson as he slammed the cell door behind him.

"Careful, Guv. Don't give him a defence. He might get some high priced trick cyclist to declare him *non compos mentis*."

"Yeah, and six months later pronounce him cured. Then he'd be out of the nuthouse and walking the streets the same as you and I."

The sergeant nodded. "Apart from the fact he'd have a piece of paper declaring him sane – whereas you and I ..."

They had reached the main cell block door. Patterson rattled the thick iron bars to catch the jailor's attention and, as they waited, Bliss put two and two together and came up with four and half. "I'm sure we're missing something important here, Pat," he began, a fog of ideas swirling in his brain but failing to coalesce into anything tangible or sensible. "Dauntsey's far too intelligent ..." he paused and thought about his choice of words. "No, it's more than intelligence: He's too cunning to get caught like this. I mean, it's pathetically incompetent to slit his old man's throat in a public place with half the town listening."

"It happened on the spur of the moment. No-one's suggesting it was premeditated – just a sudden argument."

"But what about the body, Pat? Just imagine if you were to kill me right now – no pre-planning, heat of the moment argument. What would you do with the body to ensure no-one found it?"

The sergeant put on his thinking face. "Concrete overcoat," he suggested after a moment's pause.

Bliss lit up. "Office block – new bridge, that sort of thing."

Patterson nodded, though with little enthusiasm. "There's plenty of buildings going up around here. But aren't we forgetting something, Guv?"

"What?"

"Yesterday was Sunday, and it was pissing with rain. Who's gonna be pouring wet concrete?"

Bliss got the message but was stuck on concrete.

"What about cement boots – then dump him in the river."

Patterson was already shaking his head. "The river ain't deep enough, plus the fact that'd have to be pre-planned. Where would he get a load of quick drying cement at half past nine on a Sunday night?"

"Wait a minute, Pat. You were the one who said it wasn't premeditated. I'm still not convinced. I think he carefully plotted the whole thing. Like I said, he's cunning."

"What about all the witnesses in the pub then; who's gonna be daft enough ...?" He left the hypothesis unfinished, unwilling to waste his breath.

"Could be part of the plan," mused Bliss, grateful that the arrival of the jailor saved him from having to explain his reasoning.

"Don't worry, Guv. We'll soon find the body, once the dog teams get going."

"I'd like to agree with you, but I'm beginning to think that my money might be safer on Dauntsey."

They wandered abstractly back to the CID office, both hoping to arrive at some earth-shattering explanation that would spectacularly solve the case of the Major's missing body. Neither succeeded.

"I still don't understand what they were doing at the pub," Bliss said, throwing himself into a comfort-able-looking moquette chair. "Did Dauntsey give a rea-son in his confession?"

Patterson raised his eyebrows at the chair. "That's an exhibit, Guv," he said apologetically.

"It should be in the property store then," Bliss said, rising, giving the chair an accusatory stare.

"Sorry, Guv – I'll get Dowding to deal with it. Anyway, Jonathon Dauntsey said he was visiting his father who had taken a room at the Black Horse."

"Why? He had a perfectly good house up the road."

"I assumed it had something to do with his mother being in the nursing home."

"You can't afford to assume anything in this game. You know that, Pat. Anyway, all is not lost; I'll ask his mother. Easier still – Get someone at the pub to ask the landlady if she knows."

Patterson picked up the phone and was listening to the *br-r-ring* as Bliss paced meditatively, throwing out his thoughts at random. "Doesn't make sense ... What's the motive? ... Why were they there?"

Someone at the pub answered the phone. "Let's find out, shall we?" said Patterson asking to speak to one of the detectives.

The officer was back on the phone in less than a minute. "According to the landlady, the Major didn't live down here – he ran the estate up in Scotland, and Jonathon Dauntsey told them his father preferred to stay at the pub because there was no-one at the big house to cook and clean – what with his wife being in the nursing home 'n all."

"One mystery cleared up, Inspector," said the sergeant replacing the receiver, relieved that the mystery had not been of his making.

"I wonder what did happen then."

"We'll know as soon as the body turns up."

"If it turns up," said Bliss, reflecting uneasily on the prisoner's supreme confidence. "What about a motive, Pat? Have you any ideas?"

"He says he had his reasons ... and don't forget, Guv, we've got the confession."

"I've had at least three murder cases where innocent people have confessed."

"Why?"

"Just to get their fifteen minutes I suppose. But this one's different – I've always started with the body before – two bodies in one case. Anyway, enough speculating. I guess we'd better go and see his wife; it's nearly ten."

The enquiry counter was under siege as they headed out the door. "Bloody vandals ... trampled flower beds ... tyre tracks in the grass ... half-filled a grave ..." A balloon-nosed madman in a dog collar was blasting away at the clerk with a pew-side manner he'd honed as a prison chaplain.

"What do you mean, young man – 'it's not a crime'?" griped the vicar, "I'd like to speak to someone in authority ..."

"Serg," the clerk caught them with a look of relief, "is it a crime to fill in a hole?"

"Not as far as I know, lad – never has been. Now digging one ..."

"What about the Ecclesiastical Courts Jurisdiction Act?" demanded the vicar.

Patterson flipped through his memory of legislation but couldn't place anything relevant. "Sorry, Sir, I'm in a bit of a rush."

"Wait," said Bliss, half out the door. "What did he say, Pat?"

"Something about a ... shit!" he turned. "When was this, Sir?"

"Last night ... sometime after evensong. I was ..."

"Where?" Bliss demanded hastily.

"St Paul's. In the churchyard, of course. It took three days to dig, what with all the rain. The funeral's in less than two hours. The family will be furious. They had to get special dispensation from the diocese. Officially the churchyard's been closed to new internments for the past ten years ... no ... I tell a lie, longer, probably twelve or more ..."

"Sir," Bliss tried butting in again, but the vicar, having got an ear, was unwilling to relent.

"All recently departed are supposed to go to the town cemetery," he continued. Then added, "Or the crematorium," with a little shudder and a face that said he felt that if God approved of cremation he would have equipped humans with an ignition cord.

"Sir," Bliss tried again, more forcefully. "Please tell me exactly what has happened."

"Like I said, Constable, someone's driven over the grass and ..."

"No. What did you say about a grave?"

"Filled it in – that's what I said. During the night. What I want to know is what you intend doing about it. The funeral starts at eleven."

"I'll send a team of men to dig it right away, Sir."

"Please be serious, Constable ..."

"Actually, Sir, I'm an Inspector and I am quite serious. If you'd care to return to the churchyard we'll be along in a few minutes. You can show the men where to dig; we'll have it out for you in no time."

"Well, I never," said the vicar, shuffling toward the door, his faith restored, muttering his intention of writing to both the Chief Constable and *The Times*.

Sergeant Patterson pulled Bliss to one side as soon as the old man was out of earshot. "Guv, we can't let that funeral go ahead. It's a crime scene – Forensics will be there for hours scavenging for clues."

"I know that – but I'm not going to get into an argument with the local bishop yet. As soon as we find the body we'll look as surprised as anything and we'll have no choice but to postpone the funeral and cordon off the entire area. He'll be more than happy to co-operate, but if we suggest it now he'll start bloody moaning."

"Good thinking, Guv ... And didn't I tell you he wouldn't have taken the body far?"

"Get the car warmed up; I want a quick word with our man," said Bliss, angling himself back toward the cells, refusing to offer hasty praise.

"We've found your father's body," he said, poking his head round Dauntsey's cell door, not bothering to enter fully.

"I somehow doubt that, Inspector," replied Dauntsey with a polite cockiness that immediately annoyed Bliss.

"Are you going to tell me where it is then?"

"Inspector! If you think I'd fall for a silly trick ... I don't play those sort of games."

"Suit yourself. I'm off to church."

Dauntsey's face remained impassive. "Say one for me."

"I have a feeling you're going to need it," he retorted.

No sooner had they got into the car than the question which had hovered on Patterson's lips for the past hour sprang out. "So what brings you to the sticks, Guv?"

"It's no big deal," he replied with a dismissive shrug, knowing that he was lying, knowing that it was a big deal – a very big deal – and he quickly changed the subject with a note of triumph. "I told you Dauntsey was cunning, Pat. I saw it in his eyes the moment I met him."

"Not cunning enough for you though, Guv."

Bliss picked up the sarcastic vibe and brushed it aside. "Nothing to do with me, Serg – it's just Lady Luck."

"I guess he wasn't supposed to get away with it."

"Cunning though – what a place to hide a body. Who would ever think of looking in a grave, especially when there's another occupant?"

"D'ye realise we would never have found it, even with an infra-red from a helicopter. The detector would have picked out a new grave alright – even the body ..."

Bliss nodded. "And the Vicar would have said, 'That's old Mr. So and So. We buried him this morning.'"

"Talk about a close call, Guv."

"That's Lady Luck for you – even moaning old clerics have their uses."

"It's not getting the luck, Sergeant; it's knowing what to do with it that counts."

Bliss drove to the churchyard, explaining, "I may as well get to know my way around, Pat."

But no sooner had they pulled out of the car park than Patterson started digging for more information. "So where were you stationed last?"

"Various nicks ... I got around a fair bit."

"Which ones?"

"What is this, Pat, the third degree?"

"No. I just wondered why you chose to come here, that's all."

Why am I here? he wondered, letting his mind drift, driving on autopilot.

"Watch out!" yelled Patterson, suddenly realising that Bliss had missed a fast approaching red light.

"Shit," shouted Bliss, standing on the brakes, slewing to a halt with the bonnet nosing into the junction. A cyclist, head down against the drizzle, skimmed across the front bumper, then turned in her saddle to give Bliss a pugnacious glare and stab a rude finger in the air.

"Little cow," said Patterson, then gave Bliss an accusatory look. "You nearly clobbered her."

"Sorry," he said, his voice strained by anxiety, his hands frozen so hard to the wheel he could feel the vibration, his pulse racing through the roof.

"I thought you'd seen the light," continued Patterson, unaware of the turmoil in the mind of the man next to him.

"Sorry," he said again then excused himself with a mumble about the unfamiliar roads, the lousy weather and his pre-occupation with finding the Major's body.

It only took a couple of minutes to the churchyard. The vicar was ahead of them, sheltering under the thatched lych-gate, his black robes and white collar standing out sharply against the fuzzy backdrop of the Norman church, its squat square tower drifting in and out of the murky grey drizzle like a castle's keep in a fairy tale.

Under the vicar's direction, Bliss and Patterson tip-toed toward the freshly dug grave, examining the ground ahead, skirting every depression that bore the least resemblance to a footprint or tyre mark. Bliss took the lead, warning the other two of potential evidence with the dedication of a shit-spotter leading a party of ramblers across a cattle field.

"Watch out there ... Mind that ... And there ..."

"I thought you said it had been filled in," Bliss said with annoyance, reaching the grave, and sensing the presence of the vicar as he peered into the seemingly normal grave.

"It has," he shot back belligerently. "It should be eight feet deep. It was yesterday. I checked it myself after communion. Mrs. Landrake, the widow, came with me. 'Want everything to be just right for my Arthur,' she said. Anyway, it had to be eight feet to give enough depth for her to go on top of him when her turn comes."

Bliss wasn't listening, his mind had wandered into the past, into another churchyard, standing by another grave, thinking of another body, but the vicar was unaware and prattled on. "I even fetched my measuring pole to be sure. Old Bert, the gravedigger, can be a bit spare with his measurements at times – tries to get away with the odd six inches if he thinks he can. Anyway, look at it now, it's barely six feet, and the bottom looks like a ploughed field. I want my internees to rest easy ... well, as easy as they deserve, but look at that. Like a ploughed field," he repeated. "That'd be like sleeping on a crumpled sheet ..."

With his mind miles away, an eighteen-year-old memory was consuming Bliss, edging him toward the grave, threatening to topple him into the pit. Patterson grabbed his arm. "Look out, Guv!" he called, pulling him from the brink.

Persuaded by the iron grip, he stepped back onto the duckboard, but his thoughts were still in the past, in a grave with a young woman's coffin.

"I thought you was gonna faint, Guv," said Patterson with a note of apology.

"No – No. I, I'm alright," he stuttered. But Patterson was too pre-occupied with the arrival of the search team's mini-bus to notice the shaking hands and perspiration-soaked forehead.

"We're gonna need a ladder, Vicar," said Patterson, heading off toward the mini-bus, leaving Bliss alone with the grave and his eighteen-year-old memories. He tried to break away, to take off after Patterson but the images in his mind were too strong and kept him glued to the grave. He peered in, almost expecting to see a coffin. He knew which coffin: not a flashy one, little more than a plywood box with brassy handles.

"We bought it with the honeymoon money," the occupant's husband-to-be explained at the little gathering in the local pub afterwards – sausage rolls, pickled onions and pints of best bitter ale around a pool table shrouded in a white bed-sheet.

"I would willingly have paid ..." started Bliss but the young victim's grieving mother had cut him off.

"It's alright, Constable. Very thoughtful of you, but there was no need."

Why was she so damn nice? he wondered. He'd killed her daughter, hadn't he? Hadn't he? But they didn't see it that way. They never had.

"It wasn't your fault, Mr. Bliss ... Dave, isn't it?" said Mrs. Richards, putting a chubby hand consolingly on his arm while dabbing her puffy red eyes with a Kleenex.

"Yes. It's Dave."

"Thought so," she continued, still dabbing. "Anyway, Dave, the family don't blame you. You wuz only doin' yer job. There wuz nuvving else you could've done."

I could have kept my bloody mouth shut, he thought, but found it more consoling to agree. "You're right, Mrs. Richards, but I still feel responsible for Mandy's ..."

Mrs. Richards crumpled in a gush of weeping, and the family led her to a corner couch and poured more gin into her.

"At least it was quick," said Mandy's serious-faced intended, still not fully grasping the fact that he was attending his fiancée's funeral on the same day he'd planned to marry her.

"Yes. It was quick," agreed young Constable Bliss, and he found himself repeating the old joke about a Scotsman who'd drowned in a whisky vat. "Was it quick?" the mythical coroner asked the investigating officer hoping to allay the relatives fears that their loved one lingered in agony. "Och no," replied the policeman. "He got out twice for a pee."

"I don't get it." Mandy's ex-fiancé had said, leaving Bliss praying for an earthquake or other calamitous event to cover his embarrassment.

"Sorry," he said when it became obvious that God was not on his side. "Bad joke – tasteless ... I need another drink."

Sergeant Patterson was back, a straggly line of uniform and civvy raincoats snaking along behind him. "Better rope off that area with the footprints and tyre tracks first," he called.

The line stopped, and Bliss felt the piercing stares as the men checked him out. Patterson's told them who I am, he realised, and quickly pulled himself upright and straightened his thoughts.

The first of the men dropped, uninvited into the pit as soon as the ladder was lowered. "Throw me a shovel," he shouted, with the enthusiasm of a treasure seeker – but wasn't that what it was, thought Bliss, treasure – to a policeman. He won't be so bloody keen when he's seen as many mutilated bodies as me.

"Somebody give me hand," called the man in the grave.

One look down into the slab-sided pit was enough for most of the men, and a dissenting jeer spread through the crush as some inched away. Sergeant Patterson volunteered a six-foot two-inch hulk who unwittingly drew his attention by attempting to disappear inside a five-foot ten-inch overcoat. Murmurs of derision, coupled with relief, rippled back through the crush.

"Good ol' Jacko ... Shall I 'old yer coat?"

"Get stuffed."

"At least Dauntsey gave his old man a decent funeral – more than most murderers do," said Patterson as soggy clods of earth started to land with wet thuds at their feet. "Almost seems a shame to dig him up; we could just leave the poor old beggar in peace."

Bliss stepped back, pretending to avoid the flying dirt while trying to get the memory of Mandy Richards out of his mind. You've hardly thought of her for years, he remonstrated with himself, forget it. "Messy business ... murder," he mumbled, attempting to keep the conversation alive. "Thought I'd be getting away from all this down here."

"Tell me to mind me own business if you like, Guv, but is that why you're here – to get away from summat?"

Bliss stared back into the grave looking as if he might divulge his reasons, but a shout from the grave saved Bliss from answering, not that he had an answer – not a particularly plausible one anyway.

"I think there's something down here," called one of the men in the pit, and D.C. Jackson took it as a sign to quit.

"Keep diggin', Jackson; what's up wiv ya?" shouted the sergeant.

"It's me back, Serg. You remember," he said, with a poorly executed expression of pain.

Sergeant Patterson chuckled. "Yeah, I remember Jacko, but I heard it got better after the Chief Super's visit last week."

Poorly stifled laughter animated the bystanders. Jackson turned pink and bent to his shovel.

"What's that about?" Bliss whispered to the sergeant.

"I'll tell you later, Guv," said Patterson, hearing the approaching vicar.

"Those men shouldn't be trampling over ..." the vicar was whining, but was cut off by an excited voice from the grave.

"Got it!" shouted one of the diggers.

"Got what?" asked the vicar, his voice lost in the press of men straining to peer into the pit.

"Get back," shouted Bliss, shouldering a couple of constables aside for a clearer view. "What is it? What've you found?"

The vicar's scrawny body slipped easily through the gap and he tugged at Bliss's sleeve. "What exactly did you expect to find, Inspector?"

Bliss, feeling exonerated, shot back confidently. "What else would you expect to find in a grave, Sir, but a body?"

"A body?" breathed the vicar, then he had a revelation. "Do you mean the Major's body?"

"Precisely, Vicar – no wonder Jonathan Dauntsey was so cocksure we'd never find his father. He figured that if he put it under ..."

"Sir, Sir," Jackson's voice was calling him urgently from the grave. "It ain't the Major, Sir. It's just some old bones."

"How old? Show me."

Jackson used the discovery as a means of escaping the pit and quickly clambered up the ladder with a handful of bone shards. "There's a load of 'em," he said, handing Bliss the fragments that had aged to a dark sepia.

"Ancient burials," said the vicar, dismissing the human remains with little more than a glance. "The church was erected in 1145 on the site of a Saxon burial site. The Normans commonly built on sacred ground." His eyes glazed and he took on a faraway look as if in personal remembrance of medieval Britain. "Do you know, Inspector, the Normans gave us some of our most magnificent Cathedrals and ..."

"You were saying about the ancient burials?" Bliss butted in gently, steering the vicar's historical sermon toward more relevant matters.

"Oh ... Yes. Well, people have been buried on this site for centuries, and bones have a habit of migrating under the ground. I sometimes think it is because they are unhappy where they have been placed – like uneasy spirits always wandering ..." Seemingly realising that he, too, was wandering again he paused and succinctly explained. "We clear the gravestones every few hundred years and start all over again, so wherever you dig you will probably find some remains. It's wonderful to think that all the ground we are standing on was once the mortal bodies of parishioners – the wonder of God, eh, Inspector? – dust to dust."

"Wonderful," repeated Bliss, fearing he might retch.

"There's something else," called the other digger still hard at work.

Jackson slipped back down the ladder, keener now, and two minutes later a blood stained duvet had been dredged out of the mud in the bottom of the grave and hauled to the surface.

"Any bets that this is the one from the Black Horse," said Patterson.

"Nobody will bet against it," said Bliss peering expectantly into the hole, waiting to see the Major's body emerge.

"That's it, Guv," Jackson called a few minutes later. "We've hit rock bottom. He ain't here."

"Are you sure?"

"Absolutely."

"What's that?" called Bliss, pointing, having noticed a small blob with an unnatural shape.

"Just a lump of rock," said Jackson slamming his shovel into it.

The "rock" sheared in two with a dull thud and took him by surprise. "It's soft, he said, bending. "It's metal I think, Guv," he added brushing away some of the mud. "It's an old kid's toy. A mangled horse with a rider."

"I think it's a tin soldier, Guv," said Patterson, reaching into the pit and taking it from Jackson.

"Lead, I would say," said Bliss, feeling the weight as he took it from the sergeant. "Where was it, Jackson?"

"Don't rightly know, Sir – under the duvet, I s'pose. I never noticed it 'til you mentioned it."

"It was probably dropped by one of the kids that play in here," suggested the vicar. "They're a bit of a nuisance to be honest. Or a grieving parent may have placed it in a child's coffin – favourite toy, that sort of thing."

"Why was it flattened then?"

"Jackson and his clumsy boots probably did that," said Patterson.

"Possibly," mused Bliss. "Anyway, this doesn't help us. Where on earth is the Major's body?"

Chapter Two

The press officer at Headquarters was on the phone when Bliss and Patterson arrived back at the station. Pat Patterson picked up the call then, realising Bliss had strolled into the office, smiled in relief. Sticking his hand over the mouthpiece he held it out like a gift. "Just in time, Guv, the press are fishing for some sort of statement – want to know how come we solved this one so quickly."

"You tell me," said Bliss slinging his wet macintosh over a chair and flopping down, making it clear he wasn't anxious to seize the phone.

"It was pure bloody luck to be honest."

"I'm not sure we should say that," Bliss frowned with disapproval. "We wouldn't want to dispel the public perception that we actually know what we're doing."

Daphne, rounding up dirty mugs, grunted, "You might know what you're doing, Chief Inspector, but this lot couldn't detect a bad smell in a sewage works."

Patterson ignored the quip and held the phone away from him as if it were venomous. "Will you give a statement, Guv?"

Bliss shrank back into the chair, waffling about insufficient local knowledge; lack of information; inadequate material data, leaving Patterson no option other than to release his hand from the mouthpiece and shape his mouth ready to reply.

"Wait," said Bliss, leaping forward, clamping his hand over the instrument. "I'd rather you didn't mention my name either."

"If that's what you want," Patterson said, his face clearly struggling with the intrigue of an ex-metropolitan police officer shunning publicity.

"Yeah, just stick to a few basic facts – suspect in custody – enquiries continuing – no names, no pack drill – you know the score."

Feigning disinterest, Bliss wandered across the room and busied himself with a large-scale wall map of the area. The sergeant gave a series of carefully crafted "no comment" type remarks, then put down the phone, joined him and explained the strategy. "We're concentrating on the woods and fields around the Dauntsey place ... here," he said, stabbing a finger at a spot on the outskirts of the town. "The Black Horse is just off the Market Square ... here, and the cemetery's about halfway between the two. The men we pulled off the search for the cemetery were doing the stables and outbuildings at Dauntsey's house but they'd been at it since six o'clock this morning and were pretty much finished."

"I'm a bit concerned we might be putting too much focus on Dauntsey's place," said Bliss, trying to keep his tone uncritical. "What makes you think he took the body back to his place? Surely it would make sense to get rid of it as far away as possible."

"It would – but the Super figured it might be a question of familiarity. On the assumption it wasn't premeditated murder, he would have had to act quickly and take the body to the first place that came to mind; somewhere local; somewhere on or near his own turf probably."

Bliss was nodding, "There's a degree of sense in that."

"Even more so," continued the sergeant, "Now we know where he took the duvet. The cemetery's on the flight path from the Black Horse to his place – he must have dropped it off en-route."

"That would have taken him awhile, to stop, find the open grave, throw in the duvet, scoop a load of dirt back in – it all takes time – and he still had to get rid of the body."

Patterson shrugged, "He probably knew there was an open grave."

Bliss turned from the map with a throwaway remark, "I'm beginning to wonder if there is a body."

"Of course there is – there's witnesses; blood on his clothes, the knife, the duvet; four people saw ..."

Bliss's eyes lit up with inspiration. "No!" he exploded. "What if the Major isn't dead – only wounded? It doesn't negate what the witnesses say – they heard a fracas; saw Jonathon dump him in the pick-up; found the knife and blood. But what if Jonathon stabbed him and has taken him somewhere ..."

"But, Guv ..."

"Have you checked the hospitals?" Bliss cut in.

"No ... we didn't think ..."

"That should have been routine."

"Why, Guv? Jonathon said he'd killed his dad, not wounded him."

"And what if he was lying?"

"Why on earth should he?" asked Patterson with a tired testiness bordering on insolence.

Bliss recoiled at the reproach and, feeling boxed in, felt compelled to come up with a reason. With his eyes firmly focused on the map he sifted determinedly through memories of past cases, even drifting into the realm of crime novels, seeking an explanation. "What if," he began, an idea springing out of nowhere and slowly taking shape in his mind. "What if they got into a fight, the Major gets stabbed ... accident ... self-defence ... whatever. Then he refuses point blank to be taken to hospital. I can just imagine the crusty old Major saying, 'I'm not having some snotty-nosed kid in a white coat digging needles into me. Anaesthetic – phooey – just get on with it. Didn't have anaesthetic in my day – In my day they'd stick a lump of wood between yer teeth and cut yer bloody leg orf.'"

Patterson was laughing at Bliss's impersonation. "You might be right, Guv. That would certainly explain why Jonathon isn't fazed; why he says he doesn't need a solicitor."

"Because he knows his dad will pop up right as rain once his wound has healed ... "

"Then sue the Chief Constable and all of us for unlawful arrest," continued Patterson projecting the unlikely scenario forward.

"He'd be wasting his time," said Bliss screwing up his nose and shaking his head. "All we have to show is reasonable cause – we have plenty of that."

"O.K., but why bury the duvet?"

"It was covered in blood – he probably realised the dogs would easily scent it out. Wait ... There is another possibility – what if he took him to a hospital and registered him under a false name to save the old man's embarrassment, and avoid answering awkward questions."

"But why?"

"I don't know – but try the hospitals anyway. Alive or dead, he has to be somewhere. Bodies don't just disappear into thin air."

"This one has."

Bliss ignored the comment. "Get onto it right away – All hospitals within 45 minutes – an hour to be on the safe side. Any males over sixty-five admitted since 9.30 last night. Better check all doctor's clinics as well. Shit. Why didn't we think of it before – as soon as the body couldn't be found? It explains everything."

Patterson was less sure, "Maybe."

"I'd better bring the Super up to date," said Bliss feeling pleased with the progress they had made. Selecting a phone from one of the D.C.'s desks, he dialled Donaldson's home number and listened to the ring until a gravelly sleep-filled voice answered, "Donaldson."

"D.I. Bliss, Sir."

The superintendent catapulted himself awake. "You've found the body?"

"Not exactly, Sir."

"Exactly what?"

"We found the duvet in a grave and we've got a tin soldier ..."

Excitement swung to annoyance at the other end of the line. "What are you babbling about. He didn't kill a tin soldier. He killed a real one. Tin soldiers don't bleed all over the place."

"I just thought ..."

"I said call me when you've got the body, not when you've found something to play with."

Bliss sensed that the superintendent's phone was angrily heading for its cradle. "Sorry, Sir ..."

"Click."

"Shit," he muttered, hurriedly adding. "Pat – you stay here and work on the hospitals, I'll go and see the widow."

"Do you know where the place is?"

"No, but I'll pick up Dowding from the cemetery – I can find my way back there. Oh, and I'd like to interview the last person who saw the Major alive."

"That'd be the suspect, Jonathon Dauntsey."

Bliss scrunched his face in mock pain. "Use your loaf, Pat."

"Sorry, Guv. – I don't think we know who saw him last, apart from those who saw him being dumped in the pick-up. I guess it was probably the landlady at the Black Horse."

"I'll go there after I've seen the widow."

Daphne was hovering in the foyer with half an eye on the rain as he made his way out.

"Still here, Daphne?" he called cheerily, heading for the door.

"Just look at that weather, Chief Inspector. It's getting worse and I didn't think to bring a brolly today."

Was she angling for a lift? "I'm going back to St. Paul's churchyard, if that's any help. I could give you a ride."

"If you're sure you don't mind ..."

"Not at all, Daphne. Actually I wanted a word with you," he said, scooping her in an outstretched arm and shepherding her out under his umbrella.

"How is Jonathon?" she asked as soon as they drove off.

"He seems O.K. Remarkably calm, though not what would call happy."

"Never has been, that one. Always sour. I remember him as a kid. Always sour – always walking around with a face like a smacked bum."

The wrought iron lych-gates were under heavy guard. Two bulky uniformed policeman, grateful to be out of the drizzle, were determined no-one would get through without authority while ignoring the fact that almost anyone could simply step over the two foot high stone wall forming the remainder of the cemetery's perimeter. A few disgruntled mourners were clustered under a couple of black umbrellas close-by, discussing tactics, looking, thought Bliss, as if they were deciding whether or not to rush the gates and bury their dead anyway.

"D.I. Bliss," he said, heading for the gap between the two uniformed men. They stood their ground and an arm closed the gap.

"Sorry, Sir. You can't ... this cemetery's closed today. Who did you say?"

"Detective Inspector Bliss."

"I'm sorry ..."

"Oh, get out of the way you idiot," snarled Daphne pulling off her plastic rain hood, pushing her way between them and opening the gate. "This is your new chief inspector."

"Is that you, Daphne?" said one.

"Well, I ain't one of the Spice Girls, if that's what you were hoping?"

He turned to Bliss, "Sorry, Sir."

"It's alright; you were only doing your job – and I'm the D.I., irrespective of any promotion Daphne may bestow on me."

"Yes, Sir."

With the gate swinging shut behind him, Bliss paused to look along the ancient ranks of lichen covered gravestones lolling about like disorganised soldiers waiting for a drill sergeant to shout, "Ten ... tion!" An aura of sadness hung about him as he spent a moment imagining all the suffering that had preceded the erection of each stone, and the pain in his expression caught Daphne's eye.

"What is it, Chief Inspector? Are you alright?"

"Ghosts, Daphne. Well, one particular ghost anyway."

"I thought you hadn't been here before."

"I haven't."

"How d'ye know about the ghost then?"

"Whose ghost – what ghost?"

"The Colonel – Colonel Dauntsey."

"I thought he was a major."

"No. I'm not talking about him. Not Rupert Dauntsey – the Major. He's the one you're looking for now. I mean his father – the old Colonel. His grave's over there, look – that posh job with the fancy statue on the roof."

A white marble blockhouse stood out against the back wall and appeared almost floodlit in the murk. "The mausoleum?" he enquired.

"Yes, that one, Chief Inspector – anyway his ghost is supposed ..."

Bliss wasn't listening as she steered him toward the mausoleum; he was reading the names off gravestones, half expecting to see "Mandy Richards" – knowing he wouldn't. Knowing Mandy inhabited a cemetery a world away. Not for her the tranquillity of a country churchyard with overhanging beeches and chatter of birdsong. Even the vicar's words at her funeral, "In the midst of life we are in death," had been lost to the roar of a 747 struggling to escape the gravitational pull of Heathrow Airport.

They had reached The Colonel's resting place and Bliss stood back to admire the statue soaring above the sarcophagus – a white marble winged chariot drawn by a team of flying stallions.

"Very mythical," said Daphne, following his eye-line.

"That's strange. Jonathon mentioned something about Homer's *Iliad*. I wonder if there's some connection?"

"What did he say?"

"It didn't make any sense to me – something about letting fate choose. I don't remember to be honest."

"Probably the bit about Hector and Achilles ... " she started, then cried in surprise, "Oh look! His name was Wellington ... Wellington Rupert Dauntsey."

"Didn't you know?"

"No. He wasn't the sort of man who needed a name. He was just *The* Colonel. I suppose his family called him something, but I assumed Rupert – Major Dauntsey – called his father 'Sir' or 'Colonel' like everyone else."

"'Sir,'" repeated Bliss. "You think he called his Dad 'Sir?'"

"Not a *Dad*, Chief Inspector. People like that don't have Dads. Dads are warm friendly creatures who cuddle their children, take them on picnics, play silly games and make funny noises ... People like the Dauntseys have fathers who totally ignore them for eight years, then pack them off to a boarding school saying, 'Thank God for that – children can be such an inconvenience don't you know.'"

The ornately carved wooden door to the family tomb was locked, and the huge galvanised padlock demanded his attention. "I wonder who holds the keys," he muttered, examining it carefully, noting that it did not look as though it had been opened recently.

"The family probably – The Major I expect," said Daphne, peering over his shoulder. "The Vicar will know."

"I must ask him," said Bliss with tepid intention, thinking it unlikely that Jonathon would have put his father's body in such an obvious, albeit appropriate, location. "I'd better get over there," he continued with a nod toward the knot of policemen still clustered around the open grave.

Daphne's eyes lit up. "Could I come and have a peek?"

"There's nothing to see really, just an empty grave. The Major's body wasn't in it, just the duvet."

"I always reckoned he'd have trouble getting past St. Peter, but I thought he'd manage to get as far as the grave," she whispered, as if fearful of being overheard.

"Why do you say that?"

"What?"

"That he'd have trouble getting past St. Peter."

"I don't talk ill of the dead, Chief Inspector," she said stalking off huffily. "I'm surprised you'd even ask me."

He caught up to her and tried flattery. "I just thought as how you're so much part of the police here ..."

"Not me, I'm not. All I do is clean up after the filthy beggars – you should see those toilets – piss all over the floor – young girls today wouldn't do it. Most of them would throw up at the thought."

Bliss let her cool down for a few seconds then tried again. "So, without speaking ill, what can you tell me about him – the Major?"

Daphne's face blanked to an expression of deep thought as she put together a picture of the missing man, then she screwed up her nose. "He was nothing much to look at, certainly no oil painting, but then neither was his father, the old colonel. It was the chin mainly, or lack of it. I think his Adam's apple stuck out further than his chin. He wasn't a big man either, although his rank added a foot or so to his height. It's a good job for Jonathon he took after his mother."

"When did you last see him – the Major?"

"Oh, I haven't seen him for a long time, Chief Inspector, I'm not in the landed gentry league." Then she suddenly changed her mind about inspecting the grave. "I'll walk home from here," she said, turning and heading back to the gates. "The rain's eased, and it's not far."

Bliss stopped and watched her, feeling she knew more than she'd let on. Then she paused, and swung around with an afterthought. "Where are you staying?" she called. "Presuming you're not driving back and forth to London every day."

"It's only an hour or so outside rush hour, but I've booked in at The Mitre for a few days 'til I sort something out."

"Well you won't want to eat there."

"I won't?"

"Good God no, Chief Inspector. Mavis Longbottom's cooking there – she's already lost two husbands?"

"What do you mean – food poisoning?"

"No – Lost 'em to other women – doesn't say much for her cooking though does it? ... Well you'd better come to me this evening."

"Oh, I couldn't ..."

"Don't talk nonsense, of course you can. Anyway, it'll give me a chance to tell you what I know about the Major." Then she looked at him with a cheekiest of sideways glances, "If you're interested that is."

He would have said as how he couldn't possibly impose when she held up a hand to block his refusal.

"I shall expect you for dinner at seven, Chief Inspector," she said, adding without pause for dissent. "I noticed my butcher had a nice tray of pork chops laid out this morning," as if her directive was not in itself sufficiently compelling.

Bliss folded. "Alright, Daphne. It'd be a pleasure, but we'd better say eight to be on the safe side, I've a feeling it's going to be a very long day."

"Roger Wilco. Eight it is," she said and bounced away like a ten-year-old whose best friend was coming to tea.

Still half expecting to come upon Mandy Richards name on a tombstone, Bliss made his way to the open grave. No further evidence had been uncovered, and Detective Constable Dowding was only too happy to accompany him to the nursing home. Anything was better than guarding a hole in the ground, in the rain, while photographers and scenes of crime officers bustled excitedly around, seizing on anything that may have the slightest connection to the case.

The nursing home was not at all what Bliss had anticipated. His vision of a stately stone mansion with wide terraces and sweeping lawns translated into a grubby backstreet terrace of Victorian red-brick, with a narrow raised pavement protected from the road by an iron railing that looked as though it had been hit more often than missed.

An ancient man with a crinkled spine was polishing a brass plate which was the only shiny thing about the entire place.

"We'll be sorry to lose old Mr. Davies," said the matron, answering the door herself having spotted their arrival from her office window and guessing their identity.

"Is he leaving?"

"In a manner of speaking, Inspector ..." she said, leaving the words to find their own meaning. "Now I suppose you've come to see the Major's wife," she continued, her voice as starchy as her uniform. "You do realise this could kill her," she added, as if it were his fault.

"Perhaps you could give me a bit of background information first," he half whispered anxious to be discreet.

"Like what?" she boomed, as if he'd made a smutty suggestion.

"Oh," said Bliss, taken aback. "I just wondered what you know about the Major and his wife – were they close?"

A teenaged girl, her unrealistically large bosom encased tightly in an all-white nurse's outfit, had drifted into the hallway and was hovering. The matron looked at her queryingly, as if expecting her to provide the answer, but was apparently disappointed in the blankness of the response. Am I missing something? wondered Bliss, and waited while the matron re-arranged her apron, her hair, and her face, while considering the prudence of her reply. "From what I understand Mrs. Dauntsey had been separated from the Major for sometime," she answered with obvious disapproval. "She never spoke of him, not to me anyhow. Young Mr. Dauntsey said there was a distance between them."

"So she wasn't excited at the prospect of his visit?"

"I got the impression she never really expected to see him again. I'm not aware she was expecting a visit. She certainly never said anything to me about it. Not that she would. Not her – not that one. Thinks she's too good for us does Mrs. Dauntsey."

"Has her husband visited her since she's been here?"

"Not as far as I know ... There's no need to look at me like that, Inspector. This isn't a prison, you know. Our guests don't have to get visiting orders; unlike yours."

"No, no, I wasn't being critical. I was just wondering why he should suddenly decide to visit. Maybe he was hoping to get a mention in her will."

"Oh no. Mrs. Dauntsey doesn't have much. That's why she's in here – if she had money she'd be in Golden Acres over at Fylingford." She lowered her tone reverently, "That's where all the moneyed people go – this is a council home. No – I think you'll find it is the Major who has the money, not her."

"She's got cancer, I'm told."

"Mrs. Dauntsey has Invasive Ductal Carcinoma," she said with her nose in the air. "Nurse Dryden will take you to her in the day lounge, although I think it would be wise if only one of you should visit her – two hulking great men might be too much for her – scare her to death."

"Did I say something wrong?" he asked the nurse on the way to the day room.

"Not really. It's just that saying 'cancer' round here is a bit like calling a refuse disposal officer a 'binman' We try to avoid the word as far as possible – it frightens people."

"I see."

"Mrs. Dauntsey will be in her usual place," continued the nurse, opening the door and steering Bliss toward a frail woman with parchment skin and white hair who immediately demonstrated her determination to guard her territory by picking her handbag off the floor and cradling it to her chest. "I'll leave you to it," whispered the nurse, implying that she wished him luck.

Dowding, slicking back his hair, slipstreamed the young nurse toward the kitchen with the promise of a hot coffee and the hope of something more stimulating, leaving Bliss to approach the newly widowed old woman. "Mrs. Dauntsey ..." he enquired with an overly patronising air.

She viewed him warily. "What are you going to stick in me now?"

"No. I'm not a doctor. I'm a policeman ... I wonder if we could go somewhere private," he added, aware of the anticipatory hush his presence had caused among the twenty or so inhabitants.

"Private – in here?"

"Do you have a room?"

"Don't worry about this lot," she swept a frail arm around the room. "They're all dead."

He looked: most were immobile, heads flopped, mouths agape. Some were staring at him – desperately hoping to find the eyes of a husband, brother or son, then looking ashamedly away as his eyes met theirs. He felt like the grim reaper, and some of them looked fearfully at him as if he were.

"What d'ye mean – dead?" he questioned.

"Dead is what I mean, Inspector," she said, making no attempt to keep her voice down. "No longer part of life. Oh, they all eat and sleep; most of 'em stink; some even talk sometimes – rubbish usually, but this is just a holding pen. They're just waiting for a plot at the cemetery or a slot at the crematorium." She pulled him closer with the crook of a bony finger. "Just waiting for their fifteen minutes of flame," she said, without a trace of humour.

Bliss smiled briefly then fought to select a suitable expression to presage his doom-laden message, but his face blanked while an eighteen-year-old memory came flooding back: a memory of Mrs. Richard's quizzical face, incapable of comprehending the disaster, incapable of absorbing the horror of young Constable Bliss's words – "I'm very sorry Mrs. Richards but your daughter has been shot and killed."

"Dead?" she had queried.

"I'm afraid so."

"She can't be dead; she's getting married next week," she shot back defiantly, as if he were deluded.

She's dead – and I killed her, he wanted to scream, his conscience trying to drag the admission out of him. Then a policewoman with a bush of red hair bubbling out from under her little blue hat had stepped in front of him and forestalled his confession. "Mrs. Richards," she said, softly, "there's been a terrible accident in the bank ..."

It was no accident, thought Bliss, biting back his anger. It was some petty mobster with a sawn-off shotgun.

"There's been a shooting, and unfortunately your daughter, Mandy ..."

"She's just gone to the bank to get the money for her honeymoon. She'll be back in a minute ..." said Mrs. Richards, still uncomprehending, but at least beginning to accept that the police visit was somehow connected to her daughter.

Bliss shook his head and quickly dislodged the old memory. "Mrs. Dauntsey," he started, biting the bullet, "I'm afraid I have some really bad news ... Your husband has been killed."

The news stunned her, leaving her head twitching repeatedly from side to side like a malfunctioning automaton and her mouth stuttering, "N ... N ... No."

Deciding there was never going to be a good time to tell her about Jonathon, Bliss pushed on. "I'm also sorry to have to inform you Jonathon has told us he did it." A strange look of confusion swept over her and, too late, he realised he had on the wrong face. He still had on his "This tragedy causes me as much pain as it does you" countenance, when he probably should have switched to an expression of "Your son is really in the shit."

"Jonathon couldn't have done it," she retorted with a degree of positiveness that made him realise he would have an uphill struggle persuading her any different. Every mother feels that way, he thought. The prisons are full of men unjustly convicted, in their mother's eyes. But she was still shaking her head fiercely, "Jonathon did not and could not have killed his father."

"Do you know why he would want to kill your husband?"

"But I don't understand ... He couldn't have ... It's not possible ... Not my Jonathon ..."

"Is there any reason why Jonathon might have killed your husband?" he tried again, rephrasing his question, convinced she was able to comprehend what was happening.

"Take it from me, Inspector, he didn't do it."

"He says he did."

"You just bring him in here. I'll soon get at the truth."

You're probably right, he thought, guessing she was not above giving him a clip around the ear. "I'm afraid I can't do that."

Bliss left Mrs. Dauntsey and her living mortuary after a few minutes. "I'm feeling rather tired," she had said somewhat pointedly, giving him no option but to excuse himself.

As he got up to leave a hushed voice somewhere behind him murmured, "Bloody whore."

"What?" he said, spinning around, fearing he'd mis-heard. No-one moved. The "dead" were as lifeless as ever. Had he heard it or was it extra sensory perception, a powerfully malicious thought pulsing through the ether and colliding with his brainwaves. Perhaps I dreamt it, he thought, seeking the eyes of those closest, hoping to establish contact, but the eyes were as lifeless as the bod-ies and he brushed it aside. "Goodbye, Mrs. Dauntsey."

"Fucking whore – needs locking up." There it was again. He hadn't misheard this time, and the vehemence in the words stopped him in his tracks.

"Sorry – did you say something?" he asked one old lady, noticing her eyes open. She closed her eyes slowly, as if deliberately shunning him, and he turned back to Jonathon's mother. There was nothing in her face to suggest she'd heard, although there was no doubt in his mind she was the target of the abuse. "I'll probably have to come and see you again," he said, listening carefully for the whisper, hearing nothing.

"I won't be around a lot longer."

"You shouldn't talk like that ..."

"Oh, don't worry. I used to think I'd live forever, but I guess God has other plans."

He mumbled, "Sorry," though it sounded forced, and as he turned to find the matron sweeping across the room toward him, wondered if he was sorry she wouldn't live forever, or sorry that God had let her down.

"Is there any hope for her?" he asked, his mind still spinning with the whispered accusations, as the matron guided him out onto a damp grey flagstone terrace having pointedly said, "You can get out this way, Inspector." He got the message – she doesn't want the police to be seen leaving by the front door – probably makes the undertaker carry the coffins out the back way as well.

"There's always hope, Inspector," she replied. "But whether or not one's hopes are fulfilled is a matter of perspective."

"I'm not with you."

"Most of our patients hope to die quickly and painlessly, Mrs. Dauntsey's no exception. It's her son who can't accept the inevitability of her passing."

"It's the one's who are left behind who suffer the most, Matron," he said, and felt the pain of the truth in his heart. "It's very peaceful here," he added conversationally to lighten the tone.

"Sunday afternoon is our noisy time – families coming to say goodbye to Gran or Gramps. If the kids aren't wailing and crying, their parents are."

"What about the Major? Did he ever come on a Sunday."

"Like I said before, I've never seen him. I suspect this

would have been his first visit, although I wouldn't know for certain. But her son is here all the time – even when she's asleep – the drugs you know – sits there holding her hands, crying silently. Nothing dramatic, just the odd tear, bleary eyes, occasional sniffle – pretends he has a cold. Keeps his Kleenex in a briefcase – thinks we don't notice. It's rather touching really and quite uncommon. You see this is just a dumping ground. By the time we get them most of the relatives have had enough."

"Can anything be done for Mrs. Dauntsey?"

She shook her head with a finality that eclipsed any words. "Don't tell her son though. He dotes on her. He's got a notion into his head about some sanatorium in Switzerland – some quack making a fortune out of desperate people with elaborate claims of a cancer cure. He's promised to take her there."

"Could it help?"

"Might extend her life for a few weeks – if the journey doesn't kill her, but if it did, it wouldn't be anything to do with the drugs – purely psychosomatic – even with something as physical as cancer the patient's will to survive can prolong life. Belief in a cure is often the only cure someone needs, but Mrs. Dauntsey's cancer has metastasised throughout her body."

"I reckon I could get a date with her," muttered Dowding as the top-heavy nurse was closing the side-door behind them a few minutes later.

"Would that be alright with your missus then?" asked Bliss with a smirk.

Dowding, taking the hint, slunk to the car.

"You drive," said Bliss throwing him the keys. "It'll take your mind off naughty thoughts – anyway, I don't know my way around yet."

"Sergeant Patterson called on the radio while you was with Mrs. Dauntsey, Sir," he said unlocking the door. "He's checked all the hospitals – negative."

Bliss was surprised to find the Black Horse open for business, and, by all appearances, doing a roaring trade – gawkers, he had no doubt.

"Who authorised this?" he demanded of the uniformed policeman hemmed against the bar by the throng of rumour driven drinkers.

"I did," boomed the landlady from across the bar, her voice as brassy as her hair – a Michelin woman with spidery legs that threatened to collapse under the weight at every step. "What's it got to do wiv you?"

Silence spread in a wave through the bar like a scene from, *Showdown at the O.K. Corral.*

Bliss introduced himself without pleasantries, saying, "Right. I want this bar closed immediately ..."

"Oh no you don't. You lot have caused enough inconvenience without costing me a day's takings."

"This is ridiculous. This is a murder scene – it should be entirely cordoned off ..."

"Not fucking likely – who's gonna pay me staff? You gonna pay 'em, are you? This is the biggest crowd I've had since Christmas."

The constable threw up his eyebrows in exasperation as if to say, "See what I've had to deal with."

"This is Mrs. Bentwhistle, Sir. She's the landlady ..."

"Bertwhistle ... " she corrected. "And before he gets the chance to stitch me up – I'm the one who cleaned up the mess they made here last night."

"I want to speak to you about that," said Bliss as coldly as he could.

"Don't blame me – nobody told me not to clear up,

and they're bloody lying if they say different. All they said was, "Don't let no-one go up there – and I didn't, but I weren't having those stains drying in. I only 'ad those carpets put down last year ... or maybe the year before. It were the year our Diane got married ..."

"The damage has been done ..."

"Well, don't look at me like that. I didn't do no damage; I didn't ask him to do his old man in, not in my pub, I didn't."

"What time did the Major arrive last night?"

She turned away and threw down a large gin in disgust. "Gawd – how many more of you are goin' to ask me that?"

"Sixish," answered the constable. "That's what she told me, Sir."

"What did the Major say?"

"Nothing – not to me anyhow. I didn't see him. He went straight up. Jonathon came to the bar and got the key; said his dad was tired."

"So, he didn't come through this way."

She shook her head. "Went up the backstairs."

"No-one saw him," said the constable butting in. "We've asked everyone."

"Everyone?"

"Well – all those who were in the pub and outside at the time."

Bliss was unmoved. "I still want this place closed, and all these people out until I'm satisfied there is no evidence."

"You ought'a be out catching criminals," grumbled a loudmouth as he was led from the bar. Bliss ignored him.

"Now," he said, feeling he was getting somewhere. "Let's begin again."

An hour later, without a scrap of new evidence, Detective Inspector Bliss, feeling more cheated than unjustified, allowed the bar to re-open and retreated to the police station. Superintendent Donaldson was back in his office, according to the counter clerk, and was anxiously awaiting his arrival.

Some serious bloodletting on my first day, he thought as he trod the superintendent's corridor for a second time that day. Just what I need. And, with a read-ied apology he tapped gingerly on Donaldson's door. "You wanted ..."

"Bliss ... Dave ... Come in. Sorry I snapped at you earlier ... tired you know ... lot of strain. Chocolate digestive?" he added, holding out the packet as a peace offering.

Bliss relaxed with a "Thanks."

"So, I understand from Patterson that we've made some progress even if we haven't found the body."

"Just the duvet really. His mother says he didn't do it but she's in a wheelchair in a ..." he paused, finding himself on the verge of saying, "concentration camp," reconsidered and said, "She's in an old folk's home."

"She was bound to say it wasn't him."

Bliss nodded in agreement. "The complexion of this case is changing ..." he started.

"Rapidly going down the toilet if you ask me," broke in the superintendent. "Initially, I thought we'd get the whole thing sewn up in a few hours, now we've got blokes running round in circles just bumping into each other. So what precisely have we got?"

"It might be easier to analyse what we haven't got – no body, no motive and very little physical evidence."

"No, I disagree. We've got plenty of evidence ..."

Bliss, sensing Donaldson was about to catalogue the evidence at the Black Horse, held up a hand to stop him making a fool of himself. "Patterson hasn't told you about the balls-up at the pub then?"

"What balls-up, Inspector?" The superintendent's eyes demanded a response and his entire demeanour darkened as Bliss explained how the landlady had sterilised every inch of the crime scene; wiping out footprints, fingerprints and blood stains; vacuuming up every trace of fibre and hair; even spraying disinfectant everywhere to mask scents that the dogs may have picked up.

Donaldson deflated into his chair like a punctured inflatable doll. "Oh my God, Dave. How did this happen?"

"I'm assuming everyone dashed off after the suspect, or were tied up taking statements from the witnesses."

Donaldson, realising he was personally in the firing line, pulled himself together, shot out of the chair and stomped around the office. "That's obstruction. She knew very well she wasn't supposed to touch anything. I told her ... You don't think she could be in on it do you?"

Bliss shrugged, "I shouldn't think so."

"But we've got a full confession ..."

"True, although I'm always a tad suspicious of someone who's keen to fall on his sword. I'd like to re-interview him, in light of the discovery of the duvet. By the way, what did he actually say about the body in his original statement?"

"I've got a copy of the tape here," Donaldson said, dropping it into a cassette recorder and comforting himself with another digestive.

Jonathon Dauntsey's polished accent and deep clear tone sang out of the machine and contrasted with the country brogue of D.S. Patterson as he answered the standard questions relating to his name, age and address. Patterson then launched into the scripted spiel of: date, time, place and persons present – just himself, Dauntsey and a Detective Chief Inspector Mowbray.

"D.C.I. Mowbray?" Bliss mouthed quizzically at Donaldson.

Donaldson hit the pause button.

"He's gone on leave – flying to Nairobi this morning – I didn't have the heart to tell him he couldn't go."

"What do you want me to say?" enquired Dauntsey as the machine started up again, his voice sounding more confused than contrite.

"I should remind you that you have been cautioned and we could start by asking you to describe your relationship to Major Rupert Dauntsey."

"He was my father ... but you know that, I told you that already."

"Perhaps you could just answer the questions," Patterson said, as if Dauntsey had strayed from the script and mucked up the tape. "This tape is for the court to hear."

"Sorry – shall we start again."

"No! It's alright ..."

"Well, I do think it's important to get it right, Sergeant," he continued, digging an even deeper hole. "Perhaps we should have some sort of rehearsal ..."

Exasperation coloured Patterson's tone as he firmly rebuffed the offer and began again. "Mr. Dauntsey, how would you describe your relationship with your father?"

"I would say we were quite distant," he replied, apparently leaning close into the microphone and speaking with a dictationist's metre.

"You can just speak normally – the microphone will pick you up."

"Roger," he said, then added in a stage whisper. "I think that's what you say, isn't it?"

Bliss would have sworn Patterson said, "Will you stop fucking about," although there was no trace of the sound on the tape. However, Patterson clearly did say, "Mr. Dauntsey. Please tell us where you were between nine-thirty and eleven o'clock this evening."

"I was disposing of my father."

Bliss hit the pause button this time and gave Donaldson a querying look. "What a weird answer; it sounds more like he was getting rid of a used condom."

"Perhaps that's what he thought of his father."

Patterson was making another point as the tape came back on. "A number of people have advised us that they heard a disturbance emanating from the general direction of your father's room at the Black Horse public house ..."

Bliss cringed at the witness-box jargon.

"Yes," said Dauntsey.

"And," continued Patterson, plodding on through the script he'd mapped out in his mind, "several witnesses allege they saw you placing a large object wrapped in a duvet into the rear of a Ford pick-up truck: registration number ... T173 ABP."

"It would be foolish of me to deny it, wouldn't it"

"So you don't deny it?"

"As I've already said, It would be foolish of me to do so, with so many witnesses."

"So," said Patterson clearly winding himself up to the pivotal question. "What was in the bundle?"

"I suspect you already know that, Sergeant," said Dauntsey without any indication he was being anything other than as forthright and helpful as possible.

But Patterson's tone in response suggested he was getting near the end of his tether, even admitting later that he felt like strangling the confession out of the man opposite him. "Never-the-less, Mr. Dauntsey," he continued, his voice now barely under control, "I would like you to tell me what was in the bundle, in your own words."

Dauntsey didn't respond straight away, Bliss even took a quick glance at the little window on the machine to make sure it hadn't stopped.

"Don't you think its painful enough for me without having to spell it out?" he said eventually, his voice cracking with emotion.

"Painful or not, Mr. Dauntsey, I am asking you to state unequivocally ..."

"That the bundle contained my father's body. There, I've said it. Now are you satisfied?"

Patterson gave an audible sigh, "Thank you, Mr. Dauntsey. So you don't deny killing your father?"

"No, Sergeant. I don't deny it. It was stupid of me to think I wouldn't get caught."

"Do you regret what you have done?"

"I can't help thinking it's what he would have wanted."

"To be murdered by his son!"

"Well, we all have to go sometime, Sergeant. The sword of Damocles hangs over us all. Might it not be kinder to have the thread cut by a fellow rather than a foe?"

Bliss reached over and clicked off the machine. "Amazing – the pompous ass doesn't give a shit. It's not murder as far as he's concerned – it's nothing more than the involuntary euthanasia of an inconvenient parent."

"My wife's incontinent old mother lives with us," said Donaldson, trying hard to give the impression he was joking. "She can be fairly inconvenient at times; perhaps I should do the same."

"Ah. But there you'd have an understandable motive. What was Jonathon Dauntsey's motive? From what I can gather the old Major had moved out some time ago."

Donaldson flicked the tape back on but needn't have bothered, Jonathon Dauntsey had said all he was going to say.

"So where do we go from here?" asked Bliss, surveying the ceiling, speaking to himself.

Donaldson slumped back into his chair. "I suppose I should call in the Major Incident Unit, but I'll look a bit bloody stupid now. I turned them down last night – said we had everything under control. Now I'll have to crawl cap in hand – makes me look a right imbecile – Smilie Johnston will have a field day ..."

"Smilie?"

"Chief Super at H.Q. – a miserable sod."

Bliss had other ideas. "I'm not sure we need more men; they'll just end up tripping over each other. Most of the evidence has been destroyed or contaminated so badly there's nothing to be gained by sifting through it again. Jonathon Dauntsey is banged up in the cells, and we'll have no problem getting the Beak to remand him in custody based on his confession. The Major's body is sure to surface in a day or two."

"We can't just wait and hope ..."

"I agree," said Bliss heading toward the door. "I'll have another pop at Master Jonathon – try a different tack; tell him how much he's upsetting his Mum by not letting on where the old boy is, that sort of thing. In the meantime we can give the troops a rest – there's no sense in them tearing around like headless chickens."

"And if we can't find the body?"

Bliss, hand on the door, turned. "Let's keep our fingers crossed." Then he paused, something on his mind. "The press are asking questions."

"Naturally."

"I don't want them printing my name."

"Oh. Yes. Of course. I can see that – no problem. The editor at *The Gazette* is a fellow Rotarian. I'll give him a call ..."

"Don't mention anything about ..." cut in Bliss, but Donaldson waved him off.

"It's O.K., Dave. I won't say anything."

Chapter Three

A fragrant blast of humid air rolled softly over Bliss as Daphne opened the door in response to his knock.

"It's the stuffing," she explained as he drank in the perfume with a deeply satisfying inhalation. "Fresh thyme and parsley from the garden," she added. "Please come in."

Daphne had exchanged her polka-dot day dress for a stately paisley one, with the frilliest of white aprons which fluttered as she gave a little shudder. "It's chilly for June – more like October or Oslo. You'll have to fight your way through," she added, inching her way back down the cluttered hallway.

"Are you moving?" he asked, confronted by an upended double bed; an ancient mahogany sideboard that no-one would describe as an antique; several precariously balanced stacks of books, and a stuffed goat.

She turned, her forehead crinkled in confusion, "Moving? ... Oh no ... Charity auction next Saturday –

Women's Institute." He stopped at the goat and slid his hand along the polished hairless back.

"It used to be in the butcher's," she said, seeing the inquisitive look on his face. "All the children used to sit on him while their mothers waited in line. That back's been polished by thousands of bums over the years, mine included, but the kids today wouldn't find it fun; they only want noisy toys that shake the daylights out of them and have hundreds of buttons." Pausing in remembrance, she gave the goat an affectionate pat. "It seems silly now, but sitting on that moth-eaten old thing was quite a treat in my day."

"I nearly didn't find you," said Bliss, moving on and squeezing into the dining room that seemed equally crammed.

"Jumble-sale ... Girl Guides," Daphne indicated with a sweep, suggesting that some of the clutter was not her responsibility, though not indicating precisely which.

"I was wondering if you might get lost. It's fairly isolated out here, no through traffic, and there's only the fields behind."

"Is that where you saw the lights?" he asked, taking in the view out of the back window and seeing the fresh green ripples of a cornfield lapping at the edge of her neatly cultivated vegetable garden.

"Yes – you can still see where the corn's been battered down if you know just where to look." She pointed, he strained but couldn't see anything. "Anyway," she said, turning away, "I never said they'd made circles, Chief Inspector. Dowding made that up."

"I'm sure you didn't. He was only teasing."

"He goes too far at times does that one."

Bliss looked around for something to change the subject and seized on the piano. "What a beautiful instrument. Do you play?"

"Very badly – I had loads of lessons as a child but lacked dedication. What about you?"

"A little. But I've never played one like this." He brushed his hand over the surface, "Just look at that veneer;" reverently lifted the lid and took in a sharp breath of awe, "And the keys – real ivory;" gently touched a few notes, "Perfect!"

"Quite a beauty, isn't it? Coincidentally, it came from the Dauntsey house. I bought it at an auction twenty odd years ago, and it still had the original receipt tucked inside. The old Colonel had bought it in 1903." She paused with a vague expression. "Or was it 1905? Lift up the lid, Chief Inspector, I think it's still in there."

The receipt was there as predicted. "1903," Bliss said, reading it off the faded handwritten paper. "You were right the first time." Then he sat down and started playing.

"Mozart?" she queried, recognising the theme.

"Uh-hum," he nodded.

She closed her eyes in rapture. "Oh that's so beautiful. You could make love to this." Her eyes popped open. "Oh now I've shocked you."

"No – not at all."

"There was a time, Chief Inspector ..." she cut herself off and listened for a while, her mind awash with romantic memories that softened her face and brought a touch of dampness to her eyes. "You do know that God only invented Mozart to make the rest of us feel incompetent, don't you?" she said.

"That's very clever, Daphne," he laughed.

"Yes, it is – I only wish I'd been the first to say it." Then she slipped into the kitchen, mouthing, "Keep playing."

"So, where is Mrs. Bliss?" she called as he finished the piece.

"There's no Mrs. Bliss – not at the moment anyway."

"There's hope for me yet then," she said popping her head round the door and giving him a lascivious wink that threw him off guard. "Oh don't look so nervous, Chief Inspector," she laughed, "I've no illusions about my eligibility in that direction."

"Is this you?" he asked, hastily snatching a silver-framed portrait of an attractive young woman off the sideboard.

"Uh-huh," she nodded. "I haven't always been a Mrs. Mop. I used to clean up quite nicely, didn't I?" Then she ducked modestly back into the kitchen.

She still has the same entrancing eyes he realised and, feeling her distance offered some protection, called, "Actually you haven't changed all that much."

She stuck her head back round the door, "You wouldn't say that if you saw me in my birthday suit … the ravages of gravity, " she added, before disappearing again.

Bliss looked closer at the fifty-year-old image. "Very attractive," he breathed, then noticed the inscription. "It say's Ophelia on here," he began, in a questioning tone.

"Oh really," she replied, staying in the kitchen.

He wandered into the kitchen, picture in hand. "Ophelia Lovelace," it says here. "Paris – September 1947."

Daphne closely studied the saucepan of gravy atop the stove and stirred it firmly.

"Ophelia?" he inquired, noticing the pink glow to her cheeks, wondering if it were the heat from the Aga cooker.

She didn't look up from the pot. "The truth is my name is Ophelia – Ophelia Daphne Lovelace. I'm afraid we all lie a little at times, Chief Inspector."

"That's not a lie. You can call yourself whatever you want."

She wasn't listening, her eyes and mind seemed focused on the pan. "I loathed Ophelia," she began with surprising vehemence. "Who'd want to be named after a week-willed nincompoop of a girl who drowned herself just because some bloke dumped her?"

"Suicide," mused Bliss. "Was she a relative?"

Daphne laughed, "No – *Hamlet* – Shakespeare. Ophelia was the wilting lily who jumped in the river when she thought Hamlet didn't love her anymore." Then, sticking her hands assertively on her hips, she spun on him, demanding, "Do I look like an Ophelia to you, Chief Inspector?"

"No," he laughed. "You look like a Daphne, but I wish you'd call me Dave – off duty anyway."

"I don't think I could – you're cast in the mould of a chief inspector. It suits you. There's a lot in a name you know. I actually think that some people become famous because of their names. Can you imagine what might have happened if Winston Leonard Spencer Churchill had been called Randy Longbottom – see, you're laughing already – I mean, who's going to sacrifice themselves for somebody called Randy or Matt?"

" ... or Dave," he suggested.

"Oh no. There's something very noble about David: King David, David and Goliath, David Lloyd George – Yes," she added with an admiring glance, "David is very noble."

"I don't know about that," he replied, feeling a blush of warmth from the stove.

Daphne gave him an inquisitive look. "I couldn't help noticing, in the churchyard, you looked distracted, as though you had something on your mind."

The shooting of Mandy Richards, he remembered instantly, then worked desperately hard to keep the memory from clouding his face again. "Just the death of the Old Major," he lied, "There's something very puzzling about the case. I feel as though I've sneaked into a play halfway through the first act and can't pick up the plot because I've missed some crucial bit of the action."

Daphne wasn't convinced, "And the ghost that's bothering you?"

"Just an old memory, graveyards have a way of bringing back old memories for me."

"They do for everyone – that's the whole idea of graveyards surely. If we just wanted to dispose of our dead we'd take them to the dump ... Come on," she said, brightening her tone and gathering the dishes together. "Stuffed pork chops with young broad beans, the tiniest new potatoes and a nice tender savoy. All out of my own garden – apart from the chops."

"Wherever did you learn to cook like this?"

"My mother, of course, and in France. I lived there for a while."

"Hence the portrait."

"Yes," she nodded, with a longing glance at the picture in his hand. "Hence the portrait."

"Wine?" offered Daphne as Bliss seated himself at the head of the table. "This is rather a splendid Puligny Montrachet – I'm assuming you like a red with a bit of heart."

"Oh, yes. Very much. But can you afford ..."

"Don't worry, Chief Inspector. Like I said, I haven't always been a cleaning lady; I'm not short of a few bob ... *Bon appetit*."

"You were going to tell me about the Major," he said, digging in.

"Was I? Oh yes, well I'm not sure if I have anything terribly useful to offer."

"When did you last see him?"

"Difficult to say," she started vaguely. "Time distorts time." She looked at him across the table, "Is everything alright?"

"Absolutely delicious – this stuffing ... mmm." He let a rapturous mask slide over his face then picked up where she'd left off. "Time – the Major – When?"

She gave it some thought but seemed at a loss, shaking her head. "In thirty years time you'll probably be wondering who died first, Kennedy or Diana. I won't be around then, so that's something I won't have to worry about."

"But Major Dauntsey. Can you narrow it down? Was it this year or last?"

"Good God, Chief Inspector, my memory's not that bad. No, I'm trying to remember whether it was before the Suez Crisis or after."

"But that was in the 1950s – before I was born ... I think."

"Oh – so it would have been. Yes, I suppose that does seem a long time to you."

Bliss had frozen, a piece of pork chop hung expectantly in the air in front of his face. "Are you saying you haven't seen him for forty-odd years?"

Daphne, failing to register the note of astonishment in Bliss's question answered nonchalantly. "The Major sort of kept out of the way after the war. Not that we saw much of him before the war to be honest. He wasn't usually allowed to play with us riff-raff. I sometimes caught a glimpse of him peering out at life through the hedge up at the big house, and he'd be at church on Sunday mornings during the school holidays but otherwise ..." Her words faded as she failed to come up with any other memories. "We always thought he was a bit of a nancy-boy if you know what I mean – just rumours really – probably because he had a sort of upper crust nasal whine and a silly hairstyle."

"Nancy-boy?" questioned Bliss, "Do you mean ...?"

Daphne was nodding. "Just rumours. He was at Oxford, or Cambridge, and got sent down for it we heard, not that it meant much to us, not that we cared. Although Rupert was about my age, he lived on a different planet. Anyway, he scotched the rumours a few years later when he walked into the lounge at the Mitre Hotel in full uniform, puffed out his chest and announced he was about to marry Doreen Mason, as she was then, and we were all invited."

"You were there?"

"Oh yes."

"When was this?"

"A few weeks before D-Day. Everyone scheduled to go was given twenty-four leave, and it just so happened that my twenty-four hours coincided with Rupert's."

"Do you mean you were going on D-Day as well?"

"It hardly seems possible now, does it?"

His voice rose with incredulity. "But that was more than fifty years ago."

"Was it really?" her face blanked as she looked into the past. "Yes, I suppose it was ... You can see what I mean about time distorting time. Anyway, a group of my friends were giving me a send off in the Mitre when Rupert marches in with his invite. We all thought, 'Why not?' We all knew Doreen anyway – everyone knew Doreen."

Something in the way she spoke of Doreen suggested an element of unseemliness and he quietly tucked the thought away as the basis for a supplementary question.

"They had the reception at the big house," continued Daphne, the memories flooding back. "I'd never been in there before, I don't think any of us had. I'd never seen furnishings like it – the sort of things you'd find in a stately home or a museum. Massive ancestral portraits; fig-leaved statues; settees you could hide under; and the carpets – we had linoleum and a lot of people thought we were posh, but the big house had carpets everywhere, even on the walls. Persians and Afghans, although I didn't know it at the time. Back then I wouldn't have known a Wilton from a Woolworth's Boxing Day special. Doreen was flitting around in her new home with the excitement of a bluebottle who's landed in a dung heap. 'Look at this!' she'd scream, or 'Look at this!' jumping from one enormous painting to the next, or from one statue to another ..." Daphne paused as a smile spread over her face. "I recall one statue, probably a copy of Michelangelo's *David* – Oh, there's another noble David for you – anyway, it didn't have a fig leaf, and we all giggled and dared each other to touch its thingy ..."

"Did you?" Bliss teased.

"I think I'll refuse to answer that question on the grounds I may incriminate myself," she laughed, then carried on, still with a smile. "You should have seen the food. We'd had five years of rationing, and I'd never seen so much food. There was a huge baron of beef and a mound of smoked salmon – I didn't know what it was, I'd only heard rumours. And they had a wedding cake – it was real cake! Most people had a measly Victoria sponge stuck under a beautifully iced tin that could be used for any number of weddings, but they had real cake with real cherries and real sultanas. And champagne, not the fizzy sugar water with plastic corks you get at weddings today. Real champagne." Pausing to pick up the Parisian portrait, she stared into it and sighed wistfully. "Champagne – that was my life at one time. Difficult to imagine it now. *La vie en rose.* I sometimes wonder if it was real."

"Was it real?"

"Who knows, Chief Inspector?" she replied, laying her head back in the chair, letting her eyes drift over the ceiling as if searching for images of her past. "Maybe I've just read too many novels and watched too many movies ... Anyway," she pulled her thoughts back to Major Dauntsey's wedding day. "The strangest thing was the old Colonel himself. Doreen wasn't what you would call a good catch in anybody's book, in fact she had something of a reputation, if you get my meaning, but the Colonel treated her as if she were a princess."

"So, she was a sort of Cinderella."

Daphne gave herself time to digest the thought along with a forkful of beans. "I would have difficulty imagining Doreen as a Cinderella figure," she said after careful consideration. "Put it this way: If you try to imagine Cinderella in the nude she always has the naughty bits air-brushed, whereas Doreen Mason ... well, from what I can gather, half the boys in the town wouldn't have needed any imagination."

"So what did she see in the Major?"

"It wasn't his looks, that's for sure."

"His money?"

Daphne let her raised eyebrows do the talking.

"Well, what did he look like?" continued Bliss. "Mrs. Dauntsey didn't have a photo. I found that a bit strange."

"I don't ..." She paused and picked up the wine bottle. "More?" she asked but didn't wait for a response before pouring. "If Rupert Dauntsey was a bit of a poor specimen before he went to war, when he came back ..." she shook her head in sorrow, "I didn't recognise him – no-one did." A chill shuddered through her. "Half his face was blown off; he'd lost an arm and the one he was left with wasn't a lot of use. He looked like a horror movie monster."

"Couldn't they do anything for him – plastic surgery?"

"Today they could, but not then. It was wartime. Doctors used to pray that men with injuries like his would die quickly, that way they wouldn't have to face their inadequacies. Can you imagine unwinding the bandages, holding up a mirror and saying, 'Congratulations, this is your new face – scary isn't it?'"

"It must be a bit like seeing a ghost."

"Like the one you saw in the churchyard?"

"Mandy Richards," he said inwardly, and suddenly found himself falling into a black hole. "Stop! Stop! You're going to hit something," he was shouting inside.

Dark images of the dead young woman were swirling through a dirty fog and he tried telling himself, "There's nothing there. Stop this! Stop this! You can stop this. Change the picture. Re-focus your mind. It wasn't your fault." But he was still racing onwards into the blackness, his heart pounding to keep up, and beads of sweat bursting out of his brow.

"Is there something the matter, Chief Inspector?" A voice from outside broke through the blue haze. Daphne's voice.

"Get a grip on yourself," he told himself.

"Are you alright?"

Alright – Alright. What's alright? Somebody's blown Mandy Richard's heart out with a shotgun – IS THAT ALRIGHT?

That was eighteen years ago.

No, it was only yesterday ... for her parents; her husband-to-be; her brother; it's still yesterday. It will always be yesterday. How can you move forward when Mandy can't? Mandy's still dead. It's still a week before her wedding for her. Still the day she went to get her savings out of the bank to pay for her honeymoon. Still the most joyous, expectant day of her life – and still the very last day of her life.

"Chief Inspector," a note of serious concern in Daphne's voice got through the images of Mandy and shook him back to the present.

"Oh – Sorry. I was miles away," he said, disentangling himself from the nightmarish memories.

"I thought you were having a panic attack," she said, scooping the empty crockery toward her, chattering away as if nothing had happened. "I get them sometimes. Shakes you up a bit. Makes you want to run, but you can't get away from your own ghosts."

"I was just thinking about the Major's ghost ..." he lied again.

"No – that's was the old Colonel," she cut in. "It's Colonel Dauntsey who's supposed to ride around the churchyard on his chariot. Some reckon he's still trying to get back to his regiment. He was invalided out after the first war – chlorine gas poisoning – and some say he was miserable as sin until the second one came along. But when they wouldn't let him go, he pined. I heard he died soon after Rupert was brought home – suicide some reckon, although it was never proved.

"Suicide?"

"So they say," she said, scuttling into the kitchen with the dirty crockery.

Still trying to escape the memories of Mandy Richards, Bliss got up and weaved his way around the clutter, mentally apportioning artefacts to Daphne and the Girl Guides as he went. Then he poked behind a tall umbrella stand, thinking – Girl Guides, and came upon a parchment citation in a plain wooden frame.

"What's this?" he called.

She peeked round the door and her face fell. "Oh dear. I meant to put that away."

He read from the citation, only half comprehending, "His Majesty King George VI ... Order of The British Empire ... Miss Ophelia Daphne Lovelace."

He looked up. "The O.B.E?" he questioned disbelievingly. "You've got the O.B.E."

Stepping in front of him she plucked the frame off the wall and slid it behind the sideboard, "Like I said, I should have put it away – I don't know why I leave it out ... silly pride I suppose ... It's nothing really."

"Daphne. The O.B.E. is not 'nothing.' How did you get it?"

"You don't want to hear that," she said, heading back to the kitchen.

"On the contrary."

She hesitated, hovering indecisively by the kitchen door, clearly torn between disclosing her past and fetching the next course. "Like I said," she said eventually, seeming to plump for disclosure. "I haven't always been a cleaning lady."

"Obviously."

She gave him a sharp look. "No, not obviously. Quite a few cleaning ladies have been recognised for their services over the years. Just think of the mess we'd be in without them.

"You're avoiding the question, Daphne."

"Yes, I suppose I am ... I don't want to appear rude but ..." she started to drift into the kitchen, "I'm sure you understand."

He didn't understand, had no idea why someone with such an important honour should be reluctant to discuss it, but she forestalled further questioning with a call from the kitchen.

"Treacle sponge and custard alright for desert?" she enquired breezily, letting him know that the subject of the O.B.E. was closed. "You've no idea how much I've enjoyed having someone to cook for," she continued, bustling in with a silver tray, not waiting for his reply. "As you get older, you realise why people go through all the trouble of having children," setting down the tray and not giving him a chance to resurrect the question of the award. "Treacle pudding for one just isn't worth the effort, and those tinned things are awful."

Happy childhood memories flooded back as Bliss surveyed the steaming little mountain of sponge with liquid gold dribbling down its sides. "You don't have children then?"

Daphne took on a puzzled look as if the birth of a child was something that had to be calculated. "I lost the only one I had."

"I'm sorry."

"Oh no, it's not quite what you think," she said, getting quickly up from the table and making a dash back to the kitchen, muttering that she had forgotten the custard.

"Were you married?" he asked on her return.

"I'd better put the coffee on," she said, hurriedly slipping back out. "Not every story has a happy ending, Chief Inspector," she called from the emotional safety of the kitchen. "He wasn't what you would call a good man."

"And there was no one else?"

She was back, shaking her head, "If you don't learn from experience, how do you learn?"

The splash of a car's headlights fell across the dining room window as they finished the coffee a little later.

"I wonder who that could be?" she said, stretching to peer past him out of the window.

"I'd better be going – it's late," he said, pushing back his chair.

"Would you come again tomorrow evening?"

"I can't," he started, saw the instant look of dismay on her face, and gave her a reassuring smile. "I'd love to really, the dinner was wonderful and I've enjoyed your company, but I have to go up to London in the afternoon to pick up a few things and see a man about a dog – a horse to be exact. I'll be back on Wednesday morning."

"Wednesday evening then."

"Alright – as long as nothing crops up. But only if you let me take you out to dinner one night – somewhere really posh, we could even have champagne."

Her eyes flashed with excitement, "Would you?"

"I'd love to."

"That would be wonderful. I've got an outfit picked out already."

Chapter Four

"Psst ... Psst," Detective Sergeant Patterson hissed at D.C. Dowding, catching his attention as he sauntered in the back door of the police station early Tuesday morning. "Loo," he mouthed, steering him into the lower-rank's toilets.

"What's up, Serg?"

"Do me a favour," Patterson started with a degree of sanguinity, opening his fly, aiming at the urinal and handing a note over his shoulder. "Find out who this motor's registered to."

Dowding took the proffered scrap and glanced at the typewritten number. "Sure, Serg – no problem. Whose is it?"

Patterson shot him a puzzled look. "I worry about you at times, Dowding. I wouldn't be asking you to find out if I knew would I?"

"No, Serg. Sorry."

"Thanks," said Patterson walking away shaking his head.

"Hang on, Serg. You haven't told me which case this is."

"No, I haven't, have I?" he replied, still walking, opening the door. "Use yer loaf, lad – make one up."

Dowding stared at the registration number on the scrap of paper thinking it seemed familiar. "You've gotta give me some idea, Serg."

"Know thine enemy, Dowding," said Patterson darkly, "know thine enemy," letting the door slam on its spring behind him.

Patterson was back at his desk in the C.I.D. office when D.I. Bliss walked in. "G'morning, Guv," he called cheerfully, "What d'ye think of The Mitre?'

"Good morning, Pat – It's alright. Any news on the body?"

Patterson screwed up his nose and gave his head a quick shake. "What's the grub like? I hear they do a good dinner."

Bliss was mentally moving ahead and shrugged off the enquiry. "It's O.K. – I want a full briefing this morning at ten: all C.I.D personnel; dog-handlers; search commanders and scenes of crime boys."

"Done," said Patterson scribbling haphazardly on a note-pad.

"I'll be in my office. Let me know when you've arranged it."

"It's already arranged," grinned Patterson exposing protruding gums along with a mouthful of tobacco tinged teeth, more like a snarl than a smile, and leaving Bliss mentally betting that he wouldn't be able to cram them all back into his mouth.

"Oh."

The sergeant patted himself on the back. "I guessed you'd want a strategy session so I put out an order first thing." He left the implication "Before you got out of your pit" unspoken.

"Thanks."

"So how is Daphne?" fished Patterson.

"Daphne?" questioned Bliss, as if her name needed clarification.

Patterson obliged. "Yeah. Daphne. The cleaning lady." Then he sat back, eyebrows raised questioningly, and left Bliss to wriggle.

What's he driving at? wondered Bliss. Why not simply confess to having dinner with her? But something in Patterson's tone held him back, a certain superciliousness – the tone of a blackmailer – hinting: "I know something about you that you wouldn't want broadcast."

Bliss let the silence build – though not intentionally, and was still deciding whether or not to reveal his visit to Daphne's for dinner when Patterson let him off the hook. "Dowding says she bummed a ride to the church-yard yesterday."

"Oh yes – I'd forgotten."

"How old d'ye think she is, Guv?"

Bliss, feeling the stab of yet another barb, gave him a hard stare – He's not suggesting there's something going on between us is he? "I suppose she's my mother's age – sixties, sixty-five maybe," he replied, feigning total disinterest in Daphne as he casually rooted through the morning's sheaf of crime reports.

"Ugh – I bet she's nearer seventy-five, Guv," he said somewhat scornfully.

"How come she's still working?"

"Don't ask me."

"I am," said Bliss, putting down the reports and giving Patterson critical attention.

Clasping his hands behind his head, the sergeant thrust out his legs and stretched back in his chair. "They've tried to get rid of her several times. Last year they gave her a retirement party – dinner, bouquet, carriage clock – the works. Next day she comes in regular as All-Bran, plonks the clock on the Chief's desk and says, "I won't be needing this for a while, Sir." He paused for a chuckle, all gums and teeth, then carried on. "They even stopped paying her at one time. She didn't care – didn't even know for a few months. They had to tell her in the end. "Never mind," she says,

"Give it to the widow's and orphan's fund."

"She seems harmless enough," said Bliss feeling a defence, was called for. "What do you think?"

Patterson, needing time to consider, leant forward to pick up his coffee. "She a nosey old bat really. Not that I mind personally speaking – bit of entertainment. Though some of the youngsters don't like it 'cos she knows so much of what goes on around here. I remember one case ..." he slurped some coffee as he tried to assemble the facts, gave up, and generalised. 'This'll be a tricky one,' I said once, and Daph overheard. 'Nonsense,' she said, 'Old so-and-so did it.' 'How the hell do you work that out?' I said. 'Because his father did exactly the same back in 1937,' she said. And d'ye know," he laughed, "She was absolutely right."

Bliss slid into the chair opposite Patterson and gave him something to think about. "Did I hear she's got some sort of title?"

"Title?" he queried, "Like 'Lady' – Oh yeah," he scoffed, "I can just see it – Lady Daphne Lovelace – society dame and shithouse cleaner."

"No. I was thinking more along the lines of a C.B.E., or O.B.E.?"

A mouthful of coffee splattered across the desk as Patterson exploded in laughter, "The O.B.E. Our Daphne – you are joking, Guv?"

"Shush – she obviously doesn't broadcast it, but no, I'm quite serious."

"Did she tell you that?" he queried, but didn't wait for a response. "I reckon she's having you on. I wouldn't put it past her. She's got a bit of an imagination – I mean, that story about crop circles and UFO's ..."

"Possibly," said Bliss thoughtfully.

"Possibly my foot. I'd bet my pension on it."

"You're probably right. It was just something I overheard. I probably got it wrong."

"I would say so – Daphne – O.B.E.," he guffawed.

Bliss laughed along with him.

"The Major's body?" enquired Donaldson, with more than a trace of hope, as Bliss stuck his head into the chief superintendent's office a few minutes later. Bliss strolled in, sat heavily and gave his head a negative shake.

The senior officer took on a crestfallen look. "Shit, I knew I should have called in the Major Incident Unit ... Oh," his face brightened, "I guess that's a pun ... Major Incident – searching for a major."

"Very funny," said Bliss noticing that the packet of chocolate digestives had taken a serious mauling since the previous day. "May I?" he asked rhetorically, reaching out for one of the last two.

Donaldson swiped the packet off his desk faster than a shoplifter snatching a Rolex. "Rationed," he mumbled, screwing the top and shoving it into a drawer. "One pack a day instead of fags," he explained. "Can't afford to give 'em away."

"Sorry, Sir."

"So what do you make of all this, Dave?"

"On the face of it, it seems too simple. But what if we don't find the body? What if he's disposed of it so cleverly we never find it? Furthermore, what if he knows we can't find it?"

"Where – how?"

Bliss relaxed in the chair with a shrug. "I haven't a clue. If I knew I'd just go out and find it. Do you have any ideas, Sir?"

Donaldson sat back and ruminated on a novelist's palette of barely plausible explanations, "... dissolved it in acid; burnt it to a cinder; fed it to the pigs ..."

"No, Sir," interrupted Bliss, standing up and pacing with frustration. "He didn't have enough time for any of that. In any case, the larger bones would have survived, especially the femurs."

A degree of agitation sharpened Donaldson's tone and the Newton's balls took another hammering. "Well, Inspector, perhaps you have some better suggestions."

"I suppose he might have had time to wall it up in the house or jam it under the floorboards," mused Bliss, not waiting for the steel balls to stop chattering back and forth.

"He might have had time, but the dogs would have sniffed it out."

"What about if he dropped it down an abandoned well and capped it with a load of concrete?"

Donaldson caught the swinging ball as if the suggestion were serious enough to be considered in silence. "That's possible," he started slowly, then shook his head. "Dauntsey would have been plastered in cement."

One look at the senior officer's face was enough to remind Bliss there was no cement. "I don't know then," he concluded and sat back down.

Donaldson took on a phlegmatic tone. "If it doesn't turn up we'll just go for a trial without a body – it's been done before. It may be unusual but certainly not unique."

Bliss wasn't so sure. "What if he gets in the box and recants his confession. Where does that leave us?"

"The jury will still hear the confession."

"I know – but he says, 'I was confused – we had a bit of a barney. Dad went for me with the knife. He got cut somehow – nothing serious, and ...'"

Donaldson wasn't listening, he was still working on devious methods of concealing a body. "I wonder if Dauntsey's playing some sort of intellectual game with us. He's hardly been a raving success in his life. Maybe he's just trying to prove how smart he really is."

"And he's prepared to murder his own father in the process ... I somehow doubt it."

"He's weird enough."

"Possibly, but that still leaves us seriously short of physical evidence."

"What about the duvet? Witnesses saw him bundling something wrapped in it into his truck – and the duvet was obviously missing from his father's room at the Black Horse."

"It was only the duvet," he says to the jurors. "I got blood on it and was taking it to get it cleaned."

"But he buried it in a grave."

Bliss gave it some thought then replied in a Dauntsey-like nasal whine, "Once I'd removed the duvet from the Black Horse with the intention of getting it cleaned I realised that I'd be too embarrassed to return it, so I chose instead to dispose of it. I'd be more than happy to pay ..."

"This is nonsense, Dave," said Donaldson, rising to give strength to his words.

"I know – I'm just thinking out loud. Just saying: What if the jury aren't convinced – not beyond the threshold of doubt? What if they find him 'Not guilty'? Once acquitted, he can't be re-tried. I've just got a feeling the smug little bastard's laughing at us."

"You're suggesting a good lawyer would get him off."

"I'm suggesting any lawyer would get him off. I'm suggesting that even a pox-doctor's malpractice lawyer would get him off. If you ask me we're missing something really important."

Donaldson deflated himself slowly back into his seat as if exhausted by the effort of attempting to compute an explanation for Jonathon Dauntsey's behaviour. "We are missing something – One body: Major for the use of."

"What do you make of this?" asked Bliss reaching into his briefcase and picking out a small plastic evidence bag containing the mangled mounted soldier. "This was in the grave with the duvet," he explained. "The vicar seemed to think it may have been buried with a child but ..."

Donaldson took the figurine with interest. "You told me about it on the phone. A soldier on horseback – what happened to it?"

"Dowding put his spade through it, but it was already flattened."

Donaldson shrugged and dropped it on the desk, "No idea – ask Dauntsey, see what sort of reaction you get."

Bliss retrieved the small figure. "I understand you searched Dauntsey's house, I hear it's stuffed with antiques."

"Hardly. The whole place has been stripped, apart from a couple of rooms. It almost looks as though they were moving out. They probably had to sell stuff off to pay death duties after the Colonel died. Anyway, like I said, Jonathon's never made much of himself. The three of them were living on the Major's army pension from what I can gather."

"What does Jonathon do for a living?"

"Not much – he tried writing books but didn't make a lot of money."

"How many authors do?"

The conversation hit a lull as both men sought something positive to say and Bliss wandered around the room idly setting a few of the executive toys in gentle motion. "The matron seemed to think that the Major and his wife were separated," he said, spinning a gyroscope.

"That's possible. It could explain why he'd taken a room at the pub."

"Not really – she's in the nursing home."

"Maybe it was a symbolic act – distancing himself from the family home."

"I have another source who suggests the Major may not have lived here for years."

"You are well informed, Inspector, but if he wasn't living here where the hell was he?"

"Scotland."

Donaldson digested the information slowly but then dismissed it as irrelevant. "It doesn't matter a great deal where he was living, all we want to know is where he is now. That reminds me – the marine unit are chomping at the bit to search the rivers and ponds."

Bliss cocked his head as if he'd missed something. "Is there some suggestion he dumped the body in water."

"No ... but you know what these special operations blokes are like – any excuse to put on their rubber suits and piss about on company time."

"I suppose the bloody choir will be demanding extra practice time next, so they can give him a good send off."

Donaldson acknowledged the humour with a wry smile. "What should I tell the marine unit?"

Bliss shrugged, "It's your decision boss, but I think we're jumping the gun. I reckon the body will turn up."

"And if it doesn't?"

"We'll have to make an appeal for information in the local press."

The mention of the press had Donaldson extricating the packet of digestives from his drawer. "Some bloody newshound who's had his nose snubbed by us in the past will have a field day," he exploded. "I can just see it ... banner headlines ..." he carried on, and used a biscuit as a baton to write imaginary letters in the air. "'Major loss for Hampshire Police – Anyone in possession of the body should hand it in at their nearest found-property office'..."

"Wait a minute, Sir," cut in Bliss, leaping up as an important notion struck him. "Assuming the Major came down from Scotland to stay at the Black Horse – where are his clothes; his suitcase; his overnight bag?"

Donaldson paused long enough to take a chunk out of the biscuit. "Good point, Dave – get onto it."

Sergeant 'Pat' Patterson was herding the men and women into the briefing room, sending out scouts to drag smokers away from their habit in the prisoner's exercise yard.

Patterson watched the newcomers settling while letting his feelings leak. "You're late. The new D.I. will think we're a bunch of carrot crunchers. You know what these Big City coppers are like – think we spend our time rounding up stray sheep ..."

"Or shagging sheep in your case, Serg," called D.C. Spillings from the back of the room.

A burst of laughter split the expectant air, but quickly fizzled as D.C. Dowding thundered in, his face black with anger, and he rounded on Patterson with clenched teeth and a tight tone. "I wanna word wiv you, Sergeant."

Spillings heard. "What's up, Dowding?" he laughed. "Has the Serg shagged your sheep as well?"

David Bliss marched into the room, stifling the last of the laughter, leaving Dowding scrabbling for a seat.

Patterson rattled off a preliminary assessment of the current situation, not that any of the officers needed to be reminded, and quickly handed the floor to Bliss.

"The man we are searching for only had half a face and one arm," he began after thanking them for their attendance, implying they'd had a choice. "Did we know this?" A sea of blank faces stared at him as if he were an alien. "Well, someone – anyone. Did we?"

A youngish policewoman with sparkly chocolate eyes, frizzy black hair and a smoky voice, finally caved in under his gaze and answered, "No, Sir."

Bliss homed in on her. "Do you think that this is something that we should have found out – maybe – perhaps? I mean, it does explain certain things – why he didn't go into the bar at the Black Horse to pick up the key. Why he slipped in the back way. It may also explain why he may have been living on the estate in Scotland." He glanced at Patterson. "Have we confirmed that by the way?"

Patterson's face was as blank as the sea around him and he quickly threw the spotlight on Spillings. "Have we confirmed that?"

"No, Serg."

Patterson suddenly bristled with enthusiasm, as if it had been his idea from the beginning. "Well, get onto it then. Find out where the estate is and get the locals to check it out. How long has he lived there? When he left? Who looks after him?"

Quickly rifling through his notepad Bliss added to the list. "We also need details of his doctor and dentist up there. We're still trying to establish who saw him last and we need to start putting together a full picture of this man. Talking of pictures – do we have any?"

"I'll get someone to check out the local paper," said Patterson, still bubbling with enthusiasm. "He's the sort of man who's bound to get his mug in the press from time-to-time; local elections, charity do's, that sort of thing."

Bliss stuck in a pin in his bubble. "My information is that he possibly hasn't been around here for the best part of forty years."

A gasp of amazement went round the room.

"I guess you didn't know that either," continued Bliss sweeping his eyes from face to face, feeling a certain satisfaction in the obvious fact that none of them had uncovered such basic information. "Well, what have you got? What do you know? When was he seen last?"

This is getting boring, thought Bliss, with no-one even intimating they might have a snippet of information. "Do any of you know anything about the man you're searching for?" he asked eventually, realising that the silence was becoming embarrassing.

"He's an old dead major," said one, though it was more a question than a statement.

"And ...?"

"And nothing, Sir."

"Do you mean to say that's all you know about the victim?"

D.C. Spillings had a twist of sarcasm in his voice as he answered on behalf of the group. "You'll probably reckon we're pretty stupid, Guv, but I s'pose we was working on the assumption we weren't likely to find two dead old majors on the same day."

You asked for that, thought Bliss and waited while the laughter died down. "O.K. Spillings – I take your point, but that was yesterday. As time goes on, assuming the body doesn't surface, it will become very important to know precisely who we're looking for."

Most of the meeting was consumed with practical arrangements for conducting house-to-house enquiries and interviewing everyone who had been at the Black Horse during the disturbance, but a few constructive ideas were bounced around. Spillings, still seemingly fixated on the paranormal, came up with a half-serious suggestion that the Major's body may have been used for some sort of satanic ritual.

The smoky voiced policewoman swung on him sarcastically. "What? You think they're using crippled old squaddies now in place of beautiful young virgins – I doubt it."

"No," shouted Spillings above the laughter, "I just reckon there might be some religious reason why he flung the duvet in the grave, that's all."

Even Dowding, his mind troubled by some greater dilemma, managed to come up with a proposal that merited attention. "We could do a re-enactment at the same time tonight – see if anyone's hanging about the churchyard who might remember seeing Dauntsey on Sunday. We'd get some idea how long he had to get rid of the body as well."

Arrangements were made for a re-enactment and Daphne breezed in, rounding up discarded coffee cups and stray Kit Kat wrappers, as the meeting broke up. "Good morning, Chief Inspector. How was the Mitre?" she enquired, with a curiously intimate expression.

"Fine thanks," Bliss replied guardedly, breaking off a conversation with Patterson and praying she would say nothing about their dinner engagement.

"I hope they're feeding you well," she added with a wink, obviously taking innocuous delight in having a shared secret.

Thank God, he thought. "Fine, thanks. Yes."

Dowding was prowling around in the background, just out of range, waiting for an opening. Bliss finally caught on. "Do you want something, lad?"

"I wanna speak to Sergeant Patterson." The words "in private" hung unspoken and Bliss obliged, saying he needed to ask Jonathon Dauntsey some further questions.

Bliss was barely out of earshot when Dowding rounded on the sergeant in a venomous whisper. "What the hell's going on, Serg?"

"What d'ye mean?"

"You've dropped me in the shit."

"You wanna keep your mouth shut tight then."

"Oh. Very funneee," he sneered.

"So what's your problem?"

"I did that vehicle search you asked for and it comes up no record. Then I get a very strange phone call from someone at Scotland Yard, asking me why I want to know. I says, 'What's it to do with you?' He says, 'Don't give me no flannel,' real nasty. 'I wanna know who authorised that vehicle search and what for.'"

"Oh shit – you didn't tell 'im did you?"

"How could I – I didn't know – You didn't tell me."

"I meant – you didn't give him my name did you?"

"No, I just said it were the Dauntsey case – checking all the vehicles anywhere near the scene. Must have got a wrong number."

Patterson started to move away. "Good thinking, lad. Well done."

"Wait a minute, Serg," said Dowding grasping his arm, "I wanna know whose motor it is."

Patterson shook his arm free with a scowl. "How the hell should I know? That's why I asked you to run a check."

The other detectives, sensing an approaching storm had scuttled out of the room. Dowding kicked the door shut and closed in on the sergeant, spitting a volley of abuse through clenched teeth. "Don't give me that bollocks. I'm just a fucking prawn to you, aren't I? You used me – you know damn well who that motor belongs to."

Patterson turned his attention to some papers in his hand. "So what if I do?"

Dowding played what he hoped was his trump. "Well, maybe I should tell the new inspector you're doin' dodgy vehicle searches."

Patterson rounded on him. "Are you threatening me?" Then he quickly backed off, softening his face, waving Dowding into a chair and slumping meditatively behind his desk. He sat silently for half a minute or more then spoke earnestly. "Keep this to yourself, but there's something fishy going on. That car number I gave you belongs to our new D.I."

"You ran a search on D.I. Bliss!" exclaimed Dowding incredulously. "What the hell for?"

"Like I said, something smells. It's like this guy didn't exist before he came here. I called Scotland Yard yesterday afternoon just to get a bit of background on him. I thought it was odd that a Met bloke would transfer down here. It's not as though he's from these parts, not judging by his accent."

"So what did they say at the Yard?"

Patterson angrily pulled out a cigarette, stuck it in his mouth, and gave the "No Smoking" sign a filthy look, as if holding it responsible for all his woes. "I got the run-around," he admitted finally. "'Bliss,' they said, 'Never heard of him, wrong department – try F

Division' ... 'Sorry – give Training a call' ... 'Can't help, have you tried Admin?' ... 'What's his collar number?' ... 'How the fuck should I know?' I said. ... 'Can't help you then.' ... 'Just how many blokes have you got called David Bliss?' I asked, and d'ye know what the cheeky sod said? 'Sorry, Sergeant. That's classified,' as if I were some nosey civvy."

D.C. Dowding's forehead creased into a puzzled frown, "I smell a rat."

"A mole more likely," replied Patterson

"Undercover," whistled Dowding. "Police Complaints Authority?"

"They haven't got the brains to do that."

"MI5 or MI6 then."

"Military Intelligence – now there's an oxymoron for you – but why? What have you been up to, Dowding?"

"Nothing, Serg. So, who is he? What's he after?"

Patterson shook his head. "I knew something was up when he said I shouldn't give his name to the papers – assuming that is his name ... Like I said before, know thine enemy, lad."

"Are you sure he is the enemy?"

"All senior officers are, lad – particularly ones that parachute in out of the blue."

"Right, Pat," said Bliss poking his head into the C.I.D. office on his return. "Let's take a look at the house."

"Did you get anything out of Dauntsey?" asked Patterson, stalling while he tried to think of some excuse not to escort him.

"Not much," called Bliss, already retreating into the corridor.

Chapter Five

The Dauntsey house radiated an air of neglect that had spread beyond its boundaries, even infecting the twisting lane that took them off the main road. Patterson had failed in his attempt to find a plausible excuse and they bumped their way toward the entrance gate as water-filled ruts snatched at the steering wheel under Bliss's hands, flinging globs of liquid mud high into the hawthorn hedgerows either side.

A stockade of tall poplars and old oaks surrounded the garden, though a number had been pushed over in past storms and lay, still attached to roots, like guardsmen fainting on a parade ground. A couple of sandstone lions guarding the gates had succumbed to decades of damp and frost and their fierce features had softened like butter on a warm Sunday.

"Is this the right place?" enquired Bliss, fruitlessly searching the brick gate-pillars for a nameplate, correctly guessing that, like the Colonel, the house had no need of a name amongst the locals.

"Yup," nodded Patterson, and Bliss pulled up just inside the gates to survey the sad looking building.

"Bit of a mess," he said, summing up the peeled paintwork, spalled brickwork, dislodged slates and overgrown vegetation.

Patterson declined comment as he went off on foot in search of the constable who was supposedly guarding the property, leaving Bliss to insert the heavy iron key in the ancient lock and let himself into the entrance hall.

A treacly layer of combed brown varnish had stuck tenaciously to the woodwork since the 1930s and, as far as Bliss could tell, was the only thing keeping the place glued together. Weakened joists had sagged under the stress of age and screeched in pain as he tiptoed across the desolate hallway in search of the main rooms. Realising he was treading softly, he paused, and stood silently in the middle of the vacuous hall trying to pick up vibes, attempting to assimilate something, anything, from the house's aura. But, with a slight shiver, he concluded that any warm memories of happier times had dissipated, leaving a physical coldness.

"What warm memories?" he laughed to himself as he moved forward into the house, recalling the few minutes he had just spent with Jonathon Dauntsey in the cell.

Dauntsey's appearance had degenerated. Two days of stubble darkened his chin and the paper boiler suit had picked up the grubbiness of his cell. Nevertheless, Bliss still found himself ill at ease dealing with the man. It was, he reasoned, a bit like finding your accountant has taken a Saturday job clearing tables at

McDonald's. What on earth would you say? How much should you tip?

"We'd better get you some proper clothes," started Bliss in a genuinely concerned tone, waving Dauntsey back onto the bare wooden bench.

"Are you trying to soften me up?"

"What?"

"You know the routine, Inspector, surely – good cop, bad cop."

"You didn't tell me your father was disabled," he began, ignoring the jibe.

"Didn't I?" replied Dauntsey. "I suppose I was always somewhat ashamed of the fact."

"Ashamed?"

Jonathon Dauntsey buried his face in his hands as if shutting out disturbing memories, then he slowly spread his hands like drawn curtains and revealed a face which was shadowed in pain. "My father couldn't speak," he explained. "Not real words – animalistic grunts mainly. Mother seemed to understand him quite well, but it was more a question of mental telepathy and familiarity – like knowing when your dog wants to go for a walk or the cat's thinking of spewing on the carpet."

"But he was still your father ..."

"Father," Dauntsey echoed in a far-away tone. "He was never really a father. He was ..." he paused, scouring the bare cell as if seeking somewhere to hide. "Never mind," he said eventually and veered off on another tack. "They said he was a hero but you'd think he lost us the bloody war the way the locals treated him. No-one ever came to the house, only the postman and delivery boys. I'd sometimes catch them trying to peep in the windows like we were a freak show. I'd throw pebbles at them as they went down the driveway and make howling noises to scare them off – just revenge."

"You still haven't told me what you thought of your father."

Dauntsey gave him a hard stare. "He was always very angry."

"Wouldn't you be if someone had blown half of you away?"

Dauntsey buried his face again.

"You made the reservations at the Black Horse," said Bliss eventually, realising that Dauntsey had clammed up.

"Did I?"

"That's what the landlady says."

"I must have done then."

"You're playing games again. Yes or no, Jonathon?"

"Alright. Yes. I made the reservation – so what?"

Bliss bristled at the other man's smug arrogance and swung on him viciously. "Come on, Jonathon, stop pissing us about. This isn't a game of hide and seek. Where's the body? Where is your father?"

"What are we, the bad cop now?"

Forget the decent clothes, thought Bliss, annoyed with himself for allowing Dauntsey to get under his skin. "If that's the way you want to play it," he said, then pulled the mangled mounted soldier out of his pocket. "Do you know anything about this?"

Dauntsey hardly glanced at it. "Inspector, there are times when the dead are best left buried. Digging up old skeletons only causes trouble."

"Trouble or not. That's what I'm paid to do."

Jonathon rounded on him. "Well, go and dig up somebody else's if you don't mind."

He'd had enough. "Are you going to tell us where your father's body is?" he said, his face an inch from the other man's.

"You really don't need to know, Inspector. I am fully conversant with the law and I can assure you that the absence of a body does not preclude the successful prosecution of a murderer – go right ahead, charge me."

Bliss was unprepared for the extent of desolation as he moved through the house. It was much less opulent than he had expected, certainly less than Daphne had led him to believe. Less grand, less stately, less imposing, almost as if it had shrunk with age. He had assumed that Dauntsey may have sold off some of the best pieces, but rectangular splodges of lightness hung on the walls and patterned the floors, poignantly marking the total absence of pictures and furniture. It was, he decided, not unlike visiting a neglected maiden aunt for the first time in years only to discover she's lost everything – her mind, her looks, her deportment, even her teeth – and has become just a frazzled shell.

Leaning against the fireplace in the main room he ran his fingers meditatively along the ornately carved mantel, viewed the moulded ceilings and panelled walls, and wondered if they retained memories of the more affluent times in which they had been created. Then he circumnavigated the room, tapping the mahogany panelling, speculating on the possibility of hidden doorways or concealed priest's holes where a body might lurk.

Only the huge old-fashioned kitchen displayed evidence of occupation, where a couple of armchairs, a small television and a nest of tables had been drawn up to the black range and a few other pieces of furniture lined the walls.

Returning to the entrance-hall, Bliss took the grand staircase, marvelling at the turned spindles of the balustrade and the width of the oak rail, but, as he reached the upper landing, he paused warily and checked back down the stairs. "Nothing there," he said to himself, but couldn't shake off the feeling that he was being watched or followed.

A corridor stretched before him leading to the rear bedrooms and he strode purposefully forward. Reverberations of his footfalls echoed along the empty corridor and he paused mid-step, listening hard, almost expecting the echoing footsteps to continue, but they stopped. In that moment of deathly silence he felt more afraid than if they had continued and a mysterious energy oppressed him, urging him to get out.

Pulling himself together, he rounded a corner and walked slap-bang into a shadowy grey figure striding soundlessly toward him – a tall, erect man with fuzzy features, not six feet away. Immobilised by the rising panic, he felt his body tensing, ready to run, but the ghostly figure had also shuddered to a stop and now hovered a foot or so off the floor. Bliss feinted to his right as if making to slip past the spectre but the figure seemingly anticipated his move and went with him. Nanoseconds stretched into hours as his mind threatened to explode under the pressure of trying to fathom the unfathomable, then the clogs clicked into place. "It's only a dusty mirror," he breathed with utter relief, but the blood was still coursing through his temples with the beat of a drum.

Drained of energy, he supported himself against a doorframe, asking: What did you expect? What did you think it was – a ghost? No – not a ghost – a ghostly figure from the past. A man in a Maggie Thatcher mask with a sawn off shotgun – Mandy Richards' killer. Frowning at his timidity he forced himself forward, telling himself that it was time to move on. You can't do this. You can't go through life frightened of every corner, every blind alleyway, every door that creaks open.

"Guv!"

He leapt in alarm at the shout.

"Guv. Are you there?" Patterson's voice rang out again and he quickly headed back to the landing, steadied himself on the railing and replied in a cracked voice. "Up here."

"We've got a visitor."

Patterson was at the bottom of the staircase with a gnome-like figure – an ancient man with florid cheeks and a matching jacket, doubled over a knurl-headed walking stick. "What'ye after?" puffed the self-appointed guardian.

"We're police," explained Bliss, slipping quickly down the stairs.

The old man scrutinised them warily, twisting his bent head from side to side to bring them into view. "How da I know you ain't a couple of burglars?"

Bliss got his hand halfway to his pocket before realising he still hadn't picked up his warrant from headquarters. "Show him your warrant card, Sergeant," he said to Patterson and caught the look of alarm on Patterson's face that suggested an explanation was called for. "I'm still waiting for the photos," he whispered from the corner of his mouth then turned to the old man. "You don't know about the Major then?"

The old man took a few wheezy breaths, winding himself up for a lengthy reply, then blew out his cheeks. "I live over at Mile-bottom and I ain't been out fer a day or so – me arfrightuous been playing up wiv the damp."

"So what brings you here today?"

Arnie, as he introduced himself was, according to him, something of a family retainer. An unofficial arrangement that had existed since the death of his father who'd held a more formal position as gardener and general factotum to Colonel Dauntsey. "Me father did everything 'round here," he explained as they left the house and stood under the cast iron front porch. "Now look at the bleedin' mess," he complained, scanning the surroundings and aiming his walking stick at fallen tree after fallen tree as if it were gun. "That lot came down ten years ago in the 'urricane." He shook his head mournfully. "What a bleedin mess – Me old man planted 'em for the Colonel. The whole place 'as gone to rack an' ruin," he concluded, demonstrating his contempt by forcing a few harsh coughs, then he doubled over as a genuine coughing fit took hold.

"You knew the Colonel?" enquired Bliss when the coughing subsided.

"An' 'is boy – that little twerp Rupert," he snorted noisily.

"You would know what happened to him in the war then. We understand he was badly wounded."

"No more than what 'e deserved, I dare say."

Strange reply, thought Bliss. "Why do you say that?"

"Talkin' be thirsty work," Arnie said pointedly, clearing his throat and spitting drily.

Bliss got the message and checked his watch. "I guess it's lunchtime, Sergeant," he said with exaggerated meaning. "Perhaps Arnie would like to join us for a drink." He paused, looked to the old man for a response and saw the flabby cheeks puff into a toothless smile. "That's settled then," he continued without awaiting Patterson's reply. "We might as well go to the Mitre."

"I'll just 'ave a jar a' Guinness to start. I enjoys me jar," said Arnie, his eyes roaming the opulent fixtures of the lounge bar in the hotel.

Bliss found himself straining to understand the thick country accent devoid of the "h" sound. "Sit down then," he said, noticing the way the old man was suspiciously eyeing the deeply padded wing chairs, "The sergeant will get the drinks."

Arnie wandered a little, gently scuffing the carpet for depth while surreptitiously inspecting his surroundings with the reverent intrigue of someone finding themselves taking tea with the Queen at Buckingham Palace. Apparently satisfied, he cleared his throat, tested the squab of a chair with his stick and lowered himself into it. "I usually drink in the public bar," he explained, obviously believing an explanation was required.

The drinks arrived and Bliss kicked off by playing up to Arnie's obvious dislike of Major Rupert Dauntsey. "I've heard Rupert, the Major, was a bit of an idiot. What did he do?"

"I were at Amiens meself, but we 'eard all 'bout it," started Arnie, unaware that his moustache of white beer foam made a comical addition to his red nose and florid cheeks. "The Major were a laffin stock, though t'weren't nuffin to laff 'bout fer the poor blighters unner 'im."

"What happened?" asked Bliss barely controlling his mirth at the wizened clown-like face.

Arnie was in no rush to reach the climax of his account, willing audiences needed as much savouring as a good pint, and, if he wasn't mistaken, his story could run to two or even three pints. Wiping his sleeve across his face, he offered some background information as a filler. "If it 'adn't bin that 'is old man wuz a Colonel 'e'd 'ave bin canon fodder like t'rest of us," he said, took a long pull on his drink, then spat, "Toffee nosed little twerp."

"So," started Bliss again, glancing at his watch, "what can you tell us about the Major, or the old Colonel?"

"A proud man was the Colonel," Arnie replied, noticeably stiffening his back in respect. "'E were in the life-guards ... Paschendale, Ypres, Mons ... all the mudbaths. Got gassed in the trenches but wouldn't come back without 'is men ... so they say. But that boy of 'is, Rupert – the Major, were a big disappointment. 'E wuz nowt but a little runt. Failed the h'university they say. The guards wouldn't 'ave 'im, even with 'is old man being the Colonel and all. So 'e does the next best and joins the Royal 'orse Artillery." The old man paused for a short cough and lubricated his throat with the remains of his first pint. "Good stuff that," he said, then stared wistfully at the empty glass until Bliss gave in.

"Another?"

Patterson scuttled off to the bar without waiting to be asked and Arnie, considering it respectful to await his return, fussed around with his pipe until the second pint sat in front of him. "It were a little after D-Day when it 'appened," he continued after a short slurp. "They wuz dug in outside Paris when the Major got the order to retreat – the 'igh command had got wind of a counter attack." He paused and stared out of the window with glazed eyes as he relieved the horror of war. "Massacred they wuz," he continued, his gaze, his thoughts and voice all very far away.

"Massacred?" echoed Bliss, probing gently.

Arnie turned from the window, his face suddenly pale, his cheeks sunken. "The Jerries was on 'em in a flash," he explained. "Damn near wiped 'em out. Only an 'andful got away an' they wuz all pretty badly shot-up, the Major included."

"So they didn't have a chance to retreat."

Arnie flashed him such a dirty look that Bliss realised immediately he had missed the point.

"'Course they 'ad time to retreat, plenty of bloomin' time," he spat. "But the Major was such a prissy-ass 'e weren't gonna leave the place in a such a state. Didn't want the bloody Boche accusing 'em of being scruffy so-an-so's, 'e said. So 'e 'ad all 'is troops running round tidying the place up, even made 'em pick up all the shell casings and put 'em in neat piles."

Patterson, who had been stewing in silent contemplation since Dowding's revelation about Bliss's registration number, couldn't contain himself. "You're joking."

Arnie looked offended and crossed himself, saying, "As God is my witness – 'e made 'is men pick up every last bit of rubbish – even filled in the latrines – an' all the time the Jerries were picking 'em off. Everyone hereabouts knows what 'appened – ask any of 'em. That's why when 'e come back no-one would 'ave anything to do wiv him, only old Doc Fitzpatrick. An' rumour 'as it as how the old Doc only treated 'im 'cos 'e went private an' always paid cash."

Bliss cogitated on the ridiculous spectacle of troops tidying up the battlefield under fire and, despite Arnie's invocation of the Supreme Commander, put it down to the sort of outlandish rumour that would be spread about any unpopular officer. "You'll have to carry on here," he said to Patterson, feeling he'd heard enough. "I've got some business to attend to in London this afternoon. I'll be back before nine for the re-enactment."

Patterson gave him a jaundiced look then bobbed out of his seat. "I'd better get back to the station," he said quickly, then mumbled about the need to supervise the house-to-house enquiries.

"I was rather hoping you could arrange to get Arnie home."

Arnie heard. "I could prob'ly make me own way if I 'ad another pint," he said, his voice pained in self-sacrifice, as he held out the empty glass and slumped comfortably back in the deep chair.

Chapter Six

Sidestepping a guilty feeling that he was abandoning the hunt for the Major, telling himself there was little he could do until the body surfaced, Bliss set off for London. The driver of a small blue Volvo obligingly let him escape from the Mitre car park into the High Street and, with a quick salute of thanks, he slipped his Rover into the stream of traffic heading out of town toward the motorway.

The grey overcast had evaporated into milky blue and the hazy sun was already drying off the damp pavements as Bliss navigated the narrow streets, barely aware that the Volvo was tagging along behind. As the road opened up Bliss swept aside the fears that had been with him since the morning's visit to the Dauntsey house and he found himself conducting the *1812* overture, volume blaring, bass speakers pulsating.

The music, erupting with canons, muskets and rifle volleys, rose in a crescendo and transported Bliss away from the bloody murder of the Major to another time, another place, and an altogether different scenario of violent death. In his mind he conjured formations of brightly festooned French Dragoons sweeping across the steppes, swooping out of the early morning mist, sabres and lances glinting in the sunrise, only to be mown down by a terrifying rabble of Cossacks armed with broadswords.

The triumphant chorus and jubilant peel of bells signified the finale of the orchestrated battle and Bliss savoured each chord almost as though it were the last time he would hear it. The final strains hung in his ears for a few seconds then the air stilled. The gentle buzz of the engine and the steady hum of the tyres on the road seemed only to augment the sense of tranquillity that had returned. Bliss loosened his grip on the wheel, relaxed back into his seat and glanced in the rear-view mirror. He jerked alert – the Volvo was still there and a chill rippled through him as he caught a glimpse of it slipping in behind a van. "Don't be stupid," he chided himself, dismissing immediately the possibility that he was being followed.

Why would someone be following me?

You know why. You remember what Mandy Richards' murderer had screamed across the courtroom at the Old Bailey? He remembered. The killer's words were forever burned into his brain. "I'll get you for this copper – I'll get you."

Forget it, thought Bliss. Ignore it – it'll go away. Like you ignored the threatening letters, the midnight phonecalls and the shadowy stalker, until someone put a bomb through your letterbox and took out your front door.

O.K., he conceded, but don't panic. He'll be more nervous than me.

Why? He's done it before, remember. And he's already spent one lifetime in prison: becoming acclima-

tised to the routine, inured to the coarseness and violence and revelling in the irresponsibility of institution-
al life. So how will he do it – run me off the road into a
bridge support; pull alongside and put a single bullet in
my brain; or pick off a tyre and laugh as I lose control
and career into a bus or truck.

Passing an exit ramp, he checked the mirrors again.
A small blue car was dissolving into the distance as it
slowed in the deceleration lane and he admonished himself for allowing his imagination to run away with him.
With a sigh of relief he rummaged through a glove-box
of cassette tapes, seeking something less climactic than
Tchaikovsky, and pulled himself together, telling himself
that he was being ridiculous. A hit-man wouldn't be driving a Volvo, he told himself. A hit-man wouldn't be
seen dead in a Volvo. Hoodlums don't drive poky little
Volvos with more safety features than a spermicidal
condom. He would be a Jag man, or a Mercedes or
BMW. Even the smallest of petty villains could manage
a Jaguar, especially a hot one, and Mandy's murderer
was no small time villain.

Relaxing, Bliss amused himself with the notion of a
villain turning up at a mobster's convention, wearing a
slick suit with an ominous bulge under his left armpit,
driving a little blue family saloon. But five minutes later
the Volvo was still there and his pulse raced as he spotted it tailgating a large yellow rental van with the hire
company's telephone number emblazoned across the
bonnet. Ignoring the blare of an annoyed motorist's
horn he eased out and straddled the white line as he
manoeuvred into a position where he could see the following driver. Peering deeply into the mirror he sought
a familiar face, and a familiar pair of eyes – the same icy
eyes that had stared unflinchingly at him across the
courtroom eighteen years earlier as he stood in the wit-

ness box describing the pointless murder of Mandy Richards. But he couldn't see, not clearly. His vision was obscured by distance and the constantly shifting traffic that conspired time and again to block his view.

Vowing to concentrate on his driving, he dismissed worries about the Volvo but couldn't dislodge Mandy Richards from his mind, demanding to know whether he would have ducked if he'd known someone was behind him in the bank? But he'd been through this a thousand times – knew the answer – knew there was no answer. He *had* ducked – flinging himself sprawling onto the floor as the blast ripped through the space he'd vacated – nothing could change that.

Mandy Richards' memory continued its torment as he sped along. She would have been thirty-eight, if she'd lived, he calculated, recalling that she had been twenty when both barrels of the shotgun exploded and ripped a cavity in her chest large enough to get his fist into. She had been a pretty girl, beautiful he had thought, seeing her framed photograph propped on her coffin at the funeral, though he'd not noticed at the time of the shooting. His eyes and mind had focused only on the gaping wound.

A mental snapshot of the scene in the bank hit him with the stark clarity of an unkind mirror and the road ahead dissolved into images of screaming bank customers, terrified tellers crouching behind the counter, and a tiny girl in a red dress clutching her mother's hand while a puddle of pee grew around her feet. And there, spread-eagled on the floor, the lifeless bundle of flesh that had been Mandy Richards.

He had seen the shots coming, not physically, not with his eyes. It was more of a feeling – a pulse of evil intent so strong he would have known the man was going to fire even if he hadn't noticed the fingers tightening on the triggers. He had dropped to the floor, oblivious to the fact that the young woman was standing right behind him. She'd not felt the evil stare, hadn't seen the tensing fingers. She was, in any case, too petrified to move in any direction.

The blast of acrid smoke from the gunshot still filled the air as Bliss picked himself off the floor, stared in horror for a fraction of a second at the crumpled rag-doll figure, then, without any deliberation as to the consequences, lunged at the hooded villain. Snatching the gun out of the startled man's hand he set about him, slamming the barrels into his ribs, doubling him over, then pounding him repeatedly over the head until an assistant manager vaulted the counter, staid his arm, and brought him to his senses.

The gunman, a professional mobster in a comical Maggie Thatcher mask, slumped motionless into a corner with tendrils of blood dribbling out from under the mask and creeping down his T-shirt and Bliss stood back, his elation quickly turning to horror as he realised what he'd done. It had been the mask, he reasoned later when he'd had a chance to cool down. He couldn't have beaten an unarmed man senseless, whatever the provocation, but, dehumanised by the mask, the robber had brought the attack on himself.

What else could I have done? What else could I have done? he kept asking himself as both customers and staff cringed fearfully away from him. And he was stunned by the look of revulsion on the face of the woman clutching the wet child. Who was the villain here?

"Police!" he shouted to the stunned bystanders as if justifying his actions. "Get an ambulance!" he continued, screaming at no-one in particular, rushing across the blood-slickened marble floor to tend to the young woman who had taken the blast intended for him.

"Oh my God," he sighed, seeing her pulverised chest, mentally tearing through the Red Cross first-aid manual, desperately searching for guidance on gunshot wounds – but his mental page was blank. O.K. Don't panic, he said to himself, think about the general rules. The three "B's" of first-aid flashed instantly to mind and he easily recalled the first two. "Breathing, Bleeding, and ..." but then his mind froze, unable to remember the third. He gave up and went with the first two, deciding the ambulancemen would arrive within seconds and take over before he had need of the third.

Picking up one of the girl's limp wrists he dug in his fingers desperately searching for the rhythmic beat of a pulse – nothing. He gripped harder, so hard that he felt the beat of his own heart pulsing through his fingertips and, with rising optimism, stuck his ear to her mouth. She wasn't breathing. She had nothing to breath with. A couple of hundred lead pellets had turned her lungs into pin cushions. But he wouldn't give up – he couldn't give up. It was his fault. If he hadn't been so stupid. "Armed police," he had shouted at the robber. Armed with what? A blank cheque and a ballpoint Biro.

"Get a fucking ambulance!" he screamed again as he knelt over her, still searching his memory for a meaning to accompany the third "B."

"Stop the bleeding," he ordered himself, but she wasn't bleeding, the blood pump that had been her heart was as decimated as her lungs. "Put her in the recovery position then." Recover – from this?

With his mind racing, desperately searching for a way to resurrect the dead girl until a doctor or ambulanceman could arrive with a defibrillator and oxygen mask, he set about tidying up her dishevelled chest. One breast ripped aside by the blast, still clinging to her body with a flap of skin, had flopped loosely to one side and he tenderly positioned the bloodied mound of flesh back in place but, beyond that, could think of little to do other than search for a pulse again, and again, and again.

Over the years, images of that displaced breast had sprung to mind whenever he thought of Mandy. It was her pulped lungs and pulverised heart that had ceased to keep her alive but, deep in his psyche, it was her mutilated breast that symbolised her demise.

"Where's the ambulance?" he cried, convinced that someone with the right training could work a miracle.

"Where's the police," echoed one of the survivors huddling in a corner well away from the bandit and the dead woman.

"I *am* the police," he screeched, stung by the implied criticism.

It had only been a couple of minutes since the gun's blast had fractured the air and filled the young woman's chest with lead-shot, yet those minutes had the mind-concentrating intensity of a hand grenade with the pin pulled. Do something! Do something! Bliss was screaming inside. Then he had a revelation, breathed "cardiac massage" in relief, and was convinced he had solved the first-aid riddle.

His elation wilted almost immediately as he realised that Mandy's chest offered absolutely nothing solid to palpitate. Her sternum and half a dozen ribs had been blown into shards. His heart sank and, with an impatient eye on the door, he was reduced to carefully arranging her body ready for a stretcher. Ignoring the hole in her chest, inwardly praying that it might somehow heal itself, he stretched out her legs, smoothed the creases out of her skirt which had ruckled under her bottom.

"Put her in the recovery position," suggested someone in the huddle of terrified customers.

Recover! From this? He said to himself and sat back, downhearted, to wait for the ambulance.

A close call with a speeding Rolls startled him from the nightmarish spectacle in the bank and forced him to check the mirror. The Volvo was still there. He shrugged it off as simply a coincidence, concluding that the driver just happened to be travelling to London, the same as him. However, a mile or so further on he felt himself soaring with relief as the other driver signalled his intention of leaving the motorway and swooped into the deceleration lane. Thank God, Bliss thought, switching his eyes and attention back to the road ahead. Behind him the trailing car took the exit lane and slowed to a crawl. Then, at the last moment, the Volvo swung back onto the motorway, tucked swiftly in behind a large pantechnicon and resumed the chase.

Bliss had just got his mind away from Mandy's breasts and back on the Dauntsey mystery when fast approaching road works forced him to a crawl amongst bunching traffic. Slowing, he checked his mirror and caught a familiar flash of blue. "Shit!" he shouted, although he still couldn't shift the underlying notion that a killer wouldn't be seen dead in a Volvo.

O.K., I've had enough, he said to himself, pulled into the slow lane without indication, slammed on the brakes and steered for the hard shoulder.

"Let's see what you do now," he said, telepathically addressing the pursuer.

The Volvo shot past in a blur, tangled up in a knot of cars vans and trucks, but the glimpse of the driver's profile was sufficient to tell him that the man was certainly of the right age and colour.

Skidding to a stop in a cloud of loose gravel, Bliss found himself next to an emergency phone and was already out of the car and picking it up before he stopped himself. What's the point – what's the emergency? I think I'm being followed! He dropped the phone with the realisation that he would have the motorway control officer in stitches.

"Some clown at Junction 129 reckons he's being followed," he imagined him laughing to his colleagues with his hand over the mouthpiece. "Can you give me a description?" the officer would ask with a barely concealed smirk.

"A blue Volvo."

"And the registration number ...?"

"I don't know ... S registration. I think."

"You think?"

"I couldn't see properly."

The hand would slide back over the mouthpiece, "He says he couldn't see."

"What about the driver, Sir? Could you see him?" he imagined the next question might be.

"Male, white," he would say and cringe while the control officer repeated the description sarcastically before saying, "I guess there's not more than a quarter of a million Volvo drivers in the country fitting that description, Sir. It shouldn't be too difficult working out which one was following you."

"You don't understand," he would say in frustration, "this man's a killer."

"O.K., Sir. In that case you'd better give me a full description."

That's a good point – what does he look like? he asked himself, deciding against using the phone and getting back into the car. What did he look like 18 years ago? he tried to recall, then realised that the exercise was pointless. The killer would have gone from being little more than a teenager to almost middle-age in the intervening years. And what had eighteen years in prison done to him? He'd be forty-one now, thought Bliss, feeling foolish as he drove off, quickly picking up speed.

The Volvo, bonnet up, looking like a breakdown victim, was parked on the next overpass with the driver carefully scrutinising the vehicles passing below. Bliss's Rover came into view and in a flash the blue bonnet was dropped and the small car was hurtling down the approach ramp and back on the motorway. Bliss saw. Already spooked, his senses were on high alert and he caught a glimpse of the blue car weaving in and out of traffic as the driver struggled to catch up to him.

"One more test," he mused and patiently waited until the car had settled into place behind a Volkswagen van. Then he indicated his intention of moving into the fast lane.

"Yes," he said triumphantly as the Volvo nosed out from behind the Volkswagen and began to overtake.

"Now let's see what you'll do," he said, cancelling the indicator and braking slowly. The Volvo slid smoothly back in behind the Volkswagen just as he suspected it would.

"Gotcha," he said, but took little satisfaction in proving his point. Now what? he asked as warning sirens blared in his mind: Speed up; slow down; turn off; get the number ... Yes! Get the number and write it down. At least leave a record in the wreckage and hope that, whatever happens, the Rover doesn't explode in a fireball when the bullets rip into it.

"Dauntsey played up to the old witch," Donaldson fumed as he left the court an hour later with D.S.

Patterson in one car, while Jonathon Dauntsey was carted away by his solicitor in another. "Bail!" he screamed. "Bail for a fucking murderer. Did you see the look she gave him?"

Patterson, and half the people in the public gallery, had witnessed the metamorphosis as the hatchet-faced old magistrate had preened back a few wispy strands of her silvery hair, put on a sympathetic smile, and locked eyes with Dauntsey in the prisoner's dock. "The police are asking that you be remanded to their custody for another three days, Mr. Dauntsey. Is there anything you would like to say at this time?"

Dauntsey cleared his throat affectedly, dropped his head deferentially and spoke in a soft clear tone, "I'm certain that you will make the right decision, Ma'am – I am in your hands."

In your bed as well, thought Donaldson, if the gooey-eyed look on his face meant anything.

"Are you not applying for bail, Mr. Dauntsey?" she continued with an encouraging mien and a clear implication that he should.

Superintendent Donaldson leaned into the crown prosecutor and whispered. "What the hell is she playing at?"

The rotund little prosecutor barrelled to his feet and coughed loudly. "I feel I should remind your worship that this is a murder case, Ma'am."

Her face hardened back to steel as she swung on him. "And you don't have a body, do you?"

"No, Ma'am."

The hearing had gone downhill from then on. A court solicitor had been appointed, bail applied for and, despite vociferous objections by the crown prosecutor whose bald head had turned apoplectic purple, it had been granted.

Detective Sergeant Patterson and his superintendent had hit the town centre at afternoon rush hour en-route back to the police station and Donaldson had pulled some papers from his briefcase to occupy himself, but Patterson was incensed by what had occurred and had whinged angrily about the magistrate from the moment they left the court. "It really pissed me off when she asked if he had any complaints about the way we'd treated him," he moaned angrily. "What did she think – that we'd used thumbscrews?"

"Probably," mumbled the superintendent without consideration.

"Did you hear her sweet-talking him?" continued Patterson, then he mimicked the old woman's crackly voice. "'Now then, Mr. Dauntsey. Are you going to tell the police what happened to your father's body?' And what did he say in that smarmy voice of his? 'I feel it would be best if he is allowed to remain at peace.' Huh! It's enough to make you chuck-up."

Donaldson was trying to concentrate on his work and his tone had a tinge of annoyance. "Just don't chuck up in the car, Sergeant."

Patterson wasn't listening, his mind was still back in the court. "It got me the way she says, 'In view of the fact that he won't tell me, I see no reason why he should tell you.' I do – If I had my way I'd put me boot in his bollocks – that'd make him squeal."

"I wouldn't doubt it, Sergeant, but it's purely academic. We still haven't found the body and he's been granted bail. Now ... if you don't mind ..."

But Patterson was boiling and couldn't resist grumbling. "I thought she was gonna give him twenty quid out of the poor box."

Donaldson's look of annoyance eventually shut him up but half a minute later a defective traffic light gave the sergeant time, and an excuse, to start talking again. "Bloody light's broke," he moaned, then abruptly changed the subject. "Mr. Bliss is gonna be pretty upset when he gets back."

Donaldson ignored him. The silence sat heavily for a few seconds, then Patterson tried prodding, "He's gone to London – It must have been something important."

"'S'pect so."

"He seems like a good man – our new D.I."

"Uh – huh," nodded Donaldson his head still buried in paperwork.

"I expect he'll find it quiet here after the Met."

"Probably."

"I mean ... It's not always this busy. We don't get a murder everyday."

"Thank God."

"So, was he actually at Scotland Yard? – our D.I. Bliss."

"Guess so."

"I jus' wondered, 'cos I was talking to someone at the Yard yesterday and they didn't know him."

"It's a big place."

"Yeah – but you'd think they'd ... "

Donaldson looked up and protested. "Sergeant ... Are you trying to drive this car or drive me round the bend?"

"Drive the car, Sir."

"Well shut up and drive then."

"Sorry, Sir."

Bliss was still driving; still trying to get a look at the Volvo's number plate and the face of the driver; still trying to remember the face beneath the mask.

It was the bank's under-manager who had eventually steeled himself to unmask the robber, although it wasn't concern for the lifeless man's well-being that had over-come his reticence. The manager was at lunch and he had been left in charge. Having one dead body in the foyer was going to be difficult enough to explain, he didn't want two, if he could avoid it.

Bliss, engrossed in his attempts to revive Mandy Richards, hardly noticed as Margaret Thatcher's face was peeled away revealing an unconscious thug with blood oozing from his mouth, nose and scalp.

"Oh my God!" breathed the under-manager assuming the worst, but, freed of the mask, the robber soon began to stir.

"Tie him up," shouted Bliss, but the youthful exec-utive shook his head.

"He isn't going anywhere – only the hospital."

In the aftermath of the botched robbery Bliss had found himself caught up in a controversy and knew his colleagues were weighing up the odds between him receiving a commissioner's commendation for bravery, a charge of attempting to murder the bank robber or the station "Tosspot" award for stupidity.

"You'll get something for this," everyone agreed, and in his own mind he wouldn't have felt maligned if he'd been convicted of attempted murder, or, at a mini-mum, an offence of causing Mandy's death by reckless over-enthusiasm.

The commissioner's commendation won the day, but he had quickly squirrelled the vellum certificate into a rarely visited drawer.

With his mind agitated by the disturbing memories, Bliss had been letting the car drive itself and was horri-fied to find his speed had crept to more than a hundred miles an hour. Easing his foot off the accelerator he realised that subconsciously he had been trying to out-pace the Volvo. And, once he'd slowed, he did his best to remember the bandit's face and found himself replaying the trial in his mind. What had he claimed in his defence? "I never meant to hurt no-one. It were the copper's fault. If he hadn't shouted about having a gun I would never have shot."

His assertion hadn't saved him. "You have been found guilty of murder in the first degree," the judge had said sagely, adding, "Life imprisonment is the only punishment which I am permitted by law to impose." And, despite the seriousness of his words, he obviously took great satisfaction saying it.

Following the verdict Bliss had turned to the public gallery in time to see a light of triumph flash across Mrs. Richards' face, then she crumpled under an emotional millstone and burst into tears, overcome by relief that she had finally laid her daughter to rest. But the drama wasn't over. The prisoner's dock erupted in violence as a couple of burly guards moved in on the convict.

"It's that fuckin' copper what should go down. Him and is big mouth," he yelled as the jailers tried to take him from the dock. "He's the one who should go down, not me. I'm innocent," he screamed as he flailed his fists at the men. "I wouldn't shoot no woman. What sort of scum do you think I am?"

The three bodies sank briefly beneath the dock's parapet as the guards smothered the enraged prisoner, before dragging him to his feet, with his arms painfully up his back, as the judge added fourteen days loss of privileges to his sentence.

"Take him away," ordered the judge and the prisoner shot Bliss a venomous look that penetrated his skull with a viciousness that hurt.

"I'll get you for this ... pig," he screamed, then he screamed again as one of his elbows dislocated.

"Forget it," everyone said afterwards, but the impact of the killer's words had eaten away at Bliss for weeks. Forget what? That he'd been accused of murder or forget that he had caused Mandy's death. He was innocent, everybody said so. But innocent of what? Innocent of crime. But what about impulsive behaviour and misjudgement – was he innocent of that.

"It was just bad luck," they said and he had to agree.

It was bad luck – bad luck for Mandy that he had been in the bank that day. If he hadn't been there the killer would have walked away with a bagful of loot and the only losers would have been the insurance company.

Getting off the motorway without being seen by the driver of the Volvo seemed, to Bliss, to be his safest option and, as he spotted a coach slowing to take the exit into a service area, he took a chance. Pulling sharply in front of the coach, ignoring the driver's angry fist, he slipped into the deceleration lane. Then, shielded by the monstrous vehicle, he drove into the coach park and hid amongst the herring-boned ranks of leviathans. Had the Volvo followed? He couldn't tell – the coaches blocked his view.

Keeping his head down, Bliss infiltrated the snake of passengers spilling out of one of the vehicles and had taken a dozen paces before realising he had joined a party of shrivelled pensioners. He was sticking out like a sunflower in a cabbage patch. Telling himself that it was unlikely the killer would risk accidentally hitting a little old lady mid-afternoon in a busy car park, he stayed with the group and made it safely to the self-service restaurant.

Security cameras scanned the room and, picking out a table in full view of one of them, he slunk into a seat opposite a lumpy girl with a Neanderthal brow. With his head bowed he searched the crowded room, seeking a single man doing the same. He came up blank. Everybody seemed to be in pairs or groups – but hadn't he joined a group and, looking across at the girl in the opposing seat, wasn't he now part of a pair.

The girl caught him looking. Her hooded eyes under heavy brows viewed him critically for a few seconds then, as if he were her audience, she sniffed loudly and openly swiped a dribble of snot off the end of her nose onto her sleeve. Having fixed his attention, she delved into a ragged canvas handbag and, with a victorious grunt, flourished a blue airmail envelope and began unfolding a dog-eared letter. Her rubbery mouth formed each word as she read silently from the flimsy paper for a few seconds, then she paused, looked up, and laughed uproariously. Bliss shrank himself lower in the seat as her laughter drew looks from across the room, thinking, just my luck – a loony tune.

Every few words in the letter brought another gale of laughter and the girl, seemingly unaware of the commotion she was causing, read further and laughed even louder. Bliss frantically searched for some means of escape, fearing he'd become caught up in some sort of performance art, a fringe festival event perhaps, but all eyes were on the girl. Any movement on his part would have drawn attention. He was trapped between a killer and a nutter.

"Have you been here before?" she suddenly enquired, with a fixed stare that pinioned him to his seat.

"A few times," he mumbled.

"I've been here six times."

Something in the earnestness of her tone made him suspicious. This was a motorway service area, not the Tate Gallery or even Disneyland. "Six times?" he queried.

"I was Anne Boleyn's principal lady-in-waiting once," she insisted haughtily, and leant over the table to whisper confidentially "You wouldn't believe what I used to do for Henry when she wasn't up to it."

Bliss swallowed hard. "And the other times you were here ...?"

She leant back. "I was a cat once."

Without the demented laughter the crowd began shrinking away, pretending disinterest, pretending that they had never been interested. Bliss readied to leave, waiting his moment until all eyes were elsewhere, but a strong feeling of *Deja-vu* suddenly held him in check. This wasn't a bank, the eccentric woman wasn't a killer, as far as he knew, but the whole situation seemed to have taken on the same surrealistic quality as the time he'd bludgeoned Maggie Thatcher's effigy half to death, following Mandy's murder.

As he rose, a tingling sensation on the nape of his neck convinced him the killer was present and he quickly scanned the faces searching for the Volvo's driver. No-one looked even faintly familiar. Then he paused in terror as a voice behind him shouted, "Oy!" It was the lunatic – he kept walking. "You never know," she called after him with absolute sincerity. "You might have been someone famous too."

Five miles further on the driver of the blue Volvo had pulled into an Esso station and was on the phone, his hand shaking as he whispered into the mouthpiece. "I've lost him," he admitted, and before he took a breath to explain, the handset exploded in his ear.

"Shit – How? Where? When?"

"I think he caught on."

"You useless piece of dog's ..."

"I couldn't help it – he seemed jumpy."

"Of course he was jumpy – wouldn't you be if you

were being followed by an incompetent turd like you?"

"Look, don't blame me. I didn't ask to do this. You should've done it yourself."

"All I wanted was a clean job – Oh forget it. I'll do it myself. You'd better come back."

Bliss dawdled in the service area for over an hour, vacillating between brazening it out, on the betting the killer wouldn't strike in such a public place in broad daylight, and slinking back to the car with his head down. In the end he decided to call for assistance and, without giving his name, phoned Scotland Yard from a booth and requested D.C.I. Bergen.

"He's on a course, Sir," said the operator.

Police College – Bliss had forgotten. Junior command course – having his brain adjusted and his elbow lubricated.

"What about Superintendent Wakelin?"

"Can I ask who's calling?"

"Michael – just say Michael. He'll know."

A few seconds later the dead air was replaced by the hollowness of a speaker phone, but no voice.

"Superintendent Wakelin?" Bliss enquired speculatively.

The silence continued for a split second as the man at the other end struggled to place the voice "Oh Dave – Yes ... Sorry. How are you doing?"

Bliss hesitated, "It's Michael, Sir."

"Oh shit, of course. Sorry, Dave – I mean Michael. Fuck – this is confusing, isn't it? Would you like to call back and start again?"

"No, that's alright, Sir. I'm on a pay phone."

"Thank Christ. Well what can I do for you ... Michael?"

"Can we meet?"

"Sure. When? Where?"

"Eighteen hundred hours at location B, if that's convenient."

A slight pause signalled uncertainty. "Location B," he repeated vaguely.

How the hell did this man ever become a superintendent? He's got a brain like a sieve. "Location B ..." Bliss was about to explain, then lost his patience. "Haven't you got the list of locations? ... It's that pub near Camden Lock."

Samantha was next and his daughter answered her mobile phone at the first ring. "Dad – Where are you?"

"How's your mother?" he countered, wary of giving anything away.

"Dad – I'm expecting a call."

Did he detect a touch of aggravation? "Oh sorry – I just need a few things from your attic."

"O.K. I'll be home at ..."

"No," he cut in, "I don't want to come round. Will you bring them to me at the usual place?"

"Dad – surely we don't still have to do that. It's been more than six months ..."

"I can't take the risk, Sam. I have enough on my conscience already ... if anything happened to you."

"You don't think he's still out there do you?"

"I was followed today," he admitted.

"Shit."

"Don't worry, I lost him."

The phone went silent at her end. "What's the matter, Sam?" he asked eventually.

"You know what's the matter – I'm scared shitless. I don't know why you don't just stay in the safe house until they catch him – he's a maniac."

"I'll be alright – I'm beginning to wish I'd never told you."

"Well, perhaps that goes for me too. But whether I know or not doesn't change the fact that I could become an orphan any day now."

"Sam, that isn't going to happen. Anyway, you're twenty-eight. You don't become an orphan at that age."

"Don't be picky. What do you need?"

He gave her a list, set a time, and with a final fruit-less search for the Volvo around the service centre, set off for London.

Tottenham Court Road was more or less on Bliss's route, once he'd reached London. He parked the Rover under a "No parking" sign, stuck a "Police – on duty" card in his windscreen and told himself that he would-n't be more than a couple of minutes.

The shop window was exactly as he remembered it from when he'd dragged Samantha there at the age of ten. The visit had been more his treat than hers – one of the times when a son would have come in handy. An antique bow window of tiny mullions, set in a latticework of lacquered wood, bulged out over the pavement, and a life-size guardsman, as stiff as the plywood on which he was painted, stood sentinel at the door.

The entirely appropriate smell of polished leather and Brasso had not changed, neither had a tinny elec-tronic bugle sounding reveille overhead as he opened the door under the sign, "The Little Soldier – Dealers in miniature military memorabilia."

A tall man with a well-disciplined moustache, a full head of grey hair, (fractionally longer than regulation and afflicted with an unruly curl), modelling a sharp mohair suit, came smartly to attention behind his counter. "Can I be of assistance, Sir?"

"Just looking," he lied, annoyed at being pounced upon before he'd had a chance to draw breath, and he took his time studying an army of vividly painted small soldiers artistically arranged on a battlefield of green baize. "Very pretty," he said finally sensing the man standing impatiently alongside him.

The instant frown of disapproval told Bliss he'd chosen the wrong expression. "These are historically accurate reproductions of military personnel ... not Barbie dolls, Sir," said the dealer, his officer's accent as crisp as the creases in his trousers.

Bliss mumbled something that could have been mistaken for an apology and dragged the plastic bag containing the remnants of the toy soldier out of his pocket. "I wonder if you can tell me anything about this?"

The look of abhorrence on the dealers face seemed fairly clear as he took the pieces and "tut-tutted," leaving Bliss in no doubt that, in his Lilliputian world, the miniature statuary had never been a Rodin or even a Royal Doulton. In fact, Bliss was quite prepared for him to pucker his mouth, spit drily in disgust, and drop the pieces disdainfully into a garbage bin. But he didn't. He studied them seriously, minutely examining each piece with a jewellers loupe, "tut-tutting" again and again until Bliss could stand it no longer and made a move to examine one or two of the other armies in the room.

"How did this happen?" asked the dealer without taking his eye off the magnifying glass, as if sensing Bliss's lack of attention.

"Dropped," suggested Bliss nonchalantly.

"Hmm," he hummed, then "tut-tutted" and gave Bliss an inquisitive look. "I don't think so." But he did-

n't press the point, returning to the model, leaving Bliss
with the distinct impression that he was in his bad books.

With the inspection completed the dealer put down
his glass and thoughtfully arranged the two halves of the
model on a circle of baize. "Looks as though someone
took a hammer to it," he mused, then, giving nothing
away, looked at Bliss critically and quizzed, "Where did
you get this, Sir?"

What's this – the third degree, thought Bliss, immediately riled by the dealer's demanding tone. "A friend,"
he shrugged.

"Well I can tell you it's a Britains," said the dealer.

"British," corrected Bliss with gloating satisfaction.

The dealer looked up. "Oh you really don't know
anything, do you?"

"I've led a sheltered life," retorted Bliss – mentally
equating his lack of knowledge about toy soldiers to his
ignorance of the inner workings of a dildo.

"Britains," the dealer began again, then repeated
the name for emphasis, "Britains were the world's finest
manufacturers of historically accurate fifty-four mil-
limetre military personnel." Then, weighing the tiny figure in his hand, he continued condescendingly, "This
was made in their Hornsey Rise factory on Lambton
Road. It's hollow lead alloy. It doesn't seem a big deal
today, but Britains revolutionised the whole industry
when the son of the founder, William, discovered they
could save a lot of metal, and money, by making hollow
figures. The Americans, in comparison, were still making solid models years later."

"Very interesting," yawned Bliss regretting he had
wasted so much time and becoming increasingly irritated by the man's attitude.

The dealer was unfazed. "This is ..." he glanced
down at the figure, "Or rather ... *was* a mounted officer

of the Royal Horse Artillery circa 1940."

"Oh!" Bliss exclaimed with surprise.

Wrongly assuming the exclamation was in admiration of his expertise, the dealer beamed, but Bliss was tossing Arnie's words around in his mind, recalling that Rupert Dauntsey had been a major in the Royal Horse Artillery. Suddenly the model had life.

"Sorry," he said, picking up the front half of the model with interest, now paying close attention. "I missed that. Could you tell me again?"

The dealer's face had, "Listen this time you moron," written all over it as he repeated the information.

Bliss wasn't easily convinced and peppered the dealer with questions, demanding to know how he could be so certain about the identity of such a mutilated figure. It was the paint, apparently, the khaki service dress and, "Of course," as if Bliss should know, as if everyone knew, "the steel helmet."

"The steel helmet?" enquired Bliss.

"Britains were the only company who moulded the Royal Horse Artillery wearing steel helmets in 1940 and up to May 1941."

"Oh, I see," said Bliss, dropping the pieces back into the bag. "Well thanks a lot," he added, making a move toward the door.

"Has your friend got any more?" called the dealer.

Bliss paused, "More – like this?"

"Yes – but not mangled."

Bliss shook his head. "Not that I know of."

"I might be interested, that's all."

Realising that he'd not seen any price tags Bliss swept his hand across a couple of regiments. "Are these worth something, I mean – are they valuable?"

"Depends what you mean by valuable, but ... possibly – depending on the condition."

"And ones like this," he said holding out the bag of horseman's remains.

"Maybe ... although I'd be particularly interested if there were a set."

"A set?"

"Yeah – That's the officer you've got there. A major probably. The original set had a gun carriage with a team of horses and four outriders in addition to the major. Here, take my card – give me a call. I'm sure we could come to a satisfactory arrangement if your friend was interested in selling."

Bliss drifted back to the counter, his interest piqued. "How would I know what to look for?"

"I could give you some clues," the dealer said, picking up a red coated guardsman. "For instance, this is a Britains," he said without bothering to check.

"How do you know."

He laughed. "They made a mistake with this model and painted the plume on the wrong side of the bearskin ... look," he pointed. "But don't worry, there are easier ways to tell."

"Such as?"

Flipping the figure over in his hand he pointed out the inscription "Britains Ltd." engraved on the base and laughed again – "Easy, see."

Bliss, still not certain what he was looking for picked up a few of the models then asked. "Have you got any of the Horse Guards – it would give me a better idea?"

The dealer hesitated. "No, I don't think I do, but bring in any models you can. I'll soon identify them."

Twenty minutes later Bliss pulled up in a quiet street of neat terraced houses and gazed nostalgically at the houses opposite. He had carefully gone through the routine of checking out the neighbourhood – no suspicious Volvo's, blue or otherwise – but he had spotted two large attentive men in a car half a street away, their wing mirrors trained on his house.

His house had changed and he found himself staring at it with the eyes of a stranger. The front door was different – despite the wood-grain finish and polished brass knocker it was quite obviously reinforced steel and blast-resistant. A pattern of scorch marks etched into the stone step, and fanning out across the pavement, still marked the spot where the bomb had exploded. But it wasn't the physical changes that alienated him, the house no longer had a welcoming feel. It was, he felt, more like unexpectedly finding yourself outside your childhood home – wanting to rush in and find mother at the sink and father asleep in front of the television; the sweet smell of freshly baked apple pie; the cozy warmth of laundry drying around the fire and the promise of a new *Beano, Dandy* or *Boy's Own*.

But there was no mother or father here. This was no childhood den. This was still his house – he had a key, and there was nothing stopping him from entering; only the words of the protection squad commander. "I wouldn't go back to the house if I were you, Dave – not until we've caught him. If he's desperate enough he'll try again, and next time it might be a machine gun from a passing car, *à la* Al Capone."

He drove away with a certain sadness, managed to force a mendacious smile for the two caretakers as he passed, then was forced to stop and search for a tissue. He'd bought the house for a fresh start, having finally shaken off the divorce doldrums, and now his world had been trashed again, this time by a villainous ghost from the past.

Arriving early at the pub for his rendezvous with
Superintendent Wakelin, Bliss checked out the car
park and surrounding streets for blue Volvos and jot-
ted down the numbers of a couple, though neither
looked promising.

The waitress was beautiful, stunningly so, yet
appeared to have no idea as she bustled around serving
everyone with the same innocent smile. Bliss was mesmerised by her beauty and wanted to glide his fingers
down her slender arms and stroke her soft cheeks just to
have the memory for his dotage. "I remember the day I
touched the most perfect woman," he would boast to his
peers on the bowling green. "She had stepped straight out
of an Old Master – not a Rubens. She was a Rembrandt
or Botticelli, or a Bartolini statue. Naked? Naturally.
Though nothing coarse, nothing pornographic."

She wasn't naked, but her loose fitting dress flowed
sensuously over her curves, like the robes of an Egyptian
princess, and the open smile on her fresh virginal face
left her more exposed than most women totally nude.

"Yeah, mate – What d'ye want?" Her rough cock-
ney accent broke the spell and she slipped under the
wheels of her chariot.

"Hello, Michael," called Superintendent Wakelin
pointedly, as he appeared out of nowhere and slid into the
cubicle beside him. Bliss tore his eyes off the young
woman, now just a waitress, and greeted the senior officer.

"Drink, Guv?"

"So, how are you getting on in Hampshire?"
enquired Wakelin once the waitress had wiggled away.

"They've given me an interesting sort of murder ...
local man killed his father."

"Domestic, eh! – should be easy enough for you."

"Oh yeah," he replied, choosing to ignore the minor problem of the missing body, "but they could manage perfectly well without me. In fact I don't think they quite know what to do with me. Superintendent Donaldson seems alright, although he's on his way out. I think he just wants a quiet life. I could see it on his face as he gave me the case. Here you are, son – play with this. Even the Met couldn't fuck this one up."

"So what are you saying?"

"To be honest, I want to come back. I've done my time."

He had – six months in a safe house, a padded prison with two acres of neatly tended gardens and a movie star's video library.

"Dave ... Oh fuck – I've done it again. Sorry ... Michael, this guy is determined, and he's done his homework. He knows where you work, live and probably where you play; he knows your car; he got your phone number – even though it's ex-directory, and you changed it twice; he even managed to clean out your bank account – in case you forgot."

Bliss had no argument. "I see you've still got a couple of goons doing surveillance on the place."

"We want to catch him, Dave – Don't you want him caught?"

"Of course, but that's the other thing I wanted to see you about." He hesitated while the waitress bent over to put the drinks on the table. "Pretty girl," he said to Wakelin as she drifted away.

Wakelin shrugged, "Didn't notice. Now what's the problem? What's happened? You sounded pretty panicky when you called?"

Bliss gave himself time to think as he tested the house *Cabernet Sauvignon*. "I think he's caught on," he said eventually.

Wakelin pursed his lips in a whistle of surprise. "Already?"

"I'm pretty sure I was tailed from Westchester today."

"You're gonna have to go back into the safe house then, whether you like it or not."

The mere thought was enough to have him back-tracking. "Well, I'm not a hundred percent certain. It could have been a coincidence."

Wakelin wasn't fooled. "Surely the safe house isn't that bad?"

"A padded cell is just as much a prison. Anyway, I've had other villains threaten me in the past."

"And how many of them have actually tried to kill you?"

He knew the answer. So did Bliss.

Chapter Seven

W ednesday started early and uncomfortably for Bliss.
Blue demons had tormented his sleep, chasing him
out of bed and into the office at five-thirty. He walked the
half-mile from the hotel, and took pleasure in the birthing
smells of the dawn, smells that would be swamped by
exhaust fumes within the hour. Baker's yeast, coffee, and
even pungent piles of newsprint stacked against the
newsagent's door hailed the new day, though the stench
from the fishmonger's was clearly more an odour of things
past than things to come. Without his car he found freedom in the crisp silence of the deserted streets and dawdled to relish images of the morning: the scattered
refraction of steeply slanting sunlight through a jeweller's
display of cut crystal; a tousled cat slaking his thirst at a
stone trough after the night's hunt; and a skein of Canada
geese winging noisily overhead in search of pasture.

A half-timbered Tudor Inn at one end of the High
Street had thrust its upper storey out over the pavement,

and Bliss was engrossed in the elegant sweep of the jetty when a persistent teeth-clenching screech brought him to a nervous stop and had him shrinking into a pharmacist's doorway. Mandy's killer was back in a flash and his ears pricked as he tried to identify the sound and connect it to some fearsome weapon. Baffled, he was still deciding whether or not to run, when a pile of filthy overcoats shuffled around the corner dragging a supermarket trolley with a buckled wheel and one lifetime's agglomeration. He watched silently as the white-bearded man passed, warily taking each step as though he were in a minefield, angrily muttering some unintelligible incantation. How pathetic, thought Bliss, watching the bagman struggling with his load. The poor old sod must be at least eighty and still trying to avoid the cracks in the pavement – maybe he'd do better stepping on a few.

A few minutes later Bliss slipped in the back door of the police station and headed straight for the cell block to check on Jonathon Dauntsey.

"Bail!" he screamed as the unsuspecting custody sergeant filled him in. "They gave him bail?"

"Don't blame me, Guv," replied the sergeant, fighting off a gauze of haziness as he neared the end of his night shift.

"I take a few hours off and look what happens – Bail!" he spat, marching off with the feeling that the fifteen minute stroll from the Hotel was going to be the highlight of his day.

He was not to be disappointed. More bad news waited on his desk in the form of a report from Sergeant Patterson.

The re-enactment had yielded grievously little – raising more questions than it answered. Not only were they no further forward in finding the body but, according to Patterson's handwritten note, the whole

Dauntsey case would have to be re-thought as a result of their findings.

The episode, according to the report, had gone much as planned, though Patterson had been somewhat creative in his composition. The planning had been meticulous enough: officers stationed at intervals on the route from the Black Horse to the churchyard; more officers at the pub itself; several patrol cars on the lane to Dauntsey's house; Sergeant Patterson at the grave where the duvet had been found.

Detective Dowding, since he proposed the re-enactment, had a vested interest in its success and had taken the villainous role of Jonathon Dauntsey. The pick-up truck, not Dauntsey's, though similar enough in the fading light, had first left the Black Horse at precisely nine-thirty and arrived at St. Paul's churchyard just forty-five seconds later.

"Amazing how far you can get in under a minute when there's no traffic," Dowding said to the constable sitting alongside him, observing and taking notes, then his radio burst into life with Patterson's bark. "Get back to the pub, Dowding. Half the blokes aren't in position yet."

Ten minutes later, with the stray officers rousted out of the bar of the Black Horse, Dowding re-enacted the re-enactment, arriving promptly at the churchyard, slipping out of the drivers seat and reaching for the duvet which, contrary to his wife's explicit orders, he'd borrowed from the guest bedroom. "Wait a minute," he said to himself, stopping dead. "This doesn't make sense."

"What's the hold-up, Dowding?" called the sergeant from the side of the newly filled grave fifty feet away.

"Why would he have thrown ..." he started to muse, then shouted his thoughts aloud. "Why would he have thrown the duvet away before getting rid of the body, Serg?"

There was no immediate answer and the performance shuddered to an unscheduled halt as the officers, one by one, were drawn into a debate around the grave. The conclusion was unanimous. Jonathon Dauntsey would not have ditched the duvet with the body still lying in his pick-up – it would have been illogical to do so. The only answer was that wherever Dauntsey had stashed his father's body he hadn't wanted the duvet to accompany it, but the evidence road led nowhere from the churchyard and the re-enactment was terminated in as much confusion as it had begun. Most of the men wandered back to the bar at the Black Horse where they had unfinished business. Dowding sneaked home with the duvet hoping his wife hadn't noticed.

Bliss finished the report, lay back in the chair, let his eyes cloud over, and mulled over the contents. Comprehension came slowly as the spectre of an idea slowly took shape out of a formless mist in his mind.

"The cunning bastard," he breathed slowly, then gradually opened his eyes to see if the developing idea would evaporate in the harsh light of reality.

"That's it," he said aloud, convinced he had resolved the conundrum. I've got you, he smiled wryly, recognising the genius in the apparent madness of Dauntsey's behaviour. You think you've fooled us – well, Mr. Dauntsey, you can't fool all the people ... as they say. You did drop the duvet off first didn't you – you didn't care if it was found, in fact you probably wanted it found – but why? What did it prove? Nothing really – only that someone had been bleeding. But I know why you put it in the grave ... the dogs. You guessed we'd bring in tracker dogs but, with the blood-soaked duvet in the grave, the air around would have been awash with the smell of blood, and a river of scent would have flooded all the way back toward the pub. But the trail away from the churchyard, the direction you took your poor father, would have been a trickle in comparison and the dogs would miss it. So, Mr. Dauntsey, what does that tell me? That tells me that the body must be close. Why? Because you only needed to distract the dogs if the body was within a few miles. Beyond that they'd lose the scent, especially if you drove at high speed along busy roads ... You knew that, didn't you? So, what was your motive?

Bliss closed his eyes again and stitched together a likely scenario in his mind: gamily dispute, about money probably, it usually was; Jonathon upset at the mistreatment of his mother – council-subsidised nursing home – hardly appropriate for the wife of a Major; Jonathon, wanting to take her to Switzerland, needs money – has none – asks father. Father says, "Fuck off" – No, he wouldn't have said that. "Not jolly likely, old chum." Someone starts a fight – the old man probably – hot-tempered old soldier type – not having a whipper-snapper telling him what to do, even a fifty-year-old whipper-snapper; Jonathon grabs the knife and the old man – thin skin; no flesh to speak of, blinded by rage, throws himself into battle and gets the knife stuck in an artery. Blood everywhere – bleeds to death before Jonathon's even calmed down enough to realise what has happened; Jonathon panics, bundles him up in the duvet, dumps him in the pick-up, drives off, then thinks ...

"Oh it's you, Chief Inspector – I thought I heard voices," said Daphne blundering in with a bucketful of cleaning materials. "I didn't expect you in yet."

He jerked upright and flung his eyes open. Voices? Was I talking out loud? "You're in early , Daphne," he said cheerily, hoping he wasn't blushing.

"I like to get started at six – always have."

"I should have thought someone of your age would enjoy a lie in."

The bucket dropped with a clang and she struck back crustily. "Most old fogeys die in bed, Chief Inspector – I minimise the risk by spending as little time there as possible."

"Oh I didn't mean ..." he began apologetically, but she was already laughing.

Smiling, he went back to his assessment of the Dauntsey case and picked up a sheaf of papers to give the impression of busyness.

"I've got my eye on a nice leg of lamb for tonight," she said, dusting around the boxes of his still unpacked office.

"Sorry?" he said, looking up, realising he'd missed something important.

"I said I was thinking of doing lamb tonight – have you forgotten you're coming ..."

His mind was focused on the paper in front of him – a page from a message pad. "No, I hadn't forgotten ..." he began, then drifted to silence, pre-occupied by what he was reading.

"Seven-thirty or eight?" she asked.

His mind was miles away – Scotland – a purple heather estate on the banks of a loch somewhere in the Highlands – the distant skirl of pipes, the abattoir smell of boiled haggis. "According to this, the Major didn't live there," he said waving the paper at her before scrunching it and aiming at a litter bin.

"Didn't live where?"

His brow creased inquisitively. "Didn't you say he lived in Scotland?"

"No – I don't believe I did. I suppose he may have done, but all I said was that I hadn't seen him ..."

" ... Since Suez," he interjected, suddenly remembering that it had been the matron of the nursing home who'd mentioned Scotland. "Actually, I wanted to ask you about that. It struck me as strange afterwards. Why Suez, what made you think of that?"

A look of consternation clouded Daphne's face and he worried he had offended her in some way. Putting down her can of spray polish, she scooted across to the door and checked the corridor with exaggerated care. As she returned to his desk her thoughtful expression suggested she was considering the wisdom of revealing some great secret, but she shelved the idea at the last moment, saying, "I'd rather tell you tonight – if that's alright – at dinner."

"In that case why not let me take you somewhere posh as promised – I could do with something to cheer me up."

The implication that her leg of lamb would not have cheered him smarted, but she rationalised quickly. "Thank you, that would be nice – at least I won't have to wash up."

Bliss was still trying to piece together the newly acquired information from Scotland as Daphne dragged her vacuum cleaner into the next office, and he wandered thoughtfully around the room abstractly picking at files and boxes.

"Whoomph," the low boom of an explosion shook him out of his thoughts and left him trying to identify the sound. The backfire of a car, was his first thought, but the frequency was too low – so low it was tangible rather than audible – more like a pressure wave pulsing through the atmosphere. The following silence was almost as tangible as the boom of the blast, leaving him wondering if he'd heard anything at all, even dismissing it and fleetingly returning to his inner debate over the Dauntsey murder.

Twenty seconds later he'd reached the part in his hypothesis where Jonathon was grave-side, unrolling the duvet from the body, when a second explosion hit. An explosion of instantly identifiable sounds – the pandemonium of disaster: shrieking alarms, sirens and bells; shouting men; thundering feet; slamming doors; screaming engines and squealing tyres.

Swept up in the excitement, Bliss rushed to the control room where half a dozen shirt-sleeved operators were electrified by the madly pulsating warning lights and flashing computer screens. At lightening speed the control officers were tapping buttons and flicking switches as they struggled to deal with a flood of incoming calls and alarms. And, above the electronic hum, the enlivened buzz of their voices – asking, ordering, directing, informing.

"What's happening? Where are you? Do this, do that, go there, stop the traffic, secure the area – fire services are en-route, hospitals are being alerted."

"What's happening?" whispered Bliss, leaning over one of the women, trying not to interrupt her.

"Shush," she waved him off with an irritated flick of the wrist and continued calling into her microphone. "Alpha five-niner – location, over?"

"What is it?" he tried again, a note of insistence adding authority to his tone.

She ignored him. "Alpha five-niner," she continued to call, "State your location – over? I'm getting nothing from fifty-nine, Serg," she shouted at the man on an opposing console.

"What's happening, Serg?" called Bliss, but was blanked out as the sergeant stared straight past him, treating him like an inconvenient post.

"Try fifty-four ..." he shouted to the controller. "No, belay that, I'll do it myself." He picked up the microphone. "Alpha five-four, alpha five-four. What's five-niner's ten-twenty?"

"Am I invisible?" Bliss questioned flippantly. Have I died? Did he get me? Then his thoughts darkened and left him pondering – Is this what death is like? What *was* that explosion? Maybe I am dead – maybe he did get me. "Sergeant!" he bellowed in something of a panic.

"I'm busy – what do ye want – who are you?"

The loudspeaker cackled overhead. "Alpha five-four to Delta Alpha – I've no idea where five-niner is. We're just arriving at the scene – looks a mess-over."

Unable to wait any longer Bliss harshly grabbed the sergeant's shoulder, "I'm D.I. Bliss. Will somebody tell me what's happening?"

"Sorry, Guv – There's been an explosion. One of our uniformed ..."

"Where?" insisted Bliss, cutting him off.

"Mitre Hotel in the High Street."

Bliss felt his knees giving – his hotel, the hotel he'd left only thirty minutes earlier. The hotel where he would have been shaving or showering had he waited for the receptionist's early call. "Oh God!"

"Are you alright, Guv?"

Now what? Admit I know who did it? Admit it was my fault – again?

"Yes ... yes ... I'm alright. I suppose I'd better get down there. Have you called the Super?"

"Everything's under control, Guv."

Not in Bliss's mind it wasn't. His brain was exploding with questions. How did he find me so quickly? How did he know I was at the Mitre? Why can't he leave me alone?

Snatching the keys to one of the C.I.D. cars off a pegboard he paused deep in thought. What if it's a trap –

what if he's waiting to pick me off? But he quickly shook off the notion of an ambush and ran for the car park, telling himself that the killer wouldn't risk it with the area swamped by uniformed officers. He will have been long gone, he told himself. Why hang around when the bomb's achieved it objective?

The car was already on automatic pilot as he shot out of the car park, piecing together the likely scenario in his mind: timed device almost certainly – cheap chain-store alarm clock – made in Hong Kong or Taiwan. That's prophetic, he thought – identical ones would be waking a million people around the world and this one, attached to a battery, detonator and a lump of Semtex high explosive, had woken an entire city.

He took the roundabout at high speed, slackening off the throttle as the tyres protested. It must have been planted last evening, he mused, under the bed while I was in London – careless, I should have checked. But how did he get in? Slamming the car into fourth, he pictured it in his mind as he tore along the quiet street: a fairly ordinary looking workman in blue overalls carrying an official looking toolbox. "Come to check the plumbing in 203 – you got a leak apparently," he says to the pretty Swedish receptionist who had charmed Bliss with her brilliant smile and oddball English.

"Oh. I have no understanding – I think maybe I should call to the manager?" she replies, reaching for the phone.

"Well I ain't hanging around, girl," he says, turning on his heals. "Maybe I should come back tomorrow when the place is flooded out – I can make more money that way."

"No, please – it is alright, I am sure," she pleads, handing over the keys – even placating him with the offer of a cup of tea or a miniature from the courtesy bar.

The High Street was blocked, jammed by the haphazardly abandoned emergency vehicles and the detritus of catastrophe. Bricks, tiles and baulks of timber carpeted the roadway. Broken glass had spewed everywhere, turning summer to winter as Bliss's footsteps crunched through the glistening ice-like crystals. But he couldn't hear – every burglar and fire alarm in the street was blaring; police, fire and ambulance. Sirens were still screaming in the distance, clearing a path through thin air as they raced through the deserted streets.

He ducked under the hastily strung fluorescent tape and stopped, perplexed. The Mitre Hotel seemed intact, normal even, apart from the snake of shell-shocked patrons streaming out of the door, clutching themselves in blankets and dressing gowns, and being hurried away by ambulance and fire officers. Still confused, he made straight for a fireman, his helmet and shoulders weighed down with gold stripes.

"D.I. Bliss," he shouted, hoping the other man wouldn't ask for his warrant card. "I thought it was the Mitre," he added, struggling to be heard above the cacophony of sirens.

"So did half the people in the Mitre," replied the chief, cupping his hand to Bliss's ear. "The blast shook the shit out of the place."

"So what happened?"

"Classic gas explosion I would say. I bet someone left the gas stove on and forgot to light it."

"Where?"

"Tea shop – three doors down from the hotel."

"Anyone hurt?"

The loudest of the sirens stopped abruptly, leaving the fireman shouting unnecessarily. "Yeah – one of your people, walking past at the time – caught a packet."

The flush of exhilaration drained from Bliss's face as the silent radio was explained. No wonder Alpha five-niner hadn't responded. No wonder the control room staff had been so concerned. Five-niner was already at the scene – lying under the debris. "Is he alright?"

"It's a she," replied the officer, having to shout again as the alarm burst back to life. "Yeah ... she's just shook up. A couple of your lads have taken her to emerg."

Thank Christ, he thought, asking, "What sparked it off?"

"Time switch possibly," he shrugged. "Won't know 'til we've made the place safe and had a good look. It was probably carelessness, either that or a phoney insurance claim."

"I'll get a detective working on it straight away," Bliss said moving off for a closer inspection of the wrecked building.

The siren paused again, and he stopped cold as the fire chief shouted after him. "Of course, it could have been a bomb."

He needed coffee, high roasted Arabica prefer-ably – hot and very strong, but the only café open had Cash & Carry instant – take it or leave it. He took it, but it didn't stop his hands shaking and it didn't offer comfort and warmth. Sitting on a ripped vinyl stool in a corner, he listened to the excited bab-ble of early morning workers, each having their own take on the explosion.

Bliss shut out the voices and gripped the counter tightly to stop the shaking. It wasn't fear, he tried telling himself, not fear for his own safety anyway. It was fear for others, like the policewoman, who might get caught

in the shrapnel. I wonder, was she young or old, he started thinking, then stopped himself. Does it matter? She
could have been killed.

But it was fear for his family, especially his daughter
Samantha, that hurt most, turning him, in his own mind,
into a social leper. "Keep away," he wanted to warn.
"Don't come to my house; don't stand close to me; don't
talk to me in public; don't phone me; don't even admit to
knowing me." And it wasn't only his family and friends:
Every unexpected visitor turning up on his doorstep had
been given a verbal rub down by one or other of the pro-
tective team cruising the neighbourhood. Complete
strangers, innocent people going about their daily lives,
had become tainted. People like the sorters at the post
office, using plastic tongs at arms length to pick up every
item addressed to him like pieces of shitty toilet paper,
then dropping them into a blast proof container for x-ray
examination. Even electricity, gas and phone bills got the
"contaminated" treatment.

"We can't be too careful when it comes to the safety
of our staff," the postal inspector had said, making him
feel even dirtier.

It was the elaborate routine with the garbage that
had exasperated him more than anything – three evenings
a week segregating paper, metal, glass and food; labelling
each bag with as much detail as a laboratory specimen;
smuggling it out of the house at night to be shredded or
incinerated away from prying eyes. Initially, he had complained to the commander that it seemed unnecessarily
circumspect but, inwardly, he knew very well it was not –
recognising that a single bag snatched from the kerb
under the nose of the refuse collector could yield a
Pandorian assemblage of personal information.

Shaking with frustration and anger – wanting to
scream, "Come on out you coward – fight me like a

man," he left the café, and the coffee, and walked back to the High Street. The sirens had stopped, firemen with hoses and brushes were sweeping the debris to one side and washing the glass into the gutters. Blue uniforms patrolled the tape barriers, keeping back a curious mob, allowing only shopkeepers and their staff through, to reset alarms, turn off the gas and assess the damage.

Bliss slipped under the tape and stepped gingerly through the debris toward the tea shop. The fire chief spotted him. "It was the gas," he called.

"Are you sure?"

"Yeah – the owner's over there if you want to talk to her," he pointed. "The woman in the blue pinny who looks as though she's had an accident in her drawers. She says she put some meringues in a slow oven overnight – then forgot to light it. She even worried about it when she got home but her husband said she was worrying for nothing – little did he know."

One look at the mortified woman's ashen face was enough to confirm the truth in the story and Bliss wanted to relax, saying to himself, "This wasn't the work of the killer – this was just an accident." But, he was so wound up it wasn't that simple. Since the threatening calls and letters, and especially since the bomb, he had become paranoiacally self-centred, finding it difficult to imagine that, in some way, this wasn't directed at him.

He tried stepping away from himself. "Just look at yourself. Look what he's done to you," he said. "The moment they mentioned an explosion you assumed yourself to be the target. Every time a phone rings you think it's for you, or about you. Every knock on the door and every beep of a horn or shout is to get your attention."

"Good morning, Inspector."

Bliss jumped and his head whipped around so fast his neck "cracked" audibly.

"You were miles away," continued Superintendent Donaldson chattily. "I wasn't sure you'd be back from London. How did it go – everything alright?"

"Tell him about the Volvo," whispered the voice in his mind but he brushed it aside. "Fine," he said, and immediately changed the subject. "The fire chief tells me this was gas ... owner left the stove unlit overnight apparently."

Donaldson looked around as if he'd just arrived. "It's a bloody shame. That tea shop used to do a really good cream tea ... I don't suppose you've had a chance to try their scones yet, and the strawberry ... "

"The re-enactment fizzled out, I understand," cut in Bliss impatiently.

"Patterson called me at home," Donaldson grumbled. "Interrupted my backgammon night ... just a few of us, once a week – you wouldn't be interested by any chance would you? My wife always leaves us a nice tray of sandwiches, smoked salmon ..."

"No thanks, Guv ... How come Dauntsey got bail?"

"Don't ask me. He gave the silly old bitch on the bench his 'little boy lost' act; played up to her with that poofy accent of his; she got a damp patch in her knickers and let him out."

"Stupid cow. Now he's got plenty of opportunity to cover his tracks."

"That's what I thought at first, then it occurred to me that it might be a good thing. Think about it, Dave ... We couldn't find the body when he was inside, now he's out he might lead us to it."

Bliss considered strategy for a moment. "You might be right, Sir. Twenty-four hour surveillance?"

Donaldson nodded. "Already in place – though I've had to pull men off the search details."

"No problem. I was going to do that anyway. All I'd planned for today was a thorough search of his house."

"Again?"

Bliss nodded. "Really thorough this time ... walls, floors, attics – the works."

"How about some breakfast?" asked Donaldson chummily. "I know this little place where the sausages are just ..."

"I think I'll get back to the nick," interrupted Bliss. "I've got a lot to arrange."

Donaldson seemed put out and turned cold. "Oh, alright. If that's what you want, Inspector. Was there anything else to report?"

"Tell him about the Volvo," screeched his inner voice.

What is there to tell?

"You were being followed."

Possibly.

"Definitely."

Alright, don't nag. But even if he was following what does that prove? Bliss looked around at the devastation and reminded himself that he had jumped to the wrong conclusion. You were certain this was a bomb in the Mitre ... remember. There must be a dozen possible explanations for the Volvo driver's behaviour.

"Give me two."

O.K. One ... "My wife's screwing around with someone who's gotta car like yours" ... and ... Two ... "I thought I recognised you from school and I was trying to get a closer look."

"Do you believe that?"

It's possible.

"So is my theory."

Which is?

"It was the killer, you idiot."

"Inspector," prompted Donaldson. "I said, was there anything else?"

"Sorry, Sir ... miles away again. No, nothing else."

Major Rupert Dauntsey was still on the missing list when D.I. Bliss booked off duty twelve hours later. Declining Sergeant Patterson's offer of a ride – "I'm going right past on my way back to Dauntsey's" – he walked back to the Mitre along the High Street.

"Did you hear about the explosion?" enquired the young Swedish receptionist as she handed him his key.

"I did," he smiled thankfully. Thankful that she was still there, still intact and unblemished. Thankful that it hadn't been a bomb. "Something for you," he added, slipping a five pound note into her hand.

"Zhank you very much."

"No – Zhank you."

She laughed, totally unaware of how much it meant to him to be able to give her a little something.

Bliss checked his room with care, showered, slipped on a clean shirt and took off to collect his evening's date. Then he tried to relax as they drove along knotted country lanes in the soft light of the setting sun, but his neck took a beating as he checked for the Volvo. He missed the small engraved sign, "The Limes," hidden in the bushes, but the driver knew the way and, as they crunched to a stop on the gravel driveway of the Elizabethan manor, a concierge stepped forward with military precision and snapped open Daphne's door.

Daphne lost twenty years in the warmth of the ancient house's candlelight, but, even when Bliss had picked her up from her front door in the taxi, she had been radiant. She had flounced out of the house, begging for attention in a black knee-length cocktail dress, an overconfident straw hat kept in check by a wide crimson ribbon with a huge bow and a flowing black shawl laced with gold. "Chauffer driven, Chief

Inspector – I am impressed," she had said, bouncing in beside him.

"It's only a taxi," he mumbled, then explained with unnecessary insistence that he had left the car at his hotel, not wanting to spoil the evening by being unable to drink. The truth, though he would never admit it, was that he was petrified of driving his own car and had caged it in a rented lock-up garage. A hire car had been ordered in its place – peace of mind had a price – but had yet to arrive. The journey back from London in the Rover the previous night had taken a dreadful toll on his nerves. Every blazing headlight in his mirror had been a pulse-racing Volvo forcing him to slow down and pull over. On the motorway, convoys of small blue Volvos bore down on him and transmogrified into yellow Chryslers, red Fords and black Jaguars as they swept by.

"*Oh la la*, the prices – *Mon Dieu!*" cried Daphne, glancing at the gold-framed menu as they waited in a vestibule while servants flurried around, verbally tugging forelocks, divesting them of coats and hats.

"Oh don't worry. I'm paying."

"I'm not being critical – praise, if anything – I was just thinking that anyone with the neck to charge prices like this had better come up with the goods. People have been murdered for less."

"Mandy Richards for one," he inadvertently blurted out, surprised to the extent she was in control of his mind.

"Mandy Richards?"

"Murdered for nothing – an old case," he explained, then realised even her killing had a price – the price of a couple of shotgun cartridges. But it was the robber who had been out of pocket – assuming he'd paid for them. Fifty pence, maybe one pound – was that the value of a life?

"You'll have to excuse me, Chief Inspector," Daphne continued, still thinking about the exorbitant prices as they took seats in the sombre sixteenth-century bar. "I don't get out much anymore. To be honest with you, dining alone is about as exhilarating as solo sex – I suppose it's O.K., if you're really hungry." Then she relaxed back into the chair with a comedic smile. "I bet you've never met anyone quite like me before have you?"

He laughed, "Not really."

"I'll let you in on a little secret," she said, pushing herself forward again. "Neither have I ... My body seems to have got the message about aging but my mind refuses to go along with it."

Bliss laughed, then a childhood memory of an elderly Aunt came to him. "She got 'bugger' in her mind and couldn't get it out," he explained through the laughter. "Everything was 'bugger.' She could even slide a 'bugger' into the middle of a word. We used to tell our friends we were going to see our Buggering Aunty."

Daphne shook with laughter. "Well, I'm not that bad." Their table would be half an hour, the head waiter told them dourly as he appeared from nowhere and fussed around, precisely centring a large bowl of mixed olives on the table in front of them, his stiff demeanour clearly a rebuke.

"Anal retentive," whispered Daphne behind the waiter's back and they both roared.

He was back in a flash, "You're not here to enjoy yourselves" written all over his face. "May I get you some drinks while you are waiting for the table, Sir?"

"I'll have a large Pastis," said Daphne. "I have a feeling that you're going to question me about France, so I may as well get in the right frame of mind."

"Not question," he said. "That sounds so harsh, so intrusive. I was merely hoping you'd be able to give me some background on Major Dauntsey and the war that's all. Anyway," he added, "to be truthful, I was quite looking forward to just spending an evening with you."

Daphne beamed as he ordered the drinks. "Wartime is basically the same as peacetime, Chief Inspector, only everything seems to happen so much faster, that's all."

He frowned in thought, then smiled. "That leaves me with an image of Plato and Diogenes having this great philosophical argument based on the premise that war is actually peace. And please call me Dave. We're not on duty now."

Daphne rolled the phrase round her tongue. "War is peace," she intoned. "It sounds like Newspeak but, in a strange way, it's not untrue. Things get built, damaged and destroyed in peace and war; people love and lose; friends come and go; some make fortunes, others lose everything; people die of diseases and injuries. It is just as though the movie of your life is run through the projector at ten times the normal speed. Fifty years crammed into five. So, war *is* peace – speeded up."

"You make a very credible argument, Miss Lovelace," he said as if he were an adjudicator, "and you sound as though you quite enjoyed the war."

"I can't deny it was exciting."

"Surely the constant fear of being wounded or dying takes the gloss off it."

"Haven't you heard, Dave – it's only the other chap who gets killed."

"And what about those who survive?".

She toyed with the olives, segregating the green from black and keeping those stuffed with pimento to one side. Finally, satisfied with her handiwork, she sat back and took a couple of sips of Pastis. "Survival is a question of relativity," she said eventually, without taking her eyes off the olives. "I suppose that in one way or another no-one survives war, but then again, no-one survives life either."

"But there are winners and losers in life, even if the end result is the same. Surely everyone loses in war."

Popping a stuffed olive into her mouth she chewed thoughtfully for a few seconds before replying. "I suppose the really lucky ones were those who were wounded enough to be shipped home a hero, then recovered quickly and took advantage of the sympathy before the rest got back."

"Would Major Dauntsey have been in that category?"

"I doubt it."

"I know the rumour about how he got his regiment wiped out by the way," he said as if he'd discovered some monumental secret. "Making his men tidy up the battlefield before they retreated."

"Who told you?"

He thought about teasing her then changed his mind. "Someone called Arnie."

"Agh," she spluttered. "Dear old Arnie. Trust him."

"Was he right? Is that what happened?"

"So they say, Chief Inspector," she said non-committally, then tried to change the subject. "Talking of wounds ..."

"Dave!"

"Alright . . Have it your own way ... Dave. How is the W.P.C.? The one who was hurt this morning?"

Bliss had visited the young woman in hospital, still irrationally feeling that the explosion could have been attributed to his adversary.

"Detective Inspector Bliss," he introduced himself, "How are you feeling?"

"Not too bad, Sir," she replied and struggled higher in the bed.

"Don't get up," he said kindly. "I just wanted to make sure you were alright."

The ward sister sidled up to him. "Miss Jackson will be fine, Inspector."

"Oh good. I'm pleased to hear that."

"Mainly bruises and a few cuts," continued the motherly figure, reaching in front of him and pulling back the sheet to expose the policewoman's naked torso. "See."

Later, he tried to decide who had blushed the most, him or the W.P.C., as the sister's finger pointed with great precision to each of the tiny cuts the young woman had received from flying glass. "Look at this one," she said as if Bliss were an intern. "Missed her nipple by a whisker." Bliss looked, and the policewoman's nipple stood stiffly to attention under his gaze.

Gallantly, he tried to look away but the sister wasn't finished and she tenderly lifted the other breast saying, "The cut under here will be painful for a while – see." He looked at the red welt under the fold of the breast and was flung back in time again – to the bank and Mandy Richards. To her dismembered breast.

"Thank you, Sister," he said curtly, grabbing the sheet and tenderly covering the policewoman as he mumbled, "Sorry, Miss."

"She's fine," he replied to Daphne. "They released her this afternoon. She'll be back on duty in a few days." But he couldn't help thinking that, from now on, there would be an awkward moment every time they passed in a corridor or met in the mess room.

The head waiter was back for their order. Daphne said she would take a chance on the Escargot and, as she had already set her mind on lamb, would go for the cutlets *campagnarde*. Bliss was still undecided and was interrogating the waiter on the composition of *Les Crudités* when a bellboy interrupted.

"Excuse me. Are you Mr. Bliss, Sir?"

"Yes," he answered warily.

"There's a phone call for you, Sir, in the lobby."

He started to rise automatically then froze. No-one knows I'm here, he said to himself and quizzed Daphne. "Did you tell anyone we were coming here tonight?"

She turned it into a joke, replying huffily. "Chief Inspector – I have my reputation to think of."

"I thought so," he said, sitting slowly, his mind in turmoil.

"They said it was urgent, Sir," chimed in the bellboy, waiting impatiently to guide Bliss to the phone, and collect a tip.

Bliss didn't budge. He was being jerked around by a demonic puppeteer from the past. Every time a phone rang it jangled his nerves – was it the killer: threatening; vowing; abusing; or was it a sad-sounding administrator from a hospital ... "Mr. Bliss? ... It's your daughter ... shot; stabbed; slashed." Every hand that knocked on his door held a Smith & Wesson or a stiletto. Every letter or package was a bundle of death or disfigurement. And, if he didn't pick up the phone or answer the door, and if he didn't open the mail – the killer had won.

"Who is it?" he asked the bellboy with a crack in his voice. "Did they say?"

"They didn't say, Sir. Just that it was urgent."

Three pairs of eyes were on him, urging him to go and take the call.

"You don't understand," he wanted to scream. "There's a madman with a gun or a knife just waiting for me to walk out into the lobby. No-one knew I was coming here tonight – it has to be him."

"Chief Inspector – Dave," said Daphne laying a hand on his arm. "Are you having a funny turn again?"

Bliss gave himself a shake. "Sorry – Yes," then he pulled a note out of his wallet and offered it to the boy. "Find out who wants me will you – tell them I'll call back."

"Sure – I mean, of course, Sir."

"That was ten pounds, Dave," said Daphne with a note of surprise as the boy took off. He hadn't noticed and didn't care. He suddenly had a new and more serious worry. What if the killer had rigged the phone? What if he'd crammed a walnut-sized lump of plastic explosive and a high frequency trigger into the handset?

"Mr. Bliss?" the muffled voice on the other end would have asked.

"Yes," he would have replied, pressing the handset tighter to his ear, trying to identify the voice. Then, with an inaudible beep from the other end, "Boom!" The handset would take off his head. But what if the killer doesn't wait to identify his target? What if the bellboy picks up the phone again and says, "Hello?" Ten quid isn't a lot to pay someone to be executed.

I've got to stop him, thought Bliss, starting to rise in panic, already hearing the "boom" of the blast in his mind, but he was too late. The boy was back. "It was the police station, Sir. They asked if you could you call straight back, it's very important."

Bliss slumped back in the chair and blew out a breath in relief, but he could still feel the blood pulsing through his temples. "Thanks, son," he murmured, pulling out his mobile and calling the station.

Within seconds he was patched through to Patterson at the Dauntsey house. "What is it, Pat?"

"We've found the Major, Sir." Then he paused just long enough to force Bliss's hand.

"Alive or dead?" enquired Bliss obediently.

"Very dead, Sir."

The intonation in the sergeant's voice spoke volumes, leaving Bliss simultaneously confused and annoyed at having to follow up with a supplemental question.

"Sergeant, death is similar to pregnancy in at least one respect, as far as I know – you either are or not. Which applies to the Major?"

"Oh. He is definitely dead, Sir."

"Good ... No, I don't mean ..." Then he erupted. The tension of receiving the unexpected phone call was bad enough, without Patterson piling on the pressure by playing guessing games. "What the hell are you trying to tell me, Patterson?"

"Well, Sir, according to the doctor, Major Dauntsey's been dead at least forty years."

Returning to the restaurant's lounge, in a daze, he had been surprised to find his seat occupied by a smartly dressed older man with a prosperous toupee and gold rimmed spectacles that looked to be the real thing.

"This is Andrew," explained Daphne as the man rose and politely held out his hand. Bliss looked to her for an explanation as they shook. "Andrew is a very, very, old friend," she gushed.

"Daphne ..." Bliss began, then noticed her radiance had taken on a additional glow.

"Here, less of the *old* – Daphne," laughed Andrew. "I'm just not as well-preserved as you that's all."

"Well-preserved," she echoed. "Here, I'm not a bloody pickle," and they both laughed.

"Look I hate to interrupt ..." Bliss tried again.

"Andrew's a widower," she whispered aside, making it sound like an accomplishment. "Sit down, Chief

Inspector, you're making the place untidy." Then she turned back to her friend and demurely fanned herself with her hand. "Ooh. That Pernod has gone straight to my head."

"Daphne – I have to go. Something *major* has turned up ..." he said, but Andrew talked over him.

"Well, do let me get you another then, dear heart," he said, in an accent redolent of colonial service in the 1920s – Singapore or the West Indies perhaps.

Bliss's *double-entendre* had missed its mark. "Don't worry about me," proclaimed Daphne loudly. "Andrew will take me home, won't you?"

"I'd jolly well love to, Daphne old girl. But we have to eat first."

"Oh, of course – Silly me. Well off you go, Chief Inspector. Toddle off, there's a dear. And thank you so much."

The heavy hint – the bum's rush. This hasn't happened since Samantha's teenage trysts, he thought.

"Da-a-ad," she'd whine ...

"O.K. I get the message," he'd reply. "I know when I'm not wanted."

"Nice to meet you ... See you tomorrow, Daphne."

Neither had looked up as he raced away.

Chapter Eight

7am, Friday morning and Westchester mortuary was being prepared for the last rites of Major Rupert Dauntsey, (Retd.). A cluster of spotlights flickered coldly into life above an operating table and illuminated an arctic scene. The glare of stark snow-white windowless walls reflected off the glassy sheen of steel refrigerator doors, and the milky marble floor offered neither warmth nor comfort. A couple of masked attendants, in white one-piece suits, skated around the central table, laying out trays of surgical instruments, checking the identity of the body, then blanketing the remains in a stiffly starched sheet.

"Now if you would lie perfectly still, Sir, this won't hurt a bit," jested one of the attendants, for the benefit of a small procession of sombre-faced students who shuffled into the room and hung about near the door.

Detective Inspector Bliss and Sergeant Patterson strode through the group with a bravado of experience and took ringside seats; they already knew what to expect; they knew the horrors lurking beneath the sheet.

Seating himself, Bliss scented the air with a degree of trepidation and was pleasantly surprised. It was more disinfectant than decomposition, though nothing could mask the unmistakeable ambience of death. Over the years, thousands of tortured souls had each shed a layer of agony in this room as they passed on their final journey, and he shuddered at the chilling concentration of disembodied spirits. He had been here before, many times – not this particular mortuary, but a dozen similar ones – and found himself mentally readying for the attendant's scalpel to unzip the bloated bag of flesh. With the realisation that he was steeling himself against the gagging reek of methane gas and butyric acids, he relaxed. He had already viewed the Major's body – this one would be different.

That reminds me, thought Bliss, I still haven't discovered how Patterson tracked me down at The Limes on Wednesday evening.

"Serg," he started, but the students were beginning to drift into surrounding seats. "Never mind – I'll talk to you later," he added, but the powerful memory of the fearful seconds, when he had fully expected the bellboy's head to be blown to pieces, had re-run in his mind repeatedly over the intervening thirty-six hours and did so again. He closed his eyes for a moment thinking, What if? What if? – How would you have lived with yourself after that? But it hadn't happened. The boy had returned safely.

The muted buzz of dreadful anticipation amongst the students was quelled by a sudden flurry of activity in the doorway.

"Sit," said the pathologist galloping into the room, the tails of his whitish coat flying, his footfalls still echoing along the corridor. "Good morning students and guests," he started, then snapped the sheet off the body and bowed respectfully, "and good morning to you, Sir."

Here was a man with purpose, thought Bliss, studying the boisterously dishevelled doctor – cramming life into every moment of existence; understanding better than most that tomorrow is not necessarily another day – and, anticipating that fact, he had apparently postponed shaving, combing, ironing, and shoe-shining. Watching the ebullient man, Bliss found himself wondering whatever had became of the generation of genetically engineered pathologists who had terrorised the mortuaries early in his career: beaky, balding, po-faced men, with serious glasses and superior attitudes, who frequently looked more pallid than the cadaver; men capable of verbally lashing burly policemen to the brink of tears for slip-shod investigative practices – real or imagined; perpetually angry men – angry at the carnage, angry at the waste, and, in some cases, angry that of all possible careers, they'd ended up carving dead bodies for a living.

"So, to our first case," said the pathologist racing ahead. "A white adult male we believe but, as you can see, the body now consists only of the skeleton with fragments of skin and a few strands of hair." Selecting the ulna from the body's left arm, the only arm, he held it up for inspection. "Notice that the bones have mellowed to a rather attractive butterscotch-yellow," he said, then, poker-faced, used it as a pointer to run down a list on a flip chart. "Our task this morning is to carry out an examination to assist the coroner in determining: Who this deceased was ... And, How, When and Where he met his death."

Bliss shifted his gaze away from the pathologist and found himself staring at the unveiled skeleton, thinking it looked entirely different from when he had first seen it, two days earlier, in the cramped and claustrophobic attic of the Dauntsey house. It had taken on an inanimate aspect, sterile and benign, almost as if it were a plastic copy. In the attic – throwing a ghoulish shadow in the dim light of the hastily strung inspection lamp – it clung to some essence of humanity. Slumped in a chair, encased in full uniform, seemingly at peace, the torso had shrunk, the chest caved in, but, although headless still had the shape of a human being – not just a deflated anatomical framework.

Looking at the skeleton under the mortuary's bright lights he couldn't help thinking that, in a way, it was the wrong corpse to examine. Most of the Major's mortal remains were still in the room where, in its stuffy warmth, his flesh had transmuted into the bodies of a billion flies, moths and ants. Major Dauntsey had nourished generations of insect civilisations for a while, but, as the nutrients gave out, the insects had turned to cannibalism in a downward spiral of self destruction, leaving an inch-deep layer of dust of desiccated bodies on the battleground.

The Major's skull was now before them, larger than life, as an overhead projector threw a giant x-ray onto an expanse of spotless wall. "This is what was left of the cranium," explained the pathologist, "and I would ask you to note carefully the spread of pure white speckles not commonly found in bone." Then he balanced the actual skull in his hand and spoke to it. "So then ... Yorick ... What can you tell us about yourself, eh?" He paused and looked to the audience for one of them to respond on the skull's behalf. "Anybody?" he asked, nodding questioningly to each of the students in turn.

"Was he shot, Sir?" suggested one of the students.

"Yes – well done. It would appear at this time that a single bullet penetrated the cranium through the parietal just above the lambdoidal suture."

Sergeant Patterson, taking notes, coughed and caught the speaker's eye.

"Here," added the pathologist helpfully, holding up the skull and poking his finger into a hole in the back.

"The white peppered effect we see on the x-ray is almost certainly a spray of lead fragments that shredded off the bullet as it tore through the bone."

He paused and looked around. "Any questions? ... No ... Alright. From initial observations then, before we explore further, how can we be reasonably certain that this death was not the result of a self-inflicted injury. In short – how do we know it wasn't suicide?"

A serious silence ensued, then a thoughtful young man, fingering his ginger goatee, tried, "The bullet entered the back of the skull."

"Therefore?" prompted the pathologist.

"It's a physical impossibility to shoot yourself in the back of the head."

"No, no, no. It's been done before," he said shaking his head. "Difficult, I grant you, but not impossible," he continued, and demonstrated on himself with a pistol shaped surgical instrument. "Like this," he added, pirouetting for all to see. "Any other bright ideas?"

A puritanical-faced young woman with her hair scraped brutally back in a rat's tail made a few notes then demanded in a gravelly voice. "Can I ask why it's been done before. I mean ... It seems so terribly awkward. Why would someone shoot themselves in the back of the head?"

"Maybe he wanted it to be a surprise," joked the bearded one.

She froze him with a cold stare but everyone around her collapsed in laughter. Restoring order took a few minutes and when the laughter had died down the pathologist explained. "There have been a number of cases to my knowledge where the deceased wanted someone else to take the rap. Just as murderers will often attempt to pass off their handiwork as suicide, so suicides will sometimes attempt to frame the person they believe responsible for their misfortune."

"Perhaps you would explain how you know this wasn't a suicide then?" demanded the woman, making it clear that she was not the game-playing type.

"Because, Ladies and Gentlemen, if this was a common or garden suicide, we wouldn't be graced with the presence of half the brass of Hampshire C.I.D." He bowed in Bliss's direction. "No offence, Chief Inspector – I just want this lot to realise that's there is more to determining a cause of death than a simple examination of the body."

"You've been promoted again," whispered Patterson with a malicious twist.

Bliss acknowledged the pathologist with a nod but his mind was still in the Dauntseys' attic, on the skull. He had stood looking at the body in the eerily lit space for several seconds before realising that the Major's head was still with the body. It had flopped forward under its own weight and after weeks, months or even years, the army of bugs had severed the spinal column allowing it to tumble into his lap and bury itself face down into his groin. There was only room for a few men at a time in the cramped attic and, once the photographer had finished and slipped gratefully down the ladder, Bliss, alone, had donned surgical gloves and gingerly lifted the skull to examine the remains of the face.

"Dear God," he breathed, stunned to prayer by the sheer torment still evident on the face, a face mutilated, deformed and disfigured by war. The expression "happy release" sprang to mind as he gagged repeatedly at the sight of the gruesome artefact. But, he knew, it was the agony of life not the spasm of death that had contorted the jaws into the lopsided fleshless grimace. With the bile rising uncontrollably in his throat, he dropped the head back into the Major's lap, shot down the ladder and, later, was thankful he had been called away from the restaurant before eating dinner.

"Before commencing the physical examination of the body," the pathologist was saying, tearing Bliss away from the nightmarish memory, "I shall ask Chief Inspector Bliss to relate the circumstances surrounding the death – as I would in any case of this nature ... Chief Inspector?"

Patterson dug him in the ribs. "Oh sorry ... yes ... Well, it's still a bit of a mystery to be honest, Doctor. We know that he came back from the war in a bad way: multiple injuries; badly shot-up; bits missing, including one arm; smashed face ..." he paused with the feeling he had missed something. Questioning looks from the students made him re-run the statement in his mind – he had failed to specify which war. The students were all in their early twenties. What did they know of the Second World War, or even Korea, Vietnam or the Falklands?

"He was wounded in battle outside Paris after D-Day, 1944," he explained.

"So," added the pathologist, "in the parlance of today's medical students, we might say he came back a bit of a fuckin' mess."

A student with a cascading mane of bleach blond hair choked and had to be given a glass of water, which she eyed suspiciously before sipping carefully.

"The body was discovered in a sealed attic above a sort of turret," continued Bliss, "and we believe he may have been dead for as long as forty years. The floor of the attic was covered in the skeletons of dead flies and other insects and we found a service revolver on the floor to his left side."

"I guess it was his own gun," the scenes of crime officer had said as he carefully slipped it into an evidence bag.

"It may have been army issue," mused Bliss, thinking that either way it might be difficult to trace. "I bet it's not registered, but let me have the serial number as soon as you can. I'll get someone to make some enquiries with his regiment."

Patterson, ex-army himself, standing in the room below, overheard. "I can just imagine some quartermaster-sergeant somewhere still fuming about it," he laughed and imitated a crotchety NCO. "I see Major Dauntsey still hasn't turned in his weapon – fifty years overdue – bloody officers think they can get away with murder."

"Is there any reason to suppose he was killed somewhere else and his body placed in the attic?" prompted the pathologist, but he already knew the answer, he'd studied the initial police report.

"Yes, that's a possibility," replied Bliss. "The Major's disabilities would have made it difficult, if not impossible, for him to have climbed a ladder into the attic."

"And do you have other reasons to suppose this wasn't suicide?"

"Yes ... Even if he had climbed into the attic and shot himself, he couldn't possibly have sealed the trapdoor and plastered over the ceiling behind him."

"Good point, Chief Inspector. Now," he turned to the students, "do you have any questions before we examine the rest of the body?"

The straight-laced woman was scribbling again. "Were there any personal artefacts found with the body and did he leave ...?" she began.

"One question at a time, Miss," the pathologist cut in. "Chief Inspector?"

Where to begin, wondered Bliss, the barrel-lidded wooden trunk bearing the Major's illuminated monogram or the little regiment of toy soldiers marching through the dust at his feet.

"Just look at that," the photographer had said, marvelling at the ranks of miniature soldiers. "Reminds me of that place in China where the Emperor had all those soldiers buried with him."

"Xian," said Bliss. "The terracotta army ... but these are lead." Choosing one at random he turned it over. "Britains," he said with the air of an expert.

"Do you know about these then, Guv?" asked the photographer seemingly impressed.

"Just a little ..." he paused, something catching his attention. At the head of the assorted foot soldiers was a horse drawn gun carriage with four outriders, just as the dealer had described. "That's interesting," he said manoeuvring carefully around the tableau to examine the figures. "Royal Horse Artillery," he continued, almost soundlessly, "with steel helmets." What had the dealer said? 1940 – 1941?

"Can you get some pictures of these?" he said to the photographer.

"Sure, Guv. No problem. Do you think they have some bearing on the case?"

"Put it this way – I think I know where their leader is."

"The hand-crafted wooden trunk had survived the war but had lost the battle against woodworm," Bliss explained to the students in the mortuary. "The lid disintegrated as I opened it but, lying on the top of all his clothes, was a medal, the Distinguished Service Order, and it was still shiny after all those years." He paused, thinking how proud the Major must have been of the enamelled medal with its crown and laurel leaf.

"In addition to his uniform, we found his dog-tags and, interestingly, the dog-tags of another soldier, a Captain David Tippin."

The plain-faced girl seized on the information and shook it, like a bulldog. "Maybe the Captain murdered him – tracked him down after the war – the Major seized the dog-tags ... Wait – Perhaps this Captain Tippin was the one who wounded him on the battleground – disgruntled junior officer type, lashed out at his superior ..."

"Hold on," said Bliss smiling at the woman's fervour. "Anything is possible. However, at the moment we're keeping an open mind, but the simplest explanations are usually the most accurate. Initial enquiries reveal that a captain of that name was killed around the time that Major Dauntsey was wounded. I suspect that the Major intended presenting the other man's tags to his family but never got around to it."

With the final question answered, "No – there was no suicide note," the pathologist began a thorough examination of the skeleton, picking over every piece of bone, explaining the anatomy as he went. Bliss let his mind drift. The cause of death was already clear – a single bullet in the back of the head, execution style. Wasn't the indignity of death enough without all this, he thought, recalling Mandy Richards with her breast blown off and her skirt halfway up her backside.

He had not attended Mandy's post-mortem and had not wanted to, but, because of his involvement in her death, his inspector had thought it prudent to warn him off in any case. "Not a good idea, lad," he'd said, turning an order into a piece of friendly advice. He had moped around the office that morning, picturing the grisly scene in his mind, wondering why it was necessary to dissect her scrawny body when it should be obvious to a five-year-old why she had died. What possible benefit could there be from knowing what she'd eaten for lunch? It just made everyone feel worse for the sake of accuracy.

It was her pregnancy that had caused the most grief. "A first trimester foetus was present in the womb," the coroner's clerk had said, reading the pathologist's report at the inquest. "I estimate the deceased to have been approximately eight weeks pregnant. The foetus appeared to have been developing normally."

A sudden hush had fallen around the courtroom then Mandy's mother exploded in grief. Not only had she lost a daughter but she'd also lost a grandchild. Mandy's fiancé threw his arms around her, comforting the woman who would never be his mother-in-law, but it was as much to comfort himself. He had never slept with Mandy. "We'll wait," they had agreed, throughout their two year romance. Now he had more pain to endure, as did Constable Bliss – he was responsible for two deaths now, not one. And one of them would never even see the light of day.

Superintendent Donaldson was eagerly awaiting their return from the mortuary and had taken out his frustration on another packet of biscuits. "The press are demanding some sort of statement. Someone must have tipped them off that he's been dead for ever. Where the hell does that leave us? It's the sort of thing the nationals will jump all over."

Bliss and Patterson pulled up chairs to the superintendent's desk, uninvited. "We're no further forward, Sir," started Patterson. "He took a bullet in the back of the head, but we knew that the minute we found the skull. The question is who put it there."

"What did Jonathon have to say?" asked the super-intendent offering Bliss a digestive.

"Thanks ... He gave us a long-winded no comment then stuck his nose in the air and said, "I warned you not to dig up old skeletons, Inspector." I'm pretty sure he knew the body was there but, subject to the results from the pathology lab, he couldn't possibly have done it. He couldn't have been more than ten when it happened."

"He could have done it," suggested Patterson tersely. "Ten-year-olds have shot people before."

"Then manhandled the body into the loft and plastered it up – I doubt it," sneered Bliss. "Anyway, don't you think Mrs. Dauntsey may have been a tad suspicious when her disabled husband suddenly disappears out of his wheelchair?"

"What about her?" asked Donaldson. "Could she have done it?"

"That's my bet," replied Bliss. "I wouldn't be at all surprised if she got fed up taking care of the poor specimen – it couldn't have been much for either of them. So she put him out of his misery – lightened her load. She has to be the prime suspect. There were only three of them living in the house as far as we know and one of them was a young schoolboy. That leaves Ma and Pa. Pa gets a slug in the back of the head – that only leaves Ma, and who could blame her. Ten years with a one-armed bloke in a wheelchair who can't even raise himself up for a satisfying fart without assistance. He couldn't speak and couldn't even give her a once over. He would have been less fun than a goldfish."

"You haven't questioned her yet?"

"I haven't even told her we've found him ..."

"That I found him," muttered Patterson.

"Alright, Pat – you found him – that reminds me. How did you find him? What made you rip that ceiling down?"

"There was a faint stain – very difficult to see – could've been a trick of the light. Just a ghostly smudge on the ceiling. It must have been where the juices came through when the body was still fresh, but it had been painted over – several times probably. Then, when I couldn't find a trap door, I became really suspicious."

"So what happens to Jonathon now?" asked Donaldson. "He confessed to killing someone."

"He confessed to killing his father ..." started Bliss, then paused, his mind swirling with possibilities. "Wait a minute ... what if Rupert Dauntsey wasn't his father? I think I've got it. What if he killed his real father, whoever that may have been, and we just assumed he was talking about the Major ...?"

"That makes sense," Donaldson jumped in, thinking through the confession. "I don't believe he was ever asked if he'd killed Major Dauntsey." Then he turned accusingly to Sergeant Patterson. "You never asked him, did you?"

"I ... I don't remember."

Donaldson's blood was rising. "I do – You never bloody asked him. You just took it for granted ..."

"I think we all did," said Bliss, stepping in quickly to defend his sergeant.

Donaldson smacked the Newton's balls and slumped back in his seat. "So where the hell do we go from here?"

"We can hardly re-arrest him on the strength of further evidence," said Bliss. "The only evidence we've got exonerates him. But whoever he killed has disappeared."

Donaldson reached for another biscuit. "We know that. That's why we can't find the body."

"No, Sir, you're missing the point. What I mean is, the living man must be missing. Someone, somewhere must be saying, 'Where's my husband, father or brother?'"

Donaldson caught on. "Good thinking, Dave."

"I'll get someone to do a national search for all missing persons for the past couple of weeks and we'll take it from there."

"We've got the blood on the duvet," suggested Patterson, trying to redeem himself. "At least we'll be able to do a DNA match."

The Vicar of St. Paul's was back, asking for Bliss personally, acting on a tip from the undertaker that the Major's body had turned up.

"Good morning, Inspector," he called, catching him out in the open as he returned to his office. "I'm sorry to hear about the Major ..."

"And?" said Bliss in his mind, already figuring that this was not a visitation of commiseration.

"If there's anything the church can do ..."

What had you in mind, wondered Bliss maliciously: checking up on your parishioners occasionally, perhaps, especially the sick and wounded, just to make sure that they haven't been bopped off in the past forty years or so. "I don't believe there is, not at this time, Vicar. But it's very thoughtful of you to enquire," thinking, thoughtful my ass – he's after something.

"Only I have it on fairly good authority that the poor old fellow may have left a little something," continued the vicar, cap in hand, "The church roof you know ... somewhat urgent I'm afraid, otherwise I wouldn't have mentioned it."

Bet you wouldn't. "I'm not sure it will be that much but I assume the family will get whatever there is."

"Don't you consider that to be somewhat anti-social, Inspector – passing wealth from one generation to the next? Surely each man should be a success or failure on

his merits, not because some slave-trader or royal syco-
phant in his past accumulated a stash of money."

Enough of the pussyfooting, thought Bliss, rounding on the other man. "Vicar, personally I might agree
with you entirely, but, if I were you, I wouldn't say that
too loud. I bet there aren't many bishops who grew up
in council houses and went to the local comprehensive."

Daphne was keeping her head down when Bliss returned
to his office and continued busily vacuuming the corridor
as if she'd not seen him standing in front of her.

"Everything alright, Daphne?" he shouted.

She turned a deaf ear and tried to clean behind the
door. He pulled out the plug and she looked up in mock
surprise. "Oh, it's you, Chief Inspector – you startled me."

"It's Dave – remember."

"Not on duty it's not."

"Have it your own way," he mumbled. "So, how
is Andrew?"

"Alright," she replied coldly, with a warning scowl.

He sensed an emotional minefield ahead. "How
was dinner?"

"Dinner," she spat.

He'd hit a mine. "Sorry, I ..."

"It wasn't your fault. I don't blame you, Chief
Inspector. Not at all."

"Blame me for what, Daphne?"

"For abandoning me with that wretched man, of
course."

"You seemed rather keen that I should leave."

"I think it was the drink. It was stronger than it used
to be. And that smooth talking ... I never did like him, but
I suppose I thought he would have changed with age."

"And he hadn't?"

"He's got worse. He gave me the old, 'Golly, I've lost my wallet routine,' when the bill arrived. I should have guessed what he was like. One look at that stupid wig – he's as bald as a coot."

"How do you know?"

She picked up the vacuum cleaner's plug and fiddled to get it back into the socket, her mind clearly churning in debate. Then she flung the plug down in disgust. "Do you know, Chief Inspector, that filthy pig actually tried it on, in the taxi – the one I paid for. He jumped me at my age without a bye-your-leave. I grabbed his hair to pull him off and thought for a minute that I'd ripped his head off ... you're laughing at me."

"Not at you, Daphne – I'm just laughing." He straightened his face. "Are you alright? I mean ... he didn't ..."

"Oh no. I hit him where it hurts. He soon let go."

I bet he did, thought Bliss, controlling his face with difficulty. "I am sorry, Daphne, but let me make it up to you. Let me take you out tonight and I promise not to run out on you, if you promise to ignore any dodgy old friends."

"It's Friday – have you forgotten?"

"Forgotten – what?"

"Aren't you going home? Surely you're not working all weekend."

Home, what a lovely thought that should be – Home on Friday evening. Happy memories flickered across his eyes, memories too ancient to raise a smile: contented wife and smelly baby; home cooked halibut and chips; the aroma of baking apple pie with luck. "I'll give Samantha her bath and put her to bed while you're getting the dinner," he'd murmur, his face nuzzled lovingly to her ear. And afterwards, a bottle of Côtes-du-Rhône, Brubeck or Beethoven, and a generous helping of Friday night delight.

"No. I'm not going home," he said, feelings of loss dragging his words. Then he brightened, "And I'd love to take you out."

"We can make it into something of a celebration I suppose."

"Celebrating what?"

"Finding the Major, of course."

What was there to celebrate? They had been better off without the body. At least Jonathon could have been convicted on the circumstantial evidence and his own confession.

"I'm not sure I've anything to celebrate to be honest, Daphne. We now have two murders instead of one. We're still minus one body and now were missing another murderer."

Sergeant Patterson came round the corner unnoticed, pulled up short and was trying to back away when Bliss spotted him. "Ah, Sergeant Patterson. I wanted a word with you ... my office."

Patterson turned with a hunted look. "I was just going to get that missing person search started."

"It won't take a minute," he said, turning to Daphne. "Let me plug that in for you, Miss Lovelace."

The cleaner burst into life as Bliss shepherded the reluctant sergeant into his office. "Shut the door, Pat ... can't hear a bloody thing with that machine ... That's better. Sit down, there's something I've been meaning to ask you."

By the look on Patterson's face he was wondering if Bliss intended extracting a few teeth without anaesthetic. "What, Guv?"

"I just wondered how you tracked me down at The Limes the other night."

Patterson slumped in relief. "It was nothing, Guv," he explained. "I called the Mitre, spoke to the girl with a strange accent. She said she didn't know where you were but that you'd left in a taxi. There's only two dispatchers in the whole place so it wasn't difficult. The first one I called said you'd gone to the Limes."

"Brilliant deduction, Holmes," said Bliss.

"That's why I'm a detective, Watson old chap," replied Patterson, tipping an imaginary deerstalker and sliding out.

Daphne was still vacuuming outside the office and Patterson gave her an inquisitive glance, sorely tempted to pump her for information. "So Daphne, just who was that woman our detective inspector picked up from your house in a taxi on Wednesday?" he could have asked, but what would she have told Bliss?

So, who the hell was the woman? he wondered, as he had been wondering since Wednesday when the taxi driver had blabbed, "She was quite a looker – middle aged but real smart." Had Bliss moved a mistress into the neighbourhood and lodged her with Daphne? Then a thought struck him and he poked his head back round the door, "By the way, Guv. Have you got your warrant card yet?"

"Yeah – came in the despatch this morning."

"Oh – good. I'll get on with that misper search then."

The phone rang. Bliss had another visitor vis-à-vis the Dauntsey case. A solicitor appropriately named Law, according to the receptionist, and he immediately recalled the words of the sergeant at his first posting. "There's nothing like a juicy body to bring the rats out of the woodwork," he had said.

"Law & Law," the solicitor introduced himself

with an outstretched hand. "We represent Major Rupert Dauntsey – the deceased. We came as soon as we heard."

Bliss looked behind the big man, expecting to see his partner in an equally loud herring-bone suit. The corridor was empty. "May I ask, just how did we hear?" he enquired, with more than a trace of mockery, ushering him into the room.

"It's common knowledge, Inspector – We understand there were quite a number of witnesses. The point is that the Major made a will on inheriting the estate from his father, the Colonel, whom we also represented."

"As a matter of interest, can I ask when you last saw the Major?"

"We – that is I, personally, never had that pleasure. My father drew up the will and it has remained, unaltered, in our possession since 1946."

"So who is the beneficiary? Who inherits the estate?"

"Inspector. You know we can't divulge that, not until death is confirmed. That's why we came actually, to find out who issued the death certificate, so we can lay our hands on a copy."

Explaining that the body had yet to be formally identified, and wondering who was going to do it, Bliss assured the other man that he would keep him informed, then asked, "Do you know why his son Jonathon might have wanted him dead?"

Law pulled him closer and bent to his ear. "This is absolutely confidential, off the record. We'll deny ever saying anything. We've no idea – Jonathon Dauntsey doesn't stand to gain anything at all from the will."

"That's interesting," said Bliss, then he put in a word for the church. "I'm not asking you to betray any confidences but I've just had the Vicar of St. Paul's here. He seems to think he's going to get a new roof."

The solicitor was shaking his head. "He might need to invest in an umbrella then – if you get my drift."

Bliss sloped off at 4 pm. and returned to the Mitre – exhausted. He hadn't seen a proper bed for two nights and promised himself a nap before meeting Daphne for dinner. The excitement of discovering the body and the attendant work had edged Mandy to the corner of his mind and put her killer back in his box. Even the sight of the boarded up tea shop didn't disturb him – sleep was all that interested him. He stopped at the reception desk. The smiling Swede had been replaced by a friendly local girl with wavy dark hair.

"Any messages for me?" he asked tiredly, forgetting that she'd never met him.

"Your name, Sir?"

"Sorry. Bliss – 203."

"Oh yes, Sir. Your hire car has been delivered. Here are your keys and the papers. I told them to leave it in the car park at the back."

"Thanks," he took the keys. "Nothing else?"

She checked the pigeon hole. "No – nothing there."

"Thanks," he said, turning away.

"Oh – someone was asking about you though."

The Volvo was back. The killer was out of the box. Keep calm, he said to himself, trying desperately to sound conversational. "When was this?"

"Yesterday afternoon."

Don't be pushy, don't scare her. Shrug as if it doesn't matter. "A friend, I expect. Did he leave a name?"

"No. He said he'd catch up with you sometime."

The veiled threat – he'd done it before, in the letters on the phone. "One day – when you least expect it ... I'll catch up with you."

Bliss swallowed. "Was he tall?"

"No – very short. Funny little man ... sorry, I didn't mean to be rude ..."

"That's alright," cut in Bliss, confused. "Old or young?"

"Thirtyish."

Medium height and forties would have been nearer the mark – but she could have been mistaken. "Do you recall exactly what he said?"

"Well ... he said he thought he knew you. Wanted to know if you came from London."

That's the clincher. "You didn't tell him did you?"

"No, Sir, I told him he'd have to leave a note for you – even offered him some paper and a pen, but he wanted to talk to the manager. I went into the office to ask Mr. Robbins but when I got back he'd gone."

There was something she'd omitted. Bliss saw it in her face. The mental vacillation – to tell or not to tell – making her eyes repeatedly flick away, unable to hold his gaze for more than a blink. The hotel register, the divorce lawyers best friend or deadliest foe, had lain open on the desk as she had readied to invite the visitor to sign in.

"The register was closed when I got back – I was only gone a few seconds ..." she began nervously.

"And he could've looked ...?"

"Possibly."

Thank God no-one ever checks for phoney addresses, he thought, only vaguely remembering the one he'd made up. But, combined with the Volvo, this was sobering news. "Never mind, Luv. Not your fault. Just let me know if anybody else asks for me or if you see him again would you?"

Bliss made his way to his room, his tiredness overcome by concern. Would the killer ever come into the open and put him out of his misery or would the torment continue *ad infinitum* unless he were caught and shipped back to jail? You will never escape this, he said to himself poking under the bed, then, in the dusty shadows, he saw the image of a man – a man forever scrabbling under beds, checking behind wardrobes and eyeing the postman with trepidation. This will be with you forever unless you get a new face and a new name. But a new face was out of the question, he'd already ruled that out. A new name was a possibility, although it certainly created problems, especially if he were to remain in the police force. How could he suddenly pop up as Inspector Joe Blow without a background; qualifications; a family; previous address-es; credit cards; driving licence? So many people would need to know that the risks outweighed the advantages.

Chapter Nine

"Would you mind if we didn't go back to The Limes?" petitioned Daphne, fearing it to be Andrew's regular stalking ground. She needn't have worried. Land's End wouldn't have been far enough for Bliss.

"I thought we'd drive over to Marsdon," he replied, chivalrously opening the hired car's passenger door and sweeping her in. Her sleek cocktail dress of the previous evening had given way to flouncy printed cotton, its huge tangy-yellow flowers crying out for a picnic on a grassy river bank. A parasol wouldn't have gone amiss, but she had stuck with the broad-rimmed straw hat, merely switching the crimson ribbon for lemon.

"It seems a long way to go for dinner."

"Do you mind?"

"Oh no. Not at all. It's a lovely evening for a drive."

It wasn't – not for him anyway. He was on the run again. Instead of the badly needed nap, he'd spent the first hour in his room at the Mitre poking into every conceivable hidey-hole and pacing with worry, and the next hour packing. Whoever had been making enquiries about him would be back – probably. But why hang about to find out. The strain, and the degree of powerlessness in the face of such an ethereal adversary, had worn him to the point where he was almost ready to bolt back to the safe house.

He had been sneaking out of the hotel when the Swedish receptionist spotted him loading suitcases in the car park. "Is it that you are leaving, Mr. Bliss?" she smiled, her glow-white teeth bringing a moment's brightness to an otherwise gloomy day.

"I've been called away."

"But you have already paid have you not?"

He had – two weeks in advance, twenty percent discount. "It doesn't matter – I'll probably be back in a day or so."

The High Street seemed jammed with blue Volvos, both driven by short, funny looking, thirty-year-olds, and he was glad to have got away from the Mitre hotel and his Rover. But was this the future? Trailing his suitcases around in the boot of a rented car – finding a different hotel and switching every couple of days. Was he being forced to follow the blueprint of retribution drawn up by the killer? Had the threatening letters and menacing phone calls been just a tightening of the screw, dragging out the agony in the torture chamber of his mind?

"I did eighteen years for my part," the killer was telling him. "Now it's your turn."

Even the bomb through the letterbox had been half-hearted – little more than a handful of powerful fireworks packed into a cardboard tube. If he'd wanted to kill me, couldn't he have done that already? Shoot a single bullet from a silenced .44, then walk calmly away and melt into the crowd before anyone has even realised what's happened.

"Marsdon," said the sign, taking him unawares and making him question where his mind had been for the past twenty minutes.

He baulked at the first restaurant, a pushy place with fluorescent green shades and an egocentric sign plastered with recommendations and affiliations.

"Too busy," he complained, with hardly more than a peep through the lace curtains. Too many nooks and crannies, was what he really meant; too many cozy romantic niches where who-knows-what could be going on under the tables, and who-knows-who could be hiding, waiting to pounce; too many candles and not enough light to spot a killer. Don't be ridiculous, he said to himself, how could he possible know you were coming here? He could have followed us ... The way you've had your head stuck in the mirrors – you must be crazy. You've smacked the kerb three times – good job it's a hire car.

"This looks different," he said, driving on and catching sight of a gallows sign outside a barn-like building. "The Carpenter's Kitchen," proclaimed the legend under a carved pictograph of a chef's hat surrounded by saws, mallets and unrecognisable implements.

The earthy odour of freshly milled wood hit them as Bliss opened the solid church-type door. Quickly stooping to avoid the rough-hewn beams at headache height, he ran his eye along the warped plank flooring. "It's like being below decks in an old Schooner," he said with unmistakeable delight.

"Look at this," replied Daphne dashing off to fondle a diminutive wooden replica of Michelangelo's *David*.

"'Tis all 'and carved," said a buckled old man in workman's overalls and carpenter's apron, stepping from behind a sculpted pillar. "An' 'tis all for sale ..." he added, his head screwing awkwardly on a spine fixed by years of bending over a workbench.

"We wanted dinner actually," queried Bliss. "This is a restaurant, isn't it?"

"Oh yeah, 'course 'tis – upstairs. You go on up. That boy o' mine'll look after you."

Bliss was having second thoughts, fearful the food might have absorbed the characteristics of sawdust, but at least there were no Volvos in the car park.

"I think it's rather quaint," said Daphne, dawdling to admire award-winning turnings and carvings. "Oh look at this cat," she said, stroking the life-like carving. "It reminds me of my old tom – the General."

Five minutes later the cat, elm with walnut inlay and bright glass eyes, sat alert on the dining table checking out the dozen or so other guests in the upstairs dining room.

"Sit where you like," the old man's "boy" had said, and Daphne placed her purchase on a table sliced from the bole of an ancient tree, every growth ring clearly countable.

"Cinnamon," she sniffed, then sat and picked a curled stick from a centrepiece of shaved rosewood, sandalwood and cedar. "I love cinnamon," she added, running it under her nose. "It's so Christmassy, don't you think?"

Bliss frowned. "Would you mind if I sat there?" he said, holding out the other chair for her, inviting her to move.

She caught on. "I suppose you want your back to the wall, Chief Inspector – is that a man thing?"

He laughed it off. "No – it's a policeman thing."

She moved and the "boy" came back with the menus. Fifty-five guessed Bliss, but Daphne put him in his late forties – he had young hands, she explained later.

The menus were in keeping with the general theme. "I hate this sort of thing," said Bliss, turning up his nose at the contorted literary, culinary and carpentry amalgamations. "Listen to this – Oak-smoked joint of venison with sauce of wood mushrooms and potato logs."

"Oh don't be so stuffy, it sounds rather good, and look they've got woodcock and wood grouse. Though I think I'd prefer something I can talk through – I don't want to have to concentrate, nothing finicky – no bones. And nothing awkward like lobster or spaghetti."

"I think I'll have a steak," said Bliss, reading aloud. "Grilled over charcoal burnt from Oak, Pine and Mesquite."

"That sounds good," muttered Daphne, though her face said she was still giving some thought to her selection. "You were very quiet in the car, Chief Inspector," she said, looking up from the menu. "I guess you have something on your mind."

Blue Volvos, funny little men snooping into hotel registers and untimely death. "The Major's face actually ..." he started, then paused. "It was pretty horrific. I don't want to put you off your dinner."

"No – I'm interested. Carry on."

"Well, it was only a skeleton but the jaw and cheek bones had been stitched together with silver wire. The surgeon had obviously done his best, but there simply wasn't enough bone. It reminded me of a horror movie. One of those low budget ones, *Frankenstein's Brother's Monster* or something. Anyway, the plot was that Frankenstein's brother made an even more monstrous creature out of all the bits the doctor had left over when he'd finished his monster."

"Are you making this up?"

"No – I don't think so ... Anyway, that's what he looked like. And I thought it was significant that the pathologist had removed the face bones before showing the students the skull. I guess he didn't want anybody throwing up all over the mortuary floor."

"That would be the Major alright," said Daphne, her face puckering in awful memory of the mutilated face. "He looked a right mess when he came back ..."

The barman cut into their conversation. "Would you care for drinks while you're looking at the menu?"

"I think I need an aperitif – something to bolster me up, something with a bit of body," mused Daphne. "A Dubonnet, I think, with just a twist of lemon to take the edge off the sweetness."

"A scotch for me, please," said Bliss.

"Anything with that, Sir – ice perhaps?"

"Neat, thanks."

"We do something called a Scotch Pine ..."

"Just the whiskey – thank you," he replied, his tone sharp enough to draw blood.

"That's why he got the D.S.O.," continued Daphne, her mind still on Major Dauntsey. "They say that even though he was injured and under fire, he still managed to carry one of his wounded men more than three miles toward a first aid station. He wouldn't let anyone help – said it was his duty."

"But I understood he could hardly speak."

"That was after the explosion," she nodded in agreement. "The man he was carrying literally blew up in his face and ripped off his arm. A grenade they think – on his belt or in his pocket. Either the pin jerked out or a sniper's bullet hit it. Anyway, the explosion killed the soldier and blew away half the Major."

The drinks arrived. Bliss slugged his back. "I needed that. So what was Arnie talking about? He said the Major had got them all killed because he made them tidy up instead of retreat."

"I heard the rumours," said Daphne, taking a few thoughtful sips. "He was hailed as a hero at first; given the D.S.O. for the way he'd dragged the injured man out under fire. It was only later, when the few survivors got back, that they started telling a different story; that the whole thing was his fault. But you know what the Army's like. They'd never admit a mistake – especially when committed by a senior commissioned officer."

"Sounds a bit like the police force," muttered Bliss.

"Anyway, what were they going to do – court martial a one-eyed man who didn't have a right hand to hold a bible or a voice to speak the oath?"

"But was Arnie right? Did he make the men clear up the battlefield before retreating?"

"Who knows?" she shrugged. "It's the maxim of all peons worldwide. If anything goes wrong – blame the boss."

"So you don't believe it then?"

"If he did do what Arnie said then he must have had a good reason. Only idiots set out deliberately to do the wrong thing."

"But wasn't he an idiot? Arnie seemed to think so."

"He went to university."

"Money," scoffed Bliss.

"And he became a Major," she added.

"Influence, connections. Don't forget, his father was a Colonel. What were the recruiters going to say? Anyway, it was wartime – the ability to breathe was high on the list of selection criteria."

The waiter was back with a wooden bowl overflowing with cheese sticks. Daphne was still undecided, torn between the wood-pigeon pie and the off-cuts of oak-smoked turkey, and asked for a few more minutes.

"So where do you go from here?" she asked Bliss as the waiter headed for another table.

"We're just spinning our wheels," he replied, idly nibbling a stick. "We're checking for missing persons; waiting for blood tests on the duvet; pulling Jonathon's house to pieces and digging his garden – the other body has to be somewhere, but we're stumped until it turns up. I'll have to talk to Doreen again tomorrow. Somebody has to tell her that her husband's dead."

"Well, I don't think it will come as much of a shock."

"What do you mean?"

"Chief Inspector – if anybody knew where the body was you can be sure it would have been Doreen Dauntsey. Losing your husband isn't like leaving an umbrella on a bus."

"I've been putting it off until we've confirmed his identity."

"Is there some doubt ...?"

"No – not really. It's just that Jonathon was so adamant."

"Well, personally, I've no doubt it was Rupert from the way you describe the wounds. Most people couldn't bear to look at him. Of course, he wasn't what you might call well-known in the town. He went away to one of them pricey prep schools, then onto Marlborough College – I think. And he spent most holidays in Scotland on the estate. And his father, the Colonel, was none too popular – crusty old bastard – thought he was still in the guards the way he'd order the locals about. And he seemed to think the police were his personal retainers from what I've heard."

"No wonder Rupert turned out the way he did."

"What way?"

Gay; queer; poof; fairy – he ran through the list in his mind searching for the word she had previously used to describe him and was struck by the incongruity of the situation. The woman in front of him was old enough to be his grandmother – at a stretch – yet enveloped in the wrinkled skin and white hair was a young imp. It was in her eyes – the daredevil look that said she would still take on the world, or a frisky con-artist. I bet Andrew's bollocks still ache from last night, he thought to himself. That'll teach him.

"What way did Rupert turn out, Chief Inspector?" she persisted.

Had he misinterpreted what she'd said about the Major. "You know ..." he began, suspecting she was teasing him, " ... batting for the other side."

She shrugged it off with a smile. "Like I told you – it was only a rumour, and I'm not sure I believed it myself, especially after he married Doreen."

"Well, what if I told you I'm beginning to think that the Major wasn't Jonathon's father?"

"I could have told you that."

"You could?"

"Yes, in fact I was going to tell you on Wednesday evening, then you dashed off and left me ..." her face soured at the thought of Andrew and she sweetened it with a slurp of Dubonnet. "Anyway, after our chat on Monday evening I got to thinking about what had happened, and one or two things just didn't make sense ..." She paused for a moment's deliberation, then admitted, "I've been a bit naughty, I'm afraid, but when I was polishing the custody officer's desk I couldn't help noticing Jonathon's custody record sort of sticking out of the filing cabinet. Anyway, his date of birth was the 4th of April, 1945."

Bliss laughed, "Just sort of sticking out was it? Although I must admit I didn't check his birth date."

"Well, you had no reason to, but I did a little calculation. I'm pretty sure that Doreen and the Major were married on the 27th of May 1944, it might have been the 26th but I think it was the 27th, Anyway, he went off to his regiment the following day, so, unless she was 10 months pregnant when Jonathon was born, he definitely isn't a Dauntsey."

Bliss added up the months in his head and laughed. "You're absolutely right. Although ... what about when he returned ..."

Daphne blocked him with a hand. "The baby would already have been born. In any case, according to Doreen, his thingy was one of the bits which had been blown off."

The thought set Bliss's teeth on edge. "Ooh, painful ... So who is Jonathon's father?"

"You'd have to ask Doreen – but to be honest there's a good chance she won't know. Oh dear, that sounds so bitchy, doesn't it – the sort of thing one of those Hollywood actresses would say."

The waiter was hovering for their order and Bliss expressed intrigue in the Dovetail pâté as a starter.

"Wood pigeons," explained the waiter. "Though the chef uses the whole birds not just the tails."

"Sounds interesting," he said giving a nod.

"Compote of wood mushrooms for me, please," said Daphne, adding *sotto voce*, "I do hope they use *bolets du bois* and not those tasteless white button things." Once the waiter had moved off with their order, Daphne continued, "I came across the Major in France. After he was wounded, before he was shipped home."

Everything suddenly fell into place in Bliss's mind and he held up his hand, beaming, "I've got it now, you were a nurse; Queen Alexandra's I bet; went in with the troops on the front lines – hence the O.B.E. No wonder you like looking after people, taking birds under your wing."

"Detective Inspector," she started, getting his title right for once, pointing up the gravity of what she was about to divulge. "It's rather sweet that you should imagine me in a blood covered apron, comforting the wounded, but it would be dishonest of me to let you go on believing that, and it wouldn't be sensible in the long run."

"What do you mean?"

"I'm sorry to disappoint you but I wasn't a nurse – my job wasn't to save lives."

"What did you do?"

Daphne appeared not to hear as she stroked the wooden cat. "I hope you don't put the General's nose out of joint, he can be very jealous at times," she said, then, without changing tone or taking her eyes off the statue, asked, "Do you ever tell lies, Dave?"

"Sometimes."

"That's very honest," she looked up quizzically, "unless you're lying."

"Daphne – What on earth are you rambling about? All I wanted to know was what you did during the war."

With a final stroke of the cat she seemed to make up her mind. Fixing Bliss with a hard stare she stunned him. "I killed people."

Bliss choked – seriously choked. He'd taken a sharp involuntary breath at the wrong moment and inhaled a flake of pastry from a cheese stick.

"Water," he coughed, and took several slurps before trying to speak through the spluttering – "You … killed … people?"

"I knew I should have lied … Here, have some more water, you're going red."

The waiter was back. "Something wrong, Madam?"

"He's choking."

"Don't make a fuss," Bliss pleaded, gasping for air.

"More water, Sir?"

He waved the glass away and doubled over with coughing and retching. The lights were going out – fading into a fuzzy haze, his eyes were streaming, his oxygen-starved brain was struggling for a solution and all he could think was – this sweet little old lady's a killer.

A dozen pairs of hooded eyes sneaked a look, conversations drifted to a standstill. Time held it's breath. Waiting for what? Then Daphne leapt out of her chair, ran around the table and smashed her fist into his back. Bliss exploded in a fit of coughing, panting and wheezing as he forced his lungs to inhale, but the obstruction had cleared and he gasped himself back to normality.

"You nearly choked to death," said Daphne, her voice full of concern as she re-sat.

"What d'ye expect after what you just told me?" he replied accusingly.

"I'm not proud of what I did. And quite honestly I'd rather you kept this just between us."

"But who did you kill? When? Why? – I don't understand."

She shut him out again, going back to the cat, then reminding him. "We came to talk about the Major."

"You can't do that – You can't give me a heart-attack then change the subject. This isn't the Women's Institute – 'You can finish the crochet at home ladies, now we're starting the strawberry jam.'"

"You are funny, Chief Inspector."

"No, I'm serious. I want to know."

Daphne spent a few moments brushing crumbs off the table then her eyes locked onto one of the table's growth-rings and she followed it around until it disappeared under Bliss's left hand. "People do things in wars," she began sombrely, concentrating on his fingers. "Disgusting things; things they'd never dream of doing normally; things they'd never admit having done ..." The turmoil of indecision slowed her speech. "I wish I hadn't said anything ..." she paused then looked up, pleading with her eyes. "Don't say anything, will you?"

He wouldn't, he assured her.

"I belonged to a special unit during the war," she began, explaining calmly. "French-speaking men and women trained for a specific mission during the invasion of France. The Allies were concerned the French would side with the Germans after D-Day and turn on our troops."

"Why should they?"

"Fear mainly – the Gestapo had rounded up many Frenchmen and sent them to concentration camps. Almost every family had at least one member who'd been arrested and imprisoned and the threat was clear – co-operate or they die. But the French had other reasons."

"What reasons – surely we were liberating them?"

"That's true, though some still hadn't forgiven us for deserting them at Dunkirk and don't forget we'd destroyed their fleet at Oran – killed thousands of sailors to stop the Vichy Government handing the ships over to the Germans." Checking to make sure she wasn't being overheard, she lowered her voice a couple of notches. "And they never liked us very much in the first place."

"I still don't understand. What were you expected to do – kill Frenchman before they could kill our people?"

"No – of course not. We were trained to prepare the way for the invading forces – let the French know we were coming as allies to free the country, not turn it into a British colony like the Germans claimed in their propaganda; to warn them to keep away from the coast; persuade them to dig in or hide in the cellars. We were supposed to galvanise the resistance to co-ordinate the blowing up of bridges, derailment of trains, blocking roads, that sort of thing. But the main task was to get behind enemy lines and vector artillery fire onto concentrations of German troops. Once the battle started our people wouldn't have a clue where the fleeing Jerries were and the danger was we could have wiped out the local population without even scratching the enemy. So you see, it was my job to kill people."

The first course arrived and the interruption gave Bliss an opportunity to get his thoughts together.

This wasn't bad, he thought, this wasn't the admission of some deranged old biddy who had wiped out half the inmates of an old peoples home with arsenic in the soup; this wasn't a rampaging granny mowing down the queue in the post office because her welfare cheque hadn't arrived; this wasn't a mobster in a mask ...

"It was wartime – people die. You said so yourself," he began, offering absolution, but she sliced into a mushroom with such fierce concentration that he backed off and centred on his pâté.

"How did you get there?" he tried conversationally after a few minutes.

"Parachute."

"You parachuted into France?"

"Yes."

"Wasn't that dangerous?"

"Yes."

"Was it during the day or at night?"

"Night."

"Did you have a reserve?"

"No."

"Are you going to keep this up all evening? ... I said, are you ..."

"I heard you, Chief Inspector, but sometimes it's best to leave old skeletons in the cupboard."

"That's exactly what Jonathon said."

"He was right then."

Bliss sat back with an admiring smile. "I can't get over that. You – parachuting out of a plane over enemy territory in the middle of the night."

"I sometimes wonder if it was a dream myself."

Bliss took a few moments to finish his pâté' and used the hiatus to study her with deepening respect, realising that if it were anyone but Daphne talking he'd probably not believe a word of what they were saying. But there was something so totally sincere in her manner. "So what happened?" he asked eventually.

Daphne toyed indecisively with the remaining mushroom – shunting it back and forth across her plate.

Then she edged it onto the rim and started working it around.

"Daphne – I said, what happened?"

The mushroom went round and around the plate rim, faster and faster, but there was no way out.

"Daphne?"

She stopped, stabbed the mushroom angrily with her fork and looked straight through him, focusing somewhere far off in the distance – somewhere in the past. "I was cold, wet , miserable and scared to death. My partner ... my friend ... hit a power line. Electrocuted – dead. He had the maps. I wandered – lost, disorientated, hun-

gry for two or three days – then the guns started." Her
eyes closed as the barrage went off in her mind and she
sat silent until the noise had faded.

"A young French woman, my age, was lying by the
side of the road covered in blood, screaming," she said
as she re-opened her eyes, but her voice was as distant
as her gaze. "She'd been shot or hit by shrapnel."

Mandy Richards was back, her crimson chest stip-
pled with shreds of green blouse. And her killer – blood
and snot dribbling out of his nose – his face more ghast-
ly than the mask that had been pulled off. And now
another face had got stirred into the horrific mental
morass – the Major's face, or what was left of it: half a
shattered jaw strung up with wire and a few rotten teeth
set at crazy angles.

But Daphne was having her own nightmare.

"When I bent down to see if I could help I realised
she had a baby, wrapped in a fluffy blue blanket soaked
in blood. 'Take my baby – please take my baby,' the poor
girl was screaming.' 'Where to?' I said. 'To my mother –
Mama – she will take care of him. Please, please take
him.' She paused and stared over Bliss's shoulder at a
blank wall, waiting for the pain to abate – hoping she
might wake before the worst. 'Where is your mother?' I
asked," – the horror movie refusing to stop in her mind.
"And she gave me the name of the town ... I couldn't
believe my luck. It was the town where I was supposed
to be and it was still behind enemy lines. I was desperate
... I had to get there ... I still had my job to do. Without
me our artillery would just destroy the whole place."

Burying her head in her hands Daphne tried shutting out the images, then gave up and confronted herself
with the facts. "I took her bicycle and put my radio in
the wicker carrier, you know the sort that all French
bikes have ... and ... " she paused again, fighting off the

memory, hoping it had never happened – hoping it was only a movie. "And ..." she tried again. "And ... I wrapped her baby in my shawl ... and ..." The words wouldn't come.

Bliss shook off his own demons and helped out. "And the baby ...?" he asked.

"I put him in the basket on top of the radio." There, I've said it. Now finish the story. "And I rode away. 'Good luck,' she called, *'Bon chance – Bon chance*. Tell my mother I'll be home in a day or so,' she cried. 'I'll be home as soon as the guns have stopped. Tell her not to worry.'"

She sat silent for a few moments, still staring through the wall as images piled up in her mind and she sorted them in order. "A British soldier tried to stop me at a checkpoint. He was sure I was French. Of course, I looked French – that was all part of the training. We had French instructors – girls our own age who had escaped or been in England at the start of the war. With the French it's not just the language, it's the way you stick out your bum and pout; the way you sniff everything; the way you use your hands to talk.

"'Cor blimey, Miss, you sound as though you've just come off Brighton beach,' he said.

"'Let me through or I'll ...'" She paused, "Well, you can imagine what I said.

"'Ere,' he said, 'You're English, ain't you?'

"'Of course I'm English you bloody little twerp,' I said, though I wasn't quite so polite.

"'Well I'm blowed,' he said. 'But you can't go through there, Miss. The h'enemy's up ahead. They'll mow you down,' he said.

"'Get out the way,' I said, shoving him off.

"'I'll shoot,' he shouted."

Then she smiled in memory. "'What's your name?' I said. "'Corporal something-or-other,' he said.

"'Right Corporal,' I said. 'If you shoot me, I'll wrap that gun round your bleedin' head and when I get back home I'll tell your mother what you did. Now bugger off.'" Bliss's broad grin ended in a chuckle as she continued.

"I couldn't believe how quiet it was as I cycled up that road, as if the guns were holding their breath, I even heard a bird singing – in the middle of a battle, a bird – incredible." She paused at the memory, re-creating the sound in her mind. "Then I saw my first Germans, camouflaged, scuttling into the ditches and aiming. I stopped and got off – didn't know what to do, then I thought ... wave something white. I had to use my knickers in the end, I didn't have anything else white. 'Achtung! Achtung – Stoppe,' they shouted. But I just kept going until a machine gunner took out my front wheel. I couldn't leave the bike – the baby and my radio were in the basket, so I got up and pushed it with one hand, waving my knickers in the air with the other – what must they have thought of me – a desperate *prostituée* with a wobbly front wheel I guess. I kept shouting 'Let me through' in French. 'My baby needs his father.'"

Bliss was breathless with anticipation, "What happened?"

"There were six of them, only boys really – young hoodlums. Today they'd be spraying graffiti on bridges or dealing grass in the Hauptstrasse Burger Bar, but somebody had got them up as soldiers and given them real guns with live ammo, so they felt pretty big. One of them spoke French, badly. 'What do you have in there?' he asked, pointing his gun at the basket. 'My baby,' I said. 'I live over there and I want to go home, my husband is waiting for his dinner and my baby needs feeding.' I don't think he understood, and one of the others kept screaming, 'Shoot her – just shoot her.' Then one of them said something crude. My German wasn't very good but I knew what he was suggesting 'Look,' he said, 'She's got her knickers off already.'"

The main course arrived, served on wooden platters, and Bliss started to eat, silently, dying to tell her to continue, but, sensing the fragility of her condition, left her to choose the moment. Daphne had yet to start her turkey and was pushing pieces of it around her plate, then she slammed her knife and fork onto the table making him jump. "I don't know why I feel I have to explain ..." she began, her fists clenched in fierce anger.

"You don't," he said soothingly, and reached out to comfort her. But they both knew that she did have to explain – that she would explain – that she needed to explain.

"I wish they had raped me – all of them," she began again, her voice subdued, and with the words came tears. She wiped them with her napkin then carried on crying and talking at the same time. "It wouldn't have mattered – not really. I would have got over it in time."

"They didn't rape you?" he asked kindly as she paused to wipe her eyes again.

"No," she sniffled. "They took the baby. One of them picked it out of the basket. I thought they'd see the radio – I couldn't let them see the radio, so I started screaming, '*Donnez-moi mon bébé* – Give me back my baby – Give me back my baby.'"

"'Do you want your baby?' he said, holding it high in the air, taunting me."

"'Give me my baby,' I cried." And her eyes found the distant spot again as she fought back the tears.

"He threw the baby – not at me – at one of the others, but a shell exploded and he turned just at the wrong moment. He wasn't looking." She paused to wipe her eyes and blow her nose, then looked right into Bliss's eyes.

"They just walked away – 'It doesn't matter – we'll all be dead tomorrow,' one of them said." She hesitated for a moment to compose herself, then, more calmly, continued. "I was surrounded by death yet that baby meant everything to me – I'd promised his mother you see." The tears came again and she started to get up. "You'll have to excuse me, Dave," she snivelled. "I'm just a silly old woman. I'll be back in a minute – fix up my face."

He rose with her. "Will you be alright?"

She patted him back down. "I'll be fine. Don't worry."

Bliss was on the verge of seeking her out when she returned, dry-eyed, though her face was flushed.

"I didn't come back to England after the war," she explained. I couldn't face my mother and her snotty friends. 'And what did you do in the war, little Ophelia?' they would have asked, their little pinkies poking the air as they sipped Earl Grey and pretended to be posh. What would I have said? You nearly choked to death when I told you – imagine what they would have said, 'Oh how dreadful,' she put on a plummy accent, 'How could you, Ophelia?' Then they would have asked for another cucumber sandwich."

Bliss found himself laughing – nervous relief, he assumed. Relieved she'd got over the worst – that she was able to make light of it, however dreadful it had been. But the worst was to come.

"It's not funny. You were shocked because you assumed I'd been a nurse. It's so stereotypical – men maim and women mend. But that wasn't me. That wasn't cheeky-faced Ophelia Lovelace from Westchester Church of England School, and Mrs. Fanshawe's ballet class for the daughter's of gentle folk. This was Daphne Lovelace – murderer. I killed people, Dave – hundreds of people. I picked up the dead baby, wrapped it in the shawl, put it back in the basket, then went into that town and found a whole garrison of Germans frantically packing to withdraw. And I got on my little radio and told them to bomb the fuck out of the place – don't screw up your nose like that, I was saying fuck before you were born – I wanted shells raining down on the Germans, pulping them into the ground, pulverising the life out of them. I wanted to kill every last one of them. And do you know – it felt good. It felt so good after what they did to my baby. It felt so good I didn't care anymore. If my radio hadn't worked, I would have stood in the middle of the town waving my knickers at the bombers, screaming, 'Down here – the fucking Krauts are down here – bomb the bastards to pieces.'"

"Is everything alright, Sir?" interrupted the waiter noticing they weren't eating.

Bliss testily shooed him away. "Fine, fine."

Daphne sat, eyes glazed into the distance, flicking back and forth as if she were watching the battle going on behind them. As if every flash and blast were being replayed in her brain. "And the bombs came," she carried on, with powerful emotion. "The shells came, and I was in the middle of it. It was like God had turned the volume up to 11. The noise was so loud I could see it – each new bomb or shell sending shockwaves of sound smashing into the columns of smoke, tearing them apart. Everything was shaking – buildings; trees; the ground. One earthquake after another and I was right in the middle of it. I was the bull's-eye and I didn't care."

Her eyes drifted to a close as the battle raged in her mind, then they popped open as if she had remembered something really important. "It was in colour – that was the strangest thing really. Not black and white like the documentaries and movies. More colour than I'd ever seen. Not ordinary colours – colours so vivid I wanted to shout, 'Cor look at that!' Brilliant white and yellow flashes that hurt my eyes, glowing reds and oranges like mini sunsets, spring-green fields and freshly leafed trees. And the sky – the clearest, brightest, warmest blue. It was as if God didn't know there was a war going on. I remember thinking, over and over, why doesn't God stop this – he doesn't care, he couldn't even make the day miserable. It wouldn't have been so bad if it had been drizzly and cold. Nobody wants to die on a lovely summer's day. I was so mad with God for doing that I never really made it up with him. I suppose I shall find out soon enough whether or not he ever forgave me."

"Forgave you for killing Germans?" he asked, unsure.

"Do you think they wanted to die, Dave? Do you think they couldn't see the sky or hear the birds?"

"Your dinner's getting cold," he said, not having an answer and they ate in reflective silence for a while.

"Have you ever been back?" he asked when the air had settled.

"I go back occasionally," she answered, concealing, by the languidness of her words, the hundreds of hours she had spent pacing the quaint cobblestone streets, interrogating startled strangers, desperately scouring every face for the young woman. Wanting to say, "I'm sorry about your baby." Needing to say, "I'm sorry about your baby." More than fifty years – still trying to make sense and move on, still trying to pull part of herself away. Like a harassed mother dragging a screaming kid from a toy shop window, knowing the moment she lets go he'll race back.

"What about parachuting? Did you ever do it again?" he asked as the platters were taken away.

"I was going to once, just for fun, to celebrate my fiftieth ..." she paused in thought. "Or was it sixtieth? Anyway, when I went to the place they made such a fuss – training course; medical examination; static lines;

instructors and such. I couldn't be bothered with all that nonsense and I said, 'Look here, young lady. I was jumping out of planes while your dad was still in short pants.' It didn't make any difference. They wouldn't let me – not without all the rigmarole."

Daphne ordered the Black Forest Gâteau for dessert – "There's irony for you – now I'm eating their cakes."

"The same for me," said Bliss, too pre-occupied to make his own choice, and they sat in tense silence as the pressure built in his mind. There was more to be said, he knew it – Daphne sensed it. But it was his turn, not hers. Tell her about Mandy Richards, tell her about the baby.

"I killed a baby once," he announced inside his mind, but the words wouldn't come out. "I was hoping to get away from it eventually."

What is this? he asked himself. A competition? My ghosts are more frightful than yours. Would it make her feel better? Would it make me feel better?

What would she say? One look at her sorry face gave him the answer: You'll never escape completely.

A wooden cuckoo popped out of a clock and jump started the time.

"So, I suppose you're gearing up for the auction tomorrow," he said, enthusiastically digging into his gâteau.

Chapter Ten

The driver of the blue Volvo shrank quickly out of sight as Bliss drove past on his way up the quiet street to deliver Daphne home.

"I can manage," Daphne said, as he started to get out to escort her to the door. Ignoring her, he opened the gate and accompanied her up the front path, waited while she flicked on the light and turned the key, then brushed her cheek with a chaste kiss.

"Ooh, Chief Inspector," she giggled.

"Thank you, Daphne," he said with a depth of meaning way beyond her comprehension. Thank you for your courage, your sacrifice, your modesty. Thank you for making me realise the insignificance of my fears.

"No ... *Thank you*, Chief Inspector," she replied, letting herself in. "And I hope I didn't spoil your evening,"

"I learnt a great deal," he said, heading back to the car and driving off without noticing the Volvo – too many other considerations occupying his mind, too many plans to make, too many demons to slay.

He had intended returning to the Mitre and set off in that direction, but fate snatched the wheel out of his hands and spun him around in a U-turn, leaving the driver of the following Volvo no choice but to dive for cover up a side street. By the time he re-emerged, Bliss had gone – speeding recklessly down dark narrow lanes, inspiration weighing his foot on the accelerator, feeling that, if he drove fast enough, he might somehow break through the time barrier and go back eighteen years. But if he could go back to the bank and fall dead in place of Mandy – would he?

The road became a switchback as he raced headlong into the night and he allowed the car to choose its own path – tearing through villages, laughing at speed limits and screeching at corners. Deep down he knew where he was headed and he finally knew he had run out of road when the tyres scrunched on the sand-swept tarmac of a beach-side car park. The English Channel lay ahead, and, beyond the narrow choppy sea, France.

Two cars, sinisterly dark, sat at either end of the car park and his first instinct was to seek somewhere more solitary, more remote for his deliberations, but, as he rolled to a stop, his lights picked up a flurry of activity on the beach and two figures scurried in opposite directions. Twenty seconds later the two cars burst simultaneously to life and crept away into the night without lights. "Oops," he said to himself, but isn't that the thrill of adultery – the risk of being caught.

The beach turned inky black as he switched off his lights and cut the engine, then gradually came back to life as his eyes and ears acclimatised, and he sank in his seat, exhausted, letting the gentle swishing of the surf wash over him and erase his stress. Ahead, over the ocean, a couple of hazy lights flickered hypnotically and held his attention, then an armada of grey shadows steamed sluggishly out of the mist and rolled over him. He fought off the drowsiness for a few seconds, swimming back to consciousness a couple of times before surrendering to the waves.

A thousand battleships drifted slowly out of the haze and sailed through his mind as he floated weightlessly on the sea. Above him, the deck rails of the silent ships were lined by grey lifeless men – men with faces pulled gaunt by fear. Silent men, immobile men, dead men. Men who had beaten the bullet and found death before it had found them. Wasn't it easier that way – less painful for all concerned. Wasn't it better that each sombre faced man had already accepted his destiny and said his last goodbye. "Don't worry – I'll make it back," he would have said with a forced smile, his own obituary already written and in his pocket ready for the burial party to find. *"My Dearest One – I expect you've heard the bad news by now ..."* or, more often, *"Dear Mum and Dad ..."*

Where were the happy cheering hordes that filled the *Pathé* newsreels at the Saturday Matinee? Where were the happy-go-lucky Yanks, Canucks and Aussies who always had a kitbag on one arm and a girl on the other as they headed for the gangplanks?

Endless fleets of ships with countless dead-pan faces sailed by and disappeared slowly over the dark horizon, then he slipped beneath the black oily surface; exhaustion dragging him deeper than dreams, beyond the depths of even the darkest nightmares.

An hour later the cold sea-breeze bit into his bones, rousing him sufficiently to fire up the engine and turn on the heater. Waves of warmth soon lulled him back to sleep and he picked up the dream as Daphne, (or maybe it was Mandy), rode a bicycle up a sun-soaked beach at the head of a column of dead men. Daphne – surely it was Daphne – enthusiastically waved her frilly knickers in the air, and in her basket, the wicker basket slung on the handlebars, was a skull – a grotesque skull, a skull with bulging eyes and a gaping fleshless mouth shouting encouragement.

"*Rat-ta-ta-tat.*" The staccato rattle of automatic fire burst through the dream. Margaret Thatcher with a machine gun leapt out of the scrub firing from the hip.

"*Rat-ta-ta-tat.*" Daphne crashed off the bike, blood pumping out of her chest, her skirt up around her waist, her knickers still in her hand – still waving.

"*Rat-ta-ta-tat.*" The Major's skull, still screaming orders, rolled along the beach.

"*Rat-ta-ta-tat.*" Bliss cringed as a searchlight picked him out and Margaret Thatcher turned the machine gun in his direction.

"*Rat-ta-ta-tat.*" Get down – get down. I can't, Daphne's behind me.

"*Rat-ta-ta-tat.*" "Sir … Are you alright?"

The searchlight beat into his brain and Margaret Thatcher faded in its glare.

"*Rat-ta-ta-tat.*" "Open the door."

"*Rat-ta-ta-tat.*" "Open the door, Sir, or I'll have to force it."

"What the hell?"

"Police – Open the door, Sir, and turn off the ignition please."

A few seconds later the policewoman eyed both him and his newly issued warrant card carefully, while he eyed her. Low forties, he estimated; jet-black hair; dark eyes with a hint of the orient; a complexion with a touch of Mediterranean warmth; and a trace of smile not entirely masked by her official face.

"Detective Inspector Bliss ..." She queried suspiciously, inviting him to jog her memory. "I can't say I remember you, Sir."

"Ex – Met," he explained. "Look at the date on the card. I only transferred last week."

She looked. "Oh I see – that explains it. Well, I'm sorry to disturb you ... " then she wavered. "Are you sure everything's alright, Sir?"

"Just tired." Tired of running; tired of hiding.

"You should go home then."

"Yes – I will, Miss. Thanks."

Go home, he thought, as she crunched noisily back to her car across the sand-strewn car park, that's exactly what I'm going to do, as soon as I've cleared up the case of the dead Major.

And what about Mandy's murderer?

What about him? He pulled the trigger on Mandy and her baby – not me. He's the one who should feel guilty – not me. For the past year I've been scared shitless by a two-bit hoodlum ...

Where the hell did that come from?

I've been watching too many American movies. What else was there to do in the safe house – six months solitary in a video library.

Anyway, don't change the subject, he's been killing you – strangling you with fear – you're no more alive than a soldier going to war with his obituary in his pocket. Take control – take a leaf out of Daphne's book – pedal through life waving your knickers in the air.

"Sir?"

He leapt out of his thoughts. "Oh! You made me jump."

It was the policewoman again. "Sorry, Sir, only there's a couple of messages waiting for you at Westchester station, if you'd like to give them a call."

"How d'ye know ..." he began, then smiled, "So – you checked me out then?"

"Umm ..."

"That's O.K. – Absolutely right in fact. I would have done exactly the same thing. You can't be too careful nowadays ... what's your name by the way?"

"Sergeant Holingsworth, Sir."

"Sergeant?" he said teasingly. "Funny name for a girl."

"It's Samantha, Sir."

"My daughter's Samantha ..." he began, then asked, concernedly. "Are you on your own?"

"This isn't London, Sir. Anyway, I'm a Sergeant – obviously there are some places I wouldn't go without back-up, but ..."

"Here ... get in a minute," he said opening the passenger door. "It's chilly with the window open."

The graveyard shift, he thought as she walked round the back of the car, recalling his years as a uniformed constable when he'd been glad of almost anyone's company to help pass the night.

"Thanks," she replied slipping in beside him. "I'm on suicide patrol – this is a favourite place along here," she continued, wiping a patch of fog off the windscreen and sweeping her eyes along the dark beach as if expecting to discover a body. "We usually find the car in the morning, a pile of clothes, an empty pill bottle and a note. The corpse washes ashore in a day or so when the crabs and dogfish have chewed off a few bits. The sea gulls usually get the eyes once the body's on the beach. We've had half a dozen this year already – not good for the tourist trade."

"I'm working on the murder over at Westchester," said Bliss as if to reassure her she wasn't the only one dealing with gruesome scenes.

"The old Major?"

"The very old Major as it turned out."

"I heard – been dead for years they say."

"Can I ask you something?"

"You can," she laughed. "But I'll warn you, the last inspector who said that to me in a parked car ended up with a slapped face."

"No. It's nothing like that. I just wanted to know if you've ever believed something that you later realised wasn't true."

She laughed again, "Like all the slime-bags who've put on a soppy voice and said, 'I love you, Samantha – of course I'll leave my wife.'"

"That's an occupational hazard."

"Of being a W.P.C.?"

"No. Of being a woman."

"I never thought of my gender as an occupation, Inspector."

"Please – It's Dave. At half-past three in the morning nobody can cling to a rank with any dignity ... and don't get huffy. A lot of women make careers out of being useless. 'I can't do this ... can't touch that ... I'll be sick ...' They say it in a girlish little voice and all the blokes go running. 'Oh let me do that for you.'"

"I know the type. We've got a few," she admitted.

"I meant – have you ever been convinced of something so fully, so absolutely, that when it unravels and you see the truth it leaves you totally gob-smacked."

"I believed in Santa Claus when I was a kid ..." she began, but he cut her off.

"That's not the same – every child believes in Santa Claus, even those who never get anything at Christmas still cling to the belief for as long as they can."

"But I still believed when I was about ten – my friends called me crazy, but I suppose I didn't want to believe my parents would lie to me. So – why did you ask?"

"I did something a long time ago that went pear-shaped ..."

"Pear-shaped?" she laughed questioningly.

"Yeah. It should have been as round and translucent as a crystal ball, but it got warped out of shape ... Anyway, last night an incredible old lady, with more guts than I'll ever have, made me realise that what I did was the right thing."

"So you've been blaming yourself."

"That's very astute of you."

"And why did you blame yourself?

"I suppose I confused regret with remorse."

They sat in silence for a few minutes passing telepathic messages – shall I tell you; if you want to; I want to; then tell me; I don't know if I should.

"Are you going to tell me?" she asked eventually, knowing that he would, that he was only waiting to be asked.

Thinking about it afterwards he realised there were many reasons why he had told her about Mandy's murder after concealing it from so many others. Cocooned in the dark and comfortable car he'd felt secure; Samantha had a warm persuasive voice and she had filled the car with the clean scent of pure shampoo and honest soap – nothing fancy or expensive. The sort of woman you could trust, he thought.

"I can't understand why you ever blamed yourself – I think you were very brave," she said, after he described the imbroglio in the bank.

"It was nothing ... " he began, then quickly switched subjects, conscious he had not told her about Mandy's pregnancy, nor the fact that he was being stalked by the killer. "What does your husband think of you working nights?"

"I'm not married."

"Oh," he said, confused, "I noticed the ring."

"This?" she said, deftly slipping it off. "Just a curtain ring, it saves having to fight off a bar-full of drunks – they all want to marry me – so they say. 'I'll get my husband onto you,' I tell 'em. It usually works."

"That's the trouble with pubs."

"Actually," she laughed, "I was talking about the blokes in the police canteen. What about you, Dave – married?"

"Nope."

"Let's have a look then," she said, grabbing his left hand off the wheel and holding it against the faintly luminous dashboard. "Well there's no ring mark, but that doesn't prove anything."

"You don't believe me," he protested, aware she still had a tender hold on his hand.

"I've been shafted by married men too many times," she said. They both laughed. "I didn't mean that ..." she cried, letting go and giving him the friendliest of nudges.

"I know what you meant. Anyway, believe it or not, I'm not married."

"Divorced?"

"Correct."

"And she got pissed off with the screwy hours; the week-ends; nights; bank-holidays ..."

"How did you guess?"

"Why d'ye think I'm still single – how many spouses will put up with it?"

"My ex-wife used to tell people she'd been widowed by a murderer – I suppose it wasn't entirely untrue – Anyway, I got some very funny looks from one or two people. 'Are you Sarah's second husband?' one snooty woman asked, her eyes sort of scrunched in confusion. 'No, I'm her lover,' I said, straight-faced. Sarah was furious."

An hour passed in no time: the wonders of London; the horrors of the country; the horrors of London; the wonders of the country.

"I'd best be going," Samantha said eventually. "I'd better make sure there's no frightful sights awaiting the grockles."

"Grockles?" he questioned.

"Foreigners; out-of-towners; holidaymakers," she explained. "It's a local nickname."

"Like me ..." he began, then paused, struck by a thought. "I've just realised why you looked so concerned when you couldn't wake me. You thought I was ..."

"Dead," he was going to say but she was ahead of his thoughts. "Well it happens. I've come across a couple of people who've swallowed a bottle of tablets and sat in the car waiting for them to start taking effect before braving the water. They doze off and ... Anyway," she said, getting out of the car. "Thank goodness you weren't dead."

"Don't you believe it," he muttered and was grateful that she didn't hear as she shut the door. "Goodnight, Samantha," he called, winding his window down.

"Good morning," she said pointedly, nodding toward the bright patch above the eastern horizon. And as he looked at her, framed in early dawn light, he found a most pleasing shape.

It wasn't until she was opening the door of her police car that he managed to get his mind in gear. "Samantha," he called, with only a second to spare.

She looked back with a smile. "Yes?"

"Would you have dinner with me one night?"

"Maybe – try giving me a call. But I'll warn you now – I work dreadful hours."

Watching her drive away he questioned his motives. Just dinner, he said to himself. Don't get involved with someone in the job – too many problems. She was certainly good looking. Wake up, Dave – most women look good at this time of night. Maybe a quick dip in the sea will cool you off and freshen you up – your trunks and towel are in one of the suitcases in the back.

A chilly blast of ozone laden air shocked him to life as he opened the car door. That'll do, he thought, quickly slamming it shut and starting the engine, then he had to get out and scurry to a convenient bush for a morning pee.

Detective Sergeant Patterson was already in the office at Westchester police station when Bliss phoned at six-fifteen. "He's here somewhere," said the night telephonist. "I saw him come in." He was there – ferreting through the papers on Bliss's desk and digging through his drawers.

"I've put out a call for him, he's not in his office," continued the telephonist, but there's a message here for you. A reporter from the *Westchester Gazette* was trying to get hold of you last evening – wants you to call him about the Dauntsey case."

"Tell him to go through the press office."

"I did, Sir, but he was quite insistent that he wanted to speak to you personally."

"Did he have my name?"

"Yes, Sir."

"Shit."

"Sorry, Sir – did you say something?"

"No, I sneezed. Did he leave a number?"

Giving him the number she finished by saying, "I've got D.S. Patterson now, Sir, I'll transfer you."

"Where are you, Guv?" queried Patterson coming on the line.

That's a point – where am I? wondered Bliss, pulling himself upright on the steering wheel, reaching forward to clear a patch of windscreen. Seagulls, sand dunes, a couple of beach joggers and a host of happy childhood memories. But this was neither Southend or Brighton. "Ah ..."

"Only I called the Mitre last night and that foreign girl said you'd left."

"Why?"

"I don't know. She didn't say."

"No." Idiot. "I meant, why did you want me?"

"Sorry, Guv. Well we've got the blood tests on the duvet – nothing special – O positive."

"Is that it?"

"You sound disappointed, Guv."

"With the way Jonathon's been pissing us about I half expected cochineal or paint. I suppose a small part of me even began wondering if we were chasing a dead animal."

"No – it's definitely human."

"Well I don't know whether to say 'Thank Christ' or 'Shit' but at least we now know it wasn't the Major's blood."

"You can't get blood out of a bone," sniggered Patterson.

"Very droll, Pat," he groaned, then added, "I want you to get everyone together for two o'clock this afternoon. It's time to hash this case out ..."

Patterson butted in. "It's Saturday, Guv. I won't be very popular."

"You're not paid to be popular. I've got some theories I want to run past you and the others."

"Whatever you say, Guv," Patterson said. On your head be it, he meant, already formulating excuses in his mind – Don't blame me for poxing up your weekend – blame Bliss. I just follow orders. "... Oh, Guv?"

"Yes."'

"Have you got a new car?"

"Yes – why?"

"Oh nothing, Guv. It's just that I need the details for the station car parking book, otherwise the bomb squad will blow it up."

"Right – I forgot."

"No problem. By the way, have you informed the widow about the Major yet, Guv?"

"That's my purgatory for this morning, Pat. I'll see you later."

But Doreen Dauntsey could wait for the knock on her door, after all she'd waited forty years. He checked his watch, six-forty-five, Saturday morning. Let's see how keen this reporter is.

The phone was answered at the second ring. "Peter White ... G'morning."

"D.I. Bliss, Westchester police," he was curt. "I understand you've been looking for me."

"Oh yes, Sir. Thanks for calling ..." he began, a bounce of excitement in his voice. "I wonder – could we meet? Off the record."

Bliss hesitated, "I'm not sure ..."

"It's all above board, Sir, I promise you."

"Perhaps we could meet for breakfast in an hour or so. I'm staying at the Mitre."

It was the journalist's turn to hesitate. "Um ... Would you mind if we met somewhere a bit more private – the Bacon Butty on the Marsdon Road does a good breakfast, and they open early?"

Bliss knew the place, having passed it en-route to The Carpenter's Kitchen with Daphne the previous evening, and he found himself agreeing, despite the nagging feeling that fraternising with the press was probably contrary to regulations. "Seven-thirty, then." he said, leaving no opportunity for dissent, retaining some control.

Bliss arrived early and sat for a few minutes, deliberating whether or not to go in, wishing he had a mini-cassette player with him, knowing that "off the record" had its limitations, and that reporters could be as gymnastic as policemen when it came to direct quotes.

The front door opened on a narrow passageway, the wallpaper flock erased at hip height, and Bliss followed a patternless groove in the lino into a smoky room with nicotine- yellowed walls covered in cheap prints; glitzy framed pictures oozing sickly sentimentality – fuzzy edged images of fat babies with snotty noses, a bloated cat with a budgie on its head and more sad-eyed puppies than a Disney cartoon.

"Mr. Bliss?" enquired the shrivelled occupant of a giant's sports jacket and Bliss found himself staring at the sole diner, trying to make sense of the spectacle. Nothing fitted. The man had a size six head on a size four body; his oversize nose and glasses appeared to have been borrowed for the occasion from a joke shop and his hair seemed to be slipping off the back of his head.

"Why the secrecy?" asked Bliss, ignoring the outstretched hand and sitting on a chair with an artistically ripped vinyl seat – Stanley knife, he guessed.

"I wouldn't call it secrecy, Inspector. It's just not good form for the press to be seen feeding information to the police – though it can work in both directions, if you get my meaning."

Bliss leant back in the chair, keeping his distance. "So you want to scratch my back, do you ...?"

"Well, I must admit, when I heard they'd brought in a top Scotland Yard detective to lead the investigation, I realised there was more to this than just the death of an old Major."

Bliss basked in the misplaced notoriety feeling no compunction to disillusion the scruffy little man. "And you are hoping for a scoop I take it."

"Actually, no ..." he paused to remove his spectacles for an enthusiastic clean, revealing a heavily drooped left eyelid that gave his face a lopsided appearance. "I say," he continued, "I hope I haven't given you the wrong impression."

"Two full breakfasts was that, Mr. White?" called a robust, amiable voice, above a cacophony of kitchen sounds. "Tea or coffee?" she demanded, taking the reply for granted.

"Coffee for me," answered Bliss, deciding he'd wait until he saw the breakfast, and the state of the cook, before committing himself to eat anything. "And what would the wrong impression be Mr. White, and how did you get my name by the way?"

"I was making enquiries in the Black Horse on Monday when you closed it down," said White after ordering tea. "And I can assure you I'm not here to pump you for information."

"Good – you won't be wasting your breath then," said Bliss, harsher than intended.

White turned cool, but replaced his spectacles and pressed on. "My editor asked me to prepare a biography on Major Dauntsey to run the day of the funeral. It seemed simple enough, although, to be truthful, I would have preferred to run it today."

"Why today?"

"The date, Inspector ..." he said peering over the top of his spectacles.

"6th of June – Oh, I see. The anniversary of D-Day – I'd forgotten." But then his nightmare of dead men and grey battleships suddenly had meaning, and he found himself questioning what had occurred as he had looked out over the dark sea during the night – the same sea that had swallowed thousands of screaming souls a generation ago. Was it a nightmare or had it been something more? he wondered; and his mind wandered, thinking of the ships and men steaming through the long night, arriving off the coast of France at dawn. Then what? A single shell from a strafing Stuka, or a burst of shrapnel from a mine or artillery shell, and it would all be over. Years of training, thousands of miles from home, for what – dead before you even got to the beach.

"Inspector?"

"Sorry ... Yes, please go on."

White took off his glasses again and gave them a long and thoughtful polish before taking a photocopy of a newspaper cutting from his pocket. "This was what I found in the archives," he said, handing it over.

Westchester Gazette and Herald
Thursday, July 23rd 1944

Local Major – Battlefield hero
by P. W. Mulverhill
Major Rupert W. Dauntsey,
Royal Horse Artillery, of The Coppings,
Westchester, Hampshire

A spokesperson at the War Office has confirmed to this correspondent that Major Dauntsey has been nominated for an award for gallantry, although could not confirm that a D.S.O. was in the offing.

Details are still sketchy about the action, but early reports suggest that Major Dauntsey's troops were caught in murderous crossfire as the beleaguered Hun fought a desperate rear-guard action somewhere in northern France. All reports suggest that the Bosch are running faster than rats from a sinking ship, but some are still determined to take as many of our boys with them as they can.

Major Dauntsey's wife, Doreen, (21 yrs.), married only days before "D" Day, was unaware of her husband's heroic action when contacted by this newspaper, but she stated that she was not surprised to hear of his bravery – "It is just like him," she said. "Putting other's first."

Unconfirmed reports suggest that Major Dauntsey was himself wounded in the action, but we are certain he will be pleased to learn that a hero's welcome awaits him on his return. Well done, Major Dauntsey, and God speed your return.

This correspondent will be the first to congratulate the Major and bring our readers a full account from the Major's own lips on his return.

"Sounds fair enough," said Bliss handing the cutting back. "And what did the Major have to say when he got back?"

"Nothing."

"Well, he had difficulty speaking I understand."

"He may have done – but that isn't the reason he didn't say anything. I've spoken to Patrick Mulverhill, the reporter, he's well into his eighties now, but he's no fool. He went to Oxford with the Major and remembers the day he came back from the front – trussed up like a mummy, he said, and that was the last he ever saw of him. According to Patrick, Doreen Dauntsey kept her husband locked away tighter than a duck's ass for the rest of his life – however long that may have been."

If the implication in the journalist's words left little doubt as to Doreen's involvement in her husband's demise, his tone spoke volumes. But Bliss refused to be drawn. "Thanks for your assistance, Mr. White, I appreciate it. Obviously I shall need to speak directly with Patrick Mulverhill ..."

"You could ..." he cut in, then left Bliss hanging.

"But?"

"Patrick is sort of old-fashioned about the independence of the press. He still clings to the notion that we can claim legal privilege. He probably won't tell you anything, although he can be ... shall we say undiplomatic ... he's just as likely to tell you to get lost."

"I'll take a chance," said Bliss as the kitchen door burst open and the cook, as fat and friendly as she'd sounded, fought her way through with a groaning tray. "There we are, ducks," she said. "This'll put hairs on your chest."

They ate in silence for a while, the steaming food fogging the reporter's spectacles until he removed them and looked uneasily across the table. "There is something else, Mr. Bliss," he began, then betrayed his nervousness by ferociously polishing the spectacles with a handkerchief. "I also came across this," he said eventually, taking another cutting from his pocket.

With one quick glance Bliss felt his face greying, felt himself sliding back into the miasma of concern.

"You must have trodden on some pretty important toes," continued the reporter unaware of Bliss's discomfort, quoting snippets from the cutting. "Bomb explodes at detective's home – Death threats – Underworld hit-man ..."

"I know what it says," fumed Bliss. "Where'd d'ye get it?"

White swallowed, "*London Evening Post* ..."

"I know that. I meant why ... who gave it to you? Who set you up?"

"Set me up ... I don't understand."

Calm down ... calm down. How can I calm down? He's tipped off the local press. He knows he's got me cornered – I bet he thought they'd just carry the story then I'd be on the run again. "What was it, an anonymous phone-call, or did he mail it?"

"I'm sorry ... I really don't know ..."

I thought you were going to stop this – remember – wave your knickers in the air and all that. That didn't last long did it? "Sorry – what were you saying?"

"I ... I don't know what you mean – who mailed what?"

Him ... The killer. Winding me up again. Letters and words clipped from newspapers and magazines: "You're DEAD Bliss." "I've done my time – your next."

"Who gave that to you?" he demanded, jumping up, still trying to get away, as if the cutting were explosive.

"No-one," shouted White; on the defensive, not knowing why. "It was just a routine search. We usually do a little piece 'New inspector on the beat,' that sort of thing, when a new police officer is appointed, and I came across your name and thought I'd root around for a bit of background."

What's this – everybody checking up on me today. First Samantha, now you. LEAVE ME ALONE.

He sat, consternation furrowing his brow, embarrassment flushing his cheeks. "I'm sorry," he mumbled. "I'm just a bit touchy about it."

"I can imagine," responded White, trying to modify his expression from alarm to concern.

"I'd rather you didn't print anything about it," Bliss continued. "In fact, I'd rather you didn't use my name at all."

White muttered non-committally, cleaning his glasses again.

The atmosphere was so heavy as they continued their meal that Bliss checked his watch at a politic moment and announced his departure. "Must dash," he said, laying a ten pound note next to his partly finished plate. "No – don't get up. Thanks again for the information."

Bliss drove idly for a while, a cassette of Handel's *Watermusic* calming him, then he headed into Westchester and parked next to the senior's home. Now for the merry widow, he thought, heading for the front door.

The bulbous breasted nurse whom D.C. Dowding had targeted on their first visit greeted him proudly. "Matron's off today, Sir, I'm in charge. Unless anything serious happens, then I can call her."

"I'm pleased to hear that," said Bliss condescendingly. "I'm sure you'll do an excellent job. I'm here to see Mrs. Dauntsey again."

But Doreen Dauntsey had donned the veil of widowhood and sought reclusion. Nurse Dryden's face clouded. "Mrs. Dauntsey's in her room, Sir."

"That's ideal. I wanted some privacy."

"No, you don't understand, Sir, that won't be possible – she is in her room."

What is this, a euphemism for saying she's in the toilet? "I can wait."

"I doubt she'll be out today, Sir."

Not the toilet apparently. "I'm not with you ..."

"Do not disturb," she whispered, making the rectangular shape of a sign with her hands.

"Oh. I understand. Well, I'm sure she'll want to see me."

She should have been a traffic warden, he thought ten minutes later when the nurse was still blocking his attempt to see Doreen Dauntsey – the maximum enforcement of minimum authority. "Rules is rules," she had reminded him at least ten times. "Do not disturb means do not disturb."

"But I need to tell her that we've found her dead husband," he finally told her in frustration.

"Oh – she knows that, Sir. Everybody knows about the Major in the attic. Bob was telling me all about it last night ..."

"Bob? Bob who?"

"Bob – you know, your sergeant. The one you was with on Monday."

"Dowding?" he queried. "Bob Dowding?"

She nodded enthusiastically, setting her breasts in spirited motion.

So, Detective *Constable* Dowding, he said to himself. Been promoted have you? Been playing away from home have you? Been toying with little girls with big tits?

"You'd better call the matron," he continued, without trace of conciliation.

An hour later he gave up. Doreen Dauntsey wasn't receiving visitors and, short of smashing down the door with a fire axe, he had no way to get into her room. The matron, looking veritably unmatronly in Saturday jeans and clinging T-shirt, had been empathetic to a fault, although, somewhat implausible in refusing to acknowledge the existence of a pass key. "We are very conscious of our guest's privacy," she had said, as if she were the major domo of a ritzy hotel, but she had allowed him to tap respectfully on Doreen's door.

"Go away," she had cried, and he had been forced to do so.

She's hiding, like a kid who's got into the jam, he thought. "I would have come earlier," he told the matron as they walked downstairs, "but we had to wait to get proper identification." It sounded reasonable, but was baloney. You knew it was him the minute you saw what was left of the face, he inwardly admitted.

"I think she's still in mourning." explained the matron as she saw him out. Nurse Dryden hung back behind the door and contemptuously poked out her tongue. "See – I told you."

It was only ten-thirty and Bliss found himself tossing up between returning, tail between legs, to the Mitre, or heading back to the police station and listening to Patterson moan about the spoilt weekend. In the end he ducked the question, deciding instead to visit Daphne to make sure she was alright.

A driverless blue Volvo, with a front-seat passenger reading Thursday's newspaper, sat near the end of Daphne's road. Bliss ignored it, not even bothering to note the number. Driving confidently by he congratulated himself – that's the way, Dave – wave those knickers.

Daphne was pleased to see him, and bustled around in the kitchen making tea, leaving him to stare out over the cornfield and wonder why he'd confided in Samantha when he'd kept Mandy's death from Daphne. That reminds me, he thought, I must give Samantha a call, though not too soon. I mustn't appear too keen. Surprised by the strength of his feeling, he tried to rationalise – it was dark, she was a good listener ...

"I'm glad you came round, Chief Inspector," said Daphne breaking into his thoughts. "Perhaps you'd be good enough to give me a hand in a minute. I've got to load a few things in the butcher's van, the stuff for the Women's Institute auction. George is taking it to the Town hall – Oh, that'll be him now."

The van was manoeuvring up to the front gate as they emerged with the stuffed goat.

"Will you be able to manage at the other end, George?" called Daphne.

"Yeah – the ladies are all waiting, Mrs. L," replied George, opening the back doors.

"Mrs?" queried Bliss in a whisper.

"Shh – I'll explain in a minute."

"Ahh, the old goat," he said, a crack of nostalgia in his voice. "I gave Mrs. L. this," he continued, blowing out his cheeks in pride. "And I reckon it'll fetch a pretty penny. What say you, Mrs. L?"

"What's that, George?"

"I were just sayin' to this young man as how the old goat'll be quite a 'traction at the auction today."

Daphne winked at Bliss. "I wouldn't doubt that, George. In fact I shall have my hand up for a few quid, and I'm pretty sure Mr. Bliss is keen – isn't that so, Dave?"

"Oh. Yes ... Very keen."

George beamed.

"So what's the Mrs. thing?" smiled Bliss as George drove away with the contents of Daphne's front hall.

"Oh," she chuckled, "just our joke really. I always buy enough meat for two, me and the cat, so George has his bit of fun. 'How's the General today, Mrs. L?' he always calls when I go in the shop."

"He had me worried for a minute," teased Bliss.

"Get on with you," she laughed, then added, "Come in a minute, I've got something for you."

"I've got a meeting ..." he started, examining his watch, but she talked over him. "Oh don't worry, it won't take a second. It's just that when I was going through the attic this morning, digging things out for the auction, I came across something that might interest you."

The black and white photograph had faded to a wash of tonal greys but the front porch of the Dauntsey house and the stiffly composed wedding group were instantly recognisable.

"Well. Do you recognise anyone?" Daphne asked, giving him a few seconds.

"You," he said, immediately pointing to a slender beautiful woman in a body-hugging dress that made him wish, really wish, he'd been more than just a teenager's lustful thought at the time.

"Very good, and ...?"

"This must be Doreen ..."

"Oh I remember that terrifying hat?" screeched Daphne. "It was baby-shit brown. They should have sent her to France wearing that – who needs knickers with a hat like that. If that wouldn't scare 'em off, nothing would."

"The old Colonel," laughed Bliss, pointing to the old man, ram-rod straight in his guardsman's ceremonial uniform. "And this must be Major Dauntsey, when he still had a face worth looking at."

"That's right. It wasn't much though was it?" She turned up her nose.

"What happened to his chin?"

"God knows."

"And who's this by his side?"

Daphne leaned closer for a better look. "Oh that was his best man," she sneered. "Now he was a nancy-boy if ever I saw one. He was the Major's aide-de-camp, and "camp" was the just about the right word for him. He fussed over Rupert worse than a debutante's mother. Look ..." she started, then rushed off in search of a magnifying glass. She was back in a flash, peering deep into the picture. "I thought so," she said, giving Bliss the glass. "Look in his right hand."

"What is it?" he asked, unable to recognise the object that had caught the glint of the flashbulb.

"Silver-backed clothes brush," said Daphne, clearly remembering the article. "It was very swish, chased silver with inlaid rubies. He drove me crazy with it – every two minutes brushing the Major down like he was a prize poodle at Cruft's. He was the sort who'd have creases in his underwear."

"Who was he?"

"I don't know," she shook her head, and by her tone was uninterested in recalling. "A Captain somebody-or-other."

"Could it have been Captain Tippen?" asked Bliss, remembering the dog-tags in the Major's trunk, trying a long-shot.

"I don't know … " She screwed her eyes in thought. "Yes I do!" she exclaimed joyfully. "His name was David … Oh my goodness – I'm not as senile as I thought I was."

"David Tippen?" queried Bliss.

"Oh, now that would be stretching the grey matter too far, but it was definitely David."

"I bet it was," he said, staring into the picture, trying to communicate with the characters. That would explain how Major Dauntsey got the tags – good friends; best man at wedding; dying words as he lies on the battlefield. "Give these to my mother – tell her I loved her to the end."

"Can I borrow this?" he asked, knowing the answer. "Daphne, you're a whiz."

"Thank you, Chief Inspector … are you going to kiss me again?"

He did, on the cheek, and she held onto his arm as he made his way out with the picture.

"By the way, you didn't tell me what happened after the war," he said as they neared the gate.

"I stayed in France ..." she began, the inflection saying there was more, much more, and all of it spun around in her mind until she settled on the salient feature. "Hugo, he called himself. He was an artist."

"The portrait?"

She nodded with a melancholic smile, "I thought he loved me, but, there again, I suppose I thought I loved him."

"And Hugo?"

"Hugo ... " her voice faded and her eyes drifted into the distance. "Hugo loved painting."

Chapter Eleven

The road out of Westchester hummed soothingly beneath the tyres of Bliss's liberated Rover, and the frenzied bustle of London offered the prospect of a peaceful haven after the stormy Saturday afternoon meeting.

"The men aren't very happy about this meeting," Superintendent Donaldson had snapped, catching Bliss on his way up the front steps of the police station. And the men weren't happy. Patterson had seen to that, polishing his truncheon amidst the disgruntled throng at the pre-conference moaning session.

"I'm really sorry about this folks," he had whined, smarmily. "Only this new D.I. wouldn't listen to me. He thinks he's still in the effing Met." Adding, *sotto voce*, "If he ever was in the Met. I told him you deserved the weekend off but did he care? Did he fuck!"

Bliss was still trying to puzzle out what had happened an hour later as he made for London, driving fast, trying to put the meeting behind him.

It had started badly – feigned illnesses and hastily arranged weddings accounted for the absence of more than half the officers. Detective Constable Dowding's truancy was especially notable.

"His wife seemed confused when I called," explained Patterson. "She said he'd already left – said you'd given him a special assignment to work on."

"I expect he's following up on a couple of things we came across earlier in the week," said Bliss, tongue in cheek, nurse Dryden's mammary assets in mind. "I'll discuss it with him later."

"Good afternoon," Bliss greeted the twenty or so officers as he entered the conference room, and someone ripped the air with a noisy belch.

"Afternoon," grumbled a few, leaving feet on the desks in a conspiracy of disdain.

"Sorry to spoil your weekend," he commenced, noticing the intentionally varied assortment of sport and leisurewear and feeling the glare of hostility. "Only, this case is a week old and we don't seem to be any further ahead really."

Patterson winced, visibly, but with his mind the way it was, he would have taken a congratulatory pat on the shoulder as a rabbit punch. "So, we've done absolutely fuck-all this week," he grumbled, stabbing himself in the back. "That's what you're implying, Guv, isn't it?" he continued, neatly planting the stiletto in Bliss's hand. "You're saying that getting a confession out of Dauntsey, gathering all the evidence, and finding his father's body was nothing," he snarled, his enormous fangs drawn. "That's what you're saying, isn't it?"

"I didn't say that, Sergeant ..." Bliss protested, stung by the criticism, but, with their sergeant's blood on the floor, several of the men jumped into the fray.

"I found the bloody duvet," blared Jackson, "and ruined me trousers in that damn grave."

"And I walked fuckin' miles doin' house to house enquiries," shouted another.

"And what about ..."

"Alright, that's enough," roared Bliss. "I didn't say you hadn't done anything ..."

"Sounded like it to me," muttered Patterson, twisting the blade one more time.

Bliss spun on him, enraged. "Sergeant Patterson, I said that's enough. All I meant was ... we haven't succeeded in solving this case – either case, despite all the work you and the men have put into it. That's not a criticism, it's just a statement of fact. Now, if you'll let me finish ..." Pausing, he stared the men back into their seats, then started again, this time defensively. "I called this meeting because I have some new information that may assist us. I also want to get your input on what's occurred so that I can spend tomorrow formulating a strategy, while you lot have the day off."

Although the motorway was now speeding Bliss away from the town, he was still smarting from Patterson's assault and couldn't help thinking there was more to the antagonism than an interrupted Saturday afternoon.

"This is the man we were looking for," he had said, producing the Dauntsey's wedding photograph, and Patterson had immediately jumped on him.

"It's pretty useless showing us that now we've found him."

"This man ... " continued Bliss, ignoring Patterson while pointing to the Major's aide-de-camp. "This man may have been Captain David Tippen, something of a Gay Cavalier, if you get my meaning. Anyway, who checked him out?"

"Sergeant Dobson, Guv."

Dobson rose, shaking his head. "Sorry, Guv, bad news I'm afraid. According to the Ministry of Defence, Tippen's body was never found, he was listed as missing – presumed dead."

"Where? What battle? When?"

"I didn't think to ask."

"Do you think it might be important?"

"Doubt it, Guv."

"I was being sarcastic, Sergeant. Of course it's important –'find out please."

Patterson had his doubts and sneered, "What possible relevance could that have?"

Sensing another insurrection, Bliss quickly stepped in to quash it. "We know Tippen's dead, we've got his tags, but what about his family – don't they have a right to know?"

"I thought this was supposed to be a murder enquiry," grumbled Patterson.

I'm going to belt you in a minute, thought Bliss. "Dauntsey obviously knew where the body was," he explained. "How else could he have got the dog tags. And if he knew, how come he didn't tell the Army administration, or the man's family?"

"I still don't see what that's got to do with us," griped Patterson. "I still don't see the connection."

Bliss was still trying to work out the possible connection for himself when he drove into the motorway service area where he had escaped from the Volvo earlier in the week. The nutcase was still there, sitting in the same seat, still regressing, bending the ear of some other unsuspecting traveller. "Helen of Troy was my aunty, you know?"

Bliss chuckled as he went past in search of a coffee and sandwich, then he took a nearby seat and tried to take his mind off the meeting by watching her snare unwitting listeners. "Have you ever been here before ...?"

"So what's this great theory of yours, Guv?" Patterson had asked, still in a snit.

"Personally, I think that flighty, fun-loving, Doreen Dauntsey soon got fed up living with a cabbage, especially an ugly one, so she lured him into the attic and shot him. Then she told everyone he'd gone to stay on the estate in Scotland."

"That's not much of a theory," scoffed Patterson. "Why would he go into the attic? How would he get into the attic – he only had one arm?"

Bliss looked past him again, he had no answer and was becoming increasingly aware of the disgruntled murmuring from the other officers. He needed a juicy morsel to throw at them that wouldn't be seized on by Patterson.

"What about Jonathon's victim?" asked a spiky-featured officer, giving him a seconds breathing space. "If the Major was already dead in the attic, who did Jonathon kill?"

"It could have been just about anybody," he started, then paused, half expecting Patterson to pipe up. "Follow me on this," he continued, thankful for the silence. "Jonathon was pissed off with his father, seeing him as a failure for allowing his mother to struggle financially, and for deserting them, so he flattened the toy soldier, the Major, in a symbolic act of destruction. The *trick-cyclists* call it displaced aggression, I think. But it wasn't enough, nobody even knew he'd done it. So, as his mother's health deteriorated, he had to do something more to prove he really cared – something spectacular – murderously spectacular. Obviously he couldn't attack the real man, he had no idea what had happened to him, so he chose a surrogate. But he had to have witnesses ..."

"Why?" Patterson leapt on his back again. "Why not just pull some starving old bum off the street, promise him a meal and a bed for the night, bump him off and bury him?"

Hoping to lighten the atmosphere, Bliss put on a Chinese accent. "Confucius he say – If tree fall in forest and no-one see or hear. Did it fall?" He paused, not expecting applause, but not anticipating the stone-faced silence either. Discomfitted, he pushed on anyway. "He needed witnesses because he wanted to read about it in the papers and hear it on the news, and the only way to achieve that was to sacrifice someone in public – but not somewhere so public that the victim's face would be seen."

"What about the duvet?" questioned a grey-bearded officer, showing a glimmer of interest.

"He buried it where he knew it would be found, then threw in the mangled toy as an effigy of the Major. It was all part of the illusion and might have worked if the real Major hadn't shown up."

"It's more stupid than a bloody bedroom farce," scoffed Patterson under his breath. "Someone ought'a make it into a pantomime. First we got a killer and no body, then a body and no killer, then no body ..."

"So where did Jonathon think the Major was?" asked the bearded officer talking over Patterson.

Bliss was tempted to say Scotland but knew it was an indefensible answer. He knew he couldn't explain why Jonathon had not gone there to confront the real man.

The Dauntsey estate was still there, according to the Scottish P.C. who had made enquiries. It was occupied by a tenant farmer, the son of the man who had first leased the farm from Doreen Dauntsey a few years after the war. He paid rent once a year, April 1st, rain, shine or snow – twenty and fifty pound notes just as the Major's written instructions had insisted – to be paid in cash to Mrs. Dauntsey.

"I'll happily send the Major a cheque," he'd offered numerous times. "It'll save you having to traipse all the way up here every year."

But she wouldn't hear of it. "My husband insists that I come to make sure everything is in order, Mr. McAllister," she had said more than once.

"I allus felt like I was buying off a blackmailer or paying a ransom," he told the Scottish policeman. "A bundle of used notes in a brown paper parcel. She never counted it. 'Och, I'm sure I can trust you, Mr. McAllister – good day to you,' she'd say, then take the next train away home."

"It's difficult to believe that Jonathon thought his father was still alive," Bliss told the group, "Although he may have been so much under his mother's influence that he went along with it for fear of upsetting her. She was apparently quite convincing. 'He's in Scotland – at the estate,' she'd say to anybody enquiring, and they would breathe a sigh of relief, mumbling, 'Thank Christ for that.'"

"But what about his family?" asked a thick-thighed policewoman in a brave pair of shorts. "What about siblings, cousins, uncles. Did nobody ever check?"

"Obviously not."

The street had relaxed when Bliss arrived at his house in London. It was Saturday, the double-manned surveillance car was either needed elsewhere or the crew were luxuriating in the rare pleasure of a weekend off. Unfettered residents, taking advantage of the summery weather, tarted up their cars without feeling spied upon, and children took a rare opportunity to kick a ball or throw a stone without getting yelled at by an unnecessarily anxious parent. Only Bliss, and the surveillance officers, knew the last thing in the world they cared about was what some snotty-nosed kid was doing in the street – unless it was a big snotty-nosed kid with a mask and a shotgun.

The normality of the street scene did nothing to allay Bliss's anxiety which had been mounting ever since the suburbs, when the gradually narrowing streets had closed in around him, tighter and tighter like a strait-jacket cramping his chest, making him want to turn away. But he stuck it out, determined this would be no drive-by, and he forced himself to pull up directly in front of the house. He was going in, going to stay – only a night or two, but, thanks to Daphne, it was time to stop running.

"Is there anything else that I can tell you, or you can tell me before we call it a day?" asked Bliss, wrapping up the meeting. Several checked their watches, praying no-one would ask a question or start a debate.

"What did you make of the syringe, Guv?" said a youngish policewoman in tennis gear, breaking rank with her colleagues and suffering their glares.

"What syringe?" asked Bliss blankly.

"I found it in the ashes of Dauntsey's Aga cooker," she explained, having taken the initiative to sift through the ash-bin of the coal burning stove in the kitchen of the old house, thinking it an ideal place for someone to incinerate small incriminating items. "It had exploded in the heat and was all smoky and black, but I managed to find most of it."

Bliss shook his head – completely in the dark. "Well, where is it?"

"I gave it to Sgt. Patterson on Tuesday, Guv."

"I didn't think it was significant," shrugged Patterson, leaping to his own defence. "It was obviously his mother's – being ill and all."

"She's got cancer, not diabetes," shot back Bliss, seizing a vengeful opportunity. "Where is it now? In the evidence store or at the forensic lab, I hope."

Patterson, nailed, turned bright pink. "Um ... It's in my desk actually, Guv."

"Well get it to the lab then – right away."

Patterson wriggled, unconvinced. "It's burnt ... doubt if they'll find anything. Anyway, what are they supposed to be looking for? They'll want to know."

"A sedative of some sort. My guess is he used it to tranquillise whoever he bumped off, which would explain how he got his victim up to the room in the Black Horse."

"Have we any idea who he killed, Guv?" It was the policewoman again, thinking – that'll teach them for glaring at me.

"Well, we know for sure he didn't kill the Major ..."

"We don't know that at all," complained Patterson still clinging to his conviction despite evidence to the contrary. "He confessed – I got his confession on tape."

"I strongly suggest you listen to that tape again. You've been taken for a ride, Sergeant – Jonathon Dauntsey didn't confess to killing the Major."

"But ..." protested Patterson. "He said he killed his father."

"In which case I suggest you check his date of birth. I know the pace of life has picked up in recent years but, unless Jonathon's mother was ten months pregnant, I think you'll find he is not a Dauntsey."

"Thank you for your attention ladies and gentle-men," he added quickly and was out of the door before Patterson had a chance to respond.

"Thank you, Daphne, you're a genius," he said to the corridor wall, took fifty pounds out of his pocket and poked his head back round the door. "All have a drink on me tonight," he said handing it to the nearest.

"Take tomorrow off and we'll crack this case next week." Then he raised his eyebrows at Patterson, fully expecting an argument, and was a trifle disappointed when the man begrudgingly nodded his thanks.

Two hours later he stood on the threshold of his house with more than a tingle of nervousness in his groin. You could run, he told himself – it's an option. No-one would know. You could high-tail it back to the Mitre – you've already paid. Then he thought of Daphne, knickerless, charging the German machine gunners on a bike, and he slipped the key into the lock.

Samantha had helped with the decor and choice of fabrics when he initially moved in. "You're useless, Dad," she had said.

"I'm a man. It's not my fault."

But the decor had changed, the bomber had seen to that, and the hallway was unfamiliar, hostile even as he stepped inside. He stopped, feeling as vulnerable as a naked man in a cell, realising that his home had been violated; that it had been intruded upon, first by the essence of the bomber himself, then by a slew of policemen, scientists, rubber-neckers, reporters, architects, estimators, builders, and a battalion of civil servants. Even the commissioner had been to inspect – it wasn't every day that one of his officers was bombed out of his home.

"It's like it were in the Blitz," one of the neighbours had said with a glint in his eye. "Even the King came to have a gawp then."

The heavy steel door clanged shut behind him. There, that wasn't so difficult, was it? he breathed in relief. And the decorator's have done a good job, no sign of the bomb damage ...

"*Br-rr-ing.*"

He jumped out of skin and the phone shrieked again.
"Br-rr-ing."

The killer was back – It was less than a minute and he was doing it again.

"Br-rr-ing."

He must be watching the place – get out, get out before a grenade whistles through a window.

"Br-rr-ing."

GET OUT NOW!

You are kidding? That's what he wants. He's outside right now, leering, a mobile phone in one hand and a Kalashnikov in the other.

I thought you were going to stop this.

Tell my pulse that.

"Br-rr-ing."

Answer the phone.

What – put it to my ear and listen for the "Bang" as my head gets blown off.

"Br-rr-ing."

Stand back and hit the speakerphone button then. Alright – good idea. "Yes – who is this?"

"Identify yourself."

"What?"

"I said – identify yourself."

Don't tell him – Duck! Duck! "Who are you?"

"This is Tew Park police station – identify yourself."

"Oh shit," he muttered. "I've set off the alarm."

He'd forgotten – Big Brother was watching.

"This is D.I. Bliss ..." he started, then pulled himself up. "Sorry – This is Michael."

"What's the codeword?"

There was nothing friendly in the demand – and it was a demand. The codeword? His mind was racing – what's the codeword? "Hang on, I haven't used it for six months."

"Police officers are en-route – state your codeword."

"Sarah." It came back in a flash. "It's Sarah." Ex-wife Sarah – how could I have forgotten? Well, it has been more than five years now.

"Thank you, Michael – you should have informed us you were visiting the property."

"Yes – sorry. Spur of the moment. I didn't think."

That's what had happened with the codeword, he recalled to himself. You gave Sarah's name on the spur of the moment – still living in the past – still rushing back to press your nose against the toy shop window.

"A patrol unit will be with you in just a few moments, Sir," continued the voice on the speakerphone.

"That won't be necessary officer," he was saying, but he was staring at the door – the steel anti-blast door with double deadbolt locks – still wondering if a deranged sniper with a high powered rifle was out there just waiting for a chink to appear.

"The unit is with you now, Sir. If you'd be good enough to open the door and just confirm your identity."

"Wait, wait – How do I know ...?"

"How do you know what, Sir?"

"How do I know ..." his voice faded.

This is stupid, Dave. You're making an ass of yourself. You're right.

"If you would just open the door, Sir."

His hand was on the handle but it wouldn't turn.

Bang! Bang! Bang! "Open up, Sir – Police."

"Sorry," he said a few minutes later as he sat, crammed in the kitchen with two gregarious Bigfoots in blue uniforms. "I really haven't got a lot to offer you."

"No problem, Guv."

"I could do some instant coffee ..." he started, then realised he'd have to turn on the water and scare up some mugs. In any case they were shaking their heads –

buckets of beer looked to be more in their line. "I really hadn't planned on coming back today," he continued, "but I was in the area and I thought I'd see what the old place looked like."

"You're not staying then?"

"No," he said easily. Thinking – I was going to until I stood by that door not knowing who was outside – waiting for the bullets. Sorry, Daphne old girl – guess I haven't got the bottle. "No, I'm not staying – I think I'll go to my daughter's."

"Thank Christ for that."

"Why?"

"'Cos we would have had to park outside all night if you'd been stopping."

"I'll only be ten minutes or so," he said, letting the officers out and closing the heavy door. Then he stood, fixated by the door, seriously debating whether he was inside or outside – not inside or outside the house; inside or outside the door – a mental perspective of a physical presence. With the realisation that he wanted to be the other side of the door he concluded he was actually outside, and left the house as soon as he'd rounded up one or two belongings.

"Don't wake me up too early," Samantha, his daughter, had warned, throwing a clean sheet over the guest bed. "Tomorrow's Sunday – just forget you're in the police for once."

"Roger, Sam," he had said, thinking – you sound more like your mother every day. "Don't worry, I'm so exhausted I'll probably sleep all day."

A swathe of sunlight cut through a gape in the curtains and roused him a little after nine. As he woke, "Samantha" was on his lips and he fought with his soporific memory to retrace the dregs of his last dream.

Sketchy images appeared – cozy memories: a warm dark car; moonlight on a tropical beach; a dark-haired native with an alluring body. Samantha, the sergeant, he fathomed, then realised that despite all the aggravations of the previous day she had been slinking in the back of his mind throughout.

Balancing himself on the brink of wakefulness, he played with the images until she was gambolling naked in the surf. Then the shiploads of dead men started drifting in again and spoiled the picture. Waking himself to escape the nightmare, he was annoyed to discover that Samantha had also dissolved. Be sensible, he told himself. Don't get carried away. It was 4 am and you were tired and lonely. In the clear light of day she'll be an absolute dragon. Anyway, she didn't seem overly keen.

But she said she'd have dinner.

"Maybe," was what she said. "Maybe."

"Call me," she said.

But did she give me a number? – No. Did she tell me where she was stationed?

That's easy enough to find out – you're just trying to duck out of it. What are you frightened of?

I told you – she's probably a dragon, works nights so as not to scare the horses during the day.

You're frightened of rejection – again.

Ha – ha, very funny.

"Have you upset somebody, Guv?" asked the control room officer at Westchester police station when Bliss called a little after ten.

Does he mean – apart from Superintendent Donaldson, Sergeant Patterson and half the C.I.D.? he wondered, then answered cagily. "Not that I know of. I was just calling to see if ... Why?"

The voice was guarded – circumspect. "Well ... were you expecting a delivery of any sort?"

Oh God – another bomb. Try to sound normal. "No, I wasn't expecting anything at all."

"We thought so, Guv. Well, somebody's playing a nasty joke on you."

"What is it? What's happened?" It has to be explosive, or something really disgusting like a box of cow-shit. Damn – they will have instigated full anti-terrorist procedures: evacuation; bomb disposal teams, robotic disarming devices . . . this has got to stop – one way or another.

"Guv – Are you still there?"

"Yes – Sorry, I wasn't listening. What did you say?"

"I said it were a moth eaten old goat."

"A what?"

"Some butcher delivered it this morning – reckoned it had come from an auction. I've had it put in the isolation cell. He wanted to put it in your office. 'Not bloody likely,' I said, 'You never know what it might have inside.'"

"Daphne!" he swore under his breath but he couldn't help laughing in relief. "Do you mean it could be a sort of a Trojan goat?"

"A what, Guv?"

"Never mind – it's O.K., just a mistake I expect. I'll deal with it. Anything else?"

"Three phone calls for you, Guv."

"Who?"

"Three women," he said, the suggestion of impropriety in his tone. "None of 'em would leave a message, said they'd call back, though one of 'em sounded very much like our Daphne – the cleaner."

Directory enquiries located her number in seconds. "Daphne – this is D.I. Bliss. . . did you phone me this morning?"

"Oh yes, Chief Inspector," she started, wielding formality as a shield. "I'm glad you called. I wanted to be the first to congratulate you." She paused for the words to sink in, then added excitedly, "You bought the goat."

"I did what?"

"Now, you needn't be cross. I didn't know what to do and I knew you wouldn't mind. I bid twenty pounds myself but nobody else seemed interested, then George caught my eye and he looked so downhearted. 'I thought that friend of yorn were keen,' he said, his face as miserable as a wet weekend. 'He *was*, George,' I said. 'He most certainly *was*.' 'Well where is he then?' he said, forlorn. What could I do, Dave? I didn't want you getting a bad reputation for welching on your promises, so I bid fifty quid for you."

"How much?"

"Oh don't be so ungrateful. I did it for you. Anyway, you were lucky. I thought about bidding against you and pushing the price up to a hundred, but the auctioneer was quick off the mark. "Going, going, gone," he said, and knocked it down before I could get my hand up, so I saved you fifty quid. George was so thrilled he said he would deliver it personally – he thinks you're wonderful."

"A wonderful idiot."

She pretended not to hear. "Anyway, Dave, that wasn't why I was calling really – I've got some more good news. D'you remember asking me about that Captain at Doreen's wedding?"

"The Major's aide-de-camp."

"Yes. His best man – the one with the clothes brush. Well, I thought afterwards, we were very silly."

"We were?"

"Oh yes. Very silly. You see, when I thought about it, I remembered he was Rupert's witness at the wedding. I was Doreen's ..."

"And his name will be on the marriage certificate," burst in Bliss, catching on immediately. "I'm in London, I can go to the records office tomorrow ..."

"That won't be necessary, Dave. I went to St. Paul's church this morning.

Sunday – "Communion?"

"No – to look in the parish register of course. The vicar found it in a flash. I've got it here. His name was Tippen. David Tippen, just like you said, and he gave an address in Guildstone.

"I know the place, I drive through it."

"You'll have to go there then," she said, giving him the address. "I've tried directory enquiries and they don't have a number."

"Thanks, Daphne – you're great," he said and was about to put down the phone when she announced that there was even more good news. Apparently, George, the butcher, had been so impressed by his generosity in buying the taxidermal goat he had personally delivered a joint of sirloin to her, with a request that it should be passed on. "Knowing you haven't got a place of your own," she said, "I thought perhaps I could make Sunday dinner, roast beef and Yorkshire pudding, say about 7.30 tonight. If you can forgive me by then."

"I couldn't, Daphne, really."

Her voice cracked with pain. "You won't forgive me."

"Of course I'll forgive you – already have. It's just that I don't know what time I'll be back."

"Oh I see." But she wouldn't be beaten. "I'll cook anyway, and if you're not here by eight I'll go ahead and eat on my own. I can always heat yours up later – Bye."

Putting down the phone, shaking his head at Daphne's impudence, he suddenly realised why he was still running from a would-be assassin while she had boldly walked through the German lines. She was a

woman. Even Mandy's killer had shown his prejudice –
"I wouldn't shoot no woman – what sort of scum do you
think I am?" Why? he wondered. What's the difference –
is it more horrifying for a woman to die than a man. But
what if the person in the bank had been Andy instead of
Mandy? Would the killer still be trying to exact revenge?
At least Andy wouldn't have been pregnant.

Laying back with his eyes closed, he drifted in thought,
realising it was the ethereal nature of the threat that made
it so much more frightening – he'd had no problem tack-
ling the killer head-on in the bank, and needed both hands
to count the number of armed villains he'd taken down
over the years. But he had been able to see them.

"I hope you're going to pay my phone bill," said
Samantha, bleary eyed, sliding unheard into the room
and jumping him out of thoughts.

"Well, I was going to," he said with a serious face.
"But I don't know if I can afford it now."

"Why not?" she cried, instantly wide awake.

He kept the straight face. "Well, I've just bought a
goat."

"A what?"

"That's what I said when I found out."

"Dad, it's too early to piss about ..." then her face
clouded in concern. "Aren't you taking this country
thing a bit far?"

"It's alright, Luv," he said, unable to control his
mirth, and, sweeping her into his arms, kissed her forehead. "Of course I'll pay your bill. Although," he
paused and looked to the ceiling as if in deep thought,
"perhaps you can help me out with the feed bill."

"What!"

Daphne, George and the goat were explained with a
laugh. "I've just one more quick call," he added as she
headed to the kitchen mumbling, "Coffee."

The brusqueness of the model's dealer suggested that he had stood to attention to answer the phone. "The Toy Soldier – Sunday – Closed to the public," he said, though a buzz of background voices suggested otherwise.

"Oh ... I was hoping to have a word ..."

"Call back tomorrow then."

"It'll only take a second – I was in your shop earlier in the week ..."

"Peter ..." a voice called. "I've just taken out your tank, old boy, you'd better pull your socks up."

"Blast ... Well, what is it? What d'ye want?" he questioned in a tone that said, "Get on with it man."

"The Royal Horse Artillery gun carriage – you asked me ..."

"Have you got the set?" he demanded, his enthusiasm running away with his mouth.

"Peter ..."

"Not now ... Have you got it?"

These boys are keen, thought Bliss. "Yes, I think so."

"When can I see it?"

It's only a toy – not the crown jewels. "Well ..."

"I'm here all day or I can come to you."

"It's in Westchester, Hamp ..."

"I know the place – it's eleven now, I can be there by two, one-thirty at a pinch."

"Wait, wait, wait," said Bliss. "There's no rush. Anyway, I haven't asked the owner yet ..." then he paused, thinking, who is the owner? Doreen, I suppose.

"I was only calling to let you know – you seemed rather keen ..."

"Look, I must see it ..." the dealer hesitated for a second then seemingly made up his mind. "I'll give you five hundred pounds if you tell me where it is and keep quiet about it."

Bliss's throat tightened to a squeak, "How much?"

"O.K. ... Seven hundred and fifty, as long as it's genuine and no-one else knows."

Samantha was back with the coffee and a puzzled frown. "What is it, Dad?"

He clasped his hand over the mouthpiece and took a deep breath. "I'm missing something here – hold on a minute." Then he spoke questioningly back to the phone. "We are talking about the same thing I hope. The seven hundred and fifty pounds ... that's not for buying the set?"

"No, no. That's just for telling me where it is."

Bliss held his breath and spoke slowly. "Would you consider making that a thousand pounds?"

Chapter Twelve

Captain David Tippen's house had gone. Even the street had gone – bulldozed into the foundations of a mega-store and a leisure complex. The duty sergeant at Guildstone police station remembered the street, "Crumbly old hovels – good riddance, I said. It were a bloomin' rat-hole."

There were only eight Tippens in the phone book, none David or D, but Bliss decided it was worth a few minutes of his time. The first two had left machines in charge of their phones. Three, four and five turned a deaf ear, and number six rang forever. "Hallo," said a thin voice, just as Bliss had decided to quit.

"Is this Mr. Tippen?"

"You'll 'ave to speak up."

"I said ..."

"Yeah. I heard ya. What'ye want?"

"I'm looking for relatives of a David Tippen."

"Yeah, I knows him," he replied, with a confusing use of the present tense. "He's me uncle's boy."

"No – I'm looking for a man who was a Captain in the Royal Horse Artillery during the war."

"Aye, that'd be 'im alright."

"Unbelievable," breathed Bliss.

"Who are ya anyhow?" queried the old man.

"Police – Detective Inspector Bliss."

"Police, eh? Why didn't you say so afore?"

"Can you just tell me where he is," Bliss tried again.

"Gawd knows – the poor blighter never came back, did he? Missing in action, they said."

"Oh. I thought you meant he was alive ..." started Bliss, formulating a further question when inquisitiveness got the better of the old man. "What's this all about? Mebbe you'd best come 'round here. I'm back of the old cattle market."

"I'll take you, Guv," said the sergeant when he asked for directions. "You'll never find it without a guide – unless you use your nose."

Sergeant Jones was right about the nose – though it wasn't the market giving off the stink, it was the ancient clapboard house lurking behind it.

The old man took even longer to answer the door than the phone, but each time Bliss knocked anew, his crotchety voice drifted through the splintered wood-work. "Alright, alright, I'ze a coming."

And, when the door finally creaked open, it revealed a Dickensian scene of poverty, together with a decayed man who fitted the setting perfectly. "Come in," he said amidst a waft of hot stench which hit the two officers and had them scrabbling for handkerchiefs.

"'Tis the cats," explained Tippen, a straggle-haired geriatric, sideswiping a ginger tom with his ivory-handled walking cane. "You'll get used t'it in a mo. Come along in – I were just 'aving me tea. I'll make ya a cuppa."

"Not for us," said Bliss sharply, remaining rooted to the doorstep as the old man shuffled back into the house, his shabby black clothing blending into the gloom.

"Well, don't just stand there," he called, the pallor of his face showing up as he turned back to the door. But Bliss was having difficulty motivating himself to follow into the murky labyrinth of narrow corridors, looking, as far as he could tell, as if they had been tunnelled through mountains of newspapers and ceiling high heaps of rotten clothing. It was a hellish version of Alice in Wonderland, he realised, complete with black rabbit in a waistcoat. Sergeant Jones finally nudged him into action, and together they struggled forward against the tide of decay, grateful they had passed on the old man's invitation to his tea party.

The sergeant was still retching an hour later as he sat at the police canteen bar, slugging down a third whisky, shaking his head, muttering, "I can't believe it," for the twentieth time. "I've never smelt anything like it. Did you see all that shit?"

"Everywhere," replied Bliss, scrutinising his feet at maximum range. "I'll have to throw these shoes away. I'm not having them in my car."

"I'm not sure it was all cat shit either," said the sergeant, sniffing his jacket with care.

"I'd rather not think about it."

"I'm gonna burn this uniform."

"A good dry-cleaner will probably get it out."

"Sulphuric acid wouldn't kill a smell like this."

"I'd best be off," said Bliss, rising. "I'll leave it to you to contact Social Services and make arrangements to get him out and cleaned up."

"Thanks, Guv. They're gonna love me."

"I bet you're glad you came with me now," he laughed.

Sergeant Jones scowled in mock anger. "I'm just glad you got the information you needed."

"Oh yes," he said, picking up an envelope containing the tattered remains of a photograph which the old man had miraculously found amidst the garbage. "I think I've pretty much got the case wrapped up now."

There were two uniformed men in the photo and Bliss had recognised them immediately: the Major and the Captain – two soldiers in battledress standing just a little too close; smiling just a little too much; and, fifty years on, their eyes still sparkling for each other. The picture had slotted into place in Bliss's mind the moment he took it from the grubby claws of the old man, and everything suddenly made perfect sense: Rupert's nancy-boy reputation; his whiny accent; his sudden marriage to Doreen; his retention of the dead man's dog tags. And, when he turned the photograph over, Captain David Tippen's neatly caligraphied hand spoke directly to him: "*This is me with my very best friend, Rupie.*"

"He should never 'ave gone in t'army," the old man had said with nostalgic concern. "He didn't 'ave the constitution for it, he were too much of a mummy's boy ... Killed her it did, when he didn't come back."

"Imagine Doreen," Bliss had postulated to the sergeant on their way back to the police station. "She marries a bloke who gets shipped off to war before he has a chance to get his leg over, then he comes home looking like Dracula and announces his dick's been blown off. 'But don't fret about it, my little turtle-dove,' he says, ''Cos I'm a poofter anyway.'"

"No wonder she bumped him off," laughed Jones. "My missus would kill me if I told her that."

Bliss closed his eyes in thought, "The only real problem I'm left with is – who did Jonathon kill *in loco majoris?*"

"There's no shortage of candidates," said Jones. "Have you any idea how many doddery old codgers are reported missing each week?"

"That's assuming it was a doddery old codger and not just someone who happened along at a convenient moment, and assuming whoever it was was missed. Just imagine if it was someone like old man Tippen."

"Do I have to?"

"Well, you know what I mean. Who would complain if he disappeared? He could've lain dead in that place we've just left for years without anybody caring."

"Judging by the stink I think he had."

Bliss laughed, "Did you hear what he said when I asked him where all the newspapers had come from. 'I must've forgot to cancel them when me eyes went.'"

"I wonder how he paid for them?"

"Gawd knows – he probably nicked 'em."

Parking at the rear of the Mitre hotel on his return to Westchester, Bliss couldn't help feeling a trifle foolish as he sneaked in the back way with his suitcase – feeling like a runaway lover slipping back home, red-faced, after vowing never to set foot in the house ever again, half expecting the door to be locked and another man in his bed. The smiling Swedish receptionist held the door for him and added to his discomfort by welcoming him back with professional effusiveness. "Oh. Good evening, Mr. Bliss, it is so nice that you are back – no?"

"No ... I mean, Yes, it's nice to be back."

"There's a letter for you in reception," she said, adding to his feeling of belonging. And, as he struggled his suitcases through the antique filled lounge and up the wide staircase to his room, he found himself soothed by the warm sensation of homeliness in the now familiar surroundings.

The letter intrigued him. Who knows I'm staying here apart from Superintendent Donaldson, Sergeant Patterson and Daphne? But the prospect that Mandy's murderer could have located him barely touched his mind. The plain white envelope had a fresh clean smell, and was certainly too small to contain even a trace of explosive, but it certainly gave his heart an unexpected kick as he read the short note.

"Please give me a call – Kind regards: Samantha Holingsworth." And a phone number.

"Did I leave my pen in your car, Dave?" she asked, recognising his voice immediately.

It sounded like an excuse, but he happily went along with it. "I don't think so, but I can check."

"What about ... " they started in unison.

"You go first," he said.

"No ... after you."

"I was going to ask – what about that dinner? Tomorrow perhaps?" He closed his eyes in mock pain, waiting for the crash of rejection – that's too soon – you'll scare her off.

"Sorry – I can't."

See, I warned you.

"I start late shift tomorrow," she continued. "I told you, I work lousy hours ..." she paused. "But I'm free this evening."

"Oh – I can't. I promised a little old lady."

"Oh yeah ... how old?" she asked, her voice full of tease.

"Positively ancient."

"I guess that would mean around thirty, a busty blond with a Mercedes and an expense account," she laughed. "It's alright, Dave, I know my limitations."

"Wait a minute," he said, a smile in his voice. "Do you like roast beef?"

They met in the reception area at the Mitre. The dragon he'd cautioned himself to expect had transformed into a sleek sable-haired feline with smooth round features, dark mysterious eyes and sensible white teeth set squarely behind full lips – nothing dangerously protrusive; no tombstones.

He pulled up, slack-mouthed, at the foot of the stairs, studying her profile as she chatted to the friendly Swede, and he froze – holding the moment – savouring the image.

Feeling the weight of his eyes she turned with a smile. "Hello, Dave."

Move you prat, he said to himself. "You look very nice," he said, cursing the inadequacy of polite conversation as he walked toward her.

"Thank you kind sir," she curtsied gracefully, and he took her hand and kissed it theatrically.

"Come on," he said, keeping hold, his eyes locked on hers. "Daphne will be waiting," he continued but couldn't tear his eyes free – her right pupil had taken a life of its own and was drifting slowly southward. In an instant she pulled the lazy eye back into focus and looked embarrassingly away, but Bliss was already captivated by the charming imperfection and felt a tingle of excitement down his spine as they made a move out of the lobby.

"By the way, how did you know I was staying here?" he asked, on their way to his car.

"I traced your car number," she blushed. "Mind I was a bit surprised when it came up as a hire car ..."

An implicit question hung in the air, but he chose to ignore it. He'd gone all day with barely a thought of the monkey on his back and had no intention of unnecessarily dredging up Mandy's killer and spoiling the evening.

"She's in love with you," whispered a soft voice in his ear an hour later as he sat on Daphne's couch after dinner.

"What? Don't be silly. I've only known her a few days."

"I'm a woman, Dave, believe me – I know these things. I can see it in her eyes."

Daphne bustled in with a tray of coffees. "What are you two love-birds whispering about?" she chuckled, with an edge to her laugh.

"I was just saying to Dave, what a lovely dinner," said Samantha, her face as innocent as her tone. "I can't believe you grew all the vegetables yourself."

Daphne had pulled out all the stops. The sirloin had been exquisite, and her golden Yorkshire puddings had to be held to the plates with lashings of rich beef gravy. "The trick is not to pick the vegies when the sun's on them," she explained, shrugging off the compliment.

"Well, it was really nice," said Bliss, still luxuriating in the warmth of Samantha's breath on his cheek.

Placing the tray on a Butler's table at their feet, Daphne ignored the empty armchairs and squeezed onto the settee in between them.

"Budge over, Dave," she said, giving his knee a playful nudge and Samantha shot him a cheeky smile behind her back, mouthing, "Told you so."

Returning to The Mitre, Bliss parked only yards from the back wall, behind the lounge with its deep chintzy sofas, flickering candlelight and mood music. But they stayed in the car; exchanging soft words and tender touches; breathing gently through moistened lips; savouring each other's scent; basking in each other's warmth. It would be so easy to charge full-tilt into a sexual melee, he realised: a bottle of Dom Perignon in the lounge, an indecent proposal whispered tenderly with precise timing, and it would be all over bar the shouting. But he fought the urge with ease – hastily consummated relationships with as much staying power as the Titanic were a thing of his past.

Waltzing easily into the natural rhythm of romance they melted into each other arms and their eyes locked – midnight blue on burnt sienna in the shadowy light. They floated, lips poised, and drank in each other's beauty. Then a spark of light blazed in her eyes and Bliss spun around in time to catch the fading flare of a match, and the bright glow of a newly lit cigarette, behind him.

"There's someone out there," he whispered. "Stay here," he added, easing himself out of her arms and inching toward the door.

"Are you crazy?" she said, hopping out the other side and taking off after him.

Twenty minutes later, breathless and bedraggled, they were back, standing by Samantha's car, saying goodnight.

"I do wish you'd come up to my room and clean up," he implored.

"No," she said fiercely, then immediately backed off. "I'm sorry. I didn't mean it to sound like that. I don't mean to be ungrateful. I would just prefer to go home if you don't mind, only I'm covered in mud."

"He went right through the river."

"I know, I was behind him remember."

"I thought you were magnificent."

"Just doing my job, Sir," she said in a policeman's voice, then sneezed.

"You really should come up and dry off. Look, here's my key. I'll stay in the bar if you don't trust me."

"Dave, don't get me wrong, it's just too much of a cliché – Girl meets boy; girl falls in mud; girl catches cold; girl takes off wet clothes ... well you know the rest. I've seen the movie, and read the soppy novel ... and they don't always have a happy ending."

Feeling a pang of disappointment he asked, "Can I call you?"

"You'd better," she laughed getting in and closing her door. "I can't afford to keep losing pens."

The Volvo had got away from the car park moments before Bliss and Samantha returned. The driver, breathless and drenched, stood shivering in a phone booth a mile away.

"They nearly caught me," he was bleating into the phone. "I had to run through the effin' river – got soaked."

"They? Who are they?"

"Him and the woman. The one I told you about. He picked her up again at that same house. I'm sure this guy knows you're onto him, he's real slippery. He's switched cars again ... did I tell you what he did the other night? ... He was at that house again – the woman's house, dropping her off late, then he took off, and when I started to follow he did a U-turn and left me standing. I waited at the Mitre but he didn't show up all night."

"Well don't worry about him anymore," said the voice at the other end. "It's time I turned up the heat. Time we said goodbye to Mr. Bliss."

Peter Marshall, the owner of The Toy Soldier, was as enthusiastic as a new recruit and reported early, arriving at The Mitre at seven-thirty on Monday morning.

"First stop: the police station," said Bliss, coming downstairs and marching him out of the door and up the High Street at eight o'clock precisely.

Marshall hung back. "I don't understand ... Police?"

"All will become clear," said Bliss, stepping off and refusing to give anything away.

Ten minutes later, in his office, Bliss leaned his elbows onto his desk, closely studied the man in front of him, and fired a surprise salvo. "So tell me, Mr. Marshall, just why would anyone be prepared to offer a thousand pounds simply to discover the whereabouts of a murdered man's lead soldiers?"

"I want to buy them ... What murdered man? I don't know anything about that. I just want to buy the Horse Artillery set, there's nothing sinister in that."

"That's it? That's all? You want to buy it?"

"Yes."

"And you expect me to believe that you were prepared to offer me a thousand pounds and drive all the way down here at some ungodly hour for a few bits of old lead."

"Yes. I do expect you to believe me. That 'old lead,' as you call it, happens to be fine miniature replicas ..."

"They're just kids toys ..." he cut in, then paused. "Hold on a minute – How much?"

"I don't see how that concerns you."

"Oh, I see. You won't tell me in case I get the idea I can make more than a thousand if I buy them myself. But, wait a minute ..." Bliss tilted his head and scratched his chin. "If you're prepared to offer me a thousand, they must be worth a fair bit more than that."

"Not without the major," replied Marshall with a note of triumph. "And you don't have the major, not in recognisable form."

True on both counts, thought Bliss, looking at him askance, still wondering if he knew more about the soldiers than the value. "And you do have a major, I suppose?"

"Yes. As a matter of fact I do. I have a single major."

"But that's all you've got," Bliss guessed. "And I've got the rest of the set."

"Are you trying to blackmail me, Inspector?"

Bliss laughed, "Far from it. I'm trying to protect the assets of a dying old lady, though I'm not sure she deserves to be protected. Anyway, stop beating about the bush – how much?"

Marshall put on his military haughtiness. "The last set to come on the market sold for more than twelve thousand pounds."

"Phew! – Twelve thousand quid for a toy."

"Not a toy, Inspector. Assuming your identification is correct, only the fifth set of its kind known to be in existence in the world today – a rare find indeed."

Bliss was still shaking his head, "Twelve thousand ..."

"That was a few years ago. Today, in a New York auction room, it could easily sell for twenty-five thousand dollars."

The phone rang, it was a woman – unwilling to leave her name, according to the telephonist. "Tell her to call back ... " he started, then thinking – hoping – it might be Samantha, he politely ushered Marshall out of the office and took the call.

The voice was muffled and indistinct – Samantha with pneumonia he was thinking – then he realised it was not her, it was Doreen Dauntsey, her voice cracking emotionally, "I believe you wanted to see me, Inspector."

"Yes – that's correct," he replied. "This morning please," he added, leaving little room for dissension.

"I shall be waiting for you," she said, her voice laden with resignation.

Sergeant Patterson was on the warpath over the goat and had by-passed the chain of command to take his complaint straight to the top. "Superintendent Donaldson wants to see you," he said to Bliss, spying him and Peter Marshall on their way to the evidence store.

"Tell him I'll be half an hour, Pat, would you please."

"He said it was very urgent," said Patterson, emphasising the "very."

"Sorry about this," apologised Bliss, leaving Marshall dancing in anticipation in the public waiting room.

He found Donaldson in his office furiously spinning a gyroscope. "What the hell's going on, Dave?"

"Sir?"

"What's this nonsense about you keeping a goat in the cells?"

Bliss smiled and tried to make light of it. "Don't tell me it's crapped on the floor."

"We're going to have to fumigate the whole place," he complained, whipping the little silver gyroscope again.

"What?" Bliss screwed his nose in confusion. "Wait a minute, Guv. Is somebody winding you up? Has someone told you it's a real goat – a live goat?"

"No – I know what it is," he shouted. "It's stuffed – and so will you be if you don't get it out of there PDQ."

Bliss's confusion deepened. "I'm sorry but I don't see the problem, Guv."

"You don't, eh! Well, what about Standing Orders?" He grabbed the huge book of rules and stabbed a finger at the open page – the page Patterson had found for him. "It says here," he read, "'Whenever a dead animal has been stored or conveyed on police premises, such premises, (or conveyance), shall be thoroughly cleansed by way of fumigation before any further use is made of such premises, (or conveyance).'"

"But it was nothing to do with me, Sir ..."

"I understood it was your goat."

Bliss conceded the point. "But it's been dead for ages."

"All the more reason I would say."

With both Marshall and Doreen Dauntsey waiting, he decided against arguing the point further. "I'll put it in the garage as soon as I have a minute."

"I doubt if there's room," gloated Donaldson, not concealing the fact he was being deliberately obstructive.

"It's a goat not a woolly mammoth," he said stomping out.

"Well, you'd better get it moved right now," Donaldson yelled after him. "I don't want any more complaints, and you might have to pay for the fumigation as well."

The goat seemed to have put on weight as he half carried, half dragged it, across the car park to the garage, cursing Daphne at every step. I shall have to get a pick-up to take it away, he was thinking as he rammed the old animal into a convenient corner.

"You can't leave that there," called a gangly youth in a mechanic's overall.

"Do you want a bet?" me mumbled walking away.

"Oy. I said ..."

Bliss tuned him out and set his sights on Daphne who was emptying her vacuum cleaner into a garbage bin.

"I want to talk to you about that damn goat ..." he barked but she dropped the cleaner in disgust and turned on him.

"It's going to take me all day to disinfect that cell. And have you seen all that hair? It's shedding faster than a cheap paintbrush."

Bliss stopped in his tracks. "What did you say?"

"I said there's hair everywhere, look at your suit – you're covered."

He looked, then grabbed her and kissed her wetly on the forehead. "You're a whiz, Daph old girl."

"Here, less of the old."

"Sorry," he said, rushing off along the corridor.

Detective Sergeant Patterson was shooting the breeze in the C.I.D. office when Bliss burst in.

"Yes, Guv?" he queried, as if Bliss had blundered into the women's toilets by mistake.

"The duvet in the Dauntsey case, Pat – did we have it checked for hair?"

"Not yet – we ain't got any suspects, so there's not much point."

"Do it anyway, will you please?"

"Why?"

"Just a hunch – at least we'll know if we're looking for a white-haired old faggot, or a purple haired pansy with a ring in his nose."

Patterson looked unconvinced and said so, "Waste of bloody time if you ask me."

"I'm not asking, Sergeant. Now have we got the results from the lab on that syringe yet?"

"Not yet, Guv," he said. "It'll take a week or so at least," thinking it might take considerably longer if he didn't get round to sending it.

"Well get onto them – I want it yesterday – understood?"

"Will do, Guv," he said, and slid lethargically back in his chair. "Anything you say, Guv. You're the boss."

"Thank you," muttered Bliss as he left, adding, "Now to make a modeler's day."

The Royal Horse Artillery gun carriage set, complete with original box, had not made Marshall's day, or his week – it had been the moment he'd waited for most of his life. "He was bawling like a kid," Bliss explained excitedly to a barely interested Donaldson half an hour later. "He stood with one of the tiny horseman in his hands, eyes closed, quivering in delight – like he was having an orgasm – then these tears started pouring down his cheeks."

"Humph," grunted Donaldson as he helped himself to a biscuit from a packet concealed under his desk.

"Anyway, Guv, it seems that Major Dauntsey left quite a legacy – one of the rarest sets of model soldiers in the world."

"So where does that leave us with the murder, Inspector?" he asked coldly, and Bliss heard the snap of the biscuit under the desk as Donaldson prepared for his departure.

"Nothing changes. In fact I'm just off to see Doreen Dauntsey – she called saying she wanted to talk to me. With any luck, I'll have the Major's case sewn up in an hour or so."

"And Jonathon?"

"Patterson's working on that at the moment."

"Right – And have you got rid of the goat?"

"I'm working on that."

He could have left for the nursing home immediately, but he hesitated at the front door and decided that he should take a copy of the pathologist's report with him – after all he was going to officially notify a woman of her widowhood. Returning to his office he flicked on his computer to pull up the report, then slumped as the blood drained from his face and his legs gave way.

In a daze, he picked up the phone, dialled Samantha's number, then found himself wondering why.

"Samantha ... is that you?" he squeaked as she came on the line.

"Dave, are you alright? You sound dreadful."

"I just wanted to make sure you were O.K."

"Just a sniffle – all I needed was a hot bath and a good night's sleep. Thanks for asking."

"Oh good – I'm glad."

"Dave – there is something the matter, I càn sense it."

"Remind me never to lie to you. Can you meet me tonight? ... It's rather important, I'm afraid."

"Yes, of course – I finish at ten but we could meet earlier ..."

"No, ten's fine ..." he said, quickly adding, "But don't come here. Meet me at the beach again."

"Alright ..." she replied inquisitivel,. "I will, but something's really wrong, isn't it?"

"I'll explain later," he said, slowly putting the phone down, and he sat mesmerised by the words on the computer screen in front of him.

"Your time is up – *BANG!* – *Ha-ha-ha.*"

Chapter Thirteen

Samantha Holingsworth waited with uneasy anticipation at the beach-side car park as arranged, and was surprised to spy Bliss's lonely shadow skulking along the beach in front of her.

"Over here, Dave," she shouted, assuming he'd missed her in the gloom, and he froze, like startled prey, silhouetted against the grey ocean and star-peppered sky.

"Here, Dave," she tried again, leaning out of the car window, and he straightened up and oriented himself toward her.

They sat in her car for a while, their conversation stilted by his anxieties sitting between them like an ugly little creature with halitosis.

"So, how are you?"

"Fine ... and you?" The creature's presence kept them to niceties ... the weather ... his hotel ... her car...

"Very smart," he said, meaning, "*Wow!*"

"Where's your car?" Samantha asked, craning around.

"Further up the beach," he said, without explanation.

And so it had continued: ... movies seen ... books read ... Daphne's dinner ... the weather again.

"It was really warm today."

"It's still warm now."

"Oh for God's sake, Dave," she exploded, unable to stand the suspense any longer. "Are you going to tell me why you needed to see me so urgently or not?"

He was having second thoughts – had been having second thoughts all afternoon – second thoughts from the moment he and Superintendent Donaldson had rushed back to his office to find the threatening message had evaporated from the computer screen.

"It was here," breathed Bliss, "I swear it was here."

You are going mad, he had told himself, searching the screen frantically, seeking some trace of the message – anything – even a single lingering pixel.

Donaldson laid a kindly hand on his arm. "Dave – you've been under a lot of stress ..."

"Don't give me that psycho babble, Guv," he spat, wrenching his arm away. "I know what I saw ... It was here. It said ..." he paused and buried his head in his hands. "It said ... 'Ha, ha, Bang – you're dead,' or something like that, I swear it did."

"Well where is it now?"

Looking up, blankly, he caught the superintendent unawares and saw his face pinched in scepticism. And behind the perplexed frown creasing his brow his mind was an open book. "*First he buys a flea-ridden goat – Now this – What next?*"

"Forget it, Guv."

"What do you mean – forget it. Forget what?"

"I know what you're thinking – please forget I mentioned it."

"I can't do that, Dave ..." his voice trailed off.

"Why not? ... Oh. I get it," he said, slapping his hand to his forehead. "Silly me. Of course you can't forget it – You've been told to keep an eye on me, haven't you?"

"Dave ..."

"No – it's alright, Guv, you needn't give me the bull-shit. I should've guessed. Transferring me here had noth-ing to do with the threats, did it? Somebody upstairs thought it would be a good idea to tuck me away in some godforsaken hole where I couldn't do a lot of dam-age; where it would be easy to keep an eye on me – Didn't they?"

Donaldson, caught off guard, mumbled something in the way of a platitude but Bliss's mind was elsewhere, recalling the sceptical stares of his London colleagues, together with their insidious whispers: "Maybe his nerve's gone; maybe his mind's gone; maybe he wrote those letters and made those phone calls himself." ... "Why would he do that?" ... "Guilt of course, for caus-ing Mandy's death," or, as the more cynical had suggest-ed, "He's angling for a whacking compensation package and early retirement."

As Bliss shook off old memories and brought him-self back to the present, Donaldson, conscious of his own red-face, was still scrambling to placate him. "It's not like that, Dave, honestly. People are very concerned about you that's all."

"Concerned," mused Bliss. Concerned about the reputation of the force and their own necks most likely; concerned that a rogue cop with a mental problem might rock the boat; concerned that if – and it was only "if" – if the murderer were hell-bent on revenge, an innocent bystander could be caught in the crossfire.

"Dave," continued Donaldson seriously, "I'm not disputing what you're saying – I just wonder how on earth he could have got in here."

"He got into my bank accounts and cleaned them out ..." he started, then his voice petered out as he remembered the snide suggestion from the investigating officer at the time, that maybe he'd done that himself as well, stashing away a nice little nest egg while expecting the force and the bank to club together to make up the loss – as in fact they had done.

"I haven't the foggiest idea how he got in, Guv, all I know is he did."

"Have you the slightest intention of telling me what's going on?" asked Samantha tetchily, still awaiting some response as he stared dejectedly out to sea. "Dave ... are you listening to me?"

"Sorry," he said pulling himself out of the trance.

"I said – Are you going to tell me why you dragged me out here after a hard day's work?"

He wanted to explain, but couldn't get his mouth working as his thoughts went back to the computerised death threat and reminded him of the bombing. "Thank God for the bomb," he remembered saying when it had happened, at a time when conversations withered whenever he walked into a room. At least the bomb had silenced the most vociferous rumour mongers, particularly as the chief superintendent himself had provided him with an alibi, sitting conveniently next to him at the annual widows and orphans fundraising dinner when it had exploded.

Samantha tugged at his sleeve, asking, "Dave – Are you listening to me?" – growing concern supplanting her earlier aggravation.

"Yes," he said, responding reflexively, but his mind was still stuck on the threatening message and Donaldson's obvious scepticism.

"I just can't see it, Dave," he had said, his implication clear despite the unintentional pun.

"Right, Guv," Bliss had shot back angrily. "If that's the way you want to play it. But I expect you to make it perfectly clear in your report, whoever you report to, that Detective Inspector Bliss was absolutely one hundred percent adamant that the words appeared on his computer screen."

"But, Dave – you know what our security is like ..?" he paused seeing the determination on Bliss's face, and relented. "O.K. I'll get the fingerprint boys to dust around ..."

"Waste of time, Guv," Bliss cut him off with the shake of his head. "This guy's a professional. Do you think he'd be stupid enough to leave prints?"

Donaldson bit the inside of lip as he wandered to the window, and he idly fingered the catch as he tried to fathom out the *modus operandi*. "How would you get in?" he asked, looking down at the car park two stories below, challenging himself for an answer as much as he was challenging Bliss.

"He probably strolled in with a toolbox, like he owned the place," suggested Bliss. "'Your whirly thingumajig's broken down again,' he calls to the girl on reception, as if he's fixing it every other day, and she flicks the switch to let him in without a second glance."

"Alright. Let's say I believe you ..." he started positively, turning back from the window. "There are security cameras on all external doors. All we have to do is pull the tapes and put a couple of men to go through them.

I'll get someone on it right away – satisfied?"

"Yes. Thank you, Sir," said Bliss. "And in the meantime, I'm damned if I'll let him get to me. Doreen Dauntsey's waiting to confess to murdering her old man, and I'm bloody determined to finish this case if it's the last thing I do."

Samantha had waited long enough. "Well, let me guess why you dragged me here," she said, angrily turning the ignition, preparing to leave. "You're married and you're worried your wife will find out about last night ..."

"No. No. No," he shouted, gathering his thoughts and panicking at the prospect of losing her.

She revved the engine threateningly.

"That's not it at all. I told you the truth – I'm divorced. Please don't leave. I need to talk to you ... please."

"Well, for God's sake, what is it, Dave?" she asked, switching off, her impatience suddenly muted by concern. "You look like a man facing a life sentence. Is it something to do with the Major Dauntsey case?"

"His wife did it," he replied, neatly avoiding the işsue of the death threats again. "I'm certain she wanted to confess this morning but her son, and the matron at the nursing home, kept me from seeing her."

"Let's lie on the sand," she said, grabbing a thick wool car blanket from the back seat. "And you can tell me all about it while we stare up at the stars."

"O.K.," he surrendered, wondering where to start as they walked the few yards to the beach and spread the blanket just beyond the ribbon of flotsam which marked the tide's reach.

"D.C. Dowding drove me to the nursing home," he explained as they lay listening to the gently swishing surf. "I didn't want to drive my car after what had happened. Anyway, Donaldson thought I should have back-up just in case."

"*What* had happened?" she demanded anxiously.

He froze again, still reluctant to involve her, then he carried on as if she'd not spoken. "Jonathon and the matron were in her office when I got there, working on a scheme to keep me out I guess."

Nurse Dryden had answered the bell, opening the highly lacquered front door and searching beyond him for a recognisable figure. "Is Bob with you today?"

"Bob," said Bliss vacantly, having instructed Dowding to remain with the car, forgetting that the nursing home held attractions for the detective beyond the purely professional. "Bob who?"

"Sergeant Dowding – you know, the one who was with you last week."

"Oh that Bob," he shook his head. "Day off – gone shopping with his wife I expect – probably getting something for the kiddies. You know how it is."

Her face crumpled, leaving him questioning his motive – wasn't that a bit spiteful? ... just because you're having a bad day. Maybe – But she'll thank me in the long run; so would her mother; so would Dowding's wife.

"Jonathon was spoiling for a fight," he carried on, sensing Samantha's growing agitation, "and I thought I'd teach him a lesson for getting that old witch of a magistrate to give him bail. "I'm here to visit your mother," I told him, seeing him and the matron come out of her office all buddy-buddy. "She asked to see me," I said, pushing my way past the nurse, but Jonathon, the supercilious little snot, stuck his nose in the air and put on a poofy voice." Bliss paused, furnishing himself with a passably supercilious impersonation. 'I'm terribly sorry, Inspector,' he said, 'but I'm afraid you've wasted your time. I fear my mother has changed her mind.' 'I fear you've changed her mind for her, sunshine,' I said, and told him straight, to get out of my way, that I had every intention of speaking to her myself."

"What happened?" asked Samantha snuggling up to him encouragingly.

"The bloody matron ordered me out," he said, clearly chagrined. "She rustled her apron at me like it was concealing some sort of secret weapon and waded in to protect the old lady. 'Mrs. Dauntsey has given strict instructions she's not to be disturbed again, I'm afraid.'

"'Well, I'm afraid that her wishes are no longer material,' I said. 'Either I see her now or I shall be back in an hour with an arrest warrant.' Jonathon laughed in my face. 'On what grounds, Inspector?' he asked. 'You haven't got a shred of evidence against my mother and you know it.' He was right of course – unless she comes clean we haven't a hope in hell of proving it. Anyway, I thought a bit of bluff wouldn't go amiss."

"We may have considerably more evidence than you realise, Mr. Dauntsey," he had said, before trying unsuccessfully to menace the matron with hints of prosecution for hindering the investigation of a serious crime. But Jonathon quickly stepped in to defend the matron, insisting she was merely protecting his mother's right to privacy.

"'Now, if you've quite finished ...' Jonathon said, waving me away like an annoying kid," continued Bliss as Samantha lay on an elbow studying his moonlit face. "But I wasn't leaving that easily. I told him I wanted to know how he came to be in possession of the lead soldier from his father's collection."

"But didn't you say the Major couldn't have been Jonathon's father?" queried Samantha. "I thought Daphne had worked that out from the birth certificate."

"She did," he replied, thinking – clever of you to remember. "And I was tempted to pass the information onto him, but I thought he already had enough on his plate. In any case, the man's no idiot. I assume he's worked that out for himself and has kept quiet for his mother's sake. I get the impression he'd do just about anything for her."

"Touching," said Samantha, laying back and squinting at the moon. "But what did he say about the flattened toy?"

"Not a toy," Bliss retorted, mimicking the clipped military accent of the dealer, "It's a fine miniature replica, Miss ... Anyway, Jonathon was vague ..." Then he paused in thought. "It's just struck me – Jonathon's good at vague – he does vague very professionally. In fact that's a very good description of him: white male, 5' 10", and in all other respects – vague. He's speaks vaguely – rambles on about inconsequential things that only he understands, and he's wandered idly through life living off his mother and dead father – step-father I suppose more accurately. He never seems to have achieved anything from what I can tell. In fact, up to now he's gone through fifty odd years without a scratch – then he cold-bloodedly murders someone."

"I guess he's not so vague now," chipped in Samantha.

"You're right. Anyway, not wanting to make him too happy, I told him that if he hadn't smashed up the toy ... replica ... whatever, the set his mother is now sitting on would be worth a cool twenty-five thousand dollars."

"How bloody ironic," Jonathon had laughed uproariously. "Do you read Shakespeare, Inspector – *Julius Caesar*?"

"I have ... some ... a little."

"No matter – even you would know Mark Anthony's speech – 'Friends, Romans, countrymen,' etcetera."

Bliss nodded, thinking – I'm going to enjoy bringing you down to earth one of these days, as Jonathon threw an imaginary mantel over his shoulder and posed dramatically. "'I came to bury Caesar, not to praise him,'" he began. "'The evil that men do lives after them, The good is oft interred with their bones.'"

Then he laughed again.

"So what evil did your father do?" asked Bliss, straight-faced.

"Oh, that's very astute of you, Inspector – very astute indeed. I must say I'm really rather impressed with your comprehension."

"I'm flattered, but I'd still like to know the nature of the evil."

"But what makes you think there was evil?"

"Everything else in your little speech seems to fit – you certainly put on a convincing show of burying your father, and you've just discovered he took something good, and valuable, to his grave with him. That only leaves the evil."

Jonathon looked into the distance and spoke vaguely. "Yes. I suppose it does really."

"I never did get to see Doreen," Bliss said, concluding his account to Samantha. "The matron dug in her heels and refused point blank to let me past the front hallway."

"So what are you going to do?"

"Unfortunately, Jonathon's right. I've got no evidence – not enough to get a warrant anyway. Legally, of course, I could just force my way in and drag her out on suspicion, but can you imagine what the press would do with that? 'Police today sledge hammered their way into an old people's home to arrest an octogenarian on her death bed,' he chuckled, and Samantha giggled uncontrollably as he added, "'Several of the pensioners put up a valiant fight – hurling bed-pans and dentures ...'"

"Stop, Dave," she cried through the laughter, "I'm going to wet myself in a minute."

"'Incontinent grannies manned the barricades ..'" he continued.

"I'm not a granny," she protested, thumping him playfully. "By the way, talking of grannies, how was Daphne this morning – was she still jealous of me?"

Bliss chortled, "Did you catch her face when she saw you standing at the door with me last night?"

"She looked at me as if her cat had dragged me out of the sewer."

"It was my fault really," he laughed. "I got wind of the problem when I phoned to ask if I could bring a friend to dinner. She was a bit huffy, 'Well, it's your beef, Chief Inspector,' she said, but when I said my friend was called Sam she changed her tune."

"On no," Samantha laughed. "She probably thought you were lining her up with a blind date – then I showed up."

"Poor Daphne, but I didn't do it on purpose – it only occurred to me afterwards. Anyway, it serves her right after what she did with that goat."

"Dave!" she cried. "That's sounds positively pornographic."

"Hardly," he said, then amused her with the saga of the goat; what it had cost and the trouble it had caused. And they ended up laughing together.

"You're beginning to sound more cheerful," she said as the laughing died down. "But you still haven't told me the real reason you called this morning. You had something serious weighing on your mind – I could feel it and I was miles away."

"I've calmed down since then."

"Sit up," she ordered, then ran her hands over his shoulders and round his neck. "I thought so – tighter than a Scotsman's wallet. If you've calmed down, you certainly forgot to tell your muscles. Come on, open up, tell me what's bothering you or I'm going home."

"Somebody left a nasty message on my computer," he admitted finally.

She would have laughed at the stupidity of it had she not caught the seriousness in his tone. "I guess it must have been pretty bad," she said, hoping to draw him, but when he didn't respond she tried a different approach. "There's no way it could've been a joke is there?"

"No, it was no joke," he shot back adamantly, thinking – there's more, lots more, but where to start, what to tell – the blue Volvo, the strange man digging for information at the Mitre perhaps. And what about the man who had run from them in the car park? What do I say about him? That I let you wade into a river in pursuit of a murderer. And what about the explosion in the tea shop – wait a minute he said to himself, interrupting his thoughts, surely that was an accident: Bit of a coincidence though wasn't it? You're doing it again, he warned himself, recalling what the force psychiatrist had said: "Possibly suffering from delusional paranoia." He hadn't forgotten, but neither had he forgotten that the chief superintendent himself had ripped up the report after the bomb had blasted a hole through his front door. "*Trick-cyclists*," the senior officer had scoffed. "They couldn't cure a bad case of verbal diarrhoea."

"A swim would do you good – wash away some

of that tension," said Samantha responding to his apparent distress.

"Is it that obvious?"

"If you don't start to loosen up soon, you'll snap something," she said, getting up and holding out a helping hand. "Come on, you'll enjoy a moonlight dip."

He hung back. "Much as I'd like to, I can't. I haven't any trunks."

"It's dark, Dave," she smiled. "There's no-one for miles and I promise faithfully not to peep."

"I haven't even got a towel."

"You can share mine."

Did she say share? he thought, quickly agreeing. "But what about you?"

"I was in the Girl Guides," she replied, turning her back, scrunching her flowing hair into a swimming cap that appeared from nowhere, and stripping off to reveal a slinky black costume that took on a silky sheen in the bright moonlight.

Bliss stood rock still, stunned almost to tears by the beauty of her body, entranced by her strong, almost masculine shoulders, her smoothly curvaceous waist and her firm boyish bottom. Then she turned and the swell of her full breasts took his breath away.

"Ready?" she asked, and he fought off the rest of his clothes in an instant. "Stay close," she added, taking his hand, her eyes fixed firmly ahead on the dark horizon. "And stop staring – I'm sure you've seen a swimsuit before."

He hesitated apprehensively at the water's edge and Samantha egged him on with a tug, "C'mon, it's quite warm."

But it wasn't the water holding him back – the nightmarish fleet of death ships still floated in the back of his mind and he half expected to see them, and their grisly immortal cargoes, sailing in from the shadowy distance. But the horizon was clear, the sea had stilled and the ghosts of the dead servicemen had returned to their watery graves for another year. It was D-day plus 3, in the timelessness of the hereafter, and the grim reaper had moved on to gather lost souls from the beaches and fields of Normandy.

"D-Day plus 3," Bliss mused to himself, his thoughts miles and years away – on the other side of the Channel with a pretty young Englishwoman, brazening her way across no-man's land on a liberated bicycle, to deliver a baby into the reaper's hands.

"Dave ..." called Samantha with alarm, breaking him out of his catalepsy. "You are in a bad way, aren't you?"

"Sorry," he said, clearing his mind and walking forward until the coldness of the water squeezed the air out of his lungs. Samantha sensed the contraction in his hand. "Just relax, Dave – breathe normally, you'll get used to it in a moment."

"Are you sure?" he squeaked, wondering if his testicles would ever recover.

Once fully in the water, the anonymity of darkness and the reassurance of her firm grasp dissolved his inhibitions and he bared his soul. It only took a few minutes: Maggie Thatcher's botched bank job; Mandy and her unborn baby; the killer's threats in court; the letters, phone calls and bomb; the blue Volvo; the funny little man delving through the hotel register and the final, spine-tingling message on the computer.

She said little, listened well, hummed knowingly at appropriate intervals, and clearly believed every word. "Oh, Dave ... you should've told me before," she said without censure, then queried, "Do you think that man we chased last night was him as well?"

"I thought so at first, that's why I told you to stay in the car – not that you listened. Afterwards I realised he was probably just a local car thief sussing out the car park for a worthy motor."

He questioned himself later, asking why he had confided in someone who may have mocked his apparent timidity or blabbed to his colleagues. And yet, instinctively, he'd known she would do neither. Anyway, he rationalised, had he not cornered himself by his actions. Wouldn't it be somewhat disingenuous to swim stark naked with someone late at night on an isolated beach and later claim that you wouldn't have trusted them to share a Mars bar let alone a personal secret?

As they stepped from the water Bliss hesitated and turned to give her an appreciative kiss, but she dodged his advance and ran up the beach to grab a towel.

"Lay down," she said, spreading the towel over the blanket.

"Well ... "

"Stop arguing, Dave, you're in need of serious help."

He lay, face down, and felt himself sinking into the soft blanket as he listened to the hypnotic rhythm of wavelets fizzling into the sand. Then she laid her sea-softened fingers on his shoulders and firmly massaged his rigid muscles until the tension dissolved and her fingers felt like warm tendrils playing deep inside him.

"That's wonderful," he sighed, as her hands inched down his spine, one vertebrae at a time, working their way into the small of his back. And his pulse raced with pleasure as she pushed even lower.

"Turn over," she whispered when she reached his feet.

"Do I have to?"

"Don't worry – I won't bite."

"That isn't what I was worried about exactly."

"Oh – I see ... Well, I won't look. Honestly."

He turned, eyes closed and felt her fingers dancing on his chest, then slipping sensuously over his stomach and down his thighs. This isn't happening, he cautioned himself. You'll wake in a minute and discover the psychiatrist was right – it's all a delusion.

The hands stopped moments before his mind would have burst in ecstasy and he felt her hair brushing his face as she leant over him, her fingers tracing his eyebrows – then the warmth of her lips on his mouth, and the tip of her tongue running along the length of his teeth.

"Oh Samantha," he breathed, and tried to raise his arms to embrace her, but found them pinioned to the sand by a pair of strong hands. Then she nuzzled her wet lips to his ear, "That's better, Dave – you can get dressed now."

With his arms freed he reached out to clasp her but she twisted away and sat looking out over the sea. "Don't be impatient, Dave," she said over her shoulder. "You haven't even bought me dinner yet."

"You're gorgeous, Samantha. I'd really like to make love with you."

"But you already have," she replied, leaving him questioning his memory.

"Did I miss something?"

"Close your eyes again," she commanded, squirming back across the sand to gently stroke his forehead, and he felt the warmth of her breath on his face as her soft sing-song voice played in his ears. "Love is what happens in here, Dave – in your mind," she whispered. "Surely you saw me slide out of my bathing suit: you must've seen my boobs when they slipped free – wasn't that your tongue ...?"

"*Mmmm* – You were very good, Dave," she continued after a pause, her deep breathing soothing him hypnotically. "And wasn't that your hand between my thighs," she went on, sighing breathlessly in his ear. "And your finger playing a tune on my violin ... I could feel it ... gentle but firm; soft yet hard ... And couldn't you feel yourself inside me – throbbing and pulsing ... It was wonderful, Dave ... Oh, so big; so strong; so ... *Mmmm* ... Didn't you hear the angels singing and the trumpets sounding?" He smiled at the sensual imagery and she kissed him lusciously. "You see, we did make love," she breathed softly into his mouth. "And the nicest thing is we could do it all over again the next time."

Opening his eyes, half afraid she was an illusion, he found himself staring straight into hers. "Do you mean that – a next time?" he asked. "Do you mean – for real?"

"I don't think you've been listening," she said, looking him closely in the eye and gently tapping his temple. "What's real is what's in here, Dave – what you believe – what your mind tells you is the truth."

"But what about you?"

"It was good for me too," she laughed.

"Are you teasing me, Ms. Holingsworth?"

"Maybe," she laughed. "Or maybe you're teasing yourself."

"How did you do that?" he asked as they dressed. "It felt as though your fingers were right inside me."

"I trained professionally," she explained, while using the blanket as a change tent. "I've even got a certificate somewhere."

"So – why are you in the police force?"

"I did six months as a massage therapist," she replied as if it had been a prison sentence, asking rhetorically. "How many lives do you think I saved? How many times did I go home at the end of the day thinking I'd made my little corner a safer, nicer place?"

"Yes, but you didn't have to pick dead bodies off the beach – or stand at someone's kitchen table watching them die a little as you tell them their Mum, Dad or little kid is lying on a slab at the morgue."

"Nobody said the police was perfect, Dave. I just get more satisfaction than I did pummelling flabby backsides and sweaty armpits. Most of the time I was up to my elbows in some dirty-minded fat geezer with bigger tits than mine, and I knew exactly what was going through his mind – not that he stood the remotest chance."

"Well, I know what was going through my mind," Bliss said, wondering if he qualified as dirty-minded.

She turned and kissed him tenderly. "Yeah – but you're not fat and greasy."

"So what's happening with the murder case now?" asked Samantha as she drove him back to his car.

"Patterson's pissing me about," he complained, then revealed what had happened the previous afternoon when he'd asked if results on the duvet and syringe had come back from the laboratory.

"I'll chase them up, Guv," Patterson had said, making to pick up the phone.

"No – I'll chase them up, Pat," said Bliss, adding, "They might get a move on with an inspector's boot up their ass. Which lab?"

The left half of Patterson's face twitched violently as he leafed through a stack of papers mumbling, "I'll have to look it up."

"Look up what? Which lab did you send them to? – I can get the number."

Putting his hand to his face he stilled the twitch and said, "Sorry, Guv. The courier must've forgot to take them."

"What?" exploded Bliss. "You've been hanging on to that syringe for a week – this is a murder enquiry, Pat, not kids nicking sweets from Woolie's."

"Don't blame me, Guv."

"O.K. Where's the paperwork?"

"Paperwork?" echoed Patterson.

"Sergeant – stop wasting my time. If the exhibits were packaged for transportation to the lab yesterday the paperwork would be ready to go with them, now where are the copies?"

Patterson needlessly hunted through his desk, muttering about the unreliability of couriers and the untrustworthiness of staff in general. "They seem to have disappeared," he said finally, adding nervously, "Someone must've thrown them out."

Bliss got the message. "Right, Sergeant – you will personally drive those samples to the lab now. You will grovel and beg and, if necessary, you will kiss the scheduler's backside and lick his boots ..."

"The scheduler's a she, Sir."

"Well it could be your lucky day then, Sergeant, but whatever you do, don't come back here without results."

"Right, Sir."

"And the next time the dog eats your homework – bring me the dog. Do I make myself clear?"

"Yes, Guv."

"I'm not surprised," said Samantha. "He pretty much ran that office before you arrived. Your predecessor spent more time knocking back scotch than knocking off villains, and Patterson wore his shoes for years – not that he kept them very clean, if you get my meaning."

"I think I'm beginning to."

"So. What are you planning to do about the bloke who's trying to kill you?"

"I don't know anymore. So far everything I've tried would qualify for the *Guinness Book of Cock-ups*. It started with the letters – when the first ones arrived I thought I'd just ignore him and he'd get fed up."

"But he didn't"

"He sent me the bomb instead," agreed Bliss with a shake of his head, adding. "Plan B was to hide ... just a week or so in a safe house until he was caught – but he wasn't. Plan F ..."

"Hold on," she said. "What happened to C, D and E?"

"Impractical," he said, dismissing them without consideration. "Anyway, F was to come here or some other equally out of the way place and hope he didn't find out."

"And he did?"

"Within days."

"So what's your plan now?" she asked, pulling away and looking to him for an answer.

"I'm not going to run ..." he started, then stopped, realising it sounded foolish, and admitted that he no longer had a plan.

"You've got to have a plan, Dave," she told him. "Life just sort of wanders aimlessly past if you don't have a plan."

"I used to have a plan but I somehow got off the path and I've been trying to find my way back ever since."

"Stop!" she cried. "I've heard enough."

"What?"

"You have to stop trying to find your way back. There must have been a reason why you were derailed. All you can do now is to make a new plan, and start again. You'll never find your way back onto the old

path, and if you do you won't be satisfied with what you
find at the end of it."

"Go back and start all over again at my time of life."

"Exciting, isn't it?"

He looked deeply into her eyes. "I think it would be –
with you."

"Yeah ... well don't get your hopes up – I've been
on my own a long time, and I'm quite happy not having to skivvy for man. Anyway, I've had more than my
share of men using me as a dumping ground for their
excess baggage."

Chapter Fourteen

Their goodnight kiss had been full of promise, and Bliss floated back to Westchester at midnight with Pavarotti pumping out Puccini on the stereo and God at the wheel. The High Street was as busy as a Christmas Saturday on his arrival and, in his exhuberation, he couldn't grasp the possibility that the commotion wasn't anything other than a summer festival. Abandoning his car at one end of the street, he flowed with the throng toward the Mitre, where flashing lights and costumed players seemed to be entertaining a crowd, then an electrified voice smashed him in the solar plexus: "I bet it was a bomb."

"What – what was that? What did you say?" he turned on the young man demandingly.

"I don't know mate, somebody said it was a bomb in the hotel – that's all I know."

Craning over the heads of the crowd he looked ahead, recognised the flashing lights and variously hued blue costumes and went cold: police, fire and ambulance. This was the Mitre – there was no mistake this time – this wasn't an explosion in a tea shop down the road. He stopped dead and several of the scurrying rubber-neckers crashed into him, forcing him to shelter in a shop doorway. This was not part of the plan – not his plan. What had the computer screen said? he asked himself, wringing his hands in consternation. "Bang – your time is up."

What now? he mused, but knew what he wanted to do: run back to Samantha and sink into the comfort of her arms; sink into her body.

White, the *Westchester Gazette*'s reporter, caught his attention; flashing away at the crowd with a camera. He'll just love this – "London cop bombed out for the second time." Probably sell copy to *Associated Press* or one of the nationals. It's a wonder none of the TV newshounds are here, he thought, then scouted around and spotted a microphone wielding bimbo with big hair and teeth chasing reactions from bystanders.

Keeping his head down, and wrapping his coat protectively around him, he hustled through the crowd and sidled up to the fire chief, introducing himself in a barely controlled voice. "D.I. Bliss – we met the other morning at the tea shop blast. What's happened?"

The fireman gave a nod of recognition. "Fire in the car park at the back."

The words "Oh Shit – a car bomb, the worst" went through his mind and married up with images of devastation from Tel Aviv and Armagh. Wait a minute, he questioned himself, fighting aside the carnage of dismembered bodies. Did he say fire? "Did you say fire or explosion?"

"Fire – just a fire, mind it was pretty fierce."

He paused for a breath and relaxed a notch, "That's the trouble with cars – gas tank goes up like a rocket."

"No – it wasn't a car."

"I thought someone said it was a car ..." he queried, his mind disorientated. He'd got it caught in a Möbius loop and couldn't get out. Every explosion was a bomb, every bomb had the signature of Mandy's murderer, and every one was directed at him whichever way he twisted or turned.

"No – it's not a car," repeated the fire chief. "It was an animal."

"What animal?"

"A goat, we think, a stuffed one by the looks of it – horsehair probably – tinder dry, although it's badly incinerated. Someone set fire to it right in the middle of the car park – probably a joke that misfired."

"A joke," screamed Bliss. "A joke – That was no joke," and he raced back to his car and headed for the police station.

Daphne was in early Tuesday morning and made a bee-line for Bliss's office. "I was so sorry to hear about the old goat," she said, drifting in and sitting down without as much as a tap.

Bliss cocked his head, intrigued, "How did you hear?"

"Mavis Longbottom, you know, the cook at the Mitre, she called me late last night. She's the treasurer of the Women's Institute and says you're not to worry about the fifty pounds."

"That's a relief."

"Yes – she says you can just pay half, twenty-five pounds, because you didn't have a lot of enjoyment out of the poor old creature."

Shall I throttle her or kiss her? Bliss wondered, then dug into his wallet and extracted a ten pound note. "Tell Mavis if she wants more she'll have to sue," he said, handing it over.

"Have you any ideas who might have done it?"

"One or two," he mumbled, burying his head in the daily incident log, hinting he'd rather forget.

Daphne missed the cue. "My guess is somebody doesn't like you ... or maybe they don't like goats."

"Actually, I wanted to speak to you," he said, rising to shut the door, feeling the goat was not only passé but that it had already received far more attention than it deserved. He had been right about the daily newspapers. "It's a flamin' goat," declared the caption under the picture on the front page of the *Sun,* although the details were sketchy – little beyond the fact that a spokesperson for Westchester fire brigade assumed it to be a prank.

A grinning uniformed inspector was passing as he reached the doorway. "Are you alright, Dave?" he called.

"Fine, thanks."

"Oh that's good," he sniggered. "Only I understood someone had got your goat," and went off down the corridor in stitches.

"Very droll," Bliss shouted after him and slammed the door.

"Have you thought of visiting Doreen Dauntsey?" he asked, softening his face and turning back to Daphne.

"Yes, I have, to tell you the truth – I feel I should."

"I was hoping you'd say that, only a friend of mine would like to go with you. Samantha – you remember her from the other night." Pausing, he put on a smile and offered flattery as an incentive. "By the way, she's still talking about that wonderful dinner. She thinks you're marvellous."

The flattery failed, Daphne's face fell. "You've seen her again then, have you?"

The temptation to tell her to mind her own damn business wasn't easily overcome, but he straightened his face understandingly. "Well, she is just about my age, Daphne."

It worked. "Yes – of course she is, how silly of me, but why does she want to visit Doreen?"

Because Samantha had come up with the plan, he would have told her had he felt either the wisdom or necessity of explaining, but as he didn't, he merely pushed on as if she had agreed. "It might be best if you didn't say she was a policewoman. Maybe you could say she was your companion."

Daphne bristled. "Chief Inspector. Do I look like a pathetic old witch who has to pay some withered flunky to talk to me? Haven't you ever heard them? 'Oh – this is my companion,' they say, all lah-di-dah, and you know jolly well it's only a tarted up cleaning lady putting on airs and graces. No, I shall say she's my niece, visiting from some unheard place, and if anybody starts asking awkward questions, I'll give them the illegitimate-royal routine."

"The what?"

"You lean in really close and say, 'She's actually Prince Phillip's bastard daughter. I was his chambermaid you know, but for God's sake don't let on.' It works wonders."

"That's very good," laughed Bliss. "You sound as if you've done this before."

Daphne fidgeted uncomfortably and coloured up, and Bliss gave her a critical stare as he tried to figure out what she was thinking. "You *have* done this before, haven't you?" he said, astounded, reading her mind.

The mental vacillation between admission and denial tortured her face for several long seconds before she finally plunged in. "Well, just how do you think I got the Order of the British Empire, Chief Inspector?"

"I assumed it was because of the way you crossed the line in France and wiped out the Germans ..." he began, but she was shaking her head from the start. "You don't get an O.B.E for that. That was wartime service." Then she clammed up, her face suggesting her mind was somewhere else.

"Well come on, Daphne, you can't leave me in suspense like this."

"I think I've said enough," she mumbled, getting up and gathering her cleaning paraphernalia. "When do you want me to take your lady friend to see Doreen?" she added acerbically.

"No. Wait a minute," he said, grabbing her aerosol of furniture polish and forcing a stand-off. "I want to know."

She capitulated, slumped back into the chair and started with Hugo, in Paris, near the end of the war.

"Hugo?" he queried vacantly, his mind tied up with dead goats and skeletal Majors.

"Hugo, the French artist," she reminded him, taking him back to their first evening together: pork chops and treacle pudding with custard; the portrait of a beautiful young woman; the framed O.B.E.; the stuffed goat in her hallway – forget the damn goat, he said to himself as he tried to recollect the picture and the painter. What had she said about him? he asked himself. "I loved Hugo, but he loved his painting." I wonder what she meant?

"Yes, I remember Hugo," he said in an encouraging tone.

"I was with him for two years," she began, pain, pleasure, longing and regret all coalescing into a mien that, if anything, came down on the side of happiness. But then she froze, focusing somewhere into the distance, and her face took a roller coaster ride through her emotions as she thought about what to tell. How she had wandered penniless, lonely and confused into a Parisian bar and fainted from hunger. How she'd woken to the stench of smoke and garlic in Hugo's studio as he sat, naked to the waist, quietly studying her face while he sketched.

"*Cigarette?*" he had said, offering one of the foul Galloises as she stirred, but she needed food and told him so.

He cut her a hunk of greasy dried sausage and broke a baguette in two, then, with hardly a word, she offered herself in exchange. What did it matter? The Frenchwoman's baby was dead; the German soldiers she had rained shells upon were all dead; millions more on both sides were dying or dead. Who would know, or care, if two strangers found a few moments relief from the abomination of everyday existence in each other's bodies.

"In a way it was Rupert Dauntsey's fault," she went on, catching Bliss completely off balance.

"Rupert Dauntsey – the Major?" he asked incredulously.

Her eyes went down to the floor as if in search of a memory, but when she looked up they were swelling with tears and her voice was barely audible as she bit back the sobs. "I heard on the grapevine that a Major from Westchester was in a French hospital ..." She paused, snivelling loudly into a white handkerchief pulled from her sleeve. "I didn't know it was Rupert at first, but I desperately needed something to cling on to, anything to wake me from the nightmare and return me to reality ... and I thought a friendly face from home ..." Her voice failed as the tears welled up and overcame her.

"It's alright, Daphne," said Bliss rushing to comfort her, but it wasn't alright. The horrific memories had not faded with time, nor had they become any easier to bear, and she bit her knuckles furiously as the vivid scenes forged their way to the surface: an American troop truck ... six G.I.s on 24 hours R&R, and a dozen or so others going on eternal leave.

"Don't look at the stiffs, Miss," warned the driver as he stopped to pick her up at the roadside on the out-skirts of a bombed town. Clambering in beside him she ignored the warning and turned instinctively, then found herself wondering whether the "stiffs" were the dozen or so corpses on the floor, or the six haggard-faced sol-diers staring into the clear blue sky. Following their gaze she found a screeching skylark wheeling above a moon-scaped cornfield and envied it its freedom, but looking back at the men, she realised they had not seen the bird – they were just staring.

For more than an hour decimated villages rumbled by, the ruins still quaking from the distant thunder of canon fire, and stoic-faced Normans turned their backs, burying their dead or staring in disbelief at their wrecked homes.

"Good luck, Miss," the driver shouted as she dropped down from the cab outside the hospice. "I hope your friend will be O.K."

"Thanks," she yelled, giving a friendly wave to the G.I.s as the truck roared away, but none responded – each too busy contemplating the fact that ten years of their life's movie had ripped through the projector in the past ten days; wondering how much film was left on the spool.

"I couldn't see Rupert's face at all," Daphne mum-bled through the tears. "Just bandages with a couple of holes to breathe through, and another with a feeding tube in what was left of his mouth."

"This is Major Dauntsey," the nurse had said, more by way of identification than introduction and Daphne's heart had sunk.

"He couldn't see me and couldn't talk," she contin-ued, omitting to mention that the crushing disappoint-ment had forced her to her knees. "He didn't even have a hand that I could squeeze to comfort him." Her one hope of finding someone or something to stabilise her thoughts had been dashed. For the two days it had taken to reach him she had pushed the pain of dead babies and massacred soldiers to the back of her mind, while searching for images of streets, pubs, shops and people they would have in common, fully expecting that, within seconds, they would find themselves chatting as amiably as long forgotten schoolfriends; perhaps sealing their bond with a kiss, maybe something more if he was capable – after all, it wasn't as if he were a complete stranger. And it wasn't as though Doreen was the sort who'd be too concerned, even if she found out – not that she would.

"I'm ashamed to admit this, but I screamed and ran," she confessed to Bliss, adding, "If something that horrible could happen to the shy little boy who lived up the road ..." The words failed as she sobbed in the handkerchief, then she tried again. "I think it was because I had known him. All the others, even the baby, were strangers."

"But you said that whatever happened to you had been Rupert Dauntsey's fault," Bliss reminded her. "What did you mean."

"I don't expect you to believe this," she started, looking him carefully in the eye, "but it was as if I'd somehow got on the wrong planet and didn't know how to get back to Earth. I think in some silly way I was expecting Rupert to lead me. You see, I'd done my job – killed all the people I was supposed to kill. Now what? They never told us at the training school and we never asked. I suppose we all knew, deep down, that we wouldn't survive, so it was tempting fate to even consider what to do afterwards. But, because I survived, I was lost – not physically. I was lost because my mind had already accepted the certainty of death and had made no plans for the future."

Samantha's words still buzzed in his mind from the previous night and took on a greater relevance. "You've got to have a plan, Dave," she had said and he glanced at the wall clock: 7.35 am. Superintendent Donaldson would be in at 8.00 with his sights on a chocolate digestive.

"You were telling me about Hugo," he pressed Daphne, knowing that by 8.05 Donaldson would be informed about the goat, if someone hadn't already snitched, and by 8.10 he'd feed an empty biscuit packet in the shredder and call the chief. By 8.15 the phone on Bliss's desk would ring and his career would be over. London's Grand Metropolitan Police Force wouldn't take him back and the Chief Constable of Hampshire would be happy to see him go. "We want it to be your decision, Dave," someone would tell him with a compassionate hand on his shoulder, thereby avoiding any suggestion he was being pressurised. "Of course – you *could* always go back to the safe house ... " they'd say, somehow leaving the sentence hanging, unfinished. Or I could do myself in and save everybody the trouble, he smiled to himself sardonically.

"I'm afraid Hugo used me rather," Daphne said finally, and, from her tone, expected to end it there. But Bliss was coercive, if not downright insistent. Holding her spray-can hostage he said, "Come on, Daphne, you may as well tell me. It can't be any worse."

Her face clouded in shame. It was worse, much worse.

"I have to go," she said, panic forcing her to her feet.

"I have to go," she repeated, her eyes searching frantically for a way out, and she headed for the door but was drawn back to the canister of polish. Reaching with a shaky hand she muttered "I have to go" again, and began pacing around the room, eyes everywhere, mumbling, "I have to go ... I have to go ... I have to go," like a malfunctioning robot.

"Calm down," said Bliss, and she froze in the middle of the room, unable to catch her breath.

"Daphne," he called, going to her aid, but she fended him off and began panting hysterically, her nerves going haywire, jangling her limbs and twitching her face. He grabbed her by the shoulders but she wrenched free and paced some more.

"Stop it," she told herself. "Stop it. Stop it. Stop it. Stop it. Stop it."

Then she paused again, gasping deep breaths, threatening to hyperventilate as she tried to stop the pictures in her mind.

Bliss, alarmed, picked up the phone. "Control room – call a Doctor ..." But she slammed her hand on the cradle. "No, No. I'm alright, Chief Inspector. I'll be alright."

"Sit down then," he said, easing her into a chair and giving her a glass of water.

The phone rang – the control room sergeant, confused, calling back.

"No," explained Bliss, "Miss Lovelace has had a bit of a turn in my office but I think she's alright now. I'll let you know."

"Thank you," she said and slumped back with her eyes closed, thinking – what possible difference does it make now. So you posed naked for Hugo; posed for his friends; more than posed; more than one friend. Hadn't you been flattered – so many beautiful French girls to choose from, yet they preferred *la petite tarte Anglaise.*

She didn't explain in detail, wouldn't have known how to express herself. "I let men take advantage of me," she said, simply, her head bowed in her hands. "It seemed to make them happy." Then she paused, wondering whether to elaborate; if to justify; how to justify. Yet she had justified it at the time – forcing herself to believe that she did it for food; for shelter; for love. And wasn't it love? Didn't Hugo love her? Wasn't it always Hugo who had comforted her battered body to sleep at the end of the night – on a couch reeking of hard sex and cheap cigarettes, in his studio surrounded by paintings that never showed the bruises.

"I used to sit on a canvas stool in a little square in Montmartre while Hugo painted me," she went on, skipping the humiliation and passion, recalling the brightly coloured umbrellas and the oily smell of paint. "And one day an instructor who'd taught me unarmed combat in England wandered by when Hugo was in the bar. He stopped, flabbergasted. 'You're dead,' he said, and I really wanted to believe him. It would have made things so much easier for me. I even pretended he was mistaken, told him where to go – in French, but he was insistent, and I came to my senses and realised what I was doing to myself – what Hugo and his friends were doing to me."

A dried fleck of correcting fluid on Bliss's desk caught her attention and she concentrated furiously for several seconds, scratching at it with a nail.

Is that it? wondered Bliss, and was readying to ask another question when she started again – softly, almost wistfully. "Hugo came back and I hit him, very hard. Then I grabbed a knife and ripped up all his canvasses – all the nudes; smashed him over the head with one – right in the middle of Montmartre." She paused to look out of the window, then laughed, wryly. "I remember somebody took a photo – Hugo lying on wet cobblestones with his head stuck through a painting of me in the nude ... I've often thought it may have won an award – always imagined it hanging in some pretentious photo gallery labelled 'Man's subjugation by female form,' or something equally hideous."

The phone startled Bliss; the clock had shot forward to 7.55 without warning and he reached for the receiver with trepidation. Thanks to Samantha he now had a plan. But it was a plan that would be stymied if Donaldson got to him first. "What happened next?" he asked Daphne, withdrawing his hand and letting the phone ring.

With a handful of belongings, and the one small portrait that Bliss had found on her sideboard, she had taken off with the instructor, Michael Kent, and headed east, deeper into mainland Europe.

"I didn't come home," she answered, leaving Bliss to question, "Why not?"

She found another fleck to pick at.

"Did you let your parents know?" he asked, sensing her reluctance to continue.

She looked up. "Let them know what? That I was a cold blooded killer; that I let men do things to me that nice girls never did?"

"Come on," he said, not knowing what she was talking about. "It can't have been that bad."

"I sometimes thought I might've coped better as a prostitute," she answered, leaving him slack mouthed. "At least I could have pretended it was just a job."

"I don't understand – what were you doing? Why were you doing it?"

"Where did you stay last night?" she asked, looking up, clear faced, as if she'd just walked in and had no notion of the turmoil in the air.

"At a friend's," he said succinctly. Samantha's, he meant.

Samantha's couch had been comfortable and welcoming. Which was more than could have been said for Samantha when he arrived on her doorstep, a little after 1 am, following a frantic phone call.

"If this is some misguided plot to get into my bed you're wasting your bloody time," she had said, flinging open her door, defensively tugging a thick towelling dressing gown around her while preening her hair with the other hand.

"Samantha!" he cried, stung by her mistrust. "Would I make something like that up?"

Her face broke into a grin. "Did he really cremate your goat?"

"It's not funny!"

"No, I suppose not." She straightened her face. "Well, you'd better come in then."

"I still don't get it," said Bliss to Daphne. "Your parents must have been worried sick. They must have thought you'd been killed." But, as he spoke, the faces of dead soldiers lining ship's rails winged back into his thoughts and he stopped, stunned by his perception – she'd been killed the moment she took off to parachute into France.

Daphne was crying again. "Self respect is like virginity," she choked through the tears. "Once it's gone you have to pretend for the rest of your life."

"You can get your self-respect back in time," he protested, recalling how he'd felt after Mandy's death.

"Well, I never got my virginity back," she complained ruefully. "Anyway, you've no idea what it's like."

I have, he thought, thinking of pregnant Mandy, but when he looked deep into Daphne's bloodshot eyes he realised there wasn't the slightest comparison between his hurt and hers. She'd had the killer inside her every day for more than fifty years, whereas Mandy's killer had spent 18 years out of sight and out of mind in a high-security government hotel.

The phone rang again and Bliss was out of his chair and headed for the door as if his backside had caught fire. 8.10 am and Donaldson was stomping around his office to the tune of wildly gyrating executive toys.

"The Mitre at ten this morning," Bliss said to Daphne on his way past, knowing she would understand. "And please, please, don't tell anyone."

"Matron! Matron!" Nurse Dryden cried a little after 10 am, rushing up the corridor of the nursing home, her bobbling breasts threatening to topple her. But the matron already had her hands full. Bliss was at the front door causing a disturbance, according to script: furiously waving an unsigned search warrant; demanding to see Mrs. Dauntsey immediately; claiming she was being kept prisoner; threatening to arrest anyone who stood in his way. Jonathon was still there and stood his ground challengingly, but the matron was backing off.

"I don't know ..." she started as Nurse Dryden frantically interrupted. "Matron! Matron!"

"Not now, Nurse. You can see I'm busy."

"Well," demanded Bliss fiercely, "do I get to see her or do I have to start making arrests?"

"But Matron ..." she was tugging at her arm.

"Make up your mind," shouted Bliss.

"He's bluffing," sneered Jonathon.

"Matron ..."

"Shut up, Nurse Dryden. I can't hear myself think."

"I shall have no choice but to arrest ..."

"Ignore him," shouted Jonathon.

"But Matron ..."

"Go away, Nurse. I won't tell you again – I'm busy."

"Look, Inspector. I'm sure there's some mistake – maybe we can go into my office ..."

"But Matron ..."

She turned on the nurse, purple faced, screaming, "I thought I told you to go away."

That should do it, thought Bliss, and he had a sudden change of heart saying, "I'll be back," and disappeared through the front door with as much mystery as a conjurer's assistant.

"Daphne was magnificent," Samantha laughed to Bliss a few minutes later, as they raced Doreen's wheelchair into the Olde Curiosity Coffee Shoppe just off the High Street. "'We're just going to take my old friend for a walk,' she said to that nurse with pneumatic boobs. 'Oh you can't do that, Madam,' she said, sticking out her chest like a bloody guardsman and Daphne said, 'Piss off, you silly little nincompoop,' barged her out of the way and shoved the wheelchair through the French window shouting, 'Tally Ho! Doreen. Chocks away.'"

"I'm pleased to meet you again," said Bliss, stooping to introduce himself to Doreen once they had pulled her up to a table in the restaurant.

The twin flush of excitement and fresh air coloured Doreen's cheeks, and she spent a few seconds composing herself as Daphne, her impishness returned, nudged him and drew his attention to an austerely dressed mustachioed woman in a funereal black hat across the room at a window table. "See what I mean about lah-di-dah," she scoffed, as the woman withered the waitress with a complaint about the temperature of her coffee. "She's no more a lady than ..." she paused, realising to her horror that she was just about to say Doreen Dauntsey.

"I called you the other day," piped up Doreen feeling left out. "But you didn't come to see me."

"Sorry," he said, feeling it was hardly a good time to tell her that Jonathon had stood sentinel.

"Chief Inspector Bliss bought the Colonel's goat," Daphne explained, leaning into Doreen as if the wheelchair might have affected her hearing; speaking as if such a purchase gave Bliss an excuse for his apparent tardiness while painting him as a man of substance and credibility.

"The Colonel's goat?" whispered Bliss questioningly. "You told me it came from the butcher's."

"You bought it did you?" said Doreen, seemingly impressed.

Daphne ignored Bliss and answered to Doreen, clearly and loudly pronouncing each word. "It came from your husband's home originally, didn't it, Doreen?"

"Did it?" asked Bliss, taken aback, but he was left out of the loop as Doreen reminisced with Daphne. "Oh yeah. I know all about the goat. Wellington told me about it before he died."

"Wellington?" queried Bliss, then remembered Daphne's delight at discovering the Colonel's christian name on his sarcophagus.

"Was *that* true then?" asked Doreen, ignoring him again while apparently referring to some well known anecdote of which Bliss was not privy.

"Oh yeah," laughed Doreen with the cackle of the elderly and frail. "I'd forgotten all about it. It was something of a joke apparently. The old goat was the regimental mascot and it got loose one day as he was taking the salute." She paused for a sharp breath, then continued. "He said it bolted across the parade ground, knocked a load of guardsmen ass over tit, then stopped right in front of him and pooped." She paused to join Daphne in a laugh, adding, "Ruined the parade 'pparently – men falling all over the place, couldn't stop laughing. So when he retired they had it killed and stuffed as a going away present. He hated the damn thing and swapped it for a decent bit of sirloin at the butchers."

"I don't blame him," said Bliss, finally getting in a word, mindful that he too had received the proverbial bit of sirloin. "I hate to interrupt, but we don't have long," he continued, summonsing Samantha from the doorway where she had been standing guard against Jonathon and the matron. "Sergeant Holingsworth. Perhaps you and Miss Lovelace would like to sit at that table over there."

Daphne was clearly affronted. "Will you be alright, Doreen?"

Bliss gave her a nasty look. What did she think he was going to do? Tuesday lunchtime in the middle of a restaurant – arm up her back; smack her in the gob; thumbscrews?

"What did you want to tell me?" he asked as Samantha led Daphne reluctantly away.

"Jonathon didn't kill Major Dauntsey – don't listen to him. He's a very silly boy. He thinks he's protecting me but no good will come of it," she said, leaving Bliss intrigued to note her avoidance of the word father.

"I know that, Mrs. Dauntsey, I worked that out already. But the question now is ..." he leant close, "Who did kill him?"

Technically, he should've cautioned her. She was, after all, the prime suspect, though the evidence was shaky to say the least.

"He was shot you know," she said distantly, as if recalling some character from a play or book.

"Yes, I know, Mrs. Dauntsey. But who shot him? That's the question."

"Oh – I've no idea," she said, shaking her head as if she'd got a nasty taste. "A German, I guess, although I couldn't be sure."

Bliss's face clouded in bewilderment. "Let's start again," he said. "I think you're a bit confused." Then he looked her carefully in the eye and articulated precisely. "Your husband came back from the war badly wounded – right?"

A sudden sharpness in her eyes turned her instantaneously into both hunted and haunted. Her face drained to white so rapidly that, for a moment, he wondered if

she'd died, then her hand flew to her mouth and she
started eating away at a nail.

Realising there was a problem, he gave her a few seconds to recover before asking, "Shall I try that again?"

"No ... No ... No ... I understood you," she muttered, then changed her face, and the subject, so fast he
presumed she'd had some sort of seizure. "The doctor
told Jonathon I should go to Switzerland for treatment.
Can you believe that, Inspector?"

"Yes ... but ... " he started, then his mouth froze in
indecision as an important, though elusive, thought
gnawed into his mind.

"Wouldn't that be something – Switzerland," continued Doreen, with a faraway look.

"Yes – It would ..." he said, but wasn't listening.
What was it that she had said?

"I think I'd like a fresh cream meringue," said
Doreen, cutting into his thoughts, spying a refrigerated
display case. "With a real maraschino cherry on top.
Would you mind, Inspector? Only the food at the home
is ... well, I'm sure you know."

"Sorry," he said, giving himself a shake. "Did you
say meringue?" But his mind was still miles away. He'd
found what he was looking for and was puzzling over it.

"With a maraschino cherry," she reminded him.

"Oh yes. Of course you may," he said, signalling to
a waif in a waitresses uniform.

"Mrs. Dauntsey ..." he started questioningly, but
she held up a spidery hand, indicating that the meringue
was next on her agenda, and they sat in silence awaiting
its arrival; Bliss checking his watch, wondering what
Superintendent Donaldson was doing; wondering what
plans were being concocted to oust him; wondering how
long it would take Jonathon to track them down; wondering when the killer would strike again.

The slender young woman was back with the meringue in a few seconds and Doreen eyed her critically. "Skinny as a cheap chicken," she muttered as soon as the girl was out of earshot, then took a bite. The confectionary exploded in a sugary snowstorm, dusting the bodice of her navy blue dress and giving her a coughing fit. Daphne sprang to Doreen's side with surprising agility, towing Samantha in her wake, giving Bliss an accusatory stare. "Oh look at the mess," she moaned, and set about cleaning up her old friend.

Doreen was still coughing but Bliss couldn't contain himself any longer. "When I asked what happened to your husband," he began, "you said the Germans shot him. But how did he get home with a hole in his skull ...?"

Doreen creased in another convulsion of coughing and Daphne roughly pushed him aside. "Now look what you've done."

Backing away, he focused on the diminutive grey-haired figure, a plethora of thoughts bombarding his mind, then all the cherries clinked into place and the jackpot came out so fast he had a job to keep up: The returning Major was unrecognisable; barely able to talk; refused to see Patrick Mulverhill the reporter; was in possession of another man's dog-tags; and, finally, most decisively, had been shot by a German. Bingo!

"The man in your attic wasn't Major Rupert Dauntsey, your husband, was he?" he breathed, astounded by the clarity of his own revelation.

Doreen's head went down, her hands flew to cover her face and she gave a startled cry.

"Now see what you've done," said Daphne rebukefully, as her friend burst into floods of tears. "Are you alright, Doreen?"

Doreen was anything but alright.

Chapter Fifteen

A storm was brewing at Westchester police station. Superintendent Donaldson had pressed the panic button a little before ten in the morning. Exhausted of ideas, nerve and executive toys he called the Assistant Chief Constable with rising concern about Bliss, the death threat and the goat. Detective Sergeant Patterson, summoned by phone, strolled cockily into the superintendent's office, coffee cup in hand. "You wanted something, Guv?" he said, with enough political *savoir faire* to know that indispensability outranks rank, and flopped into a comfortable looking leather armchair.

"Yeah, Pat. There's still no sign of D.I. Bliss – you've no ideas have you?"

"Like I said on the phone, Guv. I ain't his social secretary."

No need to be like that, thought Donaldson. "Well, you'd better get the men together in the parade room at eleven for a briefing ... The Assistant Chief's coming to lead the enquiry," he added as he picked flakes of chocolate from the groin of his trousers. "Bloody biscuits," he mumbled. "Well ... what are you waiting for?"

"Thought we were supposed to be searching for Dauntsey's victim," grumbled Patterson with no attempt to move, "Not poncing around after Bliss."

"I don't give a shit about Dauntsey at the moment," Donaldson's voice rose as he stood, snowing crumbs onto the floor. "Everything is on hold until we find D.I. Bliss – do I make myself clear?"

Patterson, seeing himself as unofficial envoy for the world, pushed for more information. "What's he supposed to have done, Guv?"

"What on earth makes you ask that? The man's missing for God's sake – might be murdered for all we know."

Patterson's face contorted. "Murdered?" he echoed. "Why?"

Bliss was anything but dead. In fact, in the charged moments following his revelation about the identity of the body in Doreen's attic, he found himself widely alert to his surroundings. Previously unnoticed objects now appeared as if through a lens, and he was surprised to find the coffee shoppe walls deep in bric-a-brac: polished horse brasses, gleaming like old gold, hung on black leather straps; shiny copper kettles and silvery samovars with ivory handles filled every niche; a weird collection of papier-mâché masks adorned the wainscotting: white-faced Pierrots; red-nosed clowns; devilishly horned Satans with flaming vermilion hair; grotesque, gruesome and macabre masks; whimsical, fanciful and capricious masks. And, although every mask differed, each facial image was tortured by a pair of eye holes into which, and out of which, came only darkness, and, through which he saw a mirror of Doreen Dauntsey.

Doreen had sunk into a torpor, staring rigidly into the middle distance, trying to see both into the past and future at the same time, while mentally fighting against hideous images of the body in her attic. The intensity of her mental battle spun off brain-waves that disquieted every head in the room; drawing the sour-faced woman in black from her window seat to hover, nosily, unladylike, just six feet from the wheelchair; causing a group of elderly patrons to wrap shawls and summer jackets tightly about them; dragging the spindly waitress back to their table.

"Something wrong with the meringue?" she enquired.

"No, no – it's fine," said Bliss, waving her off.

Daphne, peering unselfconsciously into Doreen's sightless eyes muttered, "I think the old turkey's snuffed it."

Samantha put her hand on Doreen's pulse. "No, she hasn't, Daphne – don't exaggerate."

Daphne, unconvinced, furiously fanned a hand in front of Doreen's stony face. "Well, she looks fairly dead to me," she said, measuring death by degrees.

"Be quiet," hissed Samantha, then softened her tone. "Doreen love. Squeeze my hand if you can hear."

The spidery fingers tightened a fraction.

"She squeezed," declared Samantha with relief and Bliss bent over her shoulder, whispering, "It could be a stroke – I'd better get an ambulance."

Doreen's thin voice whistled through taut lips. "No. I'll be alright. Please don't make a fuss."

The sinister looking woman snorted, catching everyone's attention, then returned to her table, her veiled face giving nothing away.

"Maybe she was an undertaker's scout," Samantha joked later when she and Bliss were snuggling warmly together on her couch, and, although he laughed, he couldn't help wondering if the old witch hadn't had a walkie-talkie linked to a funeral home in her black clutch-bag.

Doreen went back inside her mind: seeing a dapper little Major with a sharp brain and no chin getting married and going to war, and a ragged bundle of bandages coming home – still chinless; asking herself the questions that had tormented her for half a century: *So – Just when did you realise the major wasn't himself? When did you know the pompous little toad hadn't come back? Was it days; weeks; months or even years?*

It wasn't years. I was still pregnant when he ... when "the thing" came back. It couldn't have been years.

You weren't expecting him to come back at all were you? That was your plan, wasn't it?

No, it wasn't.

Don't lie, Doreen.

I'm not.

Bloody liar – you've always been a bloody liar.

Have not.

Why did you get expelled from school then? Why did your dad chuck you out of the house then?

"Mrs. Dauntsey – can you hear me?" asked Bliss, on the outside, but the words couldn't cut through the nagging voice in Doreen's mind.

No-one would ever have known Jonathon wasn't Rupert's son if he hadn't come back, would they?

He didn't come back smart-ass. Not in person anyway.

But you didn't know that at the time did you? You should've seen your face when the ambulance rolled up at the front door and you thought Rupert was going to pop out and point at your belly saying, "Whose is that then?"

"Mrs. Dauntsey, Mrs. Dauntsey," Samantha broke through the haze. "Can you tell us what happened?"

"I was shocked when I saw him," she said, breaking back into the real world for a second, trying to escape the voice.

Thunderstruck would be more accurate, said the voice, reminding her she would never escape. *You spewed your guts up remember; couldn't bear to look at him for weeks.* She remembered, only too well, and her face showed the pain as she thought of the nights she'd lain awake in the cold lonely bed, Jonathon swelling inside her, as she listened to the anguished whimpering of the tormented man in the turret room next door.

"I used to lie awake at night praying for him," she said, sounding compassionate, her downcast eyes looking for sympathy.

Now say that again with a straight face, sneered the voice.

I did pray for him.

Yeah – prayed he would die; prayed for ways you could bump him off without getting caught; prayed he'd cut his wrist.

That would've have been a bit tricky wouldn't it – with only one arm? Anyway, would it have been so terrible? What was life for him? – trapped inside a useless body; pretending to be someone else; mourning his lost love; stuck in the turret room all day and night – alone most of the time.

"Doreen ... Doreen," Daphne was nagging at her sleeve. "Doreen, dear. Do you think we should call a doctor?"

"Doctor?" she asked vaguely. "No – why? There's nothing wrong with me." Doctors! she swore under her breath – Bloody crooks the lot of 'em. Like Doctor Fitzpatrick, pleading poverty in his leather patched tweed jacket and cloth cap; doing his rounds in a beat-up Ford Popular – his gleaming black Bentley reserved for weekends in the city. Doctor Fitzpatrick – long dead now – the only other person to know the truth about the creature in the turreted room.

"The radiographer must have mixed up the pictures, Mrs. Dauntsey ..." the old doctor had said, pouring over the x-rays perplexedly after being called upon to examine the returned hero – expected to certify the extent of his wounds for his pension. But there had been no mistake and he had caught on eventually.

Bliss, his senses alert to the slightest shift in the atmosphere, found himself drawn to a grandfather clock which someone had appliquéd with millions of multi-coloured seeds. The tasteless timepiece was wheezing noisily as it wound itself up to deliver the hour, and, under his gaze, it stopped, a tick short of eleven and, at that precise moment, the parade room at the police station jumped to attention.

"At ease," barked Donaldson, entering with the assistant chief on his shoulder, then he faltered, seeing the measly turnout. "Christ – is this the best we can do?"

"Short notice, Guv," explained Patterson, failing to mention that he'd not put himself out; that the twenty or so men and women he'd rounded up had, in large part, been swanning around the police station in search of an excuse for swanning around the police station.

"We'll just have to manage, I suppose," said Donaldson, going on quickly to explain that their new detective inspector had not spent the night at his hotel and had been missing for the past three hours.

"Probably got lost," quipped Patterson, fixing his tombstone teeth into a ventriloquist's smile.

Donaldson, recognising the voice, directed his words at the detective sergeant, thinking – let's see if you think this is funny. "D.I. Bliss received a death threat yesterday morning," he began, straight-faced. "And last night someone stole some of his personal property and set fire to it in the car park behind the Mitre Hotel – outside his window – obviously intended as a portent."

"As a what?" asked Patterson.

"As a warning – to scare the shit out of him," explained the assistant chief, thinking: Get yourself a dictionary – moron.

Sniggers ran around the room but Donaldson barked, "This ain't funny."

D.C. Dowding wasn't so sure – he'd heard about the goat. "Can I ask what exactly was cremated, Sir?" he said with barely suppressed humour.

"It was a stuffed goat," admitted Donaldson and got the expected gale of laughter. "O.K." he shouted angrily. "This ain't Alabama – it's not the Klu Klux Klan burning crosses. This is Westchester – nobody is going to run one of our men out of town. I repeat – nobody!"

Patterson, sullen-faced, appeared serious. "It sounds more like a prank to me – kids probably ..."

"Oh for God's sake, Pat. Haven't you been listening? I said he received a death threat yesterday morning."

But Patterson sloughed it off. "I wouldn't mind a quid for every little punk who's threatened to put me in a concrete overcoat."

"Sergeant Patterson," said the A.C.C. "Have you any idea why D.I. Bliss was transferred here from the Met?"

"Haven't a clue, Sir," he replied honestly, despite all the strings he'd pulled to find out.

None of them knew – until Superintendent Donaldson filled them in.

The bizarre grandfather clock, in the Coffee House, summoned enough energy to strike only the first four beats of eleven, and time moved forward for Bliss as a pair of clacking stiletto heels announced the manageress's approach, shattering the petrified atmosphere. "Is there some sort of problem here?" she demanded, alerted by the waitress and the epidemic of worried expressions infecting her other customers.

Talk about uptight, thought Bliss, appraising the woman's clenched buttocks, over-strung brassière and tightly permed hair. "There's no problem," he said, brushing her off.

"Well – Is madam alright?" she continued, pointedly peering for signs of life in Doreen's wheelchair.

"Yes," said Doreen weakly, "I'm alright."

"She's just had a bit of a shock," confided Bliss, leading the woman out of the old lady's earshot, fearing she was on the verge of asking them to remove Doreen for causing a disturbance. "Her husband's died," he added, not untruthfully, and watched the woman scuttle back to the kitchen.

"Maybe you and Daphne should go back to the other table," he said, turning to Samantha, concerned that Daphne's presence might be intimidating her old friend.

"I didn't *have* to help get her out of the home ..." complained Daphne, her feathers ruffled, but Doreen held up a hand, saying through the tears. "You might as well stay, Daphne. I quite relish the idea that I'm still worth gossiping about."

"Just keep quiet then," whispered Bliss to Daphne, "and don't mention that damn goat again."

"I didn't realise at first," Doreen sniffled. "It wasn't as though I knew him well."

"Didn't realise what?" interrupted Daphne immediately, drawing an angry "shush" from Bliss.

"A nurse came in everyday and did his bandages," continued Doreen. "His face was such a mess that it never occurred to me."

"What about his father ... " Bliss began, then corrected himself, "I mean Rupert's father – the old Colonel. Didn't he realise it wasn't his son?"

"His eyes were bad – chlorine gas in the trenches at Ypres. He died a few months later ... heart attack." She paused in memory of the proud old man slumped, blue-faced, at the feet of his son's impersonator – his hands clawing at his chest in rigor.

"I'll put it down to the gas, Mrs. Dauntsey – shall I?" the wily old doctor had said, ceremoniously taking the stethoscope from around his neck and placing it into his bag in a gesture of finality, while giving her a knowing wink.

"Yes, please, Doctor, if you don't mind," she had replied, and Dr. Fitzpatrick's fraudulently penned death certificate had cost her a thousand pounds, but what was the alternative? "Death by shock." But who wouldn't have had a heart attack in the Colonel's place – learning, simultaneously, that his beloved son was a queer, something of an idiot, and dead? And, to cap it all, discovering the man he'd been nursing as a hero for the past few months was not only an imposter, but was also his son's lover.

Daphne was catching on. "Do you mean ..."

Samantha touched her arm to quieten her, but Doreen turned to her friend, her eyes wide open. "Yes, Daphne. I was so stupid I didn't realise I was living with the wrong man. Not that I was living with him in the true sense. He stayed in the turret room most of the time – crying I think, though it was difficult to tell."

Daphne jumped up excitedly. "So who was he?"

"You met him – the best man at our wedding – sham wedding."

"Captain David Tippen of the Royal Horse Artillery," pronounced Bliss sagely, feeling the need to prove he'd done his homework.

Daphne's face pinched into confusion. "David Tippen – What sham wedding?"

Doreen sank back into memories of her marriage, still flabbergasted to think she had been so gullible – realising she had been so bowled over by a proposal from the Colonel's son that she never really questioned his motives. But memories of the ceremony itself were murky, everything and everyone appearing through a screen of smoky glass, much as it had at the time – more alcoholic than euphoric. Rupert had made all the arrangements, even choosing her dress – and her hat. "Trust Daphne Lovelace to laugh at my hat," she remembered saying – but to whom, and when ...?

Rupert had only invited his aide-de-camp, ("Done up like a dog's dinner," Daphne had shrieked to her friends afterwards), and his father – the old Colonel. But when he announced that Arnie, the odd-job man, and his wife would be the only witnesses Doreen had dug in her heels, insisting on a "proper wedding," with a maid of honour and bridesmaids; what was the point of a wedding if it wasn't to brandish one's trophy in front of one's friends? In the end, with less than an hour to spare, she settled for Daphne and a clutch of handmaidens dragged out of the Mitre. "What about your parents?" Rupert had asked, showing some feelings at the last minute. "No," she had shot back fiercely, knowing they'd find fault with him; knowing they'd voice the same concerns which she'd worked so hard to keep buried. "Why *you*,

Doreen?" her father would question. "Why not some tight-assed little bitch with a plum in her mouth, and a stuck-up mother twittering on about how rationing was playing havoc with her dinner parties? – 'Haven't had a decent truffle for absolutely ages; and caviar? Pah – lease, don't even mention it, my dear.'"

Doreen surfaced with one clear recollection of the ceremony. "I remember the vicar with that stupid sing-song voice," she said, looking inquisitively at the faces surrounding her as if she was coming around from anaesthetic. "Major Rupert Wellington Dauntsey," he said. "Do you take this woman – Doreen Mae Mason ..." Her voice and memory dimmed for a few seconds, then she seemed to bounce back to life. "Rupert said, 'I do,' but he never did," she continued forlornly. Then she repeated, "He never did," as if to remind herself.

Three pairs of eyes forged into hers, demanding an explanation, but she sank back into her own private darkness, leaving them to watch her changing expressions as she wove together images of the wedding night out of a thick blanket of fog: Rupert, an officer and, apparently, a gentleman, in full ceremonial uniform, pouring her yet another champagne; brushing his lips off her cheek; guiding her upstairs and leaving her to marvel at the wonders of an en-suite bathroom, at a time most people still crept to the outhouse in the middle of the night, and Hollywood agents dickered over bathroom clauses in film stars' contracts.

"Mrs. Dauntsey ..." tried Bliss, concerned that time was running out, but she was already far away, her face warming to the dreamy memory of hot water gushing out of a polished brass tap – unlike her parent's stinky gas geyser scaring the life out of her every time it belched into life, then pumping squirts of lukewarm water into a tin bath until the meter swallowed the last of the coins.

Doreen had found good reason to forget the wedding ceremony, even at the time, but the joy of instant unlimited hot water was so overwhelming she had lost track of time, turning the tap on and off until she could write her name on the bathroom mirror with her finger. Finally, with the important bits washed and powdered, she staggered into the bedroom and swayed, intoxicated as much by the sight of the richly carved four-poster bed, with heavily embroidered tester, as by the champagne.

With her eyes still closed she allowed herself a cautious smile at the memory of the silky sheets; the eiderdown pillows; the giant wall tapestry depicting a mythical battle, with near naked angels lifting the vanquished from the field – someone's sanguine concept of a soldierly heaven; and the Chippendale dressing table laden with sweet smelling pomanders, and cut crystal bottles so delicate she was afraid to touch. Then her face clouded as the memory darkened and she saw herself swimming fuzzily against a tide of drowsiness, struggling into the satin nightgown, the one Daphne had hurriedly bought for her as a wedding present, then watching as the bed spun wildly away from her and she crashed, unconscious, to the floor.

"It was quite a honeymoon night," she laughed drily, rising back to the surface, greedily slurping tea to wash away the rekindled taste of bile which had made her vomit all over the bed in the morning. "I think he put something in my drinks," she added, recalling how she had struggled to pull herself awake through a porridgy sludge, testing her hooded eyes against the morning sunlight and unfamiliar surroundings, while distorted images of the previous day's ceremony swam slowly into view. Understanding had came through the fog like the beam of a car's headlights – a fuzzy glow that suddenly bursts into a blinding flash. "I'm married," she screeched, and lurched upright in bed only to find her husband, the marriage certificate and his aide-de-camp all gone. In their place was a little man with a pneumatic drill trying to hammer his way out of her skull.

"Married," she spat and opened her eyes to the realisation that those around her were holding their breath. "Rupert left me alone in that damn place," she explained. "And I was so woozy in the morning I didn't know if we had or not ... anyway, until my little visitor came a week later I was sure I was expecting."

Daphne and Bliss exchanged glances – Daphne with a lopsided "told you Rupert wasn't the father" smirk.

"Don't ask," mouthed Bliss, guessing she was itching to discover the true identity of Jonathon's father; knowing that just a month or so after Dauntsey's departure someone must have stood on guard in his place.

"He didn't want a woman," Doreen continued, head down in embarrassment, "he only wanted a wife." Then she lost her composure, simpering in shame with the admission that her husband had preferred to sleep with another man on their wedding night.

Bliss checked his watch, anxiously glancing at the door, wondering who would be first through: the matron, Superintendent Donaldson or a masked man with a machine gun. Feeling a need to speed things up he pieced together what he knew, throwing in a few guesses to fill in the blanks for the benefit of Samantha and Daphne. Explaining how, after the massacre caused by Rupert Dauntsey's stupidity, it seemed likely that Captain Tippen had carried his mortally wounded lover back from the front; that an exploding grenade had showered bits of body and uniform everywhere; that some medical orderly must have mixed up the dog tags and when the survivor, a lowly backstreet boy, found himself being treated as a major, he was more than happy to go along with the blunder.

"He'd seen the Dauntsey home and the Scottish estate," explained Bliss. "They were a vast improvement on his own home so he obviously thought: Why go back to be a burden to my mother in a Guildstone hovel? Here I have a private nurse; private doctor; a major's pension; a major's family and a major's inheritance. He knew more about Rupert Dauntsey than Doreen ever knew and, in his own mind, was entitled to the estate far more than she ever was."

Doreen pulled herself together sufficiently to add. "It was difficult for him to talk, and his face was so ugly that nobody wanted to look closely, so it was quite easy for him to get away with it."

Daphne stepped in, questioning, "But why go along with it? Why not just throw him out?" Then she gave Bliss a poisonous stare and spat, "Men!"

There had been so many reasons, so many conflicting persuasions and influences, that Doreen froze indecisively as she sounded out the most plausible and least humiliating in her mind.

"It was blackmail," she said eventually, expecting sympathy, while inwardly debating who had blackmailed whom. "He knew Rupert and me had never consecrated the marriage."

"Consummated," suggested Samantha quietly, but Doreen wasn't in the frame of mind to be corrected and carried on as if she had not heard. 'As long as I'm alive you've nothing to fear,' Tippen said, when I stuck the x-ray under what was left of his nose. 'Doctor Fitzpatrick reckons there's been a mistake,' I told him. 'He reckons you ought to have some sort of scar in your leg. Football, he told me. Broke your leg at school, he said. He reckons he set the bone himself, when you were ten, he remembers it like yesterday – said you bawled your eyes out the whole time.'"

But there had been no mistake and Tippen had superciliously rubbed in the hurt by explaining, in uncalled for detail, what fun he and his lover had in arranging the spurious wedding in order to stop tongues wagging in the regiment. "It made me sick," said Doreen, without elaborating.

"I still don't see why you didn't chuck him out," said Daphne. "Nobody would have believed anything he said, after what he'd done?"

"Tippen had worked that out for himself," explained Doreen shaking her head. "That's why he made the will."

"*The* will," not "*A* will," mused Bliss, recalling the visit from Law, the solicitor, who had made it clear that neither Jonathon nor the church would benefit from the body in the attic. "Are you saying that Tippen made a will in the name of Rupert Dauntsey?" he asked.

Doreen looked destitute as she nodded. "He left everything belonging to the Major to his own mother and the rest of his family. He called it his life insurance policy. Even gave me a copy as a reminder, telling me that when he died I would lose everything – the house, the estate in Scotland – everything. That's why I had to pretend he was still alive all those years."

"That still doesn't explain the bullet in his head ..." started Bliss, but she burst into tears at the memory of her wasted life, or was it relief that the charade had ended? "What could I do?" she blubbered. "If he'd died and I contested the will I would've had to tell them I lived with the wrong bloke for ten years."

"But, what if you'd said you hadn't known?" suggested Daphne.

"It wouldn't make any difference. He had the lawyer write in the will that our marriage was never consecrated."

Samantha let the malapropism go with a smile, but Bliss's mind was leafing through something Doreen had said earlier.

The briefing at the police station had broken up with officers fanning out across the city – clueless. Patterson was hanging back, like a kid in school waiting to pluck up courage to rat on a bully.

"Something on your mind, Pat?" enquired Donaldson.

"Sorry, Guv ..." he said, apparently coming to a decision. "No, nothing really," he equivocated, wiping his expression clean. "I was just trying to think of the best place to start that's all."

The Olde Curiosity Coffee House would have been a good place to find Bliss, where the waitress was back at his table – under pressure from the management – the bill already made out. "Will that be everything, Sir?"

"Yes, thanks," said Bliss as a trio of noisy young mothers, teeming with children, set up camp at the next table and the chaos of everyday life resumed as the women struggled with monumental decisions: cappuccino or café latte; skim milk or cream; chocolate or cinnamon topping; orange or apple juice for the bigger kids; breasts or bottles for the infants.

What must Daphne be thinking? he wondered, trying to read her mind as she eyed the mothers with their babies, realising that at roughly the same age she had parachuted into the teeth of war. Wasn't she envious of the mothers, whose carefree domestic existence would never be ripped apart by the horrors of war or Parisian artists; whose bicycles would never be machine-gunned in the street; whose babies would never be murdered. But her wide open smile hid no angst – simple acquiescence, he guessed. She was happy for the mothers, and resigned to the fact that she'd had her chance, it was written all over her face: "I didn't deserve another baby – I let someone break the one I had."

Watching Daphne, Bliss suddenly saw Doreen Dauntsey in a different light. She'd had a child, no-one had robbed her of that, and, rightfully or wrongfully she'd lived a fairly cushy life. Compassion for her predicament waned still further with the realisation that, in her own way, she had been no less mercenary than the Major who'd suckered her into a bogus marriage, or the man who'd taken his place in the house, if not in his bed. And there was something else: "Mrs. Dauntsey," he said, turning coolly toward her. "You said earlier that the doctor had examined Tippen for the army pension, that was how he discovered the fraud ..." He paused, watching the worry lines crease her forehead. "It was fraud – claiming a major's pension to which he wasn't entitled. Would you agree?"

Doreen was slow to respond, so Samantha helped her out. "Do you see what Inspector Bliss is getting at Mrs. Dauntsey? If Tippen was defrauding the government out of a pension, you'd have a good case for saying he defrauded you out of your inheritance as well."

Samantha was wrong – very wrong. Bliss knew it and so did Doreen, though neither of them let on – choosing silence instead. In the end he prodded her again. "Mrs. Dauntsey ... I said, that would be fraud, wouldn't it?"

"Yes," she hissed through clenched teeth.

Samantha sensing something in the harshness of his tone gave Bliss a puzzled look.

"I think Mrs. Dauntsey has something to tell us," said Bliss, leaving Doreen hanging.

"Oh. I suppose you'll find out soon enough," Doreen spluttered. "I was the one getting the Major's war pension not Tippen. He couldn't sign his name and they was very good at the post office – they knew he couldn't get out of the house, so all I had to do was scratch a cross on the form and they'd give me his pension."

"Didn't anyone ever check up – ever want to see him?" asked Bliss.

"No," she shook her head. "Nobody wanted to see him."

Bliss whistled. "So you were collecting Major Dauntsey's pension for what ... ten years?"

The old grandfather clock had stopped completely, halting time in the Coffee House. Even the children at the next table seemed soporific under the weight of silent anticipation. Then Doreen Dauntsey broke down. "More than fifty years," she blubbered. "I knew I shouldn't have – I knew it were wrong, but I had to pay the bills."

Those damn bills, she thought to herself, sniffling into a handkerchief – never enough money for the bills, especially with old Doctor Fitzpatrick having his hand permanently in her purse almost until the day he'd died. But what choice did she have? Then there was the cost of bringing up Jonathon in a manner befitting the supposed son of a major; the death duties when the old Colonel died; in addition to the upkeep and taxes on the house. The income from the Scottish estate had helped but she had still been forced to sell everything movable over the years. Only the land and houses remained, still registered in Rupert Dauntsey's name, and impossible to sell or mortgage while he was still alive. And, legally, he *was* still alive.

"The pension was Tippen's idea," Doreen averred when she'd calmed down. "He said we'd have to claim the Major's pension or someone would start asking awkward questions. I said I wouldn't do it, but ... " Her eyes glazed again, this time with a memory so horrific that in fifty years it had never dimmed, even for a day: Tippen, in the turret room, viciously grabbing her by the throat with the three clawed fingers of his left hand, pulling her to within an inch of his grotesque face, then slobbering with a foetid spray of bad breath and saliva as he spat, "As long as we both keep quiet nobody will ever know." Her face screwed in awful memory of the moment saying, simply, "He made me do it."

"But he forged the Major's signature on the will," said Samantha. "If you had gone to the authorities they would have soon discovered who he was and the will would have been null and void."

"Maybe," she said. "But it would still have left me penniless. Rupert never changed his will when we married. He didn't have time, I told myself; didn't want to was more like it. Anyway, his will left everything to the church because he had no other relatives. I still wouldn't have got anything."

No wonder the vicar was thinking he might see a new roof, thought Bliss, wondering why the lawyer had accepted Tippen's false signature if he had the previous will to compare it against. Then it dawned on him – Tippen alias Dauntsey didn't have a right hand. He could have scribbled anything with his left, mumbling, "This won't look anything like my previous signature."

"I decided the best thing to do was to pretend Rupert was alive as long as possible and just keep my mouth shut," Doreen continued, pulling herself together. "I couldn't think what else to do, and I thought it would all be over when Tippen died."

"But it wasn't?" piped up Daphne, seeming to surface from nowhere and stunning them with her understanding. "I bet it was worse."

Doreen nodded, sobbing. "I suppose in one way or another we're all prisoners of our dead," she said with remarkable insight. "When he was alive he had no voice. He was my prisoner and I was his. One word from either of us and we would all be out on the street: him, me and Jonathon. But once he was dead he held all the cards: His mother would get the Major's house and estate, and the pension would stop. I thought once he was dead I would be free, but he never let me go."

A sudden flurry at the front door caught Bliss's eye and he turned in time to see the matron and Jonathon Dauntsey barging in.

"Oh shit," he muttered.

"There she is," shouted Jonathon as if he'd spotted a fleeing prisoner.

"Inspector?" said Doreen, grabbing his arm as if she wanted to make a dying declaration. "The dead are the lucky ones – they never have to explain."

"Leave my mother alone," screeched Jonathon, advancing on them.

Then Doreen had her final say, "He only really makes such a fuss of me because he knows when I'm gone he'll have to live with himself."

"Mother are you alright? Has he hurt you?" said Jonathon, turning a dozen pairs of accusing eyes in Bliss's direction.

Daphne turned on Jonathon with such ferocity Bliss wondered if she might kick him. "Don't be so stupid. Of course nobody's hurt her. What rubbish – I just took my old friend for a walk and a nice cup of tea. Isn't that right, Doreen?"

"Yes. And a meringue ..."

"You kidnapped her," spat the matron, catching up to Jonathon. "And you," she spun on Bliss. "You were in on this. I shall report you to the Chief Constable. This is a disgraceful way to treat a sick old lady. I'm taking her back to the home this instant."

"I thought we were the only ones allowed to take prisoners."

"How dare you – she's not a prisoner."

"She could be," he retorted. "I have sufficient evidence to send her to prison for the rest of her life."

Something in the sincerity of Bliss's tone brought the matron up short, then she shook the notion aside. "I don't believe it."

"Are you suggesting we disregard the truth in the interest of believability, Matron?" he asked, putting on a Jonathon Dauntsey attitude, but the manageress intervened, pounding her way back across the room, demanding they should leave immediately, threatening to call the police.

Daphne started to open her mouth: "We *are* the police" on the tip of her tongue, but Bliss got to her in time and caught her arm. "Leave it, Daphne," he said, not wanting to attract any more attention, knowing that Donaldson would already have an all-units warning out for him.

"Come along then, my dear," said the matron, in baby-talk, wrestling the wheelchair from Daphne. "It's your dinner time. The cook made some tasty stewed beef and rice pudding."

"Just one question, Jonathon," said Bliss, standing in front of the man to block his exit. "When I told you we'd found your father's body, you said, 'I doubt that very much, Inspector.' Why?"

Jonathon's face puzzled as if asking, "Is this another trick question?" But Doreen was quick to respond, "Come along, Jonathon. I've told the inspector everything he needs to know." Then, giving the matron a nod to push, she added. "Thank you for the tea and the meringue, Inspector," as if nothing else had happened.

"She hasn't changed a bit," said Daphne as the three of them watched Doreen disappearing through the front door. "Still as flighty as ever."

"Possibly," said Bliss. "But I still don't know who is, or was, Jonathon's father. And I'm still not sure who blew Tippen's brains out."

Chapter Sixteen

It was not until eleven-fifteen in the evening that Samantha slipped the key into her front door.

"Sorry I'm late, Dave," she called cheerily, hanging her jacket in the closet, sighing "That's better" as she kicked off her black uniform shoes. "Shit!"

Bliss, worried, dashed out of the living room into the narrow hallway. "What is it?"

"How long have you been here?"

He looked at his watch, confused. "About nine hours, I guess."

"Nine hours," she echoed. "Nine fuckin' hours and already I'm apologising to you for being an hour late getting home from work."

"Sorry ..."

She caught the disappointment on his face. "No – it's alright, Dave. It's not you. It's not your fault."

"Maybe I should go ..." he started, half-heartedly, but she flung her arms around his neck and pulled his mouth down to hers.

"I said it was my fault," she said and clamped her lips on his until he was struggling for breath.

"I'll stay," he gave in without a fight. "Anyway, I made dinner for you."

"You cook?"

"Of course."

"You can definitely stay."

"You haven't tried it yet."

"Food's food – and it can't be worse than mine."

She rushed to the kitchen – chicken schnitzel with creamy mushroom sauce on a bed of rice. "You cooked this!"

"It didn't cook itself."

"Wow!"

"Well?" he said, dancing in anticipation. "What did you find out?"

It was the ownership of the blue Volvo that interested him. He'd spotted it behind the Mitre Hotel following the coffee house encounter with Jonathon and his mother.

"What is it, Dave?" Samantha had asked, sensing him trying to shrink behind a parked car as she, Bliss and Daphne were trying to figure out how to get at his belongings without running into an ambush of Superintendent Donaldson's men.

"Blue Volvo at ten o'clock," Bliss had said from the corner of his mouth, seeing it disappearing out of the far end of the car park.

"That's the car what's been hanging around my place a lot recently," said Daphne.

Bliss, wide-eyed in surprise, asked, "I don't suppose you got the number?"

"Of course I have," she replied, squirrelling into her handbag and coming up with a neat little diary. "Times, dates and places," she said. "Six times – seven with today – in a little over a week."

Samantha stared at the sprightly old lady in disbelief as she used the little gold pen from her diary to write the number on a scrap of paper.

"Do me a favour ..." said Bliss, not recognising the number, passing it to Samantha, "See what you can find out."

"No problem, Dave. I'm on duty at two."

"Well?" he said, still desperate to know if it was the killer himself or a hired assassin in the Volvo. But Samantha tortured him with procrastination as she insisted on trying a bite of everything from the pot.

"Orgasmic," she cried, over a mouthful of the mushroom sauce, "Mason's his real name – string of aliases ... Is this asparagus frozen?"

"Fresh – just wait a minute."

"Can't ... Wow! ... Petty villain ... How d'ye get chicken this tender?"

"You smack it around. Mason what?"

"Bomber is his street name ... Bomber Mason."

Alarms went off in his mind. His front door imploded again. "A plastics man?"

"No, just a nickname; bit of a piss artist as a youngster; bombed out of his brains most of the time. Nothing recent on the sheet – done time for burglaries; taking without consent; handling stolen goods ... I can't get over this chicken ... He's been in the frame for a couple of small bank jobs – got off."

"Why?"

"Gawd knows ... this rice is terrific ... You'd have to

ask Patterson – he's nicked him three or four times recently."

"Will you sit down ... red or white? I didn't know which you preferred so I got one of each."

"Wine as well. You certainly know how to impress a girl ... ummh – a *Grand Cusinier* ... Yes please, the red. What did you do about Donaldson?"

"I called in sick – left a message with the civvy on the enquiry desk."

"You didn't say where you were staying?" her voice rose anxiously.

"Of course not," he said, pouring the wine. "No-one knows I'm here."

It was a little after midnight. The dinner had been superb – he'd even made the chocolate mousse. Keep busy, he had told himself, take your mind off everything. And the corner supermarket had been surprisingly well stocked.

"Do you still think Doreen shot Tippen?" asked Samantha sitting next to him on the guest bed, toying with his nose as he lay back on the pillow.

"You're tickling ... She seems the only one with a motive and he meant nothing to her, neither did Rupert come to that. According to Daphne, Doreen was the town bike before Rupert swept her off her back."

"Dave ... that's not nice."

"Well ... that's according to Daphne. Anyway, she obviously liked the idea of being the Major's wife, even if it meant marrying a frog."

"But the frog's supposed to turn into a prince, not a toad."

"Now who's being unkind? But, seriously, she must've thought she'd won the lottery – big house; nice clothes; estate in Scotland."

"And the world's ugliest toad."

"Is that why they say you should be careful what you wish for?"

Samantha reached with her lips and kissed him lusciously.

"What was that for?" he asked dreamily.

"I could tell what you were wishing for," she laughed.

"What I can't understand is why she waited ten years to bump him off," said Bliss, his mind still absorbed by the Dauntsey case despite a stirring in his groin. "She'd got what she wanted, even if it came with more strings than the Berlin Philharmonic. Surely it didn't take that long to work out that nobody would care if he disappeared."

"But why leave him in the attic?" she asked, quivering at the thought.

Bliss hugged her warmly and stared at the ceiling thoughtfully, wondering what was above it, in her attic. "I suppose she thought it was the safest place. If she'd buried him in the garden she risked being seen."

The ceiling still held his attention – battleship grey. Unusual colour, he decided critically, but it matched the rest of the room: mid-Atlantic green – jade with the warmth washed out – highlighted with azure trim and accentuated by navy blue bed linen. The ensemble had a nautical, masculine feel, he concluded.

"How come I slept on the couch last night?" he asked, looking around. "You didn't tell me you had guest room."

Samantha coloured up, muttering, "I didn't want you getting too comfortable."

"You didn't believe me, did you?" he said, catching on and sitting up to emphasise his point.

"Well," she stroked his arm placatingly. "You've got to admit it was a pretty lame chat-up line: Someone left me a death threat on my computer; broke into the police garage; incinerated my stuffed goat. Ergo, I need a bed for the night. Would you have believed it?"

"It was true," he protested. "I couldn't go back to the Mitre ..."

"I believe you, Dave. I just wasn't too sure at one o'clock this morning."

Soothing him down with another kiss she lay next to him, fully clothed, and teased his hair. "Like I said, Dave, I didn't want you to get too comfortable."

"I could pay for the room."

"You will not," she shot back. "I'm not having you, or anyone else, having rights. As long as you're a guest I can boot you out anytime I get fed up with you ... Oh don't look so hurt. I'm just making sure you behave yourself, that's all."

"I'll behave," he said.

It was close to twelve-thirty. The barman in the lounge of the Mitre Hotel dimmed the lights suggestively, took off his bow tie and yawned with histrionic exaggeration. Detective Sergeant Patterson had worn out the carpet in front of the bar and was taking a circuit around the largely empty room.

"Where the hell is Bliss?" he asked, pausing to give Dowding a shake in passing.

"Oh! Sorry, Guv. I must've dozed off."

"I said, where the hell ... Oh, never mind. Go back to sleep."

Bliss was drifting toward sleep himself as Samantha soothed the lines on his brow. "I'll give you a penny for them, Dave?"

"I'm wondering what to do about Doreen?"

"She's an old lady. She's dying."

"So am I. So are you – everyday we get a little closer."

"That's morbid."

"True though. I just find it difficult to feel sympathy for somebody who thought she could sleep her way to a fortune, however small, and was prepared to live a lie for fifty years to keep hold of it. She didn't give a shit about Rupert Dauntsey – alive or dead."

"But he didn't give a shit about her."

"Two wrongs ... " he started, then shrugged. "Maybe they deserved each other, though I still can't forgive her, especially after what Daphne went through."

"What did Daphne go through?"

"I promised not to tell."

She caught the lobe of his ear between her teeth. "I could bite ... "

He told ... D-Day; the dead baby; Hugo – the works.

"Wow," said Samantha, breathless. "And I worry about finding the odd dead body on the beach. But how did she get the O.B.E.?"

"I've no idea. It's almost as if she's ashamed of it. She always manages to slide off onto something else whenever she gets close to telling."

"Goodnight, Dave," she said, slipping off the bed without warning – just a peck on his lips and a squeeze of the hand.

He tried to grab her but she jerked away, saying, lightheartedly, "I told you – behave or you'll be out. And I'll tell Donaldson where to find you."

"Sorry, Miss," he joked.

She paused, hand on the door. "Just be patient, Dave," she said, turning, clearly torn, then made a decision. "You know what they say, Dave – easy come, easy go." And she was gone.

It was nearly 1 am. Westchester had shut down for the night; the barman at the Mitre had pulled down the shutters and gone home; Patterson was close to giving up. "Why the hell didn't he tell us?" he said, putting the blame on Bliss for the hundredth time. "He should've told us somebody was after him."

Dowding stirred sufficiently to find a more comfortable position.

Bliss couldn't get comfortable. It wasn't the bed's fault. A maelstrom of thoughts kept him tossing as he tried to unravel the twisted eternal triangle between Doreen, Rupert Dauntsey and David Tippen – who did what to whom, and why? Daphne, the goat and Mandy's murderer also surfaced from time to time but, amongst the mental turmoil, Samantha was the only constant, a solid ray of sunshine at the centre of the storm – like the eye in a hurricane. And he kept coming back to her, just the other side of a hollow stud wall he reminded himself, warming to indelible images of her mysteriously dark Asiatic eyes and olive black hair.

It was eighteen minutes after one. A wash of yellow light seeped from under her bedroom door. "Samantha," he tapped lightly.

"Yes, Dave?"

"I can't sleep – do you want a cup of tea?"

"Yes please – I can't sleep either."

"Do you take sugar?" he asked, walking in, two cups in hand. "I've been thinking about Bomber Mason, the Volvo driver," he continued. But his mind was screaming: And you, Samantha. I've been thinking about you. I can't stop thinking about you.

He eyed the bed, decided against pushing his luck, slumped into a bedside chair and tried to keep his eyes off her. "This Mason bloke and Mandy's killer probably did time together ..." he began while thinking: Get out now, why torture yourself like this. "He's probably told Mason to find out my routine so he can strike at the best time."

He looked at her – it was a mistake. Oh my God – you're bloody gorgeous, Samantha.

"Dave ...?"

"Yes ... Sorry ..."

"You're staring."

"Shit! ... Sorry ... Um ... Maybe I should ... um."

"Dave."

"Yes?"

"Mason ... What are you planning to do about him?"

"Oh ... Um ... Mason ... Yes."

"So what's your plan, Dave?"

Concentrating hard he focused on the tea in his cup and got his mind in order. "Alright. First thing in the morning I'll pay him a visit and beat the crap out of him if I have to. Once I know where his buddy, the murderer, is ... You're bloody gorgeous, Samantha."

"Dave," she laughed.

"Sorry – it just sort of slipped out. I'd better go. Get some sleep. Big day tomorrow. Goodnight."

"G'night, Dave. Thanks for the tea."

It was three minutes before two. Patterson gave Dowding a shake. "O.K., Bob. Let's call it a day. He won't be back tonight and I've got to see a man about a dog first thing."

"Right, Serg," said Dowding, relieved.

It was eleven minutes past two. Bliss had lain awake counting every minute with the anticipation of a kid on Christmas Eve. I need a pee, he thought, regretting drinking the tea, and he crept out into the hallway. The spill of light from under Samantha's door lit his path to the bathroom and the noisy torrent hitting the pan reverberated around the room, turning him pink. Then, faced with the early riser's dilemma – to flush or not to flush – he flushed.

"Sorry," he said, tapping lightly, praying she was still awake.

"Come in." She was reading *Woman's Own.* "Can't sleep," she explained as he poked his head round the door, not trusting himself to go in. "I was hoping this might bore me to sleep," she laughed, flinging it aside. "You know the sort of thing – How to knit your own knickers; Haggis – boiled or fried; the joy of yeast infections."

He looked askance. She was joking? "I forgot to ask earlier. Did you get hold of the forensic lab?"

"Oh yes. Patterson took the stuff in Monday afternoon."

"I thought he would – I kicked his ass."

"Not hard enough apparently. He didn't tell them it was urgent."

"Damn."

"It's O.K. They'll make a start on the duvet first thing this morning and let us have a preliminary finding at lunchtime. The blood on the syringe ..."

"Blood – What blood?"

"Didn't they tell you? Oh no, of course not. Apparently they've found traces of blood, but it will take a while to identify because it was burnt?"

"Blood," he breathed, adding, "That's interesting," as he started to close her door. "Thanks," he said, absently, his mind absorbed as he tried unsuccessfully to find a link between Jonathon Dauntsey, the flattened toy Major and a syringe of blood. "Goodnight."

"G'night, Dave."

It was three-twenty-seven. The first shafts of midsummer sunlight had roused a cockerel in a nearby field and he was doing his best to pass on the news. Bliss needed no such alarm and was roaming the house trying to reconstruct Samantha's background through artefacts and mementos. He found little, other than a plastic coffee mug extolling the beauty of the Seychelles which had washed up on the draining board in her kitchen, a tasteless Eiffel Tower salt-cellar, a single Delft clog and a crooked Italian campanile: Souvenirs or airport presents, he wondered, finding none that bore personalised inscriptions.

A number of pictures, both painted and photographic, could have come from any high street shop, he thought; nothing garish, nothing requiring an explanation or a psychiatrist; nothing that looked more like an accident than a work of art. One picture, a family portrait in a gold frame, made him pause: a pony-tailed Samantha, aged 10 or so, together with mother and father, and a huge yellow Labrador in a green garden.

Creeping up behind him, she caught him in the act. "Are your parents still alive, Dave?" she asked, making him jump with the picture in his hand.

"I sometimes wonder."

"What?"

"Oh sorry ... I wasn't thinking. Yeah – Bungalow in Brighton. Sort of trapped in a time warp. They do exactly the same things every day – have done for at least twenty years. It starts with: 'Cornflakes dear – or would you like a change?' 'No – cornflakes are fine.' And ends with: 'Ovaltine alright?' When I first visited

Doreen Dauntsey in the nursing home she told me that all the others in there were already dead and I knew what she meant."

"I hope I never get like that," said Samantha with a shudder.

"At your age – it's a distinct possibility."

"You'd better watch what you say," she said, snatching the picture and digging him in his ribs, "or you'll be back on the couch tonight."

"Your dog?" he questioned, giving the Labrador a nod.

Her eyes misted and her voice cracked. "He was born the same day as me – my parents thought it was a good idea."

"Wasn't it?"

"He died," she replied, the simplicity of her words barely concealing the anguish.

"And what about your parents?" he asked, pointing to the vital young couple in the gold-framed photo, hoping to strike a happier note.

She took the picture and stood it back on the shelf with exaggerated care. "Split up years ago," she said, with a bitterness that evinced unpleasant thoughts for both of them.

"Is that why you've never married?" he asked, trying to duck the pain of the break-up of his own marriage.

"You make it sound as though I've left it too late."

"No ... " he started, but let the word drift as she spun on her heals and headed for the bathroom.

Picking up the gilt-framed picture again, he scrutinised the young couple and their child in their Sunday best, noted the mother/daughter likeness, recognised Samantha's intriguingly tenebrous eyes in her father's, and pieced together an explanation for the barricade surrounding her. I bet she's protecting herself, trying to guard against the pain of loss by avoidance of a relationship with anyone: men, women, pets.

She was back, tissue in hand. He challenged her with the picture. "What did you say to me the other night? You've got to have a plan, Dave – you'll never find your way back onto the old path, and if you do, you won't like what you find at the end."

"Good memory," she said, noncommittally.

"So, do *you* have a plan?" He held up his hand to block her reply. "I know what you're thinking: Stay single; live alone; don't get involved. That's not a plan, that's a coward's way out." He stopped with the realisation he was talking about himself as much as her, but she didn't answer, she just stood staring into the picture, into the faces of her past.

"I'm right aren't I?" he said, prodding her.

It was just a guess, a shot in the dark, but he'd hit the mark and she coloured up. "Maybe."

"Maybe my ass. You're a lovely woman. If you're on your own it's because you've made it that way. And don't give me the crap about working crazy hours. You'd find time if you wanted to."

"Being single has a lot of benefits ..." she began, but he cut her off.

"It's also bloody lonely."

She used the tissue without taking her eyes off the picture. "It took me years to realise that dead relationships can be as insidious as dead people. I clung to the good memories for ages, going back to the places they used to take me as a child – warm, friendly, happy places. But there was nothing there. Places I loved like the Tower of London and the New Forest had gone cold – horrible, ugly. It took me a long time to realise it wasn't the places, it was my Dad that made them special."

"That's what good Dad's do," he said, warm memories softening his voice. "But what about bad memories – didn't you have any of those?"

"Oh yeah. Lots. It's the bad memories that warn you not to get involved again."

"That's why I feel a certain compassion for Jonathon, whatever he's done," he said, feeling her pain and taking the spotlight off her. "I don't think he even knew who is father is – or was. Did you see how quick Doreen was to hustle him out of the coffee house when she thought I was going to tell him the man in the turret room wasn't his father?"

"So you think he believed Tippen was his father, and that he had deserted them by going to Scotland."

"Yes," he nodded, then paused with a puzzled frown, realising his mistake. "Wait a minute. Jonathon couldn't have smashed up the toy soldier in retaliation for being deserted."

"Why not?"

He fell silent for a second, his mind churning. "He must've taken the toy soldier before Tippen was killed. He couldn't have got it later, it would have been sealed in the attic with the rest of the set."

They had wandered back to Samantha's bedroom and Samantha had wandered into bed. Bliss hung about indecisively near the doorway, still trying to piece together the toy soldier and Jonathon.

"You might as well get in," she said, flicking back a corner of the duvet. He hesitated for half a second, slipped in beside her and was asleep before he hit the pillow.

It was 8 am. Somebody had fixed the alarm clock to sound the moment he fell asleep, at least it seemed that way, and he rolled over to find a warm empty space and a delicious memory.

The sizzling kettle hid the noise of his approach as he crept softly behind her in the kitchen and gently nuzzled his lips to the nape of her neck. "Gorgeous," he breathed. "You're up early. Where are you going?"

"With you, of course."

He shook his head. "Not a good idea. Donaldson wouldn't have bought my 'sick' story for one minute. He'll still have people out looking for me."

"So?"

"You don't want to be seen with me – not a good career move."

"Rubbish. Tea or coffee? What's your plan?"

The road back to Westchester was a race-track of morning commuters and Bliss found himself watching the other drivers – seeing aliens living in a parallel world; a world in which they would never be shot or bombed; a world where mutilated murder victims would only ever appear in artistically arranged clips on the ten-o'clock news or at the movies: sanitised death; tastefully presented death; socially acceptable death.

"Look at him with his bow-tie," said Bliss, poking fun at a Bentley driver as he swept majestically past, thinking: I bet his whole world would crash if you took away his cell-phone and cheque-book – he hasn't got a clue.

Neither Bomber Mason, nor a Mrs. Mason, answered the door at the address registered to the Volvo. The semi-detached house showed no sign of life and even less sign of care.

"Stay there," he said, leaving her on the overgrown front path as he kicked his way through a patch of nettles to peer into the front window, making a peephole through the grime with a saliva-moistened tissue.

"Nothing," he said as he came away shaking his head. "If he's a break-and-enter merchant he must have knocked over an Oxfam shop to get furniture that bad."

"I guess crime doesn't pay as much as it used to," replied Samantha, checking out the empty garage.

"The only people who make it pay today have computers and fancy corporate titles," he said, leaning heavily against the unyielding front door.

The wooden front gate fell off its hinges under Bliss heavy hand as they left. "Shit!"

"Did you do that on purpose?" laughed Samantha as they scooted back to his car.

"I didn't think it would break that easily."

"Oh yeah?"

"Honestly, Sam."

She stopped with such purpose he heard the squeal of shoes. "Don't call me that."

"Sorry ... I ... I didn't ..."

"My name is Samantha," she continued, with a resolve that spoke of past traumas and left a question in the air which she defied him to ask.

He didn't ask. "Sorry, *Samantha*."

She lightened immediately and bounced back to his side as they made for his car.

"Breakfast then," he said, assigning the contraction of her name to a past lover – one of the insidious dead relationships she'd spoken of – and headed for the restaurant where he'd met the *Westchester Gazette* reporter.

"My Dad always called me Sam," she admitted sheepishly without prompting, after a few minutes of awkward silence in the car. "It's sort of special."

He smiled warmly, "I know how he feels. I call my daughter Sam and it means such a lot to me."

If he couldn't see the darkness in her face, he certainly felt the sudden chill in the air and knew the cause. "Bugger," he said under his breath. "I've said the wrong thing again."

Now what? he worried, as the ragged edge of the town gave way to rolling hills and hawthorn hedges of the countryside, and the oppressive silence became deafening. He looked at the radio, dismissed it as too obvious, and opened his window to the rush of wind. I'll have to say something in a minute, he thought, as he slowed at the sign, "The Bacon Butty – all day breakfasts," but Samantha beat him to it.

"There's Mason's Volvo," she said, with so little surprise she might have been pointing out a pigeon or a pony.

It was just pulling out of the car park. "Gotcha," shouted Bliss, locking his back wheels in a 180° spin, shooting off after it.

Samantha spun her head around. "Isn't that Sergeant Patterson?" she asked, amazed, seeing a figure coming out the café.

"Where? Are you sure?"

"I don't know. I've only met him once or twice

Bliss stared deeply into his mirror but the man's image had already shrunk to an unrecognisable size. "Could've been anyone," he muttered.

They caught up to the small blue hatchback in seconds and Bliss mentally confirmed the number. "That's him," he breathed, as if he had never expected it to be, then, pulling alongside at a junction, he got a close look at the driver. "It's not him – not Mandy's killer," he said, full of disappointment.

"Of course it's not," said Samantha, with a touch of aggravation. "It's Bomber Mason."

"I know," he said. "But haven't you ever got an idea

into your head and can't shift it even when the truth is staring you in the face?"

"Is this déjà-vu or have we had this conversation before?"

"Oh yes. I forgot – Your childish faith in the existence of Santa Claus."

The Volvo was speeding up, the driver looking nervously in his mirror.

"He's spotted us," said Bliss

"Not surprising – any closer and you'll be up his exhaust pipe."

An hour later Superintendent Donaldson sat at his desk keeping half a dozen executive toys in motion simultaneously. Samantha, sitting alongside Bliss, was ready to scream "for Christ's sake, stop that" when a timid tap presaged the entrance of Detective Sergeant Patterson.

"Come in," shouted Donaldson with ill-concealed tetchiness.

"You wanted to see me, Guv," he began, then paled to marble as the blood drained from his face. "Mr. Bliss," he breathed in disbelief.

"Sit-down-Patterson," ordered Donaldson, stringing the words together into a single command.

"Sir ...?"

"I said sit."

He sat.

"You know Sergeant Holingsworth from Blenheim-on-sea I understand."

Patterson's brow furrowed in concentration as he stared at Samantha. "No. I don't think we've met ..."

"Take a good look," said Donaldson with uncharacteristic fierceness, not waiting for the other man to finish.

"What is this?" Patterson demanded, rising and looking at Bliss for some sort of explanation. "What the hell's going on?"

"I said – sit down, Sergeant. I won't tell you again."

"I'm leaving."

"Walk out that door and I'll arrest you myself."

"Arrest ... What for? I ain't done nuvving."

Donaldson was unyielding. "Sergeant Patterson – one more time – the very last time. Do you recognise Sergeant Holingsworth?"

Patterson wavered. It was obvious he'd missed something important but couldn't grasp it. "No, Sir."

"You don't recognise her from the description?"

"What description?"

"The one that Bomber Mason gave you."

"Patterson looked as though he'd crapped in his pants," Samantha laughed later as she shared lunch with Bliss and Donaldson at The Mitre Hotel.

"So did Mason when he had his accident," laughed Bliss as he downed a third celebratory scotch.

Bomber Mason's car accident, at the time it occurred, surprised only Bomber Mason. Bliss and Samantha knew exactly what was coming and were braced for it, though it had not been easy to arrange.

"Have you ever had a car crash?" Bliss had said, revealing his intention as they tailgated the Volvo from the Bacon Butty toward Westchester.

"One or two."

"Get ready – you're going to have another."

"Wait a minute, Dave," she said, pulling her cellphone out. "Why don't I call up a uniform car to stop him."

"On what grounds? That Daphne said he'd parked in her street a few times; that a similar vehicle might have followed me to London?"

She took a deep breath and put the phone down. "You're right, but it'll play havoc with your insurance."

"I'll risk it. Anyway, it's a hire car."

"They'll love you."

"You should have seen Mason's face," said Samantha to Donaldson between bites of pâté, "He didn't know what had hit him. Dave was brilliant. 'My dear, Sir, I am so sorry,' he said, helping him out of the wrecked Volvo. Mason didn't know whether he'd been stung, screwed or stuffed. Wham!" she laughed, "We'd rammed him straight up the ass and smacked him into a lamp post."

The "accident" had been considerably more difficult to engineer than Bliss had envisaged. "He's going too bloody fast," he complained to Samantha as Mason tried to outpace them. "I want to shake him up a bit, not put him in hospital."

"Westchester's coming up," she said, sighting the 40 mile an hour sign. "He'll have to slow down."

"Slow down, you bastard," breathed Bliss: Mind the pedestrians; watch the cyclist; slow down – slow down; mind that bus. That's all I need – send him spinning out of control into a bus stop full of schoolkids – that really would finish my career.

"Look out!"

"Fuck – those lights changed quick."

"Phew ... that was close. You nearly got that Jag."

"Sorry – Get ready, I'll try to nail him at the next light ... Hold tight. Hold tight ... Shit!"

"What is it?"

A jaywalking pedestrian. "Watch the lights, you pil-lock," screamed Bliss, adding, "And up yours!" in response to the finger.

The smiling Swedish receptionist, doubling as a lunchtime waitress, poured Bliss a glass of house Cabernet and waited for his approval. "Fine," he nod-ded, then continued to Donaldson. "Samantha was the one who cracked Mason really. All I did was pull him out of the wreck ..."

"And rub him down," interrupted Samantha.

"Just making sure you're not injured, Sir," he had said to the dazed man as he checked him for weapons before throwing him across the bonnet with his arm up his back. "So, Bomber – why are you following me?"

"You're crazy," he spat. "I dunno what yer talk-ing about."

"Who are you working for?"

"Let go. No-one. I ain't working for no-one."

"We'd better call the police then."

"You are the police ... " he started, then choked himself off – too late.

"Well. Well. Well," said Bliss, screwing the arm painfully higher. "So how would you know that, Bomber? How would you know we're police, unless you've been following me?"

"I wanna lawyer."

"I bet you do."

"Dave," called Samantha from the rear of the dam-aged Volvo. "You might want to see this."

"What is it – what have you planted on me this

time?" said Mason, already preparing his defence.

"Have you got a dog, Bomber?" asked Samantha scraping a handful of short white hairs out of the open tailgate, as Bliss frogmarched him to the badly buckled rear of the car.

"I want my lawyer. I've been framed," he squealed.

"Framed – that's a serious accusation, Bomber," said Samantha. "Framed for carrying your dog around in the back of your car. Tut, tut, tut. That would get the police a bad name if we started framing villains for carrying the pooch around in the back of the family motor. Now, on the other hand, if we were to discover that these hairs were, for arguments sake, from a stolen stuffed goat on its way to be cremated ... "

"I didn't steal it."

Bliss laughed, he couldn't help it. "Helping the police with their enquiries takes on a whole new meaning when dealing with scum like you. So, if you didn't steal it – how did it get in the back of your car?"

"I hope the steaks are better than the Pâté," moaned Superintendent Donaldson *sotto voce* as the plates were cleared away.

"I wouldn't bank on it," replied Bliss, recalling Daphne's admonition about Mavis Longbottom's culinary skills.

"Anyway," continued Donaldson, shaking his head in dismay, "I still don't know what came over Patterson to set you up like that."

"I do," said Samantha, jumping in. "He was jealous. He was in line for the D.I.'s job until Dave came along. The only thing he could do was scare him off, and he got Mason to do his dirty work ... But you weren't scared were you, Dave?"

"No," he said, hoping it sounded convincing, adding, "Patterson put the message on the computer, but Mason followed me, and Mason set fire to the ..."

"Inspector Bliss," a familiar voice interrupted and he turned to see White, the *Gazette* reporter advancing on him.

"Mr. White ..." he started, rising with outstretched hand, still fascinated by the little man's weirdly mismatched head and body.

"Oh. I see you've met at last," said the receptionist in passing.

"Sorry ..." said Bliss. "I don't understand."

She stopped. "This was the gentleman who was enquiring about you last week. I told you. Remember?"

The funny looking man delving through the register – trying to discover if he was from London. Of course, Bliss said to himself, as everything fell into place, it had been White trying to get background information for his article on the new man in town. "Well, well, Mr. White," he smiled, realising that the last of his fears had evaporated into thin air. "We meet again. Please join us. I might have a scoop for you."

Chapter Seventeen

A phone call had summoned Superintendent Donaldson back to the police station after the steak bordelaise, just seconds before the steamed chocolate sponge pudding with custard. "Probably for the best," he had said, cradling his paunch, though his tone had been less than convincing. "The Assistant Chief wants to discuss Patterson's future," he had added, cupping his hand to Bliss's ear. "Pat's finished. He'll be lucky if he doesn't get six months inside."

Samantha had gone in search of a phone, ("I'll check with the forensic lab – they said lunchtime."). And Bliss, alone, relaxed with a large Cognac and a curious sense of great achievement, as if Mandy's murderer had been caught and the Dauntsey riddle had been solved. Thank God for Daphne, he mused, mentally raising a glass, realising that had she not recorded the Volvo's number he would still be cringing in terror at every unexpected noise. And, he wondered, how many times he had cringed unnecessarily in the past six months; how many innocuous letters and phone calls had been treated as suspicious; how many entirely innocent people had answered a knock at their door to find a fully armed assault squad because, ten minutes earlier, they had quietly put the phone down when they should have said, "Sorry – wrong number." But the drained bank account? That was no mistake – somebody had swiped a little over four thousand quid. Or was it paranoia? Could it have been a bent bank employee? There was definitely no mistake about the bomb. What had the anti-terrorist commander said? "Bombs on front doorsteps are scarcer than lottery jackpots. And a thug like him won't give up until he's succeeded, or we take him out."

Just the thought of the bomb had him edgy, his eyes darting around the crowded room. Stop it – for fuck's sake stop it, he said to himself. He's not here, he never was here – not in Westchester. It was Patterson pulling Mason's strings – "You owe me big time – unless you'd rather do a stretch ...?" It was Mason in the Volvo and the reporter asking the questions. Get over it, he told himself, but knowing Mason was out of the picture didn't stop him from scanning the faces in the room: bulbous-nosed businessmen with serious drinks and high cholesterol diets, stressed salesmen struggling to keep up the appearance of success: Who would buy from a failure? "Just look at those expenses! You ate at the Mitre!" "You think I enjoy that?" And, off to one side, a party of women in smart business suits mimicking the men. Super saleswomen, guessed Bliss, Avon or Amway. Hyping each other with over-blown sales achievements and stupendous commission claims – just like the men. And by the front door, on his way in, Jonathon Dauntsey and the

Swedish receptionist cum waitress, waving in Bliss's direction. He buried his head – That's all I need, Dauntsey rampaging about the police strong-arming a confession out of his old mother.

Jonathon, pale, drawn and exhausted, floundered his way through the busy restaurant, colliding with the backs of chairs and narrowly avoiding a heavily laden waiter. But the sight of Bliss seemed to steady him. "Ah. Inspector. I was hoping to bump into you," he said, fetching up at the table with practised non-chalance; as if he hadn't been frantically scouring the town for him for several hours; as if he hadn't been up all night plotting a course.

"Yes, Mr. Dauntsey," said Bliss, struggling not to compound the situation by incivility. "What do you want?"

Jonathon pulled himself upright, held his wrists together obligingly in front of him and proclaimed loudly, "I want to confess to a murder."

A collective gasp brought conversations to a skidding halt and the whole room closed in around them.

Bliss dropped his head back into his hands. "I was having such a good day ..." then he looked up. "We've already been through this, Jonathon. You got bail – remember?"

"But that was for killing my father. This is for another one."

Bliss sharpened up with a horrible thought. "Oh God. Please don't tell me you've put your mother out of her misery."

"No, of course not, Inspector."

"Well who have you killed this time then?"

"The man in the attic, of course. I murdered him."

Bliss knew the required response, the catechism according to the Police and Criminal Evidence Act: Jonathon Dauntsey. I am arresting you for the murder of

Captain David Tippen. You are not obliged to say anything, etc. But the scene was so ridiculous he couldn't bring himself to begin. "Sit down and have a glass of wine, Jonathon, you look as though you need it. And for Christ's sake put your hands down. I haven't any handcuffs with me and if I did I wouldn't use them."

"Righty-oh, Inspector," said Jonathon, with a lilt of achievement. "As your prisoner, I would be more than happy to do whatever you ask."

"Cut the crap. Just sit down and tell me exactly how you killed Tippen."

Samantha tried interrupting from a distance, unaware of the reason for the hiatus. "Dave ... " she called, semaphoring with the handset of a phone.

"Hang on a minute, Sam ... sorry ... Samantha," he replied. Adding, in muted tones, "Jonathon's just confessing to another murder."

"You're mocking me," complained Dauntsey.

"Get on with it – How did you kill him?"

"Aren't you going to caution me?"

"I'd rather kick you in the ... Oh never mind. Yes. Consider yourself cautioned. Now, how did you do it?"

"I shot him."

"Where?"

"In his room."

"No. I meant – where in his body?"

"His head of course."

"Jonathon. I hate to disappoint you, and I really have enjoyed your little story, but aren't you overlooking the fact he's been dead at least forty years."

"Forty-four, to be precise."

"So you would have been eight at the time."

"Nine actually."

"A little young to shoot someone in the head, don't you think?"

Samantha, waving with manifest urgency, caught Bliss's attention for a second time. "Would you excuse me a moment," he said to Jonathon. "Feel free to leave if you like."

"Inspector – I'm trying to turn myself in for murder. You could at least take me seriously."

"I think you've overlooked something in your determination to protect your mother," he said, screwing up his napkin, throwing it on the table and rising.

"What?"

"The age of criminal responsibility is ten, Jonathon. If you went berserk with a machine gun in the middle of Harrods at the age of nine, I could only ask you very nicely not to do it again. So I really don't give a shit."

"Inspector – This is absolutely preposterous."

"It's the law, Jonathon," he called over his shoulder, walking away. "Sorry, old mate. Nice try. I'm sure your old mum will appreciate the gesture."

"But, Inspector ..."

Bliss stopped and turned. "Jonathon ... Bit of advice. If you're still here when I get back I'll nick you for loitering. Now piss off and stop wasting my time."

Samantha had put the phone down by the time he got to her. "They were asking if we had a control sample to match against the blood in the syringe," she said. "I didn't want to say anything in front of Jonathon, but they think they've got enough for DNA analysis. By the way, what did he want?"

"Oh he's trying to give himself up again ... " he started, paused, grabbed her wrist and dragged her back across the room. "C'mon. I think I've cracked it."

Jonathon was still at the table, still basking in the spotlight of infamy. "Are you still here?" Bliss demanded, masking his gratification with a scowl, then seemed to relent. "I suppose you'd better come with us then."

Jonathon brightened. "Are you arresting me, Inspector?"

"No – I'm taking you home."

Detective Sergeant Patterson was also on his way home, packing bits and pieces of personal items from the drawers of his office desk while Donaldson stood over him in silent anger.

Several stone-faced detectives were busily counting floor tiles when D.C. Dowding, totally unaware of the unfolding drama, entered and bludgeoned his way across the room, lashing out at desks, chairs and people.

"Serg. Any chance of a bed at your place for a night or two ..." he began, too wrapped up in a calamity of his own to notice the superintendent. "What'ye doing, Serg?"

Donaldson stepped in. "Sergeant Patterson has been suspended from duty, Dowding."

"Suspended! Is this a wind up? What for?"

"Do you want to tell him, Sergeant?"

"Bliss stitched me up," he mumbled to the desk.

"Bollocks," said Donaldson. "You stitched yourself up."

"Well *Bliss* bloody stitched me up," yelled Dowding and all eyes switched to him.

"Well, D.C. Dowding?" prompted Donaldson, breaking the heavy silence after a few seconds. "If you want to lay an official complaint against your new detective inspector you'd better tell us why?"

Dowding caught the drift in the superintendent's tone – D.I. Bliss was flavour of the month. In any case, what could he say? "My podgy wife, (thirty going on forty-five; stretch marks; cellulite; the works), up to her neck in snotty kids with shitty diapers, answers the door to a dish with big knockers in a nurse's uniform."

"Mrs. Dowding?" Nurse Dryden had queried, her face as innocent as her uniform. "Is Bob home?"

"No, he's at work. Can I help? Do you want to come in?"

"Are you his mother or his sister?" she chatted innocently as she picked up a toddler and waltzed into the living room like she owned the place, as though she wasn't about to start a world war.

"I'm his wife, actually," said Mrs. Dowding with just a trace of unease.

Nurse Dryden crumpled in a perfectly timed outburst of bawling, her hands flying to her face and churning it into a multi-coloured soup of midnight black mascara, sapphire eye-shadow, raspberry-cola lipstick, snot and tears.

Bob Dowding's wife flew to comfort the stranger fearing her three tots might catch the crying bug. "What is it? What's the matter?" she asked, cradling the young woman's head to her shoulder, offering sympathy, guessing it was man-related – wasn't it always. "Men can be such pigs," she muttered, without thinking for a moment it was her own pig she was talking about.

Wait for it, thought nurse Dryden, sniffling loudly as she prepared to ignite the fuse, then with a few shoulder shaking sobs she struck the match. "Bob told me he was single."

"Bob?"

"Yeah. Sergeant Dowding – Bob ... I said I wouldn't sleep with him unless he crossed his heart and hoped to die ..."

It was a slow fuse. "You slept with him ... my husband?"

"He swore ..."

"I bet he did."

Now for the dynamite. "I think I'm going to have his baby."

Bliss's plan to take Dauntsey home took a detour before they reached the car park. Samantha tugged at his sleeve as they made for the rear exit of the Mitre.

"You go ahead, Jonathon," said Bliss. "We won't be a second."

"I might run ... " started Jonathon but Bliss's cold stare warned him not to continue.

"Don't you want to know about the hairs on the duvet," asked Samantha as soon as Jonathon was out of range.

"Oh yes. I'd forgotten. Jonathon's chronic addiction to confession is beginning to get on my nerves. I've never known anyone so determined to go to jail. Anyway, what did they find?"

"You were right – hair, lots of it."

"And ... black; brown; grey – what?"

"White."

"White. That makes sense. I thought he would have picked someone about the same age as his father – some white-haired old bum probably, looking for a warm hay barn to spend the night ..."

"Have you finished?" cut in Samantha.

"Sorry?" queried Bliss.

"You didn't let me finish, Dave. They said it was white hair ..."

"That's what I ..."

"Shut up and listen. It was a white-haired animal, Dave."

Bliss fell against the corridor wall as if he'd been shot. "Oh no – don't tell me. I don't believe it – Yes I do. No wonder we couldn't find a body. Short white hairs, animal ... four legs. I bet it was that damn goat."

"No."

"No?"

"No."

"Well thank God for that. So, what the hell was it?"

"You know what these scientific types are like," she said, pulling out her notebook. "I had to write it down. They said it was almost certainly from a member of the *Sus Scrofa* family."

"*Sus* what?"

"A common pig."

Chapter Eighteen

Jonathon Dauntsey stalled at the top of the main staircase, steadying himself against the balustrade. Bliss strode ahead into the turret bedroom with a lightness of spirit he'd not experienced on his previous visits. "C'mon, Jonathon. Are you going to show me where you shot him or not?"

"Is this where it happened?" asked Samantha, peering into the room and up into the gaping hole in the ceiling.

"That's what Jonathon's about to tell us, isn't it, Jonathon?" replied Bliss, turning just in time to see the other man's pallid face disappearing back down the stairs. "Jonathon!" he called, but the fleeing figure didn't flinch.

"He's a strange one," sighed Bliss, turning back to Samantha.

"Aren't you going after him?"

"No. He'll come back if he wants to ... Anyway, I don't need him at the moment," he added, sidling slowly around the room, head back, examining the oak-panelled walls and ornately carved cornice just below the ceiling.

"Are you going to tell him we know it was a pig in the duvet?" she asked, staring at the walls with him.

"Not yet. He'll only say something clever like: 'That's a bit of a swine, Inspector.'"

"Dave ...?" she queried vaguely, still craning.

"What?"

"What are we supposed to be looking for?"

"That!" he cried triumphantly, pointing to a small hole in the panelling high up on the wall.

She squinted. "It looks like a knot-hole in the wood to me."

"It could be. Let's get a ladder and find out."

Jonathon was cowering in a cubby-hole behind the kitchen door when they went looking for a ladder, and they would have missed him had Bliss not thought it a likely place to search.

"Oh there you are, Jonathon," Bliss started breezily, caught off balance at finding him in such an odd place. But Jonathon wasn't there. He was miles away and his blank stare said, "Do not disturb."

"Jonathon," said Samantha, easing him out of the recess as she soothed one of his hands, "Why don't you come and sit down and tell us what's the matter?"

He moved like a man on a ledge, taking little hesitant steps; staring, terrified, dead ahead; gripping Samantha's hand with white-knuckle force as she led him toward the scrubbed pine table in the centre of the room. "Get a chair, Dave," she said from the corner of her mouth. "You'll be alright, Jonathon," she told him with a concerned kindliness, feeling she should add – don't worry, you won't fall. But the look on his face said he had already fallen.

"He's got a hole in his head, Mum," said Jonathon,

staring right through Samantha and looking deep into the past.

"Sit down ... " she started, but Bliss gently elbowed her aside. "Who's got a hole in his head, Jonathon?" he probed gently.

Jonathon's face turned to Bliss but his eyes continued to hunt the room with the apprehension of a cornered fox. "Daddy has ... Daddy's got a hole in his head."

The ambulance had probably been unnecessary. In his catatonic state they could have bundled Jonathon into Bliss's Rover and driven him to the psychiatric wing of Westchester General with as much speed and less commotion, but Bliss was concerned he might suddenly snap out of the trance and become hysterical.

"I've never seen anyone fall apart like that before," said Samantha as the ambulance pulled away. "What on earth's happened to him?"

"I think he finally solved the case of the dead captain, and didn't like the outcome."

"What outcome? I thought you said Doreen shot him. I don't understand."

"Help me find a ladder and we'll know for sure."

Arnie caught them in the act as they rummaged through a stack of dusty old planks and beams in one of the outbuildings. "Oy. What'ye doin' ...?" he began, arming himself with a handy stick, then he recognised Bliss. "Oh 'tis you again."

"Hello, Arnie – looking for a ladder. Is there one around?"

"Out back," he said, staring at Samantha, waiting for an introduction.

"Sergeant Holingsworth," said Bliss. "This is Arnie. He knew the Major; father worked for the Colonel; likes a pint."

Her smile disarmed the old man and he beamed, toothlessly, as he led them to the rear of the outbuildings and started hacking creepers off a homemade ladder. "Me old man made this," he wheezed, prompting Bliss to pull out his cell-phone. "I'll get the station to send a new one."

Superintendent Donaldson wanted to speak to him, the control room telephonist advised him and put him through to the senior officer.

"Mrs. Dauntsey's here, Dave," mumbled Donaldson through a mouthful of chocolate biscuit – making up for the missed dessert. "She insists on seeing you; claims she's escaped from a nursing home; wants to let you know she shot the man in her attic; says she used the Major's service revolver."

"Ask her where he was when she killed him, will you."

"She said he was in his room in the turret."

"In his wheelchair?"

"Yes."

"I guessed as much."

"Do you want me to have her arrested?"

"No, Guv. But I think somebody should take her to the General hospital to see Jonathon. Confessing may be good for the soul, but those two could keep the Pope boxed in for a month. They should try to get their stories straight."

"Is that a good idea?" asked Samantha as he closed his phone. "Shouldn't they be kept apart until we know for sure who did it."

"But I know already," said Bliss. "Or I will as soon as the ladder arrives."

Arnie was still struggling to free the makeshift ladder from the tentacles of a vine. "Don't bother with that, Arnie," called Bliss, and waited while the old man got his breath back sufficiently to light his pipe. "Mrs. Dauntsey tells me you took out the staircase from the turret room attic," he lied, with an expression innocent enough to fool an Old Bailey judge.

"So what if I did?" Arnie coughed through a blue haze.

"Nothing ..." Bliss turned away to conceal a smirk of satisfaction. "I just wondered where it was, that's all."

"'Tis over there amongst the stingin' nettles."

Much of the spiral wrought iron staircase had dissolved into the ground, and the remainder had been swallowed by vegetation, but its tubular shape had endured and Bliss kicked away some of the nettles for verification. "This is it," he called to Samantha, then teetered back in fright as a hen flew out of the undergrowth squawking angrily. "There's a nest here," he added with obvious astonishment, peering into the void and finding a clutch of brown eggs.

"How did you know there had been a staircase into the attic?" asked Samantha, a country girl, unimpressed by the novelty of a chicken's nest.

"I didn't. It was just guesswork – I couldn't figure how Doreen could have got Tippen's body up there on a ladder, so I thought: What if there used to be stairs?"

"So it was Doreen who killed him then?"

"Is that the scenes of crime van?" said Bliss, hearing a vehicle's tyres crunching on the gravel driveway at the front of the house. "Let's get the ladder, shall we?" he said, striding away.

"Mr. Dauntsey is here under observation," said the hospital's resident psychiatrist as Bliss and Samantha sat in his office an hour later. He might have said, "Piss off and stop interfering," the tone would have been the same.

Bliss sized him up: mid-twenties – hoping the moustache will add a few years; still practising to write illegibly; still believing everybody needs a shrink. You haven't got the faintest idea what's going on in the real world, mate, thought Bliss, saying, "I think I can help ... " But the doctor rose with his hand outstretched and a bilious smile. "Just leave him to us, Inspector. He'll be fine."

Samantha started to get up but Bliss was unmoved. "It's not that simple, I'm afraid, Doctor. You see Jonathon Dauntsey is wanted for murder ..." He waited for the word to sink in. "Personally, I'd like nothing more than to talk to him for a few moments and leave him in your capable hands, but, if that's not possible ... " He paused long enough to throw open his hands disclaiming responsibility, "If that's not possible then we'll have no option but to arrest him and take him with us."

"Murder ..." breathed the doctor, falling meditatively back into his chair. "I had no idea."

The bullet had been the clincher. Bliss had dug it out of the woodwork as soon as the ladder arrived. Samantha, Arnie and the scenes of crime officer clustered around him as he descended with it clamped between thumb and forefinger.

"Thought so," he said, peering beyond the slug to watch Arnie's reaction. "So it *was* Jonathon who killed him."

Paling noticeably from his usual florid complexion, Arnie found himself fascinated by something deep in the bowl of his pipe, and devoted himself to removing it with the sharp end of a reamer.

"How are you feeling now?" asked Bliss, with a cheery smile as Jonathon shuffled into the doctor's office and deflated himself into a padded armchair.

"Better," he mumbled, fixing his gaze on his bare right foot.

The room which had been brightly streaked by the late afternoon sun suddenly dimmed. Jonathon's depression was contagious and Bliss found himself staring at his own foot and dropping his voice in sympathy. "I've been giving some thought to what you said the first time we met, Jonathon. About the two fates of dread death – do you remember?"

Bliss felt, rather than saw, Jonathon's nod of agreement and continued. "Now I know what you meant. You had a choice, didn't you? You could only hope to save your mother by sacrificing your father." He paused – waiting; watching for a response; a sign; anything.

The psychiatrist seemed to spot something in Jonathon's face. "Just carry on, Inspector," he said quietly. "Mr. Dauntsey is listening."

"The only problem was that you didn't know who your father was ... did you? And I'm pretty sure you knew the man in the attic wasn't your father."

Jonathon's foot had developed a nervous tremble, riveting his own and everyone else's eyes, then he mumbled, as if speaking to the foot.

"Sorry?" quizzed Bliss. "Did you say something?"

Jonathon didn't look up. "I said I had no idea there was a man in the attic."

"So – if you didn't know he was there, why are you trying to convince me you bumped him off?"

The psychiatrist looked ready to kill Bliss. Hadn't they just agreed? "You can talk to him for five minutes in my presence, but you're not to confront him with the murder." Bliss had no need to ask really. He knew

Jonathon was the killer. The re-enactment in the turret bedroom had shown that.

With a high-backed Windsor chair brought from the kitchen to represent Captain Tippen's wheelchair, Bliss had quickly set the scene.

"You play the Captain," he said to Arnie, pulling him toward the seat, but the old man shied away as if it had been electrified.

"Not me. I ain't doin' it," he cried, squirming out of Bliss's grasp.

"I'll do it myself then," said Bliss, dismissing Arnie's refusal without comment, leaping into the chair and shuffling around until he was facing the hole, high up in the wooden panel, from where he had extricated the bullet. "Now ... Samantha. You pretend to be Doreen Dauntsey. Come up behind me and put a gun to the back of my head."

"I get it," cried Samantha, without even trying. "It had to be Jonathon."

"So, Jonathon. You say you killed him." Bliss continued, with no regard for the promise he'd given the psychiatrist.

"Shot him."

"O.K. You shot him. Where exactly were you at the time?"

Jonathon closed his eyes in concentration. "I can't remember ..." Then he looked up and the pain in his eyes said he was trying.

"Can you remember what you did when you were nine?" he asked in frustration.

"I remember I didn't kill anyone." Jonathon narrowed his eyes and stared accusingly. "How do you know? How can you be that positive? Until your sergeant told me you'd found a body in the attic, I remembered nothing about it."

"But you say you remember shooting him."

"I suppose it was him, I've sometimes thought about what happened but I could never get a clear picture." His eyes shifted to the ceiling as if seeking a revelation in the jumble of pipes and wires. "In the end I assumed it was a bad dream, or a book I'd once read. It wasn't real. It couldn't have been real ..." he continued, his voice failing.

"Repressed memories," breathed the psychiatrist scribbling furiously as Jonathon drew a curtain over his eyes and stared intently at nothing.

Back in the turret room, the scenes of crime officer, a civilian trained to find clues not interpret them, had failed to appreciate the significance of Samantha standing behind Bliss with a gun in her hand, pretending to be Doreen Dauntsey. "Why do you say that proves it was Jonathon?" he asked, with a vacant expression.

Bliss hopped back into the Windsor chair. "Alright," he said. "Why don't you pretend to be Jonathon and stand behind me with a gun?"

The young officer obliged and poked his forefinger into the back of Bliss's skull.

"Have you forgotten something lad?" said Bliss, spinning his head around to look up at the man.

"Sir ...?"

"Jonathon was only nine at the time. How tall were you when you were nine?"

The bullet hole in the wall stared the officer in the face and he blushed at his own stupidity. "Of course, Sir," he said, crouching down and sighting along his finger as it pointed up into Bliss's head and on up in a direct line into the woodwork close to the ceiling.

"Jonathon," continued Bliss, deciding he'd had long enough to ponder. "What do you remember about the man in the turret room?"

"He was ugly ..." started Jonathon in a rush, but his voice faded again as he gave his words some thought. "I don't know ..." Then he picked himself up, seeming to gather his thoughts, and answered directly to Bliss. "Actually, I'm not sure whether I remember him that way or whether that's a reflection of what other's have told me. He was in a wheelchair, I remember that. I only ever saw him that way. I knew he was different, and I knew people whispered about him behind my back." He smiled as a warmer memory slid over his face. "I remember his toy soldiers – his little army, he called them." Then a deep shadow fell – Jonathon had retreated into a nightmare.

The psychiatrist was on his feet in seconds. "You'd better leave," he said, his face as grey as Jonathon's.

"Nurse!" he shouted, and a plump woman in sickly green barrelled into the room. "Show these officers out ..." he started, but Jonathon unfroze with a scream that held them all rigid.

"I thought the fire alarm had gone off," Samantha said a few minutes later, as she and Bliss sat in the cafeteria trying to calm themselves over coffee.

"He was like a wild animal ..."

"A bloody werewolf," she cut in.

Jonathon's cries had stalked them down the corridor. "I killed him! I killed him! I killed him!" he was screeching, pleading for judgement, and a worried army of white coats had scurried past them, rushing to the psychiatrist's aid.

"You were right then, Dave," she said, adding extra sugar to her double-espresso.

"Looks like it. Although I still don't know his motive."

"How did you figure it out?"

"Something's been niggling me ever since the post mortem," he said, recalling the effervescent pathologist poking his finger into the entry wound in Tippen's skull. "There was no corresponding exit wound. Which meant, either the bullet didn't have sufficient velocity to break out of the skull, in which case we would have found it with the body, or, it escaped without leaving a hole."

"Through an existing hole," conjectured Samantha, picturing the scene.

"Quite," he said, impressed. "Imagine: Jonathon has got behind him with the loaded gun. He tips his head back trying to see the boy and 'Bang.' Point blank range. The bullet pierces the skull, goes through the brain like a hot knife in butter, shoots out of his eye and up into the wall."

"Ugh," she screwed up her nose at the thought.

"If Doreen or another adult had shot him the bullet would have gone down into the floor. It had to be someone short; a nine-year-old; Jonathon."

"And you think Doreen covered up for him?"

"She had too much to lose by his death. Though I doubt she did it on her own."

"Arnie?" she mouthed.

Bliss raised his eyebrows over his coffee cup.

With the re-enactment in the turret room completed, Arnie's face had dropped when Bliss and Samantha said they were heading for the hospital to check on

Jonathon. "You ain't goin' back to the Mite'*er* then?" he said, clearly salivating over a Guinness. When Bliss shook his head, he whined, "I wouldn't 'a told you about the bloomin' stairs if I'd known that."

Bliss turned on him sharply – face to face. "I should be careful what you say if I were you, Arnie, before I start wondering how Mrs. Dauntsey managed to get the body up those stairs on her own, how she plastered up the ceiling, and how you didn't notice a body when you took out the staircase. "

"He went purple," laughed Samantha as they drove away. "Talk about apoplectic. I was wondering if he was ever going to catch his breath."

"It's almost a pity we can't offer opinion in evidence," sniggered Bliss. "That's not the first time I could have said, 'The defendant looked as though he'd pooped himself, Me'lord.'"

The psychiatrist came to find them halfway through a third coffee. "I'm glad you're still here," he said, looking anything but glad. "Mr. Dauntsey is asking to speak to you."

"What's happened?" asked Samantha

"It seems as though his conscious mind has finally accepted the situation."

"That he shot the man he thought was his father?"

The psychiatrist wagged a warning finger. "Just because he admits killing him doesn't necessarily mean he did it."

Bliss gave the finger a critical stare and winced at the ragged nail-less flesh and raw cuticles. Psychiatrist, analyse yourself, he thought, and pondered what defences the doctor was cooking up for Jonathon: false memories; guilt complex; retaliation for abandonment. Should I tell him not to bother? he wondered. Should I remind him of the age of criminal responsibility? No – let him have his fun.

Jonathon was a different person on their return. ("Fascinating subject," said the psychiatrist later. "He's a nine-year-old in a man's body.") The tension had dissolved and his puffy red eyes were lowered in contrition. "I believe I owe you an explanation, Inspector."

Bliss knew he should be furious – an entire week chasing a dead pig. But Jonathon's little-boy-lost expression took the sting out of him. "I'd like to know why you did it."

Jonathon's face lit in a happier memory. "We used to play wars. I was his little captain, he said; even let me wear a cap. I'd set all the soldiers up – just where he told me." He paused to stare at the ceiling, then corrected himself. "He couldn't really talk, but he sort of grunted and pointed with his swagger stick until I got it right."

The spark in his face faded as a darker memory returned.

"If I didn't get them just right he hit me with the stick ..." he was saying when tears replaced the smile and he searched his pockets for a tissue.

"Here," said the psychiatrist offering a well-used box.

"Thanks ..." Jonathon continued, talking to the floor. "Anyway, he'd get me to move his toy soldiers around in battles; manoeuvring battalions or regiments – sometimes entire armies." He paused, marking time, an alarm sounding in his mind, holding him back, telling him to stop.

"Go on," said Bliss, and caught a glare of rebuke from the psychiatrist.

"Shush."

"Each figure represented a hundred or a thousand men," continued Jonathon after a few seconds, "and the

Royal Horse Artillery, his regiment, always had to be in the vanguard, with the gun carriage party leading the way." Then he froze, his eyes found his foot and the twitching re-started.

"I thought he was going again," Samantha had said in the car on their way back to the police station. But Jonathon hadn't "gone." He was fighting an ancient battle.

"One day I knocked over the major and knelt on him by accident," he began again, his voice faint, his eyes riveted to his foot. "He was very angry – screaming, 'Bring him here. Bring him here.' I saw the tears. I'd never seen him cry before. 'My major – Look what you've done to my major,' he was crying. 'It's only a toy,' I said, but when I gave it to him he grabbed me." He paused, tears streaming, and a bubble of silence grew around him – pressurising the small office to bursting point.

"I should have been in bed," he started again, releasing the valve with a noisy snort. "Mum told me never to go into his room alone."

"I'm not surprised," mused Bliss silently.

"But sometimes I'd pretend to go to bed then creep to his room to play with the toys. He was my dad ..." His face crumpled in tears once more. "It was all my fault – I'd squashed his favourite toy."

"What was your fault?" asked the psychiatrist, anxious not to let the silent tension re-build.

"I was in my pyjamas," Jonathon mumbled, focusing sharply on the psychiatrist, barely whispering. "And he pulled them down. It was our little secret. He made me promise never to tell."

Horrific remembrances turned his face into a battlefield of emotions and his eyes swam around the room as if trying to escape the images in his mind. "If he was asleep, I would have my own pretend battles," he continued, finding a lump of dried chewing-gum on the floor as a focal point. "But when he was awake I had to do exactly what he wanted." He took his eyes off the floor and looked pleadingly at Bliss. "You do know what I mean, don't you, Inspector?"

Bliss nodded sombrely.

"I was ashamed. I knew it was wrong, but he was my dad," he continued, covering his eyes with his hands, trying to block out the images. "I couldn't tell Mum. He said it was our little secret. Then one day I said, 'Stop, Dad – I don't like it. You're hurting me. Stop. Please stop.' But he wouldn't stop ..."

Jonathon was back in the turret room – a frightened nine-year-old with his pyjamas round his ankles. "I picked up the gun ... Please stop, Dad ... Stop, Dad ... Stop it ... Stop it ..."

The gun went off inside Jonathon's mind and the whole room jumped as he screeched. "I shot him."

Nobody spoke. What to say?

"What happened afterwards?" asked Bliss, once the air had settled, hoping to establish Doreen's involvement – just for the record.

Jonathon dabbed his eyes. "Nothing really. It was as if nothing had happened. His room was always locked and Mum told me he'd gone to live in Scotland where he wouldn't be able to hurt any other little boys. I felt so sorry for him. I think he was lonely – he just wanted someone to love; someone to love him back; someone warm and soft to touch; someone warm and soft to touch him back." He blinked back the tears for a few seconds before adding bitterly. "Loneliness is a straight road that leads you nowhere, Inspector."

Bliss looked at Samantha, but she was staring out of the window, seeking sanity in the stubby branches of a loppy tree.

"Sometimes I used to believe he was still there and Mum only said he'd gone to Scotland so he couldn't play with me. I used to call through the keyhole, 'Dad – are you there?' I was sure I could hear him crying at night when I was in bed. I wanted to say sorry. I only ever wanted to say I was sorry. But I never did."

"Did you tell your mother you'd shot him?"

"She said I'd missed, and that it wasn't a real bullet anyway. It was only like my potato gun ..." Pausing, he looked at Bliss. "Did you have one of those?"

"Yes," nodded Bliss, "I think everyone did,"

"I only ever wanted to say sorry, but I never could – he was gone forever." He looked at Bliss. "Isn't that a terrible thing, Inspector – never having the chance to say sorry?"

Mandy Richards flashed into Bliss's mind. "Yes, Jonathon, it's a terrible thing," he mumbled, seeing a picture of himself leaning over her on the floor of the bank, his ear pressed to her mouth, listening for the faintest trace of a breath, as he whispered, "I'm sorry." But it was too late, she'd gone.

"I went to the estate in Scotland to beg Dad for money so I could take mother to Switzerland," Jonathon continued, without expecting a reply from Bliss. "There's a Doctor in Lucerne who could cure her," he explained enthusiastically, oblivious to the scepticism in the faces surrounding him. "I needed twenty thousand pounds for the treatment alone – plus the expenses, but the farmer said he'd never seen my father, only my mother. He said my father had never lived there. I told him he was mistaken." Then his face and voice dropped, his eyes went back to his foot. "There was no mistake. Mum had been lying to me all those years, making excuses whenever I said I wanted to visit him. She said it would be too painful for him to see me, that I would remind him of what he'd lost."

He paused, glancing from face to face as if mystified by their presence, then focused intently on Bliss and looked straight through him. "Once I knew he wasn't in Scotland the only alternative was that Mum had killed him – Why else would she have lied to me? But I couldn't ask her could I?" He paused to look at the psychiatrist, pleading for understanding. "What on earth should I have said ...?"

The young doctor shook his head. He had no answers, only questions.

Jonathon had an answer of sort. "I thought I'd just sell the estate, or get a mortgage on the house, but when I went to a solicitor I found I couldn't. Both properties were still in Dad's name alone. Only he could sell them – unless he was dead."

"So he had to die, and be seen to be dead," said Bliss, pleased he'd been right almost from the start, "And I assume the blood on the duvet was yours. You must have bled yourself dry to get enough."

"You knew?"

"You shouldn't have thrown the syringe in the stove."

"You found it?"

Bliss nodded, with no intention of ever admitting that Patterson had disregarded it.

"I knew I should have got rid of it properly. I worried about it when I was in the cells."

"And the pig?" prompted Bliss.

"You know about the pig as well?"

They knew all about the pig. They had stopped off to see George, the butcher, on their way to the hospital. The purchase of the stuffed goat had apparently elevated Bliss to celebrity status. "Ah, my dear Chief Inspector," greeted George, using his barrelling gut to clear a path through a pack of housewives, dragging him and Samantha to the front of the counter. "What a pleasure to see you again. I've got a nice leg of lamb ..."

"Actually, I wanted a few words," said Bliss, nodding toward the back room.

"Of course," said George, yelling for his assistant to take over, ignoring the mumbles of dissent from the waiting customers. "Won't keep you a moment, ladies," he said to the crowd, and opened a flap in the counter to usher them through.

A side of pork lay conveniently on a wooden block in the back room and Bliss used it as a prop. "I was wondering, George," he pointed. "If I needed a pig in a hurry, where would I get one?"

"You wanna whole one?"

"A live one ..." he started, then stopped in memory of his first day at Westchester police station, in the C.I.D. office – D.C. Dowding ragging Daphne about crop circles in the cornfield behind her house. What had Dowding said? Pig rustling? Somebody had stolen a pig from the farm behind Daphne's.

"Sorry, George," he said, turning back to the butcher and changing the question. "What I meant was: If I had a whole pig, how would I get rid of it?"

"Eat it," suggested George, scratching his head unnecessarily.

"That would be a lot of pork."

"You could sell it then."

"Would you buy it?"

Turning to the side of pork as if it suddenly demanded his attention, he hacked at the hind leg with a meat cleaver, uttering a requisite with each downward stroke. "Ministry licence; health inspection; quality control ..."

"So," said Bliss, catching a quiet moment, "what you are saying is that even at the right price, you wouldn't buy a pig from someone who wasn't a bona fide supplier?"

"I didn't exactly say that, Chief Inspector ... " he began, his loyalty clearly torn between someone who would purchase his stuffed goat and whoever had sold him a pig.

Bliss cottoned on and turned up the heat. "You'd better start getting all your books and records together then, George. And I'll ask the tax people to come in and do an audit ... "

"That won't be necessary," he said, laying down the cleaver in resignation. "I knew I shouldn't buy it. Knew I'd get caught. But he assured me it was all above board. Reckoned he'd hand reared it in his back yard. Nothing wrong with that."

"Who?" asked Bliss, as if he didn't know.

"Jonathon Dauntsey, of course. I knew you'd find out sooner or later. He pinched it, didn't he?"

"Did he?"

"I ain't stupid, Chief Inspector. I should've known summit were up when he said he'd bring it round in middle of Sunday night."

"So what happened to it?"

"You ate it. Well some of it, anyhow."

"Me?"

"Yeah. Mrs. Lovelace bought some chops for your dinner. I remember her telling me it was for the new chief inspector. It were on Monday last week. His lordship, Jonathon Dauntsey, had left it in me cold store the night before. He must have had it a few days 'cos it were just ready for butcherin'."

"What time did he bring it round?"

"I don't rightly know. I always visit me old mum on Sunday evenings: tea, church, watch telly. Got back about eleven, an' it were hangin' up in the back just as he promised."

"Show me," said Bliss and George led them out of the rear door along a short red-brick path to an iron shed leant against a high brick wall.

"What's there?" asked Samantha, seeing only tree-tops beyond the twelve-foot back wall.

"That be the churchyard," replied George, and pointed to a narrow door let into the wall. "This is where he got in with the pig," he explained, opening the unlocked door.

Bliss stuck his head out of the door, saw Colonel Dauntsey's elaborate mausoleum only a few feet away, and the newly mounded grave where they had found the duvet only fifty feet further on, and everything became crystal clear. "No wonder we couldn't find the body," he mused aloud. "He threw the duvet into the grave to put the dogs off the scent, thirty seconds later dropped off the pig, and two minutes after he'd left the Black Horse with a dead body, all the evidence has gone."

"But the blood on the duvet was human," Samantha reminded him.

"Jonathon's own blood," replied Bliss, shutting the churchyard door. "That's what the syringe was for – not to inject an anaesthetic, but to draw out blood."

"But why?"

"Remember what Doreen said: She couldn't sell the house or estate because it was in Rupert's name, and she'd lived off his pension for fifty odd years. Jonathon obviously thought that if he could convince everyone that his father had just died, the property would go to his mother and the pension would simply stop – no questions asked."

"So he killed the pig and set the whole thing up to make it appear as if he killed Rupert Dauntsey," said George, hovering inquisitively.

"So, Jonathon. Can you remember when you first realised you had shot somebody?" asked Bliss, more for tidiness than anything else.

"He's going again," said Samantha with little finesse as Jonathon's eyes started swimming.

"I think you'd better leave now," said the psychiatrist, trying to usher them out, but Jonathon perked up.

"I don't think I understood death. People just went away when they got old and I remember thinking that I wanted to get old quickly so that I'd be able to visit Dad and tell him I was sorry."

"He wasn't your father," said Bliss, offering the information as comfort, but Jonathon already knew.

"I worked that out a few years ago. Major Dauntsey went to war before I was conceived, but I still considered him to be my father. He was the only father I ever knew, whatever he may have done."

Bliss dropped his head into his hands with the realisation that Doreen still hadn't told Jonathon about Tippen.

"I don't know how to tell you this ..." he began, then explained what he knew of Tippen and his relationship to Rupert Dauntsey. "So you see," he concluded, "not only wasn't the man you killed your father, he wasn't Major Dauntsey either."

"I couldn't understand why he would hate me so much," said Jonathon as he slowly absorbed the information.

"It was the ultimate betrayal," explained the psychiatrist later, after Jonathon had been gently guided out of the office, shuffling like a man back on a ledge, his personality a psychoanalyst's research manual. Then Doreen Dauntsey turned up in her wheelchair, still protesting her guilt.

"You'd better discuss that with Jonathon." said Bliss, as he and Samantha scurried out of the room.

"But I want to confess," Doreen shouted after them. "I did it. I killed him."

"Will she never give up?" asked Samantha as they got to his car, still laughing.

"We shouldn't mock," smiled Bliss. "You can say what you like about Doreen's morals, but you can't knock her for trying to protect her family."

"So. What happens now?"

"Well. The case is closed as far as I'm concerned and by the time the lawyers have sorted out who gets the property they'll be the only ones to benefit."

"Isn't that usually the case?"

"All I have to do is take my two favourite women out for dinner tonight."

"Two?"

Was that a trace of jealousy in her voice. "Yes, two. And there's no need to look so peevish. My other guest is Daphne, without whom, as they say, none of this would have been possible."

Chapter Nineteen

B liss shunned the elevator and rushed the grand stair-case to his room at the Mitre two steps at a time. Pausing for a breath at the top, he looked down on Samantha as she sifted through a magazine pile. "Gorgeous," he mused. "Absolutely bloody gorgeous."

"I'll wait in the lounge," she had said as he'd excused himself, saying, "I won't be a moment ... must change ... same clothes for two days."

"No problem, Dave," she had smiled, recalling he'd spent one night on her couch and the next in her bed, asleep, with only a change of shirt and underwear. "But it's almost a pity you had to invite Daphne this evening. Without her we could have had a candlelight dinner in your room."

"I had to ask her," he explained. "I owe her. I might never have cleared up the case without her. She was the one who noticed the crop circles; saw Jonathon chasing the pig; she even bought some of it – not that she knew; she put me onto Tippen with the wedding photo and even queried Jonathon's date of birth."

"Alright, Dave ... I get the point."

"And don't forget, it was Daphne who nailed Patterson's accomplice in the Volvo. And, in any case, I'm dying to find out how she got the Order of the British Empire."

"I said alright," she said, kissing him lightly on the cheek. "Maybe we can have a candlelight glass of champagne later instead."

Samantha dropped the April edition of *Cosmopolitan* into a litter bin and picked through the tourist brochures as she checked her watch for the umpteenth time. "Won't be long," he had said over his shoulder as he took the first of the stairs. Typical of a man, she thought, probably on the phone chatting to a mate. "I've got this bird waiting for me in the bar ... won't get a lot of sleep tonight if you know what I mean ... nudge, nudge, wink, wink."

Detective Sergeant "Pat" Patterson wouldn't be getting a lot of sleep either. Mrs. Patterson would see to that. Jointly charged with Mason for conspiring to steal a stuffed goat, for destroying it by arson, and for uttering death threats by computer, he faced many a sleepless night. But Detective Constable Bob Dowding would be available to keep him company – Mrs. Dowding would see to that.

Bliss's key turned easily in the lock, too easily, but he had dropped his guard. With his mind adrift in a wash of carnal thoughts, it was easy to assume the maid had left it unlocked by mistake. I hope Samantha was serious, he said to himself, as he bounced across the room shedding clothes and shoes, heading for the bathroom, carelessly missing clues in his excitement: man sized footprints in the carpet pile; a waft of aftershave; a trace of cigarette smoke from a smoker's clothing.

With only his boxer shorts remaining he eyed the huge feather bed and smiled at a fleeting image of Samantha's cute body curled into it. Shower or bath? Shower of course. She's waiting at the bar – she might change her mind. Somebody else might snap her up. The floor squeaked – It's fifteenth century, what do you expect?

Then the bathroom door opened by itself.

Samantha slipped the last of the brochures back into the rack, "Stonehenge – four thousand years of astronomy," and found herself irrationally wondering if there were a backstairs or fire-escape. Finally, with growing concern rather than annoyance, she sauntered to the reception desk.

"Yes, please. I help you," said the Swedish girl as Samantha made a show of checking her watch.

"Mr. Bliss has been a long time," she remarked, as if in passing. "He hasn't gone out has he?"

"He is talking with his friend I expect," she said, casually turning to check the key board.

"What friend?"

The receptionist looked around. "He was here earlier. Wanted to know which room Mr. Bliss was in. Said he hadn't seen him for a while."

"Oh no." Samantha's heart sank. "Tell me you did-n't tell him."

"Ah ... I don't understand."

"Did you tell him which room?"

"Yes. He said he wanted to surprise ..."

"Phone!" she screamed, nearly taking the girl's head off.

"What?"

"Give me the damn phone," she screamed, snatch-ing it from under the young woman's hand. "Get the manager. Give me a pass key. Oh Christ – you stupid, stupid girl. Have you the faintest idea ... Hello – YES – THIS IS AN EMERGENCY – Police and hurry ... You stupid girl ... This is Sergeant Holingsworth, I'm at the Mitre Hotel ... Oh, you stupid girl ... "

"Wait at the reception, Serg," the duty officer at Westchester station had said, but how could she wait? Wait for what? What would it be this time – another sawn-off shotgun, a Kalashnikov or a booby-trapped bomb?

"What's his room number?"

The girl was white. "Seventeen Madam."

"Give me the key," she screeched, already running for the stairs, then she stopped and turned with a terri-fying afterthought. "You'd better get an ambulance."

"Yes, Madam – Sorry, Madam."

"... Stupid girl ..."

A confusing maze of corridors confronted her at the top of the stairs and the rooms seemed to have been numbered by a dyslexic painter using a magnifying glass. She passed his twice, her heart pounding as she raced around the narrow twisting corridors, too blinkered by fright to spot the blind alley with his room at the end.

Eventually, on the point of returning to the recep-tionist for directions, she spotted the room and crept cautiously up the narrow alley knowing she had nowhere to duck if the door flew open and the killer came out, guns blazing.

The keyhole was peeping-tom proof and, sweeping her hair to one side, she clamped an ear to the door. Damn hotel doors, she thought, hearing only a mumble of voices. "Shoot you ... Revenge," somebody seemed to be saying.

Oh my God! Now what?

Knock?

Are you crazy?

With her blood rising, she slumped to the floor and checked her watch. Where the hell is the tactical support unit – they've had ... one minute! I don't believe it. Only one lousy minute. I'm going in.

Wait for the armed unit. He'll kill you.

He won't. That's what upset him in the first place. That he'd shot a woman.

Taking a deep breath she slid the old-fashioned brass key into the lock with the stealth of a burglar. Now stop, wait and listen. She jammed her ear back against the door – damn these insulated doors. It was only a murmur. What was it? What was he saying? "Kill you?"

Holding her breath, she turned the key with the trepidation of a bomb disposal officer. It turned forever then jumped with a solid "clunk" that shook her rigid. Run, she told herself, but it was too late, her hand had frozen to the polished marble handle and another hand was turning it under her fingers. Let go! Let go! she screamed inside, but an iron grip wrenched open the door and dragged her sprawling across the carpet into the room, flat on her face. Her hands flew protectively to her head and she was readying a scream when Bliss beat her to it.

"Samantha," he cried. "What the hell are you doing?"

"Dave?" she queried feebly as she turned to look up from the floor. "Are you alright?"

"Of course I'm alright," he said, standing over her next to a stranger. "This is Superintendent Wakelin from Scotland Yard ... Superintendent meet Sergeant Holingsworth," he laughed, dragging her to her feet.

"Oh. I see ... Super ... Superintendent ... ah ... nice to meet you," she stammered, brushing herself down, then the room exploded around them in a blast of light and sound.

They were still laughing about it twenty minutes later when Daphne showed up to join them for dinner in a new hat that could have doubled as an umbrella. "Bought for the occasion," she said. What occasion? Bliss wondered with a smirk: a ritual blinding?

"Painful pink with chicken pox," was how Samantha described it later, when they were alone. "You know what they say, Dave," she sniggered, "red hat – no drawers."

"That's our Daphne for you," he replied.

"What's happening? What's going on?" Daphne demanded as the two of them giggled over Martinis and a bowl of olives at the bar. "Oh – olives. My favourite. May I?"

There had been a bit of a misunderstanding, he explained, sliding the bowl in front of her and ordering her a Pernod, thinking there was little point in telling her about Mandy's killer.

The "misunderstanding" involved six heavyweight wrestlers wearing police uniforms and crash helmets, and a thunderflash which had scorched a hole in the carpet, shattered a mirror, and left Bliss, Samantha and Superintendent Wakelin wondering if an atom bomb had dropped on the room next door.

"It was all my fault," Samantha explained apologetically. "I was so certain the killer was in your room I told them to blast their way in."

"They did that alright," Wakelin laughed, his ears still stinging. But, when the smoke had cleared, they'd rejoiced in the bar like freed hostages as Wakelin explained the reason for his visit to Samantha. "Mandy Richard's killer has done his last blagging."

"Blagging?" she mouthed to Bliss.

"Armed robbery," he explained. "Met police slang."

"He scored an own goal," continued Wakelin, still talking in code.

Bliss checked her face for signs of bewilderment, but she understood. "When?" she asked.

"A few months ago we think. He was doing a mole job under a security warehouse with a couple of heavies. Using jelly. Looks as though they hit an old sewer – red brick – probably thought it was the building's foundations. Then *Boom!* And they were up to their armpits in you-know-what. Anyhow, they were found last week – the bits the rats had left – and a few of the fingers still had prints on them."

"Nice," said Samantha, grimacing at the thought.

Daphne watered her Pernod still looking to Bliss for an explanation. He straightened his face. "My old superintendent came to see me and told us a funny story."

She popped an olive. "What?"

"It's safe for you to come back to London now," he had said and Bliss had immediately looked to Samantha. She smiled. What does that mean? he wondered. What sort of smile is that? Say something Samantha – anything ... "Stay." "Go." ... Say something.

"Can I let you know?"

"Of course ..." Wakelin started, then viewed him questioningly. "I should have thought you'd be only too keen to get back home. We've taken good care of your place – new paintwork; new door ..."

"I'd just like a bit of time to consider it," he said, not wanting to think about the door, the steel prison door, and gave Samantha another glance. Look at me – damn you. Say something. Plead with me not to go. Beg me to stay here. Tell me there's hope; there's a chance. Being on your own's not all it's cracked up to be – ask Daphne.

Wakelin was still in the dark and blundered in the wrong direction. "I can understand you being wary about coming back. It'll take awhile to sink in ... Why not take a couple of weeks leave – as much time as you like. Call me tomorrow ... the day after ... whenever you're ready."

"I've just got a few loose ends to tie up here."

Loose ends – Samantha Holingsworth you mean. Go on – tell her how you feel about her. Look into those mysterious eyes and say, "I think I love you." But I hardly know her. I thought I said no more Titanic relationships; no more trails of emotional debris.

"I'll call in a day or so, Guv. Like I said, I've just got a few things to do ... can't leave them in the lurch."

"Understood, Dave. No pressure. You do what you've got to do."

What have I got to do? You could keep running. From what? And what about Samantha? Can you stop her running – running from relationships and commitment?

She's not unlike Daphne – waving her knickers in the air for England then spending the rest of her life running from the consequences. And Doreen – her race almost over. If ever a woman had a reason to run it had been Doreen, and yet in some strange way she had not run, or had she – from the truth.

"I'll let you know, Guv."

Daphne was still awaiting an explanation of Superintendent Wakelin's visit and Bliss straightened his face as he turned. "An old acquaintance of mine has dropped himself in the shit," he said, causing Samantha another fit of the giggles, leaving Daphne none the wiser. "Shall we go into the dining room?" he added, rising from the bar. "And I want you two ladies to order whatever you'd like – my treat. And," he gave Daphne's arm a complicitous squeeze, "we'll have champagne."

The long-stemmed red rose on Samantha's side-plate brought a thoughtful glance in Bliss's direction as she carefully placed it to one side. Daphne stuck hers to her nose. "That's nice of you, Dave. I haven't been given a red rose since ..." The heavy scent reddened her eyes and she pulled a lacy handkerchief from her sleeve, " ... Silly me."

Robert, "Your waiter for this evening," introduced himself as "Robêrre" with a gallic roll despite his unmistakable Hampshire accent. "May I take your order?"

Bliss, still overawed by the fact Samantha, armed with a handbag, had burst into his room fully prepared to confront a madman with a machine-gun, simply followed her lead – Venison pâté followed by salmon. Daphne, with a mischievous wink, ordered in French, forcing Robêrre to acknowledge his linguistic shortcomings, and as he slunk away, pink-faced, Bliss turned to her.

"Come on, Daphne. I'm dying to hear how you got the O.B.E."

Her face went from day to night.

"I could always dig up the honours list and find out," he nudged gently.

The handkerchief resurfaced. "I was a courier," she admitted and might have meant UPS or Federal Express had it not been for the agony on her face.

"I've never seen so much pain in someone's eyes," said Samantha, after Daphne had excused herself to find a bathroom.

"Was it pain or fear?" asked Bliss rhetorically, wishing he had never asked about the O.B.E.; wishing he'd never seen it on her dining room wall.

Samantha shook her head in wonderment. "Who would have imagined it? Daphne, the police station cleaning lady, smuggling defectors out from behind the iron curtain. I simply can't believe it."

"I can," replied Bliss. "I can see her crossing over on forged papers; leading men across minefields; hiding them in false-bottomed boats; fast-talking them past itchy-fingered border guards. I can see it."

"But who was Michael Kent?"

It was Michael Kent who had caused the pain in her eyes. Michael Kent who had grabbed her from the clutches of Hugo in Paris, and the man who'd talked her into snatching people trapped by the advancing red army after the war. Michael Kent who'd been caught, tortured, tried and executed. Michael Kent who'd taken her heart to the grave and had sent her scurrying to the sanctuary of the Mitre's bathroom.

"Michael Kent was the guy who found her in Montmartre after the war," he explained to Samantha, though he knew nothing more – only what he could read into the look of dread on Daphne's face.

"No wonder she had no problem getting Doreen out of the nursing home," laughed Samantha. "It was hardly in the same league as smuggling a rocket scientist out of east Germany under the Rusky's noses."

With the ghosts out of her attic, Daphne returned to tackle the remaining escargot with enthusiasm, announcing, "I've decided to give up my job."

"Why?" asked Bliss and Samantha in tandem.

"Oh, I only did it for a little extra pin money to top up my pension."

That's rubbish, thought Bliss, knowing she'd not bothered to take her wages unless they were forced on her.

"It was a bit selfish of me really, when there's so many young mothers who could do with the money," she continued, failing to mention that Superintendent Donaldson had finally put his foot down, telling her point blank to hand in her keys.

"It's time I looked for something a little more challenging," she added.

"Parachute instructor perhaps," joked Bliss and got a frosty stare.

"Don't mock, David. I'm not over the hill yet."

"Sorry, Daphne," he said. Sorry that despite her knowledge, and capabilities, at aged seventy-five nobody was likely to give her a chance. And sorry that such a gutsy old lady was about to join Doreen on the downhill slope to the graveyard. "I'm sure you'll find something ..." started Samantha, but Bliss was quick to change the subject.

"There's only one thing that still puzzles me," he said, speaking to his reflection in a silver salt-cellar. "Who the hell was Jonathon's father?"

Daphne laughed. "You still haven't worked it out?"

"Do you know?"

"I asked Doreen."

"She told you?"

"Not exactly – but she wouldn't deny it."

"Deny what? Come on, Daphne, spill the beans. Who was it?"

"Do you remember when I told you about the day Rupert and Doreen were married, just before D-Day?"

"And you rushed around touching statues' thingies," he laughed.

"Only one," she protested. "Anyway, you're getting away from the point. Do you recall I said the most surprising thing was that the crusty old Colonel treated her as if she were a princess."

"And I asked you if you meant like Cinderella."

"Well ... What do you think the King would have done with Cinderella if the Prince went dragon slaying the day after the ball? Played scrabble maybe?"

"Well I'm damned," laughed Bliss. "You mean the old Colonel stood picket duty while his son was away fighting for God and Country."

"That's the long and short of it, Dave," she nodded. "I suppose somebody had to keep the home fires stoked. Quite a man was the Colonel – gawd knows how he sired such a poor specimen as Rupert."

"That's incredible," breathed Samantha. "So that means Jonathon is actually a Dauntsey. He's actually half-brother to Rupert."

"And heir to the Dauntsey estate in his own right," added Daphne, having already given it some thought.

"Wait a minute – my entire case has just fallen apart," said Bliss, slumping back in mock disappointment. "Jonathon killed Tippen, but wasn't responsible because of his age. The money from the estate in Scotland was lawfully his, so his mother didn't steal it. And he was perfectly entitled to batter the toy soldier and throw it away – it belonged to him."

"But what about the Major's pension?" protested Samantha. "They certainly weren't entitled to that, and over fifty years it must have run into hundreds of thousands, even a million."

"That was fraud," agreed Bliss. "But it wasn't Jonathon's fraud, it was his mother's, and I've no intention of prosecuting her on her death-bed. Anyway, it may sound Clintonesque, but she could claim that because she was never actually informed of the Major's death, she was entitled to assume he was technically still alive."

"Nobody would believe that," cried Samantha.

Daphne gave a little shudder. "I can't help feeling that life, purely as a technicality, gave Rupert little satisfaction."

"Satisfying or not, he may have achieved something none of us ever will," replied Bliss.

"What?"

"Immortality."

"I don't understand."

Bliss cupped his wine glass in his hands and peered meditatively over the rim. "Can you imagine how much red tape you would have to cut to change military records more than fifty years old? It could take forever to get the Army eggheads to admit they sent the wrong man home. The chances are that, on paper at least, Major Rupert Dauntsey will outlive us all."

"Jonathon stole the pig," piped up Samantha, still determined to pin something on him, though her tone suggested it was an academic exercise.

"But where's the evidence?"

"You ate it," she laughed. "But you've got his confession. He confessed to killing his father."

Bliss threw up his hands in mock horror. "No more confessions, please. I can't take any more confessions. I will never believe another confession as long as I'm on the job."

"He was actually telling truth ..." started Samantha, but he cut her off shaking his head.

"You mean he would have been telling the truth if Captain Tippen had been Major Dauntsey, and if Major Dauntsey had been his father."

"Complicated, isn't it?" muttered Daphne concentrating on the escargot.

"Anyway. Whoever he confessed to killing, he obviously didn't believe it at the time. It must have come as

James Hawkins

quite a shock when he looked into the turret room this afternoon and it all came back to him."

"What did the psychiatrist say?" asked Daphne.

"Selective amnesia, amongst other things. In fact I reckon he could retire on this case. I can imagine him touring the country with Jonathon standing in the wings. 'Ladies and Gentlemen, kindly allow me to introduce the world's most screwed up man.'"

"Talk about a dysfunctional family," mused Samantha. "No wonder Jonathon's weird."

What had Doreen said about the power of the dead over the living? thought Bliss, recalling that Tippen had kept her trapped for over fifty years. And what about Jonathon? He must have known in the back of his mind that he'd killed the man who had abused him – the man he thought was his father. "The whole thing is a saga of death," he said, looking slowly from Samantha to Daphne and speaking of life in general. "Dead people, dead relationships and dead animals ..." He paused, almost daring anyone to mention the stuffed goat, preparing to scream, then added. "It was so horrific that Jonathon's mind just shut it out."

"I don't blame him, I think I'd shut out something like that," said Samantha.

The main course arrived. Poached wild salmon on a concasse of oyster mushrooms with a creamy dill sauce.

"Absolutely superb," they agreed.

"It must be Mavis Longbottom's night off," muttered Daphne maliciously.

Bliss leaned into her and whispered consolingly. "Don't worry, Daphne. The food here isn't a patch on yours."

She looked up, beaming. "Actually, Dave, I was meaning to speak to you about that. Now I've decided to give up my job I'll have more time on my hands and I was thinking of taking in a paying guest. I was wondering if you'd be interested – all home cooked food of course."

"That's very tempting ..." he began, but Samantha reached across the table, took his hand tenderly and looked deep into his eyes. "That's very nice of you to offer, Daphne, but he's coming to live with me. Aren't you, Dave?"

The End